DAWN AND DUST

HAYLEY WHITELEY

First published in the United States on April 9, 2025 by Storm Hollow Press.

Paperback ISBN: 979-8-9890476-4-2

Hardcover ISBN: 979-8-9890476-5-9

E-Book ISBN: 979-8-9890476-2-8

Line Editing by Sarah Wentworth of Indie Editorial.

Cover by Stefanie Saw of Seventhstar Art.

Map by Rachael Ward of Cartographybird.

For Nick,
my husband, my love,
my constant source of encouragement.

By Hayley Whiteley

The Kerafin Chronicles Trilogy

Ink and Ore
Dawn and Dust
Fate and Frost (coming soon)

Short Stories

"The Rabbit's Foot," first published in *Four Names of Fortune: Tales of Luck and Destiny*

Author's Note

Dawn and Dust is intended for ages 13+. It includes depictions of violence in a fantasy setting, as well as mentions of off-page sexual assault, specifically child sexual abuse (CSA). This is mentioned in the form of a character opening up about past trauma to a loved one using non-graphic terms. The purpose of including this topic in a novel intended for teens as well as adults is to represent overcoming shame and to represent sharing difficult past experiences with others. This topic will not be discussed in more detail in future books, nor will it ever be included on-page in any form.

This novel also includes a character with a visible disability. Sensitivity readers were consulted to ensure this representation was authentic and positive.

ICEMARK GLACIER
FROZEN WASTES
FIR KELT
YULE VALLEY
LINDEN
THE NORTHERN MOUNTAINS
BAR KUR
KLOSTERN
HALSTAT
A'SLENDERIA
BALLYNACH
CLON KILLY
SLONDE RIVER
FORMER BORDER OF DREZCHY
AFDOT
FORT DONOUGH
FORT CAJETAN
JINENSIN
FORMER BORDER OF DREZCHY
TIBEDO
BEIRA BAIJA
PIZEMAC

ROSKEBORG
SEVERN ISLES
NEW DREZCHY
VINCENCIM
TRAIN LINES
POLITICAL BORDERS
CAPITAL CITIES
CITIES AND TOWNS
FORTRESSES
THE CONTINENT OF
KERAFIN
AND
NEIGHBORING LANDS

Anton

Four Months Before the Assassination of King Stefan XIV

Anton Dvorsky wasn't sure which was worse: being surrounded by idiots, or not being one of them.

Anton slinked down the dimly lit hallway in silence, his dark suit blending into the background as his brainless cousins barreled past in a ruckus of grunts and cheers. This evening, King Vadim of New Drezchy had called the full court in a mandatory summons, and knowing his uncle, the so-called meeting was going to be a bloodbath.

The typical court session started with a severely expedited criminal trial, followed by some poor soul getting his fingernails ripped out or his tongue chopped off. Then the revelry would begin with rounds of drinking and dancing while the court waited to see if the condemned bled out. If they didn't, they were considered redeemed of their crimes and released. Whenever Uncle was the torturer, survivors were rare, which was one of the many reasons Anton avoided court as much as possible.

Although—now that he thought of it—his cousins hadn't been heading to the throne room, but to the amphitheater. That could only mean one thing—someone was taking the Blood Raven. The ritual consisted of peeling the victim's ribs out through their back, one by one, followed by their lungs—all while they remained alive. There was no chance of survival, but remaining silent throughout the ritual would redeem one's honor.

A chill crawled up Anton's spine at the memory of the last Blood Raven he'd witnessed, and he desperately hoped he wasn't today's victim. While he was confident he could stay silent, he didn't want to die with so many half-drafted inventions left unfinished.

When Anton pushed open the double doors that led to the courtyard, he took in the sight with clenched teeth. Designed as a reminder of the historic Drezchy, the amphitheater consisted of a pyre on a raised dais, perfect for spectators to witness the glorified brutality. A dirt pit—reserved for nobility to ensure the best view—surrounded the stage.

Beyond the pit, the steep, grassy hillside was open to the public and provided a view not only of the festivities but into the rest of Karolinum, the fortified castle in the city center that commoners viewed as mysterious and intriguing. Anton, meanwhile, had the misfortune of knowing exactly how dull the place actually was, having lived here his entire life.

The loose dirt gritted under his fine shoes as Anton sidled up next to Nev, his only sibling, waiting at the back of the pit. Without the slightest flinch, she asked, "Who do you think today's victim will be?"

Anton didn't have time to say what he honestly thought—that it might be him—before Uncle's voice echoed across the amphitheater, as loud as if he held a horn.

"Crown Prince Anton Alexandrei Gregorovich of House Dvorsky, come forward."

It *was* him, then. Dread coated Anton like wax, but he steeled his features into indifference and stepped toward the pyre. He stole a glance at Nev, but his sister didn't look as distraught as he would have expected, as if she knew something he didn't. Perhaps he might not die today, after all.

Uncle Vadim stood on the wooden platform surrounding the pyre. The king wore a thick cloak of black bear fur and mink tails despite the late spring heat to mask his small stature. At the lowest step of the wooden stairs, Anton halted and clasped his hands behind his back, waiting to receive further instruction.

Uncle wasted no time before making his proclamation. "The crown prince is hereby stripped of his title and reduced to prince."

Anton hung his head, knowing better than to object. His uncle held absolute power over the line of succession, able to alter it without so much as stating the grounds for this monumental decision.

"As you all know, I boast neither queen nor heir. I do still possess uncommon luck, however, for I have thirteen nieces and nephews to speak of, all over the age of fifteen—the correct age for a successor."

Anton scowled, the cruelty of the statement not lost on him. If Nev were to be counted, there would be fourteen possible successors. At nineteen, she was a year older than Anton and should have been first in the line of succession, but she'd been born with her legs not fully formed. The condition left her unable to feel or move them, so once she grew older, she began using a wheeled wicker chair to get around. Shortly after Nev's birth, Uncle had declared her unfit to rule, and worse yet, due to the Drezchy cultural value of physicality over intellect, there were many who called the decision prudent and even just.

As for his own demotion, Anton was neither offended nor particularly surprised to be stripped of the hereditary title. He had long known the depths of Uncle's hatred for him. In truth, he was grateful for it, considering Uncle was the vilest human being he'd ever known. Favor from him would have been the most painful type of insult. Besides, Anton had never wanted the crown, and he'd made no attempt to hide that from the court. He hadn't even bothered to wear it to this very meeting.

"Further, as you all are undoubtedly aware," Uncle continued, "come Yuletide, I will reach fifty, the most honorable age to pass into the Veiled Eternity. Thus, I am now declaring the ancient Rite of Conclave to choose a successor, and prevent further unrest among the kingdom once I have passed. The worthiest among them will become my successor, the king or queen of New Drezchy, at the end of the year when I take the solemn Blood Raven for myself."

The crowds of both the hillside and the pit burst into applause, whooping and cheering at the prospect of a Conclave.

Anton took the distraction as his cue, stepping away from the dais before Uncle had the chance to dismiss him. He crossed the pit in long strides, sparing Nev a nod on his way past, and halted at the tunnel entrance that led into the castle, waiting for Uncle to finish explaining the rules of the ritual.

The Conclave was the stuff of legend—literally. Anton could scarcely believe even his crazed uncle would attempt one. In short, it was a months-long tournament to the death, and the last one standing was the victor. It was said that their Drezchy ancestors on Kerafin chose monarchs exclusively by Conclave, though enough time had passed to blur the line between fact and fiction.

While there would be several official trials, Uncle emphasized that killing the others outside of them was fair game. From the moment this meeting adjourned, Anton would have a target on his back. With that sobering thought, he continued into the castle, the wheels already turning in his mind. He had a plan. He could survive this—if he left the country immediately.

When he reached the library, his closest friend, Simeon Mendev, was exactly where Anton had left him: restocking books atop a perilously high ladder. Simeon's father was the head librarian at Karolinum, and Simeon worked under him as an apprentice. It was how Anton had befriended him, actually, since the library was his favorite haunt.

With a single look down, his friend's face grew grave.

The news had evidently traveled fast, but Simeon needn't be concerned. Anton held quite the advantage, seeing as he was a genius and the other competitors idiots. He could merely wait for them to pick each other off and then outsmart them during the trials—which he already had the perfect plan to do.

"Pack your bags," Anton declared to his friend, smirking as Simeon raised a questioning brow. "There's been a change of plans. That research trip we were planning to A'slenderia has just been rescheduled for tomorrow."

1

Katiel

Two Days after the Rescue of the Esteemed Royal Family of Bar Kur

The coastal city of Afdot sloped down into the glimmering harbor, and the crisp sea breeze was said to cure a multitude of ailments. Katiel Salzbruck, however, had no energy to appreciate any of it.

She was here for one reason, and one reason only—to find Anton Dvorsky and force him to return her stolen ore. The first time she'd been separated from the ore while away from home, she had passed out within seconds, but this time, she'd managed to stay conscious long enough to make it to Afdot, a port town in southern A'slenderia. Her only conclusion was that she still had some lingering ore residue on her hands or lodged deep in the hiding space between her teeth—enough to keep her functional—but it seemed even that meager supply was dwindling, because she grew increasingly fatigued.

After leaving Ballynach, Bar Kur, where she'd used the last of her ore to free the Barkurian royal family from the clutches of the corrupt General Taregh, she'd stayed alert long enough to stow away on a train back to her home country. She'd fallen in and out of consciousness throughout the train ride and the subsequent carriage ride to Afdot. By the time she entered the harbor, she was doubling over with every step. She told herself it would only be a few more paces until she could make out the faces in the bustling harbor, and one of them had to be Anton's.

Anton was the first person to tell her she could wield the ore. He was the most handsome man she had ever seen, whose kiss made her lose track of every sense she possessed. He'd travelled with her across the continent only to swipe the ore once she finally trusted him.

He even had the nerve to leave a note with a coded message asking her to meet him here. Her jaw twitched just thinking about it. All of her was shaking, really, as she stood on the sidewalk, hunched over with her palms propped on her knees.

Fishermen and sailors paid her no heed as they bustled past, carrying nets and ropes to set out for a morning at sea. She had been to this harbor once with Father when she was ten—nearly eight years ago, now—but she hadn't remembered it being nearly this crowded. Most of the people looked like her, with blond hair and fair skin. Anton, on the other hand, had light olive-toned skin and thick waves of deep brown hair, and there was no one like that milling about.

He wore the finest of clothes, but after stealing her ore, Katiel wondered if those were stolen, too. He might not even be from New Drezchy, for all she knew.

She took a few more steps down the sloped path, the small effort wrenching the air from her lungs. Slow and steady, she told herself. She could take as many breaks as she needed, but she wouldn't give up on finding him. Not when she was this close, and not when he possessed the exact thing that would heal her.

"It's her!" a man called in the distance, spiking the hairs on the back of her neck. Her instincts knew from those two words alone that the statement was meant for her. "The sorceress from the wanted posters!"

And that was enough for her to run.

Or at least, run as fast as she could manage in her current state.

After she and Brenna rescued the Barkurian royal family, Katiel was no longer wanted in Bar Kur, so she could only assume these men were bounty hunters who hadn't heard of her pardon. She thought she'd spied them back in Ballynach, but evading them had been easy enough in the crowded city. Now, with her ore withdrawals making even walking difficult, she might not be able to get away.

Her thighs screeched in protest as she broke into a sprint, but she pressed on. Gravity would do most of the work getting her down the hillside path, if only she could keep her footing.

Behind her, the crowd issued grumbles and protests as the men pushed through, but the road ahead was blissfully clear, lending a picturesque view of the morning harbor.

That was when she saw him.

Anton stood at the helm of the largest ship in the harbor, a three-masted clipper flying the flag of New Drezchy. From this distance, his features were still a blur, but from the posture alone, she knew it was him. He faced the town with his hands clasped behind his back as he surveyed the shoreline.

She would not allow herself to consider that he might be looking for *her*, and she ignored the fluttering that sprang up in her chest at the mere sight of him. He wasn't trustworthy, and she wasn't the naïve girl from when they met. She refused to be.

Her chest burned as the ground leveled out, forcing more exertion to keep up her speed. With a painful snap, her ankle twisted against a jagged paver that she noticed a second too late. Suddenly, she tumbled, her bare forearms scraping against the stone street.

She braced her palms against the ground to stop herself and stole a glance behind her. The fall had cost her—her pursuers were pushing past the last of the pedestrians, mere feet from her, and the impact had knocked away what remained of her breath. She had the errant thought to call out for Anton, somehow forgetting that he was her enemy now, too, just as much as these men were.

No, she would not call for him. Instead, she feigned helplessness, leaning back onto her elbows to conserve the last bit of her strength. The element of surprise might be the last weapon she possessed.

As she hoped, when the two reached her, they didn't bother speaking, instead reaching down as if to haul her to her feet. With all her might, she kicked upward, her boot colliding with the head of one man and slamming him directly into the skull of the other.

It was enough to stun them—enough time for her to get away.

She leapt to her feet in a last mad dash. The tops of her thighs and backs of her calves locked up like she was a wooden marionette, but she pushed through. From the sounds of the footfalls, her pursuers were still close behind, and after her and Brenna's treatment by General Taregh, she would not risk being captured again.

Ahead, the sky itself seemed to point to Anton's ship as a single beam of sunlight shone through the clouds. Mercifully, there was no one on the gangway as she approached. Anton was no longer on the upper deck, but she had no time to check for him elsewhere as she bounded over the gangplank in one last stride. She heard someone shout for her to halt, but she had no strength to turn back as she collapsed onto the deck and broke into a coughing fit.

There was no air left in her lungs. Her palms pressed into slimy muck on the damp wooden deck, but she was too weak to move her hands away.

A guard stepped in front of her, and Katiel wrenched her neck up to look at him, trying unsuccessfully to suppress her cough. He wore a coat with silver shoulder pads and pins across his chest, a regalia she did not recognize.

"Mad woman," he addressed her. "You have three seconds to convince me not to throw you off of this ship."

"Anton," she panted, unsure if the words were even intelligible. "I am here for—"

"How dare you—" the guard began, only to be interrupted by the two pursuers. Another guard blocked them as they tried to storm onto the main deck.

"Hand her over!" the one she had kicked in the head shouted. "She's ours."

Katiel tried to protest as indigo splotches cut across her vision. Only tiny slivers of the world peaked through, the spots growing with every blink.

"How fortunate for her that this craft belongs to me." It was Anton's voice, but with a soulless edge she had never heard before. "Now leave my ship before I gut you both."

Katiel could not see him or anything else. She tried to breathe again, but it came slower, staggered.

"And the girl, your highness?"

Everything was indigo. Her hand slipped out from under her, and her forehead collided with the deck.

Ice coated Anton's voice. "She belongs to me as well."

And then an arm reached around her, cradling her back, and another scooped up her knees, lifting her into the air. Her face fell against a swath of velvet as she went under at last.

2

KATIEL

WHEN KATIEL OPENED HER eyes, she was lying atop an itchy comforter in the same pattern as the black-and-gold filigreed canopy stretched over the bed. She hurried to sit up, only to notice a strange substance above the square neckline of her lavender dress. Peering down, it took her a moment to make it out, and she scrunched her nose when she realized. Right across her collarbone, someone had smeared a thin layer of ore, the dark pewter dust glimmering even in the dim lighting.

"Katiel," Anton breathed, drawing her attention. He stood next to the bed, gnawing at his thumbnail. "Are you feeling better?"

Katiel scoffed. "Yes, but please save us both the trouble, and don't pretend you care again. You stole my ore. You're the reason I fainted at all."

Anton sucked in a breath, but he didn't object. "What happened to your necklace?"

Katiel fumed, for once not bothering to hide the extent of her feelings. "The guards took it when I was sent to prison!"

His feigned concern for her wellbeing was bad enough, and now, he even had the nerve to look sorry. "I thought you kept extra hidden in your teeth," he said, reminding her of the suggestion he'd given her back in A'slenderia to keep a small amount of ore on her person at all times, in case something happened to her pouch of ore. In retrospect, the advice foreshadowed Anton's own plans to steal the rest.

"I do brush my teeth, you know," she snapped, the intended barb sounding better in her head. "But I'm surprised you didn't try to steal it with your mouth when you kissed me."

That sounded better in her mind as well.

Still, it seemed to have the intended effect, because the color drained from Anton's face.

A throat cleared from the opposite corner. Katiel shifted her gaze to find Simeon, Anton's closest friend, shuffling his feet in the opposite corner and pushing his glasses up to cover his widened eyes. "Shall I leave you two alone?" he asked.

Katiel spat, "No!" at the same moment that Anton said, "Please." Then Anton gave a tiny nod, and Simeon left the room.

In the momentary silence that followed, Katiel took in her surroundings. She supposed this was the captain's quarters, though she'd never been aboard a ship before today. Dark wood stretched into every corner of the space, and on the far wall was a grand bay window, the floor-to-ceiling glass divided into tiny square panes.

Katiel had a mind to ask where they were, but she had a feeling that she already knew—Anton's chambers. Which meant she was lying atop his bed.

She rushed away, nearly colliding with a large globe on a three-legged wooden stand in her haste. From where she stood, the horizon line where the ocean met the sea was barely visible, and her breath hitched as a thought occurred to her. "Have we left the shore?"

"No, we're still docked," Anton rushed out, like speaking faster might prevent her from leaving. "I wouldn't set off with you on board, not unless you agreed to come with me."

"*You* wouldn't...?" Katiel started, confused by his role. He pretended to be a scholar when they met, but the truth could be anything. At the moment, he wore a silver-trimmed navy jacket with dual-breasted silver buttons and several pins across the shoulder, along with knee-high black leather boots. "Who are you pretending to be now, a pirate? A ship captain?"

"I was never pretending, Katiel," he replied, his tone infuriatingly kind.

"You weren't? When?" she demanded. "When you claimed to be a university student, studying my culture? Or when you pretended to be interested in me just to get close enough to untie the pouch of ore from my waistband?"

He stalked over to the window, gazing out with his hands clasped against his lower back. If she didn't know better, judging by his sagging shoulders and sullen expression, she would have believed him to be remorseful.

"You know what, never mind," Katiel said, deciding she didn't want to wait for more excuses. It was maddening to see him so calm when her insides were a thunderstorm of raw anger. "I couldn't care less about you or your reasons. Return the rest of my ore so I can be on my way, before this vessel departs A'slenderia."

Anton glided to a tall dresser beside the bed, his heeled boots soundless against the wood floor. He reached into the top drawer for only a moment, craning his arm under linens to pull out a parcel—a mouse-gray velvet pouch, the one she used to store her ore. Wordlessly, he handed it to her.

Katiel untied the strings of the pouch and peered in. The platinum dust shimmered back at her, the stores appearing untouched. "I don't understand. Why steal it and then give it back so easily?"

Just then, a knock sounded, and the door to the stateroom creaked open. The same guard who had addressed Katiel earlier stepped in. "Your Royal Highness, the captives are demanding to be released," he began, before noticing Katiel standing there. Instantly, he ducked his head and stared at his shoes. "Forgive me, my liege. I did not realize you had company." He didn't look up as he rushed out of the space, colliding with the doorframe in his hurry to get away.

Katiel scoffed. She didn't know quite what to make of this, but whatever game Anton was now playing at, she wanted no part in it. Whether he was pretending to be a pirate, or royalty, or someone else entirely was of no consequence to her. Her pouch of ore in-hand, she made for the door.

"Wait, Katiel, please. Let me explain myself."

He reached out like he might grab her wrist, but the searing hatred she felt must have shone in her eyes, because he recoiled from her glance like he'd been burned.

"*Bitye.*" He repeated the request in Aslen, the language of her home valley, that she still could not believe a foreigner could speak. "*Lasen siet mit erklarn.*"

How dare he, was her first thought. How dare this man speak her language to her now, to manipulate her further after all he had done.

She almost told him that, too, but something in his expression held her back. His doe eyes bore into hers, contrasting against his chiseled features, set in fierce determination. He didn't look like a thief, but rather someone who had something important to accomplish—someone who felt like she had when she set off with Brenna to stop the false war. Katiel wondered if he was already fooling her again, if he was that skilled at manipulation.

Anton always has his reasons. The last words Sera spoke to Katiel flashed across her mind. While secretly working for the mysterious mastermind, Sera had betrayed her and Brenna, but then returned to save them when they needed her help the most. She was the ex-girlfriend of Anton's older sister and a trained assassin, and it seemed like she would have no reason to lie on Anton's behalf. Unless there was some key piece to this puzzle that Katiel was missing.

When Katiel had first agreed to let Anton come along on their quest, it hadn't been because she found him to be trustworthy, but rather because he'd known things that no one else had. Today, she felt the same. The war was not over, and between his intellect and unexpected connections, Anton may prove useful to her yet.

So, she said, "Fine."

She took a seat at the ornately carved table by the windows, hoping to hide how winded she remained as she waited for him to continue. But when he hesitated for a second too long, she snapped, "Explain yourself."

"It's a long story," Anton said, pacing from the table to the bed and back again.

Katiel scowled, rubbing at the shimmering layer of ore on her chest. "If you truly command this ship, then we have plenty of time."

"I do." Anton's eyes flashed. "I've had us docked here for days waiting for you. I trusted you would discern my note in time."

Katiel wanted to ask how he knew she would come, and how he could have possibly known she would make it out of Bar Kur alive. But instead, she swallowed hard and said, "Then explain."

"Very well." Anton nodded, a muscle ticking in his square jaw. "I'm going back to New Drezchy to kill the mastermind behind this war."

His eyes locked on hers, imploring her to understand. She could hardly form words to reply.

"You know who it is?"

"Yes," he said, his expression ablaze with a fire she had not seen before. "It's my uncle, King Vadim of New Drezchy."

The room spun around her, a ship rocking on the calm sea.

King Vadim, the cruel ruler across the ocean, who seemed to her more of a storybook villain than a living, breathing human, was the puppetmaster pulling General Taregh's strings all along. If this were the case, it changed everything. And some deep instinct told her that Anton spoke the truth.

"I didn't know it was him when Mara first mentioned 'the boss,'" Anton continued, still pacing. "It was that night in the hostel when it hit me, the night I left. Before we—erm, retired—I was thinking about who would benefit most from this war, and I realized it should have been obvious."

Katiel couldn't help the thought that passed—that it almost sounded like talking to her gave Anton mental clarity, the same way he did for her. But she knew that was just wishful thinking—and she shouldn't still wish it, anyhow.

"An allied war across Kerafin," he explained, "would finally provide an opportunity for what every New Drezchy ruler has promised since the country was founded: reclaiming our former lands. Reclaiming the Old Drezchy, the homeland we lost to the continent of Kerafin in the Ten Years' War. A war would weaken the continent enough to reclaim it. It would require sacrificing many innocent lives, but my uncle's ruthless enough to do it."

Katiel pursed her lips, letting the information sink in. Though it wasn't the motive she'd expected, she had to admit that the logic stood to reason.

"There's just one thing that doesn't add up," Anton added with a wry smirk. "How my uncle came up with such an elaborate plan, considering he's an absolute idiot."

Though he clearly meant it as a joke, Katiel only stared at him as she processed his theory. It all made sense, and at the same time, none of it made any sense at all. "Please, go back. Start from the beginning. Who are you really, and what were you really doing in A'slenderia when we met?"

With that, Anton leaned against the back of the chair opposite her, and launched into one of the strangest tales she had ever heard. From the beginning of the story to the end, which was the day she and Anton met, she found herself leaning closer and closer. She could honestly say she hadn't expected any of it, least of all the bloody competition for the throne.

"If you were the crown prince, then does that also mean you're the Ghost?" Katiel asked, recalling one of the only bits of information she had ever heard about the Drezchy royal family. The Ghost, who Katiel had always assumed was the king's son rather than his nephew, was said to be as cruel as the notorious monarch.

Anton smirked down at her, but she could swear his knuckles grew whiter as he gripped the chair. "So, you *have* heard of me."

"Very little," she amended. "I had never seen your portrait or a sketch in the newspaper, and I'd never once heard the Ghost was called Anton. I've never seen a portrait of your uncle, either."

He scoffed. "You're not missing much."

Katiel wanted to laugh, but she held back. He clearly despised his uncle, though she wasn't about to inquire as to why. "Why did you come to A'slenderia, though? Why not hide out in the Drezchy countryside, where no one would ever find you?"

"My cousins aren't like me. They're all around my age, but they're massive. They fight with axes and maces above guns—just to show they can. I wanted to let them pick each other off while I was gone, but when I returned, I wanted to win."

She waited for him to continue, not quite following.

"In my uncle's court, wielders are far from ancient history. We've employed at least six official court wielders that I can remember, though we haven't had one for a few years now."

Katiel couldn't imagine growing up in a world where wielding was ordinary. Then again, she could hardly imagine growing up in a royal court at all.

"I've drawn blueprints for a catalogue of powerful weapons," he went on, "but didn't have the time to prototype, much less build them. My plan was to come to the Northern Mountains, the homeland of the wielders, and hire a new court wielder myself. If they could wield my deadliest inventions for me, it would ensure my victory."

Katiel let the information sink in—let it line up with everything that had happened. Anton's interest in her, his ability to recognize her necklace and the symbols of the wielders and keepers, suddenly shone with new clarity. Sera's ability to instruct her in wielding, despite only posing as a keeper, finally made sense as well. Since Sera was from Anton's court, she would have seen wielding demonstrated before. Anton must have let Sera take the lead in instructing her to further conceal his identity, though she did recall him cutting in quite often.

"So, what happened?" she asked. "Why didn't you hire a wielder for your court and return home?"

"You know what happened," he said, flashing his perfectly white, straight smile. "I was looking for an old man with a long beard, like the wielders I remembered as a child. Instead, the one I found was the most beautiful girl I'd ever seen, who had no idea of the ability she possessed and who was on a more important mission than I was."

Katiel scolded her chest for fluttering. She was falling into the exact same trap she had when she'd traveled with him before. But the prince didn't truly believe his own words. He was a flatterer, who'd say whatever he could to win her over.

"You never asked me to work for you, though," she reminded him. "You just stole my ore and left. And I don't understand how the raw ore would help with your uncle, anyway. You can't wield it."

"I thought perhaps if I had enough of it to study, I could use it myself," Anton said, his eyes falling as though he weren't telling her everything. He stepped away from her, heading for a line of maps above the dresser that Katiel had not noticed until now. "But I was wrong. I shouldn't have taken it, and I regret what I did immensely."

He seemed sincere, and he had given it back. She didn't know how to respond.

"Besides, none of that matters now." He flung his hand in the air at the declaration. "You and Brenna were right to try to end a false war.

The competition for the throne doesn't matter to me anymore, and neither does finding a court wielder. I'm done with playing Vadim's games. I intend to end the war the simplest way I can. The day I return to Vincencim, I'm going to kill my uncle."

"Then who will rule in his place?" Katiel asked, her nose wrinkling. "Won't they continue with his plot?"

Anton shook his head. "No one is as crazed as him."

"It would not guarantee the war would end though, not really," Katiel said, as much to herself as to him. A plan was forming in her mind, painting itself into a clearer picture as the room before her blurred. She didn't know how many people might still come after her, and she didn't want to lead them home to her parents. If Anton meant what he said, and his intention of ending the war was true, eliminating his uncle would accomplish little. Securing his place on the throne, on the other hand, could guarantee New Drezchy's compliance in a peace treaty.

"What if you try something else?"

Anton looked over his shoulder, a mischievous grin creeping across his face. "What do you have in mind?"

"You said your uncle would hand over the throne to whoever won the contest and end his life with the rite of the Bloody Bird."

Anton winced. "Blood Raven."

"Yes, that," Katiel said in a rush. She needed to suggest this plan quickly, before she thought better of it. "So, go with your original plan and hire me. I will help you win the throne, if you promise to end all of New Drezchy's meddling and promote peace once you're in power."

The prince's eyes were spinning in amazement, gawking at her like she was a scientific experiment that had finally yielded the right results. "You would do that?"

"To end the war before more lives are lost," she answered, standing as Anton walked around to her side of the table, "I would, yes. I would do anything."

"Then it's settled." He extended his hand, and she gave it a firm shake, the smirk never leaving his lips. "Welcome to the court of New Drezchy."

3

Brenna

Two Weeks After the Coronation of Queen Stefana I

As usual, Brenna Malley was struggling to hold her tongue.

She stood near the wall in the Grand Hall, only a few paces behind Queen Stefana—who Brenna had taken to calling Steffi, at least in private. After Brenna and Katiel rescued the then-princess and her two younger brothers from where the corrupt Barkurian General Taregh kept them imprisoned, Steffi had asked Brenna to be her lady-in-waiting. Since her parents, the king and queen of Bar Kur, were betrayed by their confidants, Steffi wanted someone she could trust by her side.

This morning, Steffi headed a long mahogany table, with ten of her advisors and cabinet members seated along each side, while the group discussed the ongoing war with Tibedo and A'slenderia. Since Brenna accepted ladyship weeks ago, state meetings had touched on little else.

"Our units have made progress on the main front," said Lord Ovach, the Secretary of Internal Affairs. An impish man with a curled mustache, he always spoke as though he were trying to be heard in a crowd, even if he were the only one speaking. "Thursday's battle was a success."

"Fine progress indeed," Lord Walsh agreed, stroking an off-white beard that had likely once been red. He was the new Secretary of War, the replacement for General Taregh—whose treachery was conspicuously never mentioned in these meetings. "A couple more victories will surely have Tibedo ceding to us."

"But what will they have to cede?" the Secretary of the Treasury, Lord Byrne, objected. "Tibedo will have nothing left once they've paid A'slenderia off for their aid."

The longer she listened, the more Brenna wanted to scream.

As far as the Barkurian public knew, the Tibedese assassin Inigo Farro shot King Steven XIV during a parade. That catalyst prompted Bar Kur to declare war against Tibedo in retaliation, before Katiel's home country of A'slenderia joined on the side of Tibedo. As it turned out, not only had a Barkurian, General Taregh, framed Farro, but Farro's tip led to the royal family's rescue. Despite it all, neither the queen nor her cabinet had made any move to broker an amicable end to the conflict.

Brenna knew she wasn't meant to contribute during these meetings; she was simply on-call in case the queen needed a handkerchief or her skirt straightened. Still, every minute, she fought the urge to interject. Her eighteen-year-old brother, Henred, had already died fighting during an early battle at the border, after Brenna begged him not to volunteer. She'd received the tragic news of his passing the same day she became lady-in-waiting. Ever since, hearing a joke he would've laughed at, or seeing Steffi sitting with her brothers at dinner, would remind Brenna of her brother. Each time, she excused herself to go bawl in her tiny bedroom in the castle. In her hometown of Fir Kelt, surely someone would have noticed her perpetually swollen eyelids, but here in Ballynach, no one paid any heed to her blotches and puffiness.

To make matters worse, her friend—*perhaps more than friend*—Dakier was still fighting on the opposite side of the war, having been drafted to the Tibedese army. Every day of delaying the ceasefire was a chance that he might be killed, and Brenna's only hope was that she could persuade Steffi to end the war before Dakier met the same perilous fate as her beloved brother.

"It sounds as though everything is proceeding as expected," Steffi decreed, sounding far older than her age. "If there are no further inquiries, I call this meeting adjourned."

And not a moment too soon, Brenna thought.

"Forgive me, your highness. There is one further complication to the matter that we might discuss," Lord Walsh said, placing his elbows on the long oak table with a *thunk.* "After our recent victory, now is the time to advance into Tibedo."

Lord Byrne hummed his agreement. "Agreed," he said, his thin lips twisting into a graceless smile. "Ensuring their swift defeat is the only way to protect our queen and the continuity of her sovereign line."

The way he spoke about protecting the queen set Brenna's worries alight. What if the statesmen *didn't* know the truth about Farro? What if, for some incomprehensible reason, Steffi never told them what really happened, and all this time, the war was a single warning away from ending?

"You know that isn't the truth, don't you?" Brenna blurted out from her post at the wall, well and truly unable to contain herself. "Tibedo doesn't pose a threat. There was no Tibedese assassin. General Taregh killed the king, but Taregh is out of the picture now. Bar Kur could enter into a new treaty and reach a truce."

Nausea washed over Brenna as every eye in the room turned to her with a mix of pity and derision. It was clear that no one was considering the merit of what she'd said, not even for a moment. It was like she spoke a different language, or was a child so small that anything she said could be a fairy story.

Lord Walsh cut his eyes toward her for a fleeting second before focusing again on his hands, his discomfort evident. "Yes, we are all aware of those unfortunate events regarding Taregh and Inigo Farro, though Farro's whereabouts remain unknown."

Brenna clenched her teeth, his backtracking confirming what she'd suspected—that he knew protecting the queen wasn't their true concern. The lords could recommend a ceasefire, but they didn't want to—likely because they saw the peaceful resolution as a threat to Bar Kur's power. What Brenna didn't understand was why Steffi was going along with it.

"Let us return to the discussion at hand," the queen declared, though her tense shoulders betrayed her steady tone.

As one, the furrowed brows relaxed and heads turned, bringing the focus back toward the center of the table. No one felt the need to dignify Brenna's outburst with any further response. Steffi didn't look at her at all.

"As I was saying, we must plan our advance into Tibedo," Lord Walsh continued. "Fort Cajetan is along the path to Jinensin, and would be a suitable target if we mean to take the city. What say you, gentlemen?"

Brenna's cheeks burned, and her lower lashes filled up with unwept tears. She knew the lord was still talking, but she could scarcely make out the words. Her humiliation filled the room like a gas leak.

At least speaking up had done one thing—it had confirmed that all of them knew the truth, but no one was willing to put their own neck out to change anything.

Not the way Brenna had just now, not the way she had all summer, and not the way she was willing to again if things didn't change soon.

THE SECOND THE MEETING ended, Brenna rushed out a back door alone, rather than trailing the queen like she was meant to. She had to admit that she wasn't the best lady-in-waiting, and her role often felt like play-acting. The sole reason she'd taken on this title in the first place was to guide the queen toward peace, but she faced opposition at every turn.

She walked down the series of halls that led to the queen's chambers and drew out her key to enter the suite. There were several dressing and reclining rooms before one reached the queen's actual bedroom, and a nondescript door off of the last dressing room led to the tiny bedroom that Brenna now called home.

The space was more of a glorified wash closet than a bedroom, but it was elegantly appointed, with a hand-carved writing desk and a bed covered in the softest linens and a fine, forest-green tartan comforter. Living here also came with the unique perk of being the only person other than Steffi herself who carried a key to the suite, since the queen didn't even trust the royal guards after her parents' deaths. Actually, Brenna recalled, that wasn't entirely accurate, since Prince Eoghan held a key to his sister's room as well, but the thought brought a fresh wave of agony as Brenna's own brother came to mind.

A salty tear stung Brenna's cheek as she sat at the writing desk, pulled out Henred's final letter, and reread the worn page for the thousandth time. It was the note he'd sent after she'd left with Katiel, where he said he was proud of her for leaving home to make things right, and his penned words meant everything in his absence.

"Brenna?" Steffi called into the chamber, snapping Brenna out of her reverie.

The young queen stood just beyond the threshold, and Brenna hastily wiped at her eyes as she stuffed the letter back into the drawer. Mere weeks ago, at just twelve years old, the now-queen had witnessed the assassination of her father during a public parade before being kidnapped and kept in inhumane conditions for weeks. During her imprisonment, Steffi's mother, the queen, had died right beside her, but had remained chained to the wall next to her children for days after passing. The young girl was traumatized, even if she didn't show it, and Brenna didn't want to burden her further with her own loss.

In fact, that was why she'd started calling her "Steffi" in private rather than "Your Royal Highness Queen Stefana I." After only a few days as lady-in-waiting, Brenna noticed that, aside from her two younger brothers, the queen had no friends. There was an emotional chasm between the queen and even her closest subjects, and Brenna felt for her. When Brenna's own father passed away, and her mother became emotionally unavailable, Brenna had Katiel, Henred, her older sister, Derenta, and countless friendly acquaintances in town who were at least her equal.

So, when Brenna noticed the queen's brothers called her "Steffi," she took a chance and tried it herself, and was rewarded with the first genuine smile she'd ever seen on the queen's face. At that moment, she'd vowed to be the queen's friend instead of her subject, even if the rest of the court found Brenna impertinent for her casual manners.

"Were you crying?" Steffi asked, her auburn ringlets spilling over her shoulders as she dipped her small, heavily freckled face. "Do not fret over the meeting today. The lords are calling for you to be removed from your position, but I will do no such thing."

Brenna's eyes shot wide, unaware of the alarming demands. "Thank you?" she said feebly, and then coughed. "Thank you, Steffi."

"After you left, the discussion continued a bit further," the queen explained, supplying the answer to Brenna's unasked question, "but I do want to end the war. Truly, I do."

Brenna brightened. "You do?"

This was exactly what she wished the queen had said during the official meeting, rather than privately afterward. It occurred to her that perhaps the queen was afraid of her cabinet members, since one of them had already murdered her parents. It would make sense for her to fear herself becoming the next target if she didn't go along with their wishes, but Brenna hoped she'd have the courage to do the right thing.

Steffi nodded, her narrow mouth pressed into a soft smile. "I do. And I've decided that I'm going to send word to the Tibedese High Magisters, to see if they'd be willing to send a delegate to begin negotiations for peace."

Brenna gasped and leapt to her feet, throwing her arms around the queen a second after she finished her sentence.

This was amazing, and perfect, and everything Brenna could've hoped for. Henred may be gone, but others like him could return home soon.

4

Brenna

Several days later, Brenna walked into the castle dining hall, a spacious room with stone walls covered in ten-foot tall portraits and a comically long, polished wood table in the center. Barkurian flags hung on vertical wooden support beams, and green pennants streamed overhead, drooping to form little smiles every few feet.

Brenna paused as a servant pulled her chair out for her, and she awkwardly nodded her thanks. She would never get over being waited on like this, when just a month ago she was waiting on hostel guests passing through her tiny hometown.

Steffi sat at the end of the table, and Brenna's place was directly opposite hers, underscoring her role as the queen's right hand. Prince Eoghan sat opposite her, with little Prince Muiread beside him on a stately, tasseled cushion to help him reach the table. The other thirty-odd seats remained empty. Eoghan's shaggy, strawberry-blond bangs flipped as he shot the two girls a wave, but Brenna's smile was forced as she waved back. The last two times she'd been to dinner, everything had turned out fine, but—

Brenna shifted her empty dinner plate the tiniest bit, just to check, and her stomach dropped. Peaking out from beneath the silver plate was the corner of an envelope, and the unwelcome sight sent sweat beading at her hairline.

Though she'd never been particularly stealthy, Brenna tried to keep her features neutral, and thankfully, the others paid her no mind. As usual, Steffi engaged her brothers in conversation, asking about their studies like a mother might, while Brenna slid the envelope out and pushed it beneath the table.

Brenna thumbed the paper in her hands, keeping it out of sight between the folds of the deep green tablecloth. She traced an index finger over her full name, penned in capital letters on the envelope. No return address was listed, and once again, she hadn't seen who placed it. It was the third letter like this she'd received. Each time, the bearer had evidently waited until the hall was empty to slip the note under Brenna's plate unnoticed, and this instance was no different.

She had a feeling the menacing contents on the inside would be the same as well.

Brenna glanced at the others, still engrossed in their conversation, before she popped open the seal, a burgundy wax circle with no stamp or signet to lend a clue as to the sender. Inside was a close variant of the same message the others had borne.

Leave Bar Kur, murderous traitor, while you still have a life to leave with.

A chill crept up her neck and slithered around to the back of her ears. She could only assume that the "murderous" part referred to General Taregh, though technically Katiel had killed him. The "traitor" portion, she reasoned, meant her association with Katiel. Still, the notes struck Brenna as nothing short of bizarre. The nation's queen herself had cleared Brenna of all charges, and even honored her with a noble title.

Though the cabinet members weren't exactly fans of hers, she'd received the first two before she spoke up in the state meeting, so she didn't think the letters were coming from them. No, she held the sickening feeling it was from the mastermind behind the war, or at least from someone doing their bidding.

The mastermind had ordered the execution of the King of Bar Kur, so Brenna knew what they'd be willing to do to silence her. She knew she should tell Steffi about it, but didn't want to bother the queen with anything other than reaching a ceasefire.

Strangely, like the other two notes before it, this missive was written in green ink, something Brenna never recalled seeing before. The notes also all bore several smudges with criss-crossing, uneven lines not unlike a fingerprint, and as Brenna tucked the note back under the tablecloth, she wondered if that could be a clue as to who wrote it.

She covertly looked down at her own hands as she ate, pondering if it was indeed a fingerprint, when she realized that she had a black ink mark down the heel of her left palm from writing home earlier that day. The heel of a hand—that was it! The mystery author was left-handed, which was a clue indeed.

Brenna told herself she could leave the note in her lap and enjoy her dinner, but she barely tasted the braised beef and potatoes. She found herself tugging at the collar of her dress repeatedly, wondering when it had gotten so warm, and she wound up excusing herself before the waiters brought dessert. It might not be the right time to tell the queen, but she couldn't stand to sit before the others with false smiles when her insides were a whirlwind. For now, she would walk around the city and clear her mind. Or, more accurately, worry about the same thing while getting some exercise.

Rather than wait for a footman like she was supposed to, she closed the dining hall doors herself and set off down the hall, her heeled slippers clanging noisily against the smooth stone tiles. All the halls in the castle looked alike, with rows of windows stretching floor-to-ceiling along one side and perpetually abandoned, tufted chairs lining the other.

When she finally reached the southern exit, she placed her hands on her hips and blew a stray red curl from her forehead. The grand doors loomed in front of her, but the footmen were nowhere in sight. A previous scolding had taught her not to pull the levers and unlock the thick metal drawbar herself, though it hadn't taken much to figure out the supposedly secure system.

She figured she could slip out the servants' exit by the kitchens, but she scarcely had time to turn around before the bronze latches began creaking of their own accord. The rope-and-pulley system pried the doors apart with surprising speed, and Brenna had to jump back to avoid getting smacked by the heavy oak.

Immediately, the guards who normally stood watch shuffled into the hallway, followed by a small legion of soldiers. They weren't wearing the deep green uniforms of the Barkurian army, though, but rather drab brown, collared, short-sleeve shirts tucked into belted, pleated trousers of the same color—Tibedese soldiers.

Steffi's request had already reached the Tibedese, and Brenna's heart soared. They'd agreed to a peaceful deliberation even after the false accusations against one of their own, and soon, the countries of Kerafin would be in harmony once again.

Short, flat-topped hats adorned their heads of thick, black hair, and nearly every soldier had a copper skin-tone, notably different from the fair skin that was most common in her nation. Each soldier moved in unison, with arms swinging in step at their sides and eyes focused straight ahead.

She watched, waiting for the half-dozen men to file through so she could make her exit. But when she glimpsed the final soldier marching into the castle, Brenna's breath hitched.

In front of her, wearing the same standard-issue uniform as the rest, was Dakier.

If she'd been holding something, she surely would have dropped it. It took all her willpower not to race up to him that very second.

Dakier was alive.

Dakier was *alive.*

Somehow, he'd avoided the battlefield for a different sort of position, the sort that was sent for peaceful meetings in foreign castles. But as to what his role actually was, she could only guess.

Since he was the tallest of the group, he was easy to track, but his gaze was locked firmly forward. The shoulders of his shirt were too tight, and his cheekbones were so sharp, making him somehow even more gorgeous than he'd been when they'd parted mere weeks ago. And when he'd picked her up and kissed her—

Quickly, she slipped off her noisy shoes and pinched the backs between her fingers, trailing the group. If anyone questioned her, she could simply say she'd hurt her foot. After all, she was allowed to be here, and there was no chance she was leaving the castle for a walk now.

The soldiers stopped outside the throne room, which was strange, since Steffi didn't have any appointments on her calendar after dinner. And if someone else was meeting with the Tibedese procession—

Suddenly, the group lurched forward and into the throne room, jerking Brenna from her thoughts. To her surprise, Dakier hung back, bending down to tie his loose shoelace.

It was a momentary delay at most, but it was more than she'd expected. Now was her chance.

"Dakier," Brenna hissed, hanging back by a corner where the hallway veered to the east. "Dakier!"

When they locked eyes, the strangest series of expressions passed over him. First it was relief, his features softening like she was the one person in the world he wanted to see, then sheer panic, his square jaw locking with an unnatural clench.

"Brenna?" he whispered back, darting a quick glance toward the throne room.

She waved him toward her. "Hurry!"

With another glance over his shoulder, he complied, crossing the hallway to where she lingered in the shadows. Wasting no time, she enveloped him in a tight hug. But instead of wrapping his arms around her like she expected, he stiffened, not reaching for her at all.

He gave her a tense pat on the back before he stepped away. His face was frozen, unreadable, with his jaw still clenched. "What are you doing here?"

"I could ask you the same." Brenna scrunched her nose in confusion. It was strange that he sounded concerned for *her* safety when *he* was the one in the heart of enemy territory. "It's a long story, but I'm the queen's lady-in-waiting now."

One of Dakier's eyebrows swung down while the other shot up to his hairline. "You're what now?"

"Never mind that." Brenna needed to know he was safe before his group discovered he was missing. "Why are you in Bar Kur?"

"They made me a translator after I was injured in battle."

"Injured?" The word sent a pang of anxiety into Brenna, though he looked perfectly healthy. "In a battle?"

"Yes," he said, staring down at her with strange, disconsolate eyes. A bitter pang touched his voice as he turned toward the door behind him. "I need to go."

"Of course." Brenna nodded fervently, fearing she'd already gotten him into trouble for his absence. "Will I see you again?"

"I'll try."

And with that, he slipped into the throne room, leaving Brenna alone in her stockinged feet.

She couldn't stop thinking about that strange look on his face at the sight of her. The flicker of warm light was missing from Dakier's dark eyes, like his short time in the army had already changed him. He could've simply been terrified by combat, but she knew Dakier. Nothing that happened *to* him would haunt him like that. It wasn't in his nature to worry for himself—but it was certainly in his nature to regret his own actions. As cruel as it was to assume, she couldn't help but wonder if he'd hurt someone in the line of duty.

Or even killed someone.

If he had, he would need her more than ever.

5

Dakier

Dakier crept into the throne room as quietly as he could manage and took up his post beside his superior, Captain Pereira. They stood at attention with the rest of the unit, Dakier ready to translate the negotiations should anyone bother showing up to meet them.

After getting drafted to the army in his home country of Tibedo, Dakier had quickly bonded with Pereira after the captain discovered Dakier's affinities for smithing, tending to horses, and speaking foreign languages. Since he'd lived with Katiel's family in A'slenderia for years before receiving his draft notice, Dakier spoke three languages fluently—Aslen, the regional language of the Northern Mountains; Endran, the language spoken in Bar Kur and in most of A'slenderia; and Tibedese, his own native tongue, which was spoken throughout Tibedo.

Tibedo ran on a federal system, with eleven regions that each elected a magistrate to govern their region and convene in the capital when national decisions had to be made. When his unit was assigned to accompany Magister Jao to Ballynach for peace negotiations, Pereira selected Dakier to come along as the translator, and after a week of travel, their unit had finally arrived at the castle. Pereira had repeatedly warned them to be on guard against an ambush, fearing that the entire invitation was a trick, but Dakier's hyperawareness had vanished the moment he saw Brenna.

"Didn't peg you for the type," Captain Pereira remarked as soon as he spotted Dakier.

"Sir?" Dakier gulped. He'd been hoping that, somehow, his superior officer hadn't noticed his absence.

"I didn't see you being the type to shirk your duties to flirt with foreign courtiers." Pereira smirked. "And on our first day in Bar Kur, no less."

"Oh no, sir, you've got it all wrong," Dakier stammered, though the captain didn't sound entirely disapproving. "She—erm, she merely tripped going past me. Her heel broke, and I helped her to her feet."

The excuse didn't sound plausible, he knew, and Pereira was no fool.

"You sure picked the prettiest girl in Bar Kur to conveniently help," was the officer's dry quip as he turned to face forward, ending the conversation.

Though the captain seemed more amused than angry, Dakier wished he could set the record straight. Unfortunately, the truth was far worse than the immature flirtation Pereira assumed.

Actually, I'm not the type. That girl is the one I've had a crush on for years, then finally confessed my love to right before I arrived for the draft. And if it wasn't bad enough that I had a secret Barkurian girlfriend while I fought for Tibedo, I accidentally killed her beloved brother in combat, so although she doesn't know it, she should actually hate me.

No, that didn't sound any better.

On the long journey from Fort Cajetan to Ballynach, Dakier had thought of little else. Each time, shame filled him at the memory of what a coward he'd been—slashing and slaughtering every Barkurian soldier in his path in a desperate bid to survive, his vow of pacifism forgotten.

During the battle, he hadn't thought. He'd only acted. But now that the rush of adrenaline was long in the past, he didn't know if dying that day would've been such a bad thing.

At least he wouldn't be here now. Being in Ballynach—no, being in Bar Kur at all—was far too close to Brenna for comfort. Though the possibility of seeing her had been in the back of his mind all day, the last thing he'd expected was to see her wandering around the castle, jovial at the sight of him.

The way she'd looked at him when he pulled away from her embrace just moments ago, stricken at his rejection—Dakier couldn't bear to see the hurt on her face. By now, she had likely already heard the news of her brother's passing, and his coldness had probably made her feel even worse.

The queen was late to greet them, but since they were in her throne room, Dakier supposed that meant they were simply a half hour early. Brenna walked behind her throughout the short introductory procession and then stood behind the thrones for the rest of it. Her expression was uncharacteristically sullen throughout, and Dakier found himself worrying over how well she was adjusting to this role. Being a lady didn't suit her free spirit, though in the full-skirted mauve-and-violet plaid dress she wore, she certainly looked the part. His traitorous eyes kept sneaking glances at her when he was supposed to listen to the queen.

By the end of the uneventful meeting—which consisted of one unnamed statesperson filibustering and Dakier doing his best to rapidly translate before being dismissed—he was certain he'd see Brenna many more times again before the negotiations made any progress.

If he had to be around her for this assignment, he would have to come clean to her and take responsibility for what had happened. Learning the truth would hurt her, but it would hurt her even more to find out after showering him with kindness. He couldn't put her through further betrayal.

Though he wished he could explain himself to Brenna after the introductory meeting concluded, Pereira ordered him to tend to the Tibedese horses before retiring to the delegation's appointed rooms.

He would have to find a more suitable time to break the terrible news to her.

When he parted ways with his fellow soldiers, a Barkurian lord assigned a nameless guard to escort him across the castle courtyard, since the Tibedese weren't allowed unaccompanied on the castle grounds—or in the capital at all—during wartime.

The two of them walked outside into a nondescript castle side-yard, where stable hands tended to the royal horses and servants stowed a carriage next to a row of others. The sky was a shade of burnt orange that seemed exclusive to Bar Kur, and gravel crunched beneath Dakier's standard-issue army boots. In no time, they reached the stable assigned to the Tibedese delegation, where Kranich, one of the Salzbruck family's horses that Dakier had brought along with him when he reported for the draft, was being housed alongside the others.

The stallion gave a merry whinny when he spied Dakier. He hurried over to the horse, stroking the side of Kranich's neck in greeting, but then he realized with a jolt that the guard was no longer behind him. Dakier angled out of the covered stable, craning his neck until he spied the guard. He was standing on the opposite side of the path, leaning in the open washhouse window to flirt with some maids.

With a shrug, Dakier went back to Kranich and got to work, keen on getting to bed after the long day of travel, but he'd only just finished re-plaiting the horse's mane when he heard a strange yelp. He ducked behind the door, anxious as he scanned the courtyard that his countrymen had already been ambushed. But there was no sign of activity, save for the guard laughing at his own joke before he told another.

"So, a fisherman, a barber, and an A'slenderian walked into a bar—"

"Argh!"

The cry sounded again, but the guard didn't take any notice. Dakier ventured farther into the gravel path between the buildings, craning his head toward the yell. The only building it could've come from was the blacksmith's forge adjacent to the stables, and Dakier noted the flames flickering through the narrow, glassless window with a pleasant familiarity. It had been ages since he'd crafted anything himself in Feniel's shop back home. His curiosity got the better of him as he peered into the open doorway of the narrow smithy.

Inside was a lad of no more than eight or nine years of age, wearing a raggedy gray shirt and matching pants, with a burgundy newsboy cap pulled low over his eyes. He was clearly trying to forge something, holding a rod of black metal over the open fire with a pair of long tongs. But when the metal glowed orange, he panicked, dropping the tongs and the metal into the fire. Sparks went flying, two landing in the straw by his feet, and he frantically stomped them out before sighing in relief.

Dakier already didn't like seeing such a young kid working the forge by himself, but after witnessing that, he was certain the kid would hurt himself before long. Against his better judgment, and hoping the guard was as bad at his job as he seemed, Dakier cleared his throat.

"Need any help?"

The boy turned to him, pushing back a chunk of strawberry blond hair from his eyes, and Dakier waved.

"Do I?" the boy exclaimed. He spoke with a crisp, posh Barkurian accent, different from the ones Dakier was used to hearing from the citizens of Fir Kelt. Then, he stiffened abruptly. "I mean...that's alright. I'm fine on my own."

The kid was abnormally skinny—emaciated, even—and Dakier wondered why the royal household would employ such a slight child in such a dangerous role. One would think a skilled adult blacksmith wouldn't be terribly hard to come by.

"What are you working on?" Dakier asked, careful to keep one foot in the courtyard, lest the guard come looking. "Adjusting some shoes?"

"Yes," the boy said, idly shuffling his polished boot in the soot littering the forge's dirt floor. "No, actually, I was trying to make a decorative snake. A wall-hanging of sorts."

Dakier was skeptical about where anyone would want to hang that, but he forced an encouraging smile. "Well, why don't you have another go? I've never made a snake before, but I can try to help if you need it."

"Alright," the boy said, picking up the tongs and placing a small, black cube between them.

Dakier fought hard not to grimace as the lad made several feeble attempts. On his first try, the boy dropped the tongs in the fire again, and on his second, the hammer slipped and nearly landed on his toes before Dakier rushed to catch it. By the third, Dakier leaned over to guide the boy's hands before he injured himself.

"What are you doing?" the boy squeaked in alarm.

Dakier flinched away from him, immediately regretting his attempt to help, and in the commotion, the boy dropped the piece of metal into the forge. Strangely, instead of landing amid the flames like Dakier would have expected, the piece crumbled and collapsed into ash, disappearing into the rest of the coal at the base of the fire.

"What kind of metal were you using?" Dakier asked, leaning as close to the fire as he dared to get a better look.

"Oh, it's alright," the boy said, using the tongs to lift another metal cube from the anvil next to him. "I've got more."

The boy moved the cube over the fire in the open, circular forge before them, hands wobbling even with the simple motion. Dakier sucked in a nervous breath, but when he did, he must have accidentally inhaled some soot, because his throat suddenly burned. He coughed to clear it, sending a massive cloud of ash swirling into the air, and Dakier waved his hands to try to dissipate the dust.

"Come on, snake!" the lad cheered, oblivious to the mess Dakier was making, as the boy heated the new piece of metal.

Dakier was about to remind him that the process would take longer than that, but when the ash cleared from the air, Dakier's eyes widened in astonishment.

The boy's mouth hung agape as he held his empty tongs over the forge. Beneath them, in the flames, was what appeared to be a black, metal snake. Quickly, the boy plucked the finished piece from the fire with the tongs and set it on the anvil to cool, and Dakier drew closer to get a better look. Inexplicably, the snake sculpture was fully formed, complete with two almond-shaped divots for the eyes and subtle imprints down its back to represent scales.

Dakier stepped back, searching for a logical explanation that wouldn't come, when the stomping of boots behind him interrupted his thoughts. The guard who'd been assigned to escort him stood in the open smithy doorway, his pale face ripe with confusion. "What's going on here?"

"I—" Dakier stammered. "He sounded like he needed help, so I came over. I thought he was going to hurt himself."

"Jimmy doesn't need any help—" the guard started, his words cutting short as he took in the scrawny kid. "Aye, you're not Jimmy. Who are you?"

"I must go." The boy leapt to his feet, pulling his cap down to cover his face before frantically patting his pockets.

"Soldier, just get back to the stables," the guard ordered, shaking his head as he addressed Dakier. Then he turned to the child. "As for you, kid, you're too young to be in here. You're coming with me."

The guard stepped forward as if to grab the boy's arm, but the child was too quick. He ducked under the guard's outstretched hand and bolted out of the forge, leaving his newly hewn snake behind.

6

Alfien

When he spied a blond braid bobbing through the crowd in Afdot Harbor, Alfien Weiberung could hardly believe his eyes. The girl rushing past looked exactly like Katiel, his ex-girlfriend from back home. Only, it couldn't be. There was no reason for her to be anywhere near the A'slenderian coast, which was hundreds of miles away from his hometown. The only reason Alfien lived so far away now was to attend university. Not to mention, this girl appeared to be alone, and Katiel would never travel without her father.

Still, he found himself trailing after her, as if his feet had a mind of their own—just in case, by some strange stroke of fate, it was her.

When he noticed her, he was busy working the docks, one of the odd-jobs he'd picked up to make extra marks between university semesters. He'd been offloading shipments for hours, and between his exhaustion and burning curiosity, it didn't take much to convince himself to leave work for a while to investigate.

Whoever she was, the girl did not look well. She was breathing heavily, her skin was sallow, and even from a distance, he could make out huge bruise-like bags beneath each of her blue-gray eyes. A second later, Alfien noticed two gruff-looking men with auburn hair following her, and he decided that he had to help her, whether it was Katiel or a stranger.

He trailed the group until the girl picked up speed and raced onto a large clipper. She was nimble on her feet as she darted across the narrow gangplank, but then, without warning, she began swaying and fell to the deck. At the unexpected fall, Alfien dashed to the edge of the dock to get a better look.

On the ship, the crewmen went deathly still, a hush falling over them. Instead of helping her, they all stared—first at her, and then toward the bow. A sole pair of footfalls sounded as a man dressed in Drezchy royal regalia crossed the deck, the brocade on his shoulder matching the emblem emblazoned on the main sail. The crew bowed their heads as he passed.

It took Alfien a second to piece together what he was seeing. The man crossing the deck was far too young to be the king, but was being shown all the deference that a king might expect. In fact, it wasn't just deference that shone among the crew, but fear. And Alfien knew what that meant: this man was the Ghost.

The Ghost was the nickname of the crown prince of New Drezchy, whose ruthless reputation preceded him. He oversaw law enforcement at the highest level in his country, and he was said to be particularly fond of cutting off appendages as a form of punishment: tongues, ears, and the ilk. Alfien had heard the Ghost had been seen stalking around Afdot, and it took no time for rumors to spread about why he was prowling an Aslenderian harbor, during wartime, no less. Some speculated that A'slenderia and Tibedo might be gaining a new ally in the ongoing war with Bar Kur, but Alfien thought that seemed unlikely. He was a history major, after all. After Bar Kur and Drezchy lost the Ten Years' War, A'slenderia and Tibedo had split the Drezchy lands between them. As a result, the Drezchy people had been forced to leave Kerafin and form New Drezchy in a penal colony across the sea. That didn't seem like the kind of history a nation would easily forget.

Yet, the crown prince was here, and in plain sight at that. For a moment, the Ghost stared down at the girl lying on the deck, but when his guards bent down to her, the prince waved them off. From the edge of the dock, Alfien watched in disbelief as the prince lifted her into his arms himself, then turned toward the stern, in the direction of the cabins. To his dismay, it was only then that Alfien got a good look at her face. When he did, he knew for certain that it was Katiel.

And that was how Alfien wound up in the hallway of a Drezchy vessel, deciding how best to break into the captain's quarters and rescue his ex.

He took a deep breath, starting the countdown in his head. He could start high. Give himself a minute.

Sixty, fifty-nine, fifty-eight...

At one, he took another steadying breath. Perhaps that hadn't been high enough.

One-hundred, ninety-nine, ninety-eight...

He'd made it no further when the door swung open.

"Alfien?"

Katiel stood in the doorway, mouth agape at the sight of him, but otherwise unharmed. The cream-colored frock peeking out from under her purple *dirndl* was rather low-cut—he noticed with a frown—and above it, a strange, metallic gray pigment was smeared across her skin.

"Did he do something to you?" Alfien asked in a hushed tone, dipping his head toward the odd silver smudge.

"No!" Katiel's cheeks flushed a rosy pink. "No. Nothing like that."

"Are you—?" Alfien started to ask if she was certain, but instead grabbed her upper arm to lead her down the hallway. "Never mind. Let's just get out of here."

That was when the Ghost walked up behind Katiel, his hand grazing the small of her back. To Alfien's surprise, Katiel didn't so much as flinch, even with the prince standing less than a foot behind her.

"Is something the matter?" the Ghost drawled, sizing up Alfien pointedly. They were around the same height, but the Ghost was nearly half Alfien's mass. Not exactly intimidating, except for the fact that he could legally cut Alfien's ears off so long as he remained on this boat.

"Nothing at all," Alfien gritted through his teeth, extending a hand to Katiel. "We were just leaving. Sorry to disturb you."

But instead of taking his hand and running, like Alfien expected, Katiel cleared her throat. Her eyes darted between him and the Ghost, like she wasn't afraid but, rather, embarrassed. "Anton," she said, surprising in her informality, "this is a friend from back home. Alfien Weiberung."

"This is Alfien?" he asked, like he'd already heard of him. It dawned on Alfien then that Katiel *knew* him. Judging from the way the prince stood possessively close to Katiel, she might know him very well.

Alfien could scarcely believe what he was witnessing. Back home, Katiel had always been meek, timid, and honestly, a bit boring. It hadn't come as much surprise to him that she'd stayed home instead of going to university last year. She made an excuse about her parents preventing her, but truthfully, she just wasn't the daring type. Alfien knew she would hold him back from the grand adventures he had planned, so he broke up with her, hoping to meet a more like-minded, worldly girl while off at school.

The last thing he would have expected was for Katiel to have an exciting secret life that he knew nothing about.

"Wearing a shirt would suit you, honestly," the prince said, jolting Alfien from his thoughts.

He had nearly forgotten he was shirtless, having discarded the sweat-soaked garment earlier after working in the sun for hours. Katiel, for her part, looked mortified as she fixed her gaze anywhere but on his chest, while the prince was still spewing nonsense.

"I have some excellent merchants to recommend. Or, if you like, you can take two of my spare shirts and sew them together."

"Actually, we *will* be going," Katiel said, stopping either of them from saying anything else. She gave a slight curtsy before grabbing Alfien by the elbow. "Good day, Your Highness."

The Ghost held a gaze of cool indifference as Katiel dragged Alfien down the hallway, saying only, "We leave at first light tomorrow," as he turned back into his quarters.

Though she'd referred to him formally that time, Alfien could tell the formality was forced, an afterthought—which meant that Katiel definitely had secrets.

And Alfien suddenly found himself very interested in finding them out.

The second they were out of the Ghost's earshot, he reeled on her. "What did he mean about leaving?"

She looked away at the question, fidgeting with a stray lock of hair and pressing her lips together to hide her very slightly crooked tooth. In an instant, she'd turned into the same meek Katiel he'd always known, so he was all the more shocked by her next admission. "I'm going with him to New Drezchy."

"What?" Alfien grabbed her shoulders, forcing her to look at him. "Why would you do that? Don't you know who that man is, Katiel? He's dangerous."

But she shrugged away, her tiny nose crinkling in anger. "*I'm* dangerous."

"What?" he repeated, somehow more confused than before. "What are you talking about? Just go home, Katiel. This isn't like you.."

"I was about to explain myself," she said, taking a determined step away from him, "but I don't know why. You've never understood me, and nothing I say will change that. Now please go."

"Absolutely not," he said, heat rising in his cheeks. "I'm not going anywhere unless you leave with me. You can't just run off by yourself. What would your father say?"

At that, her eyes flashed, but then she glanced behind her as if searching for someone. In a second, the Ghost was standing between them, earning his nickname over again with the stealthy arrival.

"Is he bothering you?" the prince asked Katiel, cutting a cold glance at Alfien.

"No, it's not that..." she began, but from the sheepish way she looked down at her feet, the defense was anything but convincing.

"Guards." The prince spoke casually, not even projecting his voice, but instantly two men were upon Alfien, each grabbing one of his upper arms.

Katiel, to his surprise, said nothing as the guards hauled him across the deck, his feet working overtime not to trip.

"I should've stopped you back when you and Brenna came to the outpost with that ludicrous plan of yours!" he yelled, seeing red as the guards led him back over the gangway and plopped him down on the dock. Even with the distance between them, he knew she could hear him, and he wouldn't leave without getting the last word. "This time, I'm telling your father where you're going! And he's not going to be happy about it."

7

Katiel

Katiel leaned against the ship's railing, her braid waving like a flag in the wind. The salty sea air had already shaken free every hair that it could, the loose tendrils now wildly framing her face, but she didn't particularly care how she looked. The sea was calm tonight, and everyone else had long since retired for the evening.

It had been three days since the vessel had departed Afdot Harbor and set sail for New Drezchy's capital—three days that she had avoided Anton, which was a feat considering he'd insisted she take the cabin directly next to his. She hadn't missed the displaced first mate's grumbles about being relocated, but having a room to herself did help her feel safe at night. It had hardly mattered, though, since the ship's sickening rock ensured she couldn't sleep a wink.

That was why she was out now, watching the moon cast its curved reflection across the water's surface. Alone with her thoughts, she couldn't help but wonder if taking the court wielder position had been the right decision. It was risky and impulsive, to be sure, but it felt like her last chance to make a difference.

Before they set sail, she'd written to Brenna with an address where she could be reached in New Drezchy, and Alfien's knowledge of her journey left her with an odd sense of reassurance. She'd been too afraid to write to her parents herself, but if anything happened to her, at least Alfien would tell them she'd been trying to do something good.

Trying being the operative word. She may have successfully wielded twice now in life-or-death situations, but she was far from a skilled wielder. It would take a lot of practice to be of any use in the Conclave, so she may as well start practicing now.

A quick glance around the deck confirmed she was still alone, so she drew out her familiar pouch of ore and plucked out a single piece, no bigger than a grain of sand. When she blew on the ore, the dust swirled around her, filling the deck with a twisting, glimmering cloud and that strange, otherworldly stillness that only the ore could conjure.

With a flick of her wrist, she formed a compass, its chain swinging as it fell into her upturned palm. It looked just like Father's—the one he'd used on all their trips together to sell their farm's wool and cheeses. She hadn't realized until then that his compass likely served the same purpose her ore-filled necklace had.

Forming the simple object was refreshing. She had gone seventeen years without ever having wielded, but once she'd started, she craved the sensation in a way that wasn't entirely pleasant. The yearning gnawed at her almost constantly, a dull ache deep under her skin.

Wielding again was like taking a swig of cold water from her canteen after a long day watching the sheep, but as she looked down at the compass, she realized it wasn't working. No matter which direction she turned it, the needle spun wildly, never landing on a true north. It seemed she needed more practice wielding automated mechanisms—yet another thing she would need to master in very little time.

"Trouble sleeping?"

Katiel gasped, tucking the compass into her pocket on instinct, and feigned nonchalance with a glance over her shoulder. She already knew who it was, but as she took in the familiar figure, her chest fluttered despite herself. In the short time they'd been apart, Anton's sharp jawline had somehow sharpened even more. He looked like he hadn't shaved in a few days, and the shadow of dark facial hair lent him an older, manlier air. She had forgotten how easily he rendered her spellbound, and she loathed him for it.

With as much contempt as she could muster, she turned back to the water. "No."

"Come, Katiel." The prince stepped forward, the light from a nearby lantern flickering off of his dark brown hair. "You can't convince me you're out here night-wielding for your own enjoyment. Something must be troubling you."

Katiel pursed her lips. "That is none of your concern."

Anton leaned his forearms against the railing, bringing him down to her height. "The first female court wielder in the court of New Drezchy, and she already despises me." Despite his words, his voice held the hint of a smile. "I should have known."

Though she wanted to tell him to leave, the thought of other wielders piqued her interest. It was undoubtedly why he'd brought it up in the first place. "Your court truly had other court wielders, then?"

He smirked. "Yes, we had several of them when I was young."

She was feeding right into his entrapment, but she didn't particularly mind. Questions had been mounting since she'd discovered her heritage as a wielder, and she welcomed answers, even if they came from him. "What were they like?"

"They all had long gray beards. One of them always wore a pointy hat, and a star-patterned cloak, actually."

Katiel raised an eyebrow. "Truly?"

"No!" He had nearly burst out laughing before giving his answer, and now he was cackling at her heartily, his mouth hanging open without shame. She smacked his shoulder with the back of her hand, trying to suppress her own grin.

"Honestly, though," he went on, "I thought they were astounding. How quickly they could create things, how wondrous their creations were—as a young boy, I was obsessed with them. I think that was part of what made me want to invent, to be like the wielders."

Katiel squirmed. In a way, it seemed like he was still obsessed with them—with her. And Katiel was not sure she wanted to be someone's obsession.

"What happened to them?" she asked, focusing instead on what she could glean from the conversation at hand. "Why doesn't your court employ wielders any longer?"

Darkness clouded Anton's expression, a look she recalled seeing on his face the last time he spoke of the king. "My uncle."

"He fired them?"

"He executed them." The darkness changed into something worse, something that Katiel had not seen before. It was a cold rage, like ice and fire all in one, and scarcely contained. His hatred for his uncle was fierce, even stronger than Katiel had initially realized. "He found excuses to kill every last court wielder, claiming they each committed some act of treason while in his service. Everyone knew those accusations were fabricated, though. He took them out because they posed a threat to his power."

Katiel whirled on him with gritted teeth. "Why did you not tell me this before I took the position?"

"I thought you would've assumed as much," he explained, his soft one lacking any hint of a challenge. "Though I suppose you've had the blessing of growing up"—he paused—"*differently* than I did. But you will learn. The powerful people of the world—they make it their business to know who else is powerful. And every single person in power wants the wielders—wants to use them, control them, or snuff them out entirely."

When she made no reply, he went on with a grating softness.

"I can't stand for you to worry, Katiel." If she didn't know better, the ardent tone with which he said her name might suggest he cared about her. "Please, don't fear him. My uncle will know you are under my employ, and he wouldn't dare cross me. He and I have come to an agreement."

The way his voice hitched on the last word, Katiel wondered just what sort of agreement that was. It certainly didn't sound like an amiable one.

Her anxiety at the thought must have shown, because Anton added, "Truly, do not fret. Court is vicious, but my reputation precedes me. You'll be under my protection, always. If anyone lays a finger on you, they'll answer to me."

His eyes met hers with an infectious intensity, and it was abundantly clear to Katiel that she needed to return to her cabin—before she acted as foolishly as ever.

"Court's not all bad, though," he said, his eyes still melting into hers. "You'll get to meet my sister. Nev's a genius. She's the smartest person I've ever met, save for Simeon, perhaps. You're going to love her."

The mention of his beloved sister reminded her of the first time he'd brought her up by the riverbank on their journey to Halstat. The memory of that first kiss they'd shared brought all those thrilling, joyful feelings back to the surface, and Katiel feared her resolve to hate him was wearing thin. With a pointed clearing of her throat, she said, "I should be getting back."

"Wait," Anton said, far too loudly, before regaining his usual composure. "Wait a moment, please. I have something for you before you go. Actually, two things."

He reached into the pocket of his fur-lined cloak and pulled out a tiny, ashen wood box and a toy horse. The latter was made of crocheted yarn, black with white above the hooves and a white muzzle, exactly like her favorite horse, Gunnel.

Katiel fixed him with a smirk. "Do you always keep that in your pocket?"

He laughed outright, loud enough that he could wake the sailors below deck. Katiel widened her eyes at him in mock annoyance.

"Of course not." His slightly crooked grin contrasted his intensity from the moment before. "I've been trying to give it to you for days, but you were incredibly hard to find. I was beginning to worry you'd come to your senses and jumped ship in the harbor."

Katiel tucked a loose strand of hair behind her ear, avoiding considering what he meant about coming to her senses. "Where did you find it?"

"At a street vendor's stall in Afdot," he supplied, placing the plush Gunnel in her hands. "Once I learned you lost your necklace, I went out to get a replacement before we set sail, and of course, I thought of you when I saw that creature. It looked just like Gunnel."

He remembered her horse's name, she realized with a jolt. It should not make her so happy, but it did.

Before she could thank him, he opened the box to reveal a necklace—a thin gold chain with a single charm of frosted, amber-colored glass shaped into a delicate heart. She could tell it was hollow, with as much space to store ore as her old one. It was perfect, exactly what she would have chosen for herself.

It should be easy to hate him after he'd stolen from her, but for reasons beyond her understanding, it wasn't. Perhaps because he did things like this.

"May I?" He held one end of the pendant's chain in each hand, offering to put it on for her. Katiel lifted her braid and turned her back to him, the crisp night air biting at her now-exposed skin.

He looped an arm over her head, allowing the necklace to fall into place. For a moment, his head dipped dangerously close to her nape, his warm breath brushing against the sensitive skin. Instantly, she was back in that shadow-cast hallway with him, spinning with his lips on every part of her neck and shoulders and collarbone. How badly she wanted him to lean down and kiss the back of her neck now.

He'd tensed, halting, her hand still holding her hair. Energy flickered in the air between them, and she knew he could feel it, too. Perhaps she could let him continue and forget about what had happened, just for the moment. She didn't have to like him—

No. Katiel hated herself for even considering it. She was not falling into the same trap yet again. The second the metal clasp clicked shut, she stepped away, turning on her heel to face him. The way the color drained from his face was not lost on her.

"Anton," she started, working to keep her voice emotionless. "You're my employer now. I'm walking into a court where I am unknown, where I assume rumors can start quickly. The situation is not as it was before. Things between us must be strictly professional now."

The prince's eyes widened as he backed away a step further. It was clear from his expression that he thought he'd misread her, misread that she was interested in him...*intimately*, again. She almost felt bad for him, since he hadn't misread her at all, but she wasn't about to correct the misconception now.

"My sincerest apologies," he said, sketching a bow. "Of course. We shall keep things strictly professional. Your council is wise, as always. I should not think to jeopardize your reputation at court."

Katiel gave a small curtsy in return, and Anton turned to leave, suddenly in such a hurry that Katiel thought he might depart without bidding her farewell. "Ahem," he added as he turned back to her again, seeming to remember himself. "Was there anything else I could help you with before I retire for the night?"

She started to shake her head, before she thought better of it. Anton had already shown her he was cunning and conniving—not the sweet person he sometimes pretended to be. But she could be every bit as calculating, and she ought to remind him of it—that she was listening, and she was not to be taken for the fool again. Steeling her face into indifference, she asked, "What do you plan to do with me?"

He blinked twice, his thick brows furrowing. "Come again?"

"Use me, control me, or snuff me out entirely," she clarified. "Which one do you plan to do with me? You said that's all people in power want with the wielders."

"Oh, no, Katiel. You misunderstand." Anton pulled his cloak tighter around himself, glancing at the yarn horse in her hand like he sorely regretted bringing her a gift. "I may be a prince, but with you, I'm powerless."

As he drew away, his voice grew so low that she wasn't sure if she misheard him, but the words echoed in her mind for the rest of the night.

8

Brenna

Brenna didn't have to wait long for a chance to see Dakier again. The evening after the Tibedese soldiers arrived, Steffi announced a court social to welcome the foreign guests.

Disgust crept up in Brenna's throat as she surveyed the adjoined rooms set aside for the soiree. Trays of libations were being passed around among the guests, and on tables felted in hunter green, games of dice and billiards were well underway. It was as if everyone were comfortable pretending that their respective infantries hadn't been killing each other just days ago. On the other hand, this night could be the first step toward peace, if the Barkurian diplomats' intentions were sincere. Though based on the state-of-affairs meeting earlier that day, Brenna feared they might not be.

She also had a sinking feeling about the letters, which she'd stuffed in her dresser as proof in case she found the author. Before the fete, she'd found the time to visit Jay, her brother-in-law, who represented their remote home region in the Barkurian Cabinet. She'd spent the whole day walking to and from his rented city apartment to speak with him away from the prying ears of the castle, but he'd had neither leads nor guesses as to who might be threatening her, though he promised to keep a lookout.

As if on cue, Jay walked up to her, holding two goblets of red wine. Handing one off to her, he took a long swig of the other himself. At her inquisitive glance, he said, "It'll give you something to do with your hands."

Brenna shrugged, opting to take a sip for her nerves, and then two more immediately after. If she could only see Dakier. After their conversation was cut short, she was itching to talk to him again.

"Are you looking for someone?" Prince Eoghan asked as he ambled up beside her.

At ten years old, the prince was whip-smart and easy to talk to, but small for his age, his green-and-black tartan drapes engulfing him much more than they should. She wasn't sure if his small stature was from being starved for weeks at the hands of General Taregh, but he had taken to hanging around her at events, possibly due to a mistrust of the government officials after all he'd been through.

"No," she lied at the exact moment that she caught sight of Dakier, her raised eyebrows betraying her. He was walking in with a Tibedese man in his thirties—a captain, if the bronze stars along his shoulder were any indication.

Though she hoped to remain inconspicuous, she'd obviously failed, because Jay and Eoghan both followed her eyeline to the soldiers. While her brother-in-law scowled, the prince outright flinched when he saw the two Tibedese officers. The reaction gave her pause, but she didn't have time to ponder it before Jay started a lecture. "Brenna, now I don't think it wise—"

"Be right back," she said, darting off before he could finish.

She downed the rest of her wine in one gulp and discarded the goblet on a card table, earning a scoff from the dealer she set it in front of. Though she wanted to apologize, she was on a mission, and she couldn't draw any more attention to herself. Jay and Eoghan were both notable exceptions, but she didn't think the rest of the court would let her keep her position if they knew of her association with Dakier. Some might even suggest she should face jail time for the illicit relationship—or worse.

Come to think of it, she could really use another glass of wine.

But there was no time, not if she wanted to talk to Dakier tonight. Steffi was approaching the dais, about to officially welcome the Tibedese delegation. In any sort of Barkurian state procession, the opening statements were notoriously long-winded, creating an ample opportunity to get time alone with him away from prying eyes.

If only Brenna could muster the courage.

Suddenly, a plan hatched in her mind.

Dakier's back was now to her as he chatted with a handful of other soldiers, and Brenna hurried across the room to him. On her way, she grabbed a goblet of white wine from a servant's tray, but this one she didn't bother drinking. Instead, she waited until she was but a step behind him, and forced herself to trip, sending the liquid sloshing onto Dakier's back.

Dakier looked behind him, his eyes lighting up in surprise as they met hers.

"I'm so sorry, *sir*," she said, fighting the urge to wink. She retrieved a handkerchief from her pocket and held it out to him. When he took it, she stepped closer, and pretended to trip again. The move sent her head falling into his chest, and he grabbed her shoulders to help her to her feet. "My apologies."

It would look natural to anyone watching, or so she hoped—just a very clumsy lady-in-waiting struggling to walk in her heeled slippers—but it gave her an opportunity to whisper low where only Dakier could hear. "Follow after me in ten minutes. Down that hall"—she cocked her head—"first door on the right."

Dakier's eyes widened, but she couldn't wait for his agreement without arousing suspicion, so she gave a tiny curtsy and darted off.

SHE CHOSE ONE OF the spare game rooms that wasn't being used tonight. A burgundy-felted billiards table stood in the center of the room, and she jumped up to sit on its edge while she waited.

As the minutes ticked on with no sign of Dakier, her anxiety mounted. Had he been detained, somehow? It might be difficult to slip away from his regiment, so it would make sense if he couldn't come see her. But something had been off about him, and she couldn't help but worry that he didn't want to see her at all.

Then the door creaked open, and she released a breath. There he was, stepping into the darkened room and clicking the door shut behind him.

"Brenna, I—"

"No, I'm sorry. I know we shouldn't be seen together," she said, the words escaping in a rush. "And I'm sorry for getting wine on your clothes. I just missed you, but I didn't know if we should be seen talking to each other, and—"

"Brenna." Dakier stepped up to where she sat on the edge of the billiards table, close enough that if she let her knees part, he might press between them.

She blushed at the thought, but then scolded herself for it as she reached for his hand, pulling him to her. "I really missed you."

His gaze lingered too long on her mouth, and she tilted her head back, letting her palms fall back against the soft fabric of the billiards table.

For a fleeting moment, he appeared to angle down to her, his eyes glazing over, before he straightened and stepped back. "I can't." He blinked furiously and shook his head, like he was waving spots out of his vision. "I can't. And I need to explain to you why."

When he didn't go on, Brenna grabbed his hand, rubbing her thumb across the back of it in reassurance. "It's alright." She was sure he was ashamed of the things he did during the war, actions that were no fault of his own. "You can tell me."

"Brenna, I..." His deep brown eyes pierced hers before darting away. "I did something in battle, something horrible. If you knew, you wouldn't want to be around me right now. You wouldn't ever want to see me again. That's the reason I can't let you close, as much as I want to."

Just as she suspected, Dakier was riddled with guilt over the normal actions of a soldier. "You did what you had to do. Even if you had to kill someone, that's part of battle. You're too hard on yourself."

"No, that's not all." He dragged his fingers through his hair, which was longer than Brenna would expect for a soldier. Her wanton imagination didn't seem to be slowing down, because she desperately wanted to do it for him. "That's not what I'm trying to explain. I—"

"Did you kill someone? A Barkurian soldier?"

"Yes, but—"

She hopped off the table and pressed a finger to his lips. "That's all you have to say." Her hand drew away, and he sucked in a startled breath as she slinked her arms over his shoulders. "I understand what you had to do."

Dakier's cheeks blanched, his mouth falling open like someone had slapped him. "Please, listen, Brenna. *Please.* We can't see each other again. If you knew the truth, you would understand, but I'm afraid knowing the truth will only hurt you more."

His all-consuming guilt confounded Brenna. It was as if he had done something even more terrible than killing Barkurian soldiers during the battle. But what could be worse?

"When you got on that train, I thought I might never see you again," she said, hushing her tone to add weight to the words. "While you were gone, I thought of you all the time. You're perfect for me, and I had been too blind to see it. I kept thinking about our kiss, and when you told me you loved me. My heart grew fonder every day we were apart."

This time, when their eyes met, he didn't look away. She inched forward, her arms still slack around his neck. When she angled her mouth up to his, he didn't pull away.

"Don't push me away now," she whispered, their mouths now inches apart, "just because you're feeling guilty. We can get through this—whatever it is—together."

For a fleeting, blissful instant, his lips slid past hers, soft and thick and greedy. But then he pulled back, the conflict still ripe in his features as he shook his head.

"I can't."

She pressed her palm to his chest, a last plea to stay with her, and his rapid heartbeat thrummed beneath her fingertips. Then, slowly—achingly slowly—he backed up, and her hand fell away. Her fingertips dragged down his torso before he slipped from the room, not looking back at her as the door clicked shut.

9

Dakier

Dakier rushed out of the gathering hall, anxiety coursing through him. He clutched his throbbing head, brushing the shoulders of Barkurian statesmen as he weaved his way to the door. Pereira tried to flag him down, but he blew past, pretending not to see him. Even when he knocked a stray glass of wine to the ground, he didn't stop. He couldn't speak, couldn't think—not until he got some air.

When the crisp evening wind stung his cheeks at last, he pressed his back against a stone wall overlooking the castle courtyard and tried to steady his breathing. Everything had happened too fast.

At first, he'd told himself he was trying to tell Brenna the truth about what he'd done—about him killing her brother, about the mementos he'd saved from Henred's pocket for her. But then he'd seen that sweet, kind look in her eyes, and he'd lost his nerve. If he told her then, she would have to go back to the party and pretend that everything was fine. In her shock, she might even cry out, revealing their secret rendezvous to the other revelers, and get in trouble for being associated with him.

And yet, knowing how wrong it was, he'd let her kiss him. The way she'd looked, leaning back over the billiards table in her dangerously low-cut gown—the mere thought quickened his pulse in a strangled mix of lust and shame. She was heavenly, and he was deplorable. Shaking the memory from his mind, he pushed his palms harder into the stone, concentrating on his breaths.

After a few moments, his pulse slowed and clarity returned. There never would be a good time to deliver such horrendous news, but for now, all he could do was resolve to tell her soon—and head back inside before his absence was noticed. As a Tibedese soldier, he knew he wasn't permitted on the castle grounds alone, and his rash actions could get the captain in trouble as well.

He scanned the courtyard, hoping he at least hadn't been spotted. Mercifully, the grounds stood completely empty, the staff presumably all occupied with the night's fete. But if he went in the same door he'd come out of, he'd end up directly in the center of the soiree, and it would be obvious he'd been out here alone. Instead, he decided to enter through the door he and the guard had used on the other side of the courtyard, and return to the gathering through the center hallway. The queen's address should begin any moment, and with the crowd's attention turned toward the dais, it was the best chance he stood of slipping in unnoticed.

Dakier headed off at a brisk but casual pace, thinking he would claim to be checking on his horse if anyone stopped him. But just as he passed the blacksmith's forge, a blur of black shot out the door, zipping straight for his feet across the gravel courtyard. Dakier jumped back, his arms flailing as he landed in a pile of hay. He propped himself on his elbow and shook the spots from his vision. It took several long blinks to see what monstrosity lay before him—but it was nothing more than a small, black snake. Though it had been slithering at top speed just seconds before, it stopped directly in front of him, turning to face him in a peculiarly alert manner.

Growing up by the Tibedese coastline, he'd seen plenty of snakes, from harmless grays to poisonous serpents banded in gold and red, but a snake this far north was an odd sight. Since this one bore no bright colors, he ventured a closer look. He crept to his feet, not wanting to startle the serpent, which lay motionless in the center of the gravel footpath. The animal was of an unnatural onyx shade, like the creature itself was made of shadow. Instead of proper eyes rolling in their sockets, it had bizarre-looking indents where eyes should be. Between the eyes, burrowed into the flesh, was the six-pointed shape of a crystal.

Dakier shook his head, trying to make sense of what he was seeing, when the serpent suddenly seized. It launched itself into the air, its body tightening unnaturally at a series of right angles, almost as if it were slithering down a set of stairs. The reptile let out what Dakier could only describe as a bleat, if such a thing were possible, and his temples pounded at the grating screech.

He didn't move, hoping to avoid the animal turning its attention toward him. But even standing still, the snake watched him, continuing to make the horrid sound.

Come to think of it, the snake looked uncannily familiar. It was exactly like the one he'd helped the boy forge the other day in the shop.

But now, it was definitely alive, which meant—

That boy.

The boy in the shop that day had wielded the ore, or so it seemed. The forging method was quite different from what he'd seen Katiel try back in A'slenderia, blowing a great cloud of dust to form, which was an anomaly that Dakier couldn't explain. Regardless of the method, though, wielding was a serious crime on the continent, and Dakier had helped him.

Dakier had aided the boy in creating this animal—this abomination—and its screams made it clear the animal was suffering. As much as he hated the idea, he needed to end its misery. Drawing in a breath, he turned his head away, lifted his boot above its almond-shaped head, and stomped, crushing it against the ground.

His teeth clattered uncontrollably as he walked off, unable to look at the poor animal while his mind reeled with the implications.

If the boy were indeed a wielder, he would be the first Dakier had met from outside the Yule Valley. And since the century-old Kerafin Pact also outlawed wielders from reproducing, he was far too young to be born without his parents violating that stipulation as well. The kid had worn ragged clothes, but his soft hands had clearly never seen a day's work.

Suddenly, it dawned on Dakier. Earlier that night, when he'd first walked into the soiree and spotted Brenna, there had been a young boy in royal regalia standing next to her. Dakier had mused then that the royal looked oddly familiar, but the thought left his mind when Brenna ran into him.

But his smattering of freckles and small, upturned nose were features that rags couldn't hide. The prince of Bar Kur wielded the ore—a practice that the Kerafin pact deemed illegal and Barkuian culture deemed an abomination.

It was no wonder he'd donned a disguise.

Dakier chewed the inside of his cheek, considering what to do next. While he could keep this knowledge to himself, he felt obligated to tell Captain Pereira, lest the secret lend some leverage to Tibedo in their negotiations.

The question was—could he really use this secret against a child? Despite him being a royal of the enemy nation, Dakier felt oddly protective of the boy. He didn't want to see him suffer for a crime that was no fault of his own.

The last thing he was supposed to do was inform a member of the Barkurian court who could help the lad. And yet, Dakier's feet were hurrying back toward the gathering as if of their own accord. Hopefully, Brenna would still be there, and after she concocted some brilliant plan to protect the prince, she wouldn't have to see Dakier again.

The air had stilled as he approached the festivities, and Dakier pressed his ear to the side door, hoping to hear the queen addressing his delegation so that he could enter without drawing notice.

To his surprise, the chorus of voices inside had grown quiet. Even if the address were finished, the party wouldn't have ended just after it began, so he waited, expecting more revelry to commence at any moment. But strangely, even after a long pause, he heard nothing.

Out of nowhere, a gunshot fired from within, the sound jolting him back. On instinct, Dakier clapped his hands over his ears to muffle the ringing. A vision of the battlefield flashed in front of him, even as he tried to push it from his mind.

Black ash, flying through the air. A field of thick mud where grass had been only moments before. A dying horse's panicked eyes, staring up at him in a plea for help. The acrid taste of blood hitting his tongue as he shoved his bayonet forward—

His hands flexed open despite himself, dropping the rifle he wasn't holding.

The castle door flung open, bringing him back to the present, and a handful of Barkurian ladies rushed out, screeching as they ran. They screamed even louder at the sight of him, like he might be poised for the attack, but he raced around them, his pulse still pounding from the unwelcome flashback.

Inside, the rest of the revelers were just as frenzied as the women, each rushing toward the nearest exit. No one noticed him in the chaos as he stepped aside and pressed his back to the wall.

A quick scan revealed no sign of Brenna, but amidst the fleeing courtiers stood the Tibedese soldiers, encircled by Barkurian guards. It was just as Pereira had feared all along—the invitation to Ballynach Castle was nothing but a ruse to capture Tibedese leadership.

Though no one else noticed Dakier in the frenzy, his captain spotted him immediately. Pereira locked eyes with him and mouthed, *"Go."*

Dakier held his eye contact, shaking his head emphatically to signal his unwillingness. Both his captain and the rest of his unit were surrounded by guards, and he couldn't leave them helpless.

In response, Pereira mouthed something else. The movement of the captain's lips was so slight, the words were almost imperceptible, but Dakier caught them all the same.

"That's an order."

Suddenly, he understood. The Barkurians hadn't realized he was missing, and if he tried to help his comrades now, he would only be captured along with them. There would be no way to escape or send word to their Tibedese countrymen, but if he left now, he could wait until the moment was right and try to break them out. Nodding, he turned back to the door he'd come in from, only to see a Barkurian guard posted there, looking directly at him.

With no time to waste, Dakier bolted for an open door that led into the castle hallway. It was only a few feet from him, and he made it before the guard moved a muscle.

As his boot crossed the threshold, a man cried out behind him—Captain Pereira. Several courtiers shrieked, crashing into Dakier and pushing him into the fleeing mob. The frantic crowd jostled him fully out the door, but not before he stole a last glance over his shoulder.

In the center of the guards, Pereira was on the floor, struggling on his hands and knees as he reeled from the blow. Then a boot collided with his face, and he fell to the side.

Squeezing his eyes shut, Dakier sprinted down the hall, praying all the way that his captain made it out alive.

10

Brenna

"What are you doing here?" Brenna shouted. She'd been in the lady-in-waiting's chamber when she heard a commotion and rushed out to investigate, only to find Dakier of all people sprinting down the hall outside the queen's chambers.

When he saw her standing in the doorway, Dakier halted so abruptly that one long leg swung up in front of him, and he almost lost his footing. "Brenna?"

She rubbed at her eyes with the back of her hand, hoping the smudged lash-coal there didn't reveal she'd been crying, and looked down the empty hall. No one was supposed to be this far into the royal wing, not common subjects and mostly certainly not Tibedese soldiers. If the guards found him, he would be killed without question.

"Down there!" a man called from down the hall. Several sets of banging footfalls echoed through the passage, growing closer at a rapid pace. "He went that way!"

Dakier met her eyes in a wild panic, like he was about to run for it, but it would be of no use. The passage led to a dead end, and he'd be cornered within minutes. Before she could think better of it, Brenna grabbed his arm and yanked him into the queen's private chambers. She dragged him through the receiving room, then through the dressing room and into the queen's bedchamber beyond, since she knew the empty room to be affixed with several locks and deadbolts.

She also knew that if either of them were caught like this, they'd both be dead.

Taking in the finery and splendor that outfitted the space, Dakier's mouth dropped open. "Brenna, where is this?" he asked, keeping his voice low. "Is this the royal chambers?"

"The hall was a dead end," she whisper-yelled, pointing an accusatory finger in its general direction. "I couldn't let you die."

He gulped, the strangest look passing over his features. "You should have. Without a doubt, you should have."

He turned toward the door, like he actually meant to leave and turn himself in to protect her, so she reached out and caught his wrist, or at least she tried. Her hand was too small to wrap around it, and she wasn't strong enough to restrain him. But he waited, anyway. "We're alone here. They won't find you if you let me help," she said, her eyes imploring him before she dropped his hand. "Why were they chasing you?"

"I think the invitation for our unit to come here was a trick. The guards ambushed our group—the Tibedese soldiers, I mean—and they captured my captain."

Brenna gasped. "Where were the queen and prince?"

"I didn't see them," Dakier said, shaking his head. "We were outnumbered, so I ran, hoping I could find a way to free my unit when the dust settled." He paused, breaking eye contact like he was ashamed of his cowardice now that he recounted it aloud.

"You did the right thing," Brenna said, nodding fervently. "If you hadn't fled, they would've just captured you, too."

"Right," Dakier replied. His thousand-yard-stare suggested he was trying to formulate a plan to help the others. "It sounds like the guards may have gone past the door—" he started, but Brenna was hardly listening.

"I just can't believe Steffi would agree to this," she interrupted, unable to contain her thoughts. "I know she listens to her stodgy old advisors too much, but I thought she was better than that. I thought she wanted to end the war."

"Steffi?"

"That's what I call the queen," she explained, yet Dakier's brow only crept higher. "You know, because it's a nickname for Stefana."

"Right." Dakier swallowed hard. "So, I should go now, before—"

"If you're going," Brenna cut in, "then I'll go with you. I know the way to the dungeons, since that's probably where they took the captain. In fact, I broke out of—"

"No, please." He shook his head. "Don't come with me. I promise you, if you knew what I'd done, you would never, *never* consider helping me again. I've used too much of your kindness today already."

"Dakier," Brenna said, grabbing his hands in hers and squeezing them tight. "I thought of you every day while you were gone. There's nothing you could have done that would change my mind about you."

A bleakness fell across Dakier's expression, something strange and haunted in his once-soft eyes. It pained her to see it, and without knowing where her boldness came from, she reached up to cup his cheek. But he shrugged away from the touch, and the words that tumbled from his lips were so strange that she almost couldn't make them out.

"I killed Henred."

11

Katiel

The voyage across the sea took weeks—weeks that felt like both months and hours simultaneously. Katiel passed the days by herself, switching between retching bouts of seasickness and avoiding eye contact with the crew, though she occasionally took Simeon up on a card game, deciding it a necessary consolation to avoid going mad in solitude.

From the rumored conduct she'd heard of sailors, Katiel was fearful at first as a young woman traveling alone, but it was clear early on that Anton commanded tremendous respect on his ship. When he passed down the halls, even the burliest crewman averted his gaze, and when he was on deck, there was never any idleness or chatter. She knew he was royalty, and yet, the behavior struck her as odd.

The respect he cultivated seemed to be based more on fear than on admiration. An ordinary prince might order a punishment if he found a crew member disagreeable, but these men seemed to fear Anton as a person, like he himself was worse than any punishment. Then there was the matter of his ominous nickname—the Ghost.

It was this that she thought of as she crossed the gangplank onto a whole new continent—not her new role, or all that she intended to learn about wielding. Not about ending the war, or the terrifying position she had volunteered for, but him.

A sailor offered a steadying hand as she took her first steps on the soil of New Drezchy. The first to depart, Anton strode on ahead while the other crewmen unloaded his numerous leather trunks, and his eyes bore daggers into the one who took her hand. Noticing this, the sailor let go of Katiel before she had gotten her balance, and she had to take several quick steps to avoid falling over.

The harbor at Vincencim was a dusty, arid place, with swaths of sand stretching between the walkways and the dark, spired buildings. Though the air was dry, it wasn't overly warm, and a stale cold nipped at Katiel's exposed hands and nose as pedestrians surveyed her with curiosity.

Many of the men around, including Anton and his crew, wore thick capes in blacks and browns, with furs lining the neckline and edges. Others donned minimalistic, gray or off-white robes in a canvas-like material, with rope sashes securing the garments at the waist. It was a strange juxtaposition that made sense only in New Drezchy. Before the Ten Years' War, this area had been occupied by sparse populations of native inhabitants, as well as a penal colony for serious offenders who were banned from Kerafin.

The punishment was effective not only because the prisoners were sent so far from home, but because the climate was harsh, with oppressive heat in the summer and freezing temperatures in the winter. Katiel supposed it was lucky her visit was in the fall—generally the mildest time of year—though it might not make much difference considering the worrisome prospects that awaited her.

The city grew denser as the party made their way into a large square, the buildings a curious patchwork of topsy-turvy rooflines and more swirling black spires. Along the northwest edge of the plaza, they ducked under a nondescript archway, through a thick, black door, and into a long, grand hallway, void of any furnishings, with white-and-black square marble tiles dotting the floor.

A servant in burgundy coattails scurried up to them, with a deep bow and a curt, "Your Highness."

Gold frames highlighted what had to be hundreds of oil paintings, covering close to every inch of the walls, and the ornate, black crown molding was punctuated with sculptures of ravens dotted every few feet around the perimeter. At first, Katiel thought they might have stepped into a macabre, overcrowded art museum, but then she realized with a jolt that they were already in the Royal Palace of Karolinum.

"Anton," she said quietly, meaning to inquire about how many of the mismatched buildings she'd seen were part of the palace.

The servant—a large, burly man despite the scurrying—raised his brows, and she recognized a second too late that she was not meant to address the prince by his given name. Behind the man's broad shoulders, the group of servants and courtiers who had arrived to greet the visitors looked her up and down, sneering like she'd offended them already.

"Ms. Salzbruck is here on official business," Anton said, projecting his voice as he addressed the small crowd of courtiers. "I have appointed her as the new court wielder. While she will serve the entire court at large, let it be known that she reports directly to me."

Katiel slouched involuntarily, shrinking into herself as though it could make her invisible, when a high-pitched, lovely voice rang out through the hall.

"Brother!"

At the far end of the hallway, a young woman in a wicker wheelchair rounded the corner and made her way toward them. She wore a velvet dress in the deepest shade of sapphire, cut wide to show her pale skin and jutting collarbone, with a black ribbon stringing a sizable blue gemstone tight around her slender neck. She looked so much like Anton, with a delicate jawline that curved inward along the edge and eyes that were like the thick-lashed orbs of a doe. Thick, midnight brown curls spilled out from a chignon high up on her head, and her petite frame was swallowed by a brown fur blanket that covered her lower half completely.

Though she pushed the wheels at a considerable pace, Anton met her with a few long strides. As he leaned down to hug her, the dazzling, snow-white smile that Katiel glimpsed only a handful of times before stretched across his face, but to Katiel's surprise, the siblings didn't linger and catch up after their long time apart. Instead, they both made straight for her.

"Is this Katiel?" Anton's sister asked immediately, with a melodious voice that echoed through the hall like a yule-bell chorus.

Katiel quirked a brow. "How—?"

A mischievous twinkle crept up into her soft gray eyes, her upper lip drawing back to reveal a sharply pointed canine. "He wrote to me about you, of course." She glanced up at Anton before making conspiratorial eye contact with Katiel again. "I suggested right away that he bring you here. I had to meet the first girl who could charm my cold-hearted brother."

Katiel had no worldly idea how to respond to that, but Anton saved her by clearing his throat far louder than was necessary.

"Katiel Salzbruck," he said, gesturing a gloved hand from her to his sister, "allow me to introduce Her Royal Highness Princess Ananevia Alexandrina Minevechy of House Dvorsky."

Katiel nodded, mentally making a note that Dvorsky was his house name, rather than a casual surname, as he had implied when he introduced himself back in Linden. "Honored to make your acquaintance." Hesitantly, Katiel extended her arm for a handshake, unsure of how a member of court was meant to greet a royal.

But the princess paid her awkwardness no heed, instead clasping Katiel's hand in both of hers with a warm shake. "Please, call me Nev. Everyone does."

"Of course," Katiel said, trying to match her warmth but finding herself lacking. She could see why Anton had said before that he cared for his sister more than anyone else. Though he had misled

Katiel about so many things, that admission seemed to be a kernel of truth amid his manipulations.

As they made their way through the checkerboard-floor hall—which Nev explained was a side entrance—and descended the stairs into the main palace, Katiel could see where all the famed Drezchy ghost stories came from. The gas lamps were dim, most of the walls were draped with black velvet curtains, and the cream wallpaper was patterned with an eerie black botanical. The design reminded Katiel of an invasive plant species growing throughout, though perhaps that was the intended effect.

After another labyrinth of hallways, the group arrived at a door. Anton shooed the flocking courtiers away, leaving only him, Nev, and Katiel. When they entered the chamber, Katiel knew immediately that it must be Anton's private apartment. There was a monstrous canopy bed centered in the room, draped on all sides with thick, brown velvet curtains. The walls were covered with floor-to-ceiling bookcases that ran the length of the room and wrapped around the fireplace, each shelf stocked full of scattered tomes.

"Does Karolinum not have a library?" Katiel asked, overwhelmed by the sheer volume of knowledge in this single room.

"Oh, it does," Anton assured with a vigorous nod. "The Karolinum Library is the biggest in the world, or so they say. Simeon's father is the caretaker. That's how we met, actually, but I digress." He gestured to the books surrounding them. "This is my private collection."

"I see," Katiel said simply, craning her neck back to read the spines of the stretching expanse of titles. *Static and Dynamic Principles of the Modern Carriage*, *Methods of Post-Aslen Optics Volume IV,* and *Kinematics of Geared Automation* were the first three titles she spied, making it abundantly clear that she and Anton had very different tastes in reading. "What are we doing here?"

"Seeing as there's no time like the present," said Anton, "I thought we could work on my chief project to help you warm up before we focus on the competition."

Katiel gulped, already regretting agreeing to work for him. Far from home and separated from any allies, she could hardly refuse whatever he asked of her, regardless of if she was comfortable wielding it.

He grinned down at Nev, like they were sharing a private joke about her wariness. Without another word, he walked over to the drawers at the bottom of the bookshelf and began opening them, one after the next. Each drawer was filled with leather tubes that Anton spun around, reading the label, but each time he huffed and moved on to another. It seemed he forgot his organization scheme in the time he had been away, or perhaps it was the lack of an organization scheme that was the problem. At last, he pulled out a tube that looked the same as all the rest, and hissed a triumphant, "Finally."

Unscrewing the cap on the end, he pulled out a blueprint and laid it flat on the nearest desk, waving Katiel and Nev to his side. It was a blue-green sheet of thin parchment, with faint, straight lines sketched across it in both directions. On the grid was a detailed drawing of a wheelchair, similar to Nev's, but with tracks on either side in place of wheels. Around the perimeter of the drawing, measurements and footnotes were enumerated in a neat, tight scrawl.

It took Katiel a moment to realize what it was, but when she did, her eyes shot open wide to meet Anton's expectant gaze. It was a chair for Nev that could traverse varied terrain, allowing her to go wherever she wanted. To travel to Kerafin with him, like she hadn't been able to the last time.

Katiel's heart gave a little unwanted leap, touched that this was the project that meant so much to him. On the other hand, this machine was complex, and she couldn't even make a compass work.

"This is a wonderful idea," Katiel began, measuring her words carefully, "but I'm not certain I can wield it. That machine looks quite complicated."

"Nonsense." Anton waved off the notion. "This need be no different from wielding any other object." He pointed to the drawing. "If you follow this exactly, it will work."

Anton was focused on the feasibility of his creation, but behind him, Nev examined her cuticles, her lips pressed together tightly. She hoped Anton had discussed this with his sister ahead of time, but Katiel decided against mentioning it to him. Nev could speak up if she wished, and besides, it wasn't Katiel's place to interfere between siblings. She was his employee now, she reminded herself, not his friend and certainly not anything more, like she fleetingly—foolishly—had once hoped.

"Not today, then," Katiel said, buying herself time with a resigned sigh. As much as she wanted to help, she'd never be able to complete this machine, and she couldn't bear to disappoint them both. "Tomorrow. I'm still weary from traveling."

Anton looked like he might object, but Nev cut in, not at all meekly despite her high-pitched voice. "Truly, brother, you get ahead of yourself. She hasn't even been shown to a room or had time to freshen up. This is hardly the way to treat a member of the court."

At that, Anton looked rightfully abashed, his thick eyebrows shooting up and his closed mouth dropping slightly. "Quite right." He straightened a cufflink, though it didn't appear to have come undone. "Would you like to show our wielder to her rooms?"

"Absolutely," Nev said, spinning around and making for the door as Anton stayed behind. Katiel was unsure if Nev was annoyed with her brother, or simply preferred to travel quickly, but Katiel had to hurry to keep up with her.

The siblings had apparently already discussed her sleeping arrangements, because the princess led Katiel straight to her appointed room—the suite directly across from Anton's. Though she didn't love being thrust into this space without any choice, being close to him admittedly eased her mind a bit. He'd vowed to protect her from anyone who opposed her at court, and after seeing how his subjects treated him, she believed he could.

The spacious bedroom was four times the size of her real bedroom back home, and adjoining it was a bathroom with a clawfoot tub fed by indoor plumbing. The armoire was filled with more Drezchy fashions—all dresses of either black or deep blue, with black lace sleeves and collars that Katiel could tell would itch even before trying them on.

After showing her how to work the faucets, Nev left Katiel alone to rest, a consideration she was immensely grateful for after the jarring tour. New Drezchy was much more intimidating than she expected, and the second the princess left, Katiel locked the door, drew a bath, and spent the rest of the day hiding in her room.

Though she imagined a castle to be bustling with servants, Nev informed her that she and her brother preferred their privacy, and no servants visited their wing save for one afternoon a week for cleaning. For the rest of the day, her only interaction with another person was when a steward came to deliver an unrequested dinner of roast quail, the entire bird disgustingly intact on the plate. She obviously could not eat a creature as it actively stared back at her, so she skipped dinner and opted to retire early.

As she stared up at the canopy draped over her newfound bed, wearing an uncomfortable nightgown with scratchy lace trim, Katiel's stomach began grating from more than just hunger.

Tomorrow, she would have to wield. She'd obviously known she would have to when she took on the role of court wielder, but that fact did nothing to stemmy her dread. On the ship, time and distance had kept her anxiety at bay, but alone in the dark, the reality of what she had done fully sank in. She was alone, on another continent, with no way home, and obliged to do the bidding of a cunning prince who she knew she shouldn't trust.

For the rest of the night, sleep eluded her, and she could only think of one sentence, repeating on a never-ending loop in her mind.

What have I done?

12
Anton

Katiel shouldn't trust him.

She shouldn't have trusted him when they met. She shouldn't have let him join her quest back in Linden. And after everything Anton did, she certainly shouldn't trust him now.

But she did, anyway. She followed him to another continent. Honestly, her faith in him was terrifying.

Not that he was tricking her this time. No, Anton fully intended to honor everything he claimed and take the throne from his cold-blooded uncle. But Katiel had no reason to believe that other than naïvety and blind optimism. In this court, those traits could get her hurt—or worse.

That concern nagged at him throughout their voyage and now, back in the halls where so many of his nightmares had happened, the worry was positively gnawing. He already warned her to avoid Uncle Vadim and his cousin, Ludvig, in particular, but he would still need to keep a close eye on her to make sure none of his cruel relatives could harm her.

On Kerafin, physical distance had given him the chance to breathe, but being back in New Drezchy, it was like his fears were eating at him.

Chewing, and chewing, and chewing—and before long, they were going to spit him out.

There would be no harm in checking on Katiel, surely.

Except she wanted space from him. Their relationship was to be strictly professional going forward.

He tried and failed to ignore the constriction in his chest at that.

She wanted space from him. Anton could handle that. It was good, actually. It meant she was learning to be wary. He couldn't be around her constantly, and she needed to protect herself.

But there was nothing unprofessional about an employer checking on the newly appointed court wielder on her first day. In fact, he would check on any non-beautiful employee without hesitation.

So, he was actually doing as she'd asked as he abandoned his untouched breakfast and made straight for her quarters. After a sleepless night, he'd gone to the dining hall long before the crack of dawn, and the sun had only just begun rising as he knocked on her door.

He rapped twice with a deliberate lack of urgency. It would not do to have her think him a tyrant, after all.

With surprising swiftness, she opened the door, as if she'd already been standing there despite the early hour. Behind her, the room was untouched, the plush bed still made. Her hair was plaited and twisted atop her head, with a couple of alluring pieces floating loose by her cheekbones. Nev had assured him she'd had time to outfit her wardrobe with enough new garments to last throughout the season, but the wielder was wearing the same dress she wore on the ship, a traditional A'slenderian frock with the *dirndl* and the adorable, puffed sleeves on the shoulders.

Biting his lip, he forced his gaze back to her forehead. It was a habit he'd picked up at court, appearing to make eye contact when doing so would be too disarming. And with her looking like this first thing in the morning, he was feeling particularly distractible. "Did you not sleep well? Were the appointments not to your liking?"

"Oh, no, the lodging is as comfortable as can be," she assured, her delicate hands clasped in front of her, though he noticed she did not answer the first question. "It's quite literally a palace."

"Why then—?" He began to ask about the made bed, since he'd specifically ordered the servants to keep their distance, but caught himself. She must have made it herself. Of course she would. People like her and her friends did things for themselves, a fact he always had to remind himself of. "Never mind. Did the new clothes not fit properly? Were they too large?"

Katiel wasn't overly petite, actually. She was curved and strong—perfect in his eyes. But judging from her blush, he said the right thing.

"No, they fit well, actually." At that, she blushed again. "But they are very...Drezchy."

"Hmm," he mused. Anton could see what she meant. The Drezchy preferred brown, black, and slightly lighter black. Katiel was much too lovely for it. "I'll put in an order for some A'slenderian styles."

Her eyes brightened, but she bit back her smile. "So, what are we to do today?"

Right. That's what he came for. He smirked as he peered down at her, unable to contain himself. "Wielding, of course."

Katiel was going to love this. She didn't even know how much.

Taking to the spacious grounds of Karolinum, Anton led them to the last of the walled courtyards, the perfect place to practice wielding with privacy. Only members of court were allowed, and between the long walk it took to get there and the lack of anything but grass and a single willow tree, this yard saw few visitors.

"Why do you look like that?" she asked from where she followed a step behind him.

He might consider slowing—he always walked quickly when he was excited—but they were stepping into the courtyard now, so he came to a full stop instead. "Look like what?"

She flicked her wrist, effectively gesturing to all of him. "So grinny."

Since she pointed it out, he grinned wider just to annoy her and whipped out a rolled blueprint from his satchel. "Because you're going to love wielding with me."

Katiel scoffed, but she took the paper, regardless. "Nev's maneuvering chair." Her nose drew close to the charcoal as she read the tiny notes etched in the margins. "So, the chair absolutely must be able to move on its own?"

"Naturally." He nodded. "She can push herself on level ground with ease, but this chair needs to climb stairs, go over a fallen log on a woodland walk, and stay level on a rocking ship deck. The wheels will have to not only move of their own accord, but expand and contract in size as the situation requires."

Immediately, her jaw sagged. "Can such a thing be wielded?"

"Katiel," he said, at which she sucked in an odd little breath, "you aren't thinking big enough. You have the power to create anything. Think about it. *Anything.*"

"No." She shook her head, her mouth pressing into a hard line. "Some might. Not me."

"Anything. You." He winked. "You need to start associating those two ideas."

She said nothing as he shoved his hand into his satchel, rifling around for the book he'd brought her. He had entirely too many stray papers crammed inside, and it took a moment to grab the tome beneath them. When he finally pulled it out, her eyebrows fell into flat, unimpressed lines.

"A guide to the basics of wielding," he supplied. "To begin your training. The practice may be banned on the great and honorable continent of Kerafin, but Karolinum's library houses many resources on the subject."

She traded him the book for the blueprint and opened it to the page he'd marked with a thin ribbon. Her light eyes darted side to side as she scanned the text. "So, I must wield each component and then manually assemble them? That's not how I did it when I wielded the pistol." He didn't know what she was referring to, and he was about to ask when she supplied, "The one I shot General Taregh with."

Anton whipped around to face her. As he was already leaning over the book, the movement forced him to step back to avoid touching his forehead to hers. "You shot General Taregh?"

Her small mouth pulled taught, clearly only just realizing she'd omitted that detail when she'd relayed the events. At the time, she'd merely said that Taregh died when she rescued the Barkurian royals. "I killed him."

The pitiful tone she struck clawed at his heart. It was like she already felt less human, like she knew no one would ever see her as she'd once been. Though he'd loathe to admit it to her—or even himself—he'd felt the same after his first execution. "You did what you had to do."

She said nothing in return, and he couldn't say much else without revealing everything he wanted to hide from her. So, back to wielding it was.

"No, those are separate from the chair. That you will wield fully formed, as usual," he explained, answering her original question. "I thought it would be nice to practice smaller, easier objects and work up to something more complex."

She looked over the blueprints again, brightening the slightest bit. "You made this whole guide to teach me?"

"Yes, well—" Anton stammered, hoping she didn't think him overstepping. "I *have* been studying the practice for years."

"Thank you, Anton," she said, and heat instantly flared in Anton's chest.

He coughed and sat down a few paces back, leaning back on his elbow in the short grass.

"Remember," he said, tapping his index finger against his temple. "You can create anything. These simple items will be easy."

Katiel nodded and set to work, but after hours of practice, she hadn't successfully crafted a single thing. The best she'd done was wield an iron shield, only for it to evaporate in a puff of dust before the piece touched the ground. This was worse than he expected, and Anton couldn't figure out what was going wrong.

"Do you recall doing anything differently last time, when you were able to wield?" he ventured, hoping a jog of her memory might help.

"I had to clear my mind," she said, her chest heaving with exertion, "and allow myself to feel."

"That's a bit cheesy, no?" he joked, and was met with a glare that he admittedly deserved. "What allows you to clear your mind and feel?"

For him, it was her.

But as for her answer, the only response she gave was a flash of the eyes.

He got the message—his help was only making things worse—and he was about to say as much when the Karolinum clock tower chimed twelve.

Noon. He'd already forgotten. High court had started in the throne room thirty minutes ago, and he hurried to his feet, brushing the errant blades of grass from his suit.

The sudden motion startled Katiel, and the vague shape she was forming collapsed along with her shoulders. "Is everything all right?"

"Quite," he outright lied. "I've a bit of business to attend to, but good luck with your practice."

He rushed back into the castle, unwilling to look back at Katiel lest she appear hurt by his sudden departure. He was late, and not to just anything. At breakfast, Uncle's valet had informed Anton that he would oversee today's criminal proceedings at court—as well as carry out the punishments.

Only crimes of the most heinous nature made it all the way to the top, and by the time they reached Karolinum, the accused was all but condemned. He'd never left court without at least one person put to death. Anton had been seven when he was deemed old enough to spectate, and fourteen when he began filling in for his uncle in executing the guilty.

When most performed the punishment—his uncle included—they'd elongate the torture, claiming that anyone who survived would prove themselves innocent, but no one ever survived. Once Anton took over, his swift executions had earned him a reputation for brutality, though he saw it as mercy.

At first, he'd been excited to take on the role. Having a slight build in a kingdom that valued brute strength meant Anton needed a boost in public favor—favor he would sorely need when he inevitably became king. Or, at least it had once been inevitable, before his uncle declared the Rite of Conclave.

Anton never wanted Katiel to learn of his role as the Ghost, and even more so, he never wanted her to find out he volunteered for the position. She could hardly stand herself for killing a monster who was seconds away from killing her best friend if she didn't act. He could only imagine what she'd think of him courting favor via cold-blooded public spectacle. His only consolation was that formal court only took place twice a week. As long as he scheduled Katiel's mandatory practice sessions during them, she would never have to know.

When he reached the amphitheater, Nev and Sera were already waiting there. Sera stood a step behind her, like she still occupied her former position as his sister's guard.

It was how they'd met years ago, when their mother insisted to their uncle that Nev needed a full-time protector. Their mother—may she forever rest in the Veiled Eternity—had decided that the sentinel must be a girl around Nev's age, for her safety and happiness both, and many girls began training from a young age for the permanent role. Of all of them, Sera had been the best.

When he approached, Sera was bent down to his sister as they both snickered at some private joke, and Anton's chest warmed at them getting along again. Sera had been crazy about Nev when they'd dated, and he couldn't get his sister to tell him why she'd broken up with her in the first place. Perhaps she'd gotten past whatever had bothered her during Sera's year-long absence from New Drezchy.

"You're late," Nev teased as he drew to a halt next to her, clasping a wrist behind his back in formality. She hauled up her satchel from where it hung off the back of her chair and pulled out a cheese wedge and a small loaf of sourdough. "Here, I brought you lunch. I assumed you had not eaten since you were busy practicing."

Anton beamed and thanked her. She was always doing kind and thoughtful things like that. With her inherent goodness and stellar intellect combined, it was a crime that she couldn't hold court herself—or compete in the Conclave, for that matter. She'd make a better ruler than any of them, himself included, so it was a travesty that the people of New Drezchy would never go for it. They saw kindness as weakness, and a weak monarch, to them, was a death sentence.

"Anton," his uncle snapped, yanking him out of his thoughts. The raw bellow of the unfortunately familiar voice scraped down his spine. "Would you do the honors?"

"Very well," Anton said, but he ground his teeth as he stepped forward.

He'd held out hope that he would be relieved of his duties as crown prince when he lost the title, but of course, he hadn't been. Uncle knew Anton had grown to dread the gruesome task, and since Anton's own late father—may he forever rest in the Veiled Eternity—was Vadim's younger brother and greatest rival, his uncle had always done absolutely anything he could get away with torturing his nephew.

The fate of the men chained atop the dais was decided before Anton arrived, each one brought forth with a pile of evidence against them. It wasn't that he believed they were innocent, not at all. Unfortunately, even with the severe laws, violent crime ran rampant in his kingdom. Carrying out executions, though—that was what he hated.

The blood, the smell, the hollow pit in his stomach as he forced himself to disassociate from the corpse in front of him—it all made him want to refuse and return to his library, to escape the nightmare that was sure to follow.

But he stepped up to the dais despite his wishes. Because if there was one person Anton would never allow himself to show weakness in front of, it was his uncle.

13

Katiel

Katiel practiced for hours after Anton left, but to no avail. She wasn't sure what was wrong with her. On the ship, she'd at least formed a compass, even if it couldn't locate true north. Now, being here in this anxiety-inducing role, with the first trial threatening to commence at any moment, it seemed her nerves were too fried to concentrate on anything.

When the sun had just begun sinking behind the edge of Karolinum's roofline, Katiel rolled up the blueprint and crossed the grassy courtyard. She reached the side entrance leading into the palace, but the door opened of its own accord before she could grab the handle. A small gasp escaped her lips as Nev appeared in the doorway, dressed in a deep-maroon, long-sleeved velvet frock with a low neckline and a fine jeweled choker.

"There you are!" she exclaimed, her curly, dark brown updo bouncing in emphasis. "I've been looking all over for you. If you don't hurry, you're going to miss the state dinner. And you're the guest of honor!"

The princess turned around and took off down the hall, and Katiel scurried up to her side. "Pardon. The guest of honor?"

"Yes," Nev said with a series of quick nods. "Uncle is to proclaim the appointment of the new court wielder."

"I'm surprised that Anton did not tell me of this," Katiel admitted, the uncharacteristic candor tasting strange on her tongue.

"My brother has been," Nev said, cutting her eyes downward, "indisposed with another appointment."

"I see." Katiel wasn't sure what exactly being a crown prince entailed, much less a newly demoted one.

She imagined it was something similar to Jay Donnell's position, though on a much larger scale. According to Brenna, he mostly did a lot of bookkeeping and traveling to the capital to request aid for his town. Katiel had to admit, it was hard to picture Anton in such a role. To her, he seemed better suited for idle studies than important matters of state.

The princess headed straight for Katiel's suite, where Katiel quickly chose one of the Drezchy-style dresses from the wardrobe to change into. They were all heavy, with thick, stiff materials and unnecessary layers of skirts, and each one was of a dull, unflattering hue. She tried a few on, but none looked right, so she had to try half of them again. Finally, she selected the frock that most closely matched Nev's—a black velvet full-skirted dress with an equally low neckline—and paired it with a diamond choker featuring a large, oval-shaped pearl in the center.

While she hurriedly applied coal to her lashes and a swipe of red stain to her lips, Nev waited patiently, not appearing even slightly irritated that Katiel was keeping her from arriving on time. The princess wasn't prickly like her brother, and Katiel found herself warming to her already. As they entered the formal dinner together and every eye turned to them, she was especially grateful for Nev's presence.

The hall was long and ominous, with a vaulted ceiling looming high above the two tables that ran the length of the room. A smattering of ornate candelabras speckled the air, casting a dim glow that somehow made everyone look uncannily attractive. Though on second thought, it was largely Anton's own family in attendance, so perhaps that was just how they looked.

"Here," Nev said, tapping Katiel's elbow to steer her toward the far end of the hall. "You'll sit by me."

In her chair, Nev had to look up at everyone to hold a conversation, Katiel included, yet she managed to cast the most confident, important presence in the room. Katiel could see why Anton believed she should be the queen.

Katiel slid into a seat near the head of the banquet table, waiting for Nev's lead on what to do next. From the place the princess had selected, they could easily survey the lot, and the princess wasted no time in filling her in on the important players. Anton, meanwhile, was nowhere to be found.

"So, Katiel, you must acquaint yourself with your competitors, first and foremost." Nev leaned toward her, and Katiel followed suit so they could speak in a hush. Now at eye level, it was easier to converse with the princess, and her beauty was striking. She had the most angelic features Katiel had ever seen, next to her brother. Her heart-shaped face was perfectly balanced under her halo of thick curls, and up this close, the eyes that Katiel had thought were gray were actually of a distinctly purple hue. "There are six male cousins competing and four females. See him, there?"

Nev nodded toward a tree trunk of a man, laughing raucously with a group of other men and women of similar stature. He was blond, with a strong, rectangular nose and matching chin. His fine suit was trimmed with brown fur pelt lapels, making him appear at first glance to be even larger than he already was. "That's Ludvig," Nev went on. "He's eighteen, just like Anton, so they've always seen each other as rivals. Forget about any legitimate complaints—they hate when the other so much as breathes near them."

Katiel smirked. That sounded like the Anton she knew.

"The Conclave trials are always physical competitions, tests of strength. Naturally, Ludvig was elated when it was declared. Uncle may as well have handed the crown to him directly."

"Anton is strong in his own way," Katiel said aloud without meaning to, thinking back to when he pulled her unconscious body out of the rushing Slonde river with one arm.

Nev didn't bother to hide her surprised giggle. "If you say so."

At that, Katiel had the good sense to blush.

"Surrounding Ludvig are his four siblings. The one next to him is Signy," she said, indicating a tall woman with blond hair cropped just above her muscular shoulders. "She's a very, *very* strong woman, not unlike our own mother was. Then Agneska, Yaro, and Inek—all of them the children of my eldest aunt and her various suitors." The three others looked like near-copies of Ludvig and Signy, though slightly smaller and much quieter. "None of the five are particularly sentimental, but they care for one another enough to be interesting to fight. I think they'd prefer not to kill one another, but none will risk being seen as soft enough to admit it to the others. Therefore, I imagine they will break up early on instead of defending as a unit, hoping Anton or another cousin will pick the others off. None of them will want to make it to the end alone with a sibling."

"That would be seen as soft?" Katiel asked, shaking her head. "Soft to not want to kill your own sibling?"

"Yes, that would mean you love them," Nev replied, as matter-of-factly as if she were informing her of the weather that day. "Love is weakness."

Katiel had always heard the Drezchy were ruthless, but this was more than she expected. "Tell me more about the competitors," she urged, hoping to forget the topic without having to chime in about how much she disagreed.

"Then there's Halina." Nev dipped her head toward a slender woman with near-black, pin-straight hair who might be taller than Ludvig. "The best way to describe her is, 'intense.' She trained with Sera as a child for the position to guard me, so agility is second-nature to her. She's the youngest daughter of my youngest uncle, so she wanted the position to gain some influence, having grown up behind thirteen others for the throne in our generation alone."

"Thirteen?" Katiel asked, expecting the count to be one higher.

"I'm not in line," Nev explained. "New Drezchy will never accept a ruler with unformed legs." She said it as emotionlessly as she'd said love was a weakness, like there was nothing unjust about the concept at all. To Katiel, the throne should be hers as much as anyone's—more so, since she was the eldest child of the current king's eldest brother.

"Then, last of all, we have Cezary, Havel, and Ferenc, all siblings." Each of them had a sturdy, muscular build, and thick, dark waves that matched Anton's and Nev's, but with deep, olive-toned skin. "They took a cue from Anton and left Vincencim until a few days ago, once their eldest brother, Jindrich, was killed out-of-round by Ludvig."

The top of Katiel's ears grew several degrees colder as most of the people milling about began taking their seats for dinner. All the casual talk of cold-blooded murder was so foreign to her that she didn't think she'd be able to eat a bite of her meal when it was served. When all but the last of them had found their places, Anton stepped into the hall, a harsh shadow cast by the broad iron chandelier hanging directly above him.

He was dressed more lavishly than ever, in full tails and a high white collar stretched around the thick column of his neck. His choice of outfit made it clear that he was nothing like his cousins, with their gaudy furs to make themselves larger. The shine of a silver pocket watch chain contrasted the all-black ensemble, and the simplicity of it highlighted his elegance.

Katiel forced her eyes back to Nev, away from his perfect face and the stylish suit covering the presumably perfect body underneath—which she vowed resolutely to never imagine again. Starting now.

After the first course was served, Katiel attempted to rekindle the previous conversation with Nev while she pushed her uneaten food around the gilded plate. "What were you saying about out-of-round"—she flinched, the word heavy in her mouth—"*kills*? Is that allowed?"

"Yes, they're allowed, of course. What would the punishment be?" Anton quipped as he came into earshot. "Death?"

He let his fingers graze along the back of her chair as he went past, and Katiel clenched her teeth in response, reminding herself of all the reasons she had to hate him. Something about him looking the way he was, and standing above her, behind her but just out of view, was quite distracting. But then he sat on the opposite side of Nev, allowing Katiel some much-needed physical space.

"What about the other cousins?" Katiel asked the princess, forcing herself to cut into her steak and pretending to take a bite, knowing she couldn't stomach it while on the subject of the Conclave.

Nev blinked and took a hearty bite herself. "What other cousins?"

"I thought there were fourteen total," Katiel said, pausing for a quick mental tally. "Counting you and Anton, that's only eleven you've introduced so far."

"Oh, well, the other three have already been killed by Ludvig and his siblings. Berta and Varya, who were Halina's older sisters, and the one I already mentioned, Jindrich."

If she wasn't merely pretending to eat, Katiel would've choked on her food. "Three killed before the first trial?"

Nev nodded like she didn't understand the fuss. Meanwhile, a sweat was breaking out on Katiel's temples from sitting amongst these people. Here they were, dressed in finery for a civilized meal, knowing that they would murder the others at the first chance they got. Knowing Anton had grown up among this savagery, it astounded her that he was as kind as he was.

No—that line of thinking would lead her nowhere worth going. She knew he wasn't trustworthy from the second she met him, and she had to remind herself of that before she let her guard down again.

Just then, a round of applause and hearty cheers interrupted her thoughts. At the head of the center table stood a man wrapped in the most massive fur cape Katiel had ever seen, the oversized apparel casting strange proportions on his clearly small frame. He had thick, dark hair with a few flecks of white peeking out from under his bold platinum crown, and a dark goatee to match. With a pint of ale sloshing in one hand and the other hand clutched to his chest, he laughed boisterously as he waited for the crowd to quiet.

King Vadim of New Drezchy, mere feet away from her.

The thin lines on his cheeks and forehead revealed his age, but with his well-proportioned facial features and doe-eyes, he was clearly handsome once—which was strangely at odds with what Katiel had expected. He was the boss; the mastermind; the epitome of evil. He started a war under false pretenses, throwing away innocent lives in a quest for power, and he called a Conclave for all his nieces and nephews to murder each other. Then again, being unusually handsome may have helped him get away with wrongdoing, something she absolutely must not forget when it came to his nephew.

"Now, now," he started saying to those closest to him, as though they were sharing a private joke, "I must make the announcement."

Katiel leaned forward an inch to steal a glance at Anton. His face was passive, unreadable, and forced—a look that she was starting to think meant pure hatred.

"As you all know, we're gathered here tonight for multiple esteemed purposes. The first is to celebrate our new court wielder, an appointment made by our very own *former* crown prince." The king's emphasis on the word "former" couldn't be missed, but it still baffled Katiel to hear someone refer to their own relative so condescendingly and in such a public manner. "Kaltey Salzbrick, would you stand for us, please?"

It took Katiel a moment to realize that the butchered name was meant to be her own, and she stood, giving a slight bow as she looked toward the room full of courtiers. "She's not your usual court wielder, eh?" Vadim looked back to the room, and several people agreed with raucous laughter. Then he added with a wink, "She'll be nice to look at, even if she won't be of much use."

Katiel's cheeks burned, and she took a seat without being asked to, swiping at her already-straight skirts to retain as much composure as possible. Hot tears prickled at the corners of her eyes, and she hastily took a swig of water from a glass goblet to obscure her face.

Anton noticed, though. Even without looking his way, she could feel his eyes on her. The absolute malice coming from his direction was palpable, like he was considering walking onto the dais and strangling his uncle right there. She wondered if anyone else could feel the wrath emanating from him.

"Now onto other matters," King Vadim continued, addressing the congregants as a whole. "Since we've all returned to New Drezchy, I've chosen a date for the first trial of the honorable Rite of Conclave."

Gasps and murmurs sounded around the room. Clearly, Katiel wasn't the only person who hadn't expected it to begin so soon.

"The Conclave will consist of three trials, which I've thoughtfully selected to ensure only the worthiest rises to the monarchy in my stead."

The worthiest. According to Anton, that was Nev, who wasn't even allowed to compete. Thoughtfully selected, indeed.

"For the first trial," the king proclaimed, "each competitor will be permitted to bring one weapon only, anything you choose."

Katiel already knew that Anton intended for her to wield him a magically-imbued weapon. Although the court wielder served the royal court at large, Anton assured her that she would only have to wield for him during the Conclave. Though the idea of Anton being dangerous was still strange to her, she was assuming he meant to keep his cousins from requesting her services through violent threats.

"During this trial," the king went on, "we'll remain in Vincencim, so all of our fine citizens will get quite a show. No one but the competitors will be permitted in the streets, but there are an abundance of balconies in our fine city, and spectating is *highly* encouraged. The final six competitors will advance."

He winked again, and the crowd nearest to where he stood broke out in a series of whoops. It seemed he had a fan club among the court, which notably included none of his nephews or nieces—not even Ludvig.

"For the second trial, we'll head outside the city. The arena for this round will be the Changing Maze."

At that pronouncement, groans and gasps sounded throughout the hall. Katiel had no idea what the Changing Maze was, but it must be terrifying if even people who'd trained as warriors all their lives didn't favor competing in it.

"Since this terrain may prove challenging, I've decided to make things interesting. Each competitor can bring in a single mercenary. After all, a ruler must know how to lead and strategize. From this round, two will go on to compete in the third and final trial."

It was such a bizarre, callous way to say that only two of his nieces and nephews would remain alive to participate in the last round, but it strengthened Katiel's resolve to help Anton win the crown. Despite his faults, he wasn't anywhere near as barbaric as the country's current ruler, and deep down, she did think he'd make a good king.

"The third trial's rules are simple—no weapons, no tools, no help. A bare-bones arena in the amphitheater. Brawn versus brawn. Because it simply wouldn't do to have anyone but the strongest rule New Drezchy."

Katiel hoped he was done. The venom dripping from his every word was enough to make her queasy, and for what had to be the thirtieth time that hour, she wondered why she had ever come to this Creator-forsaken continent.

But the king wasn't finished speaking yet, not until he concluded his announcement with the worst part of all.

"The first trial begins in three days."

14

Brenna

"I killed Henred."

At Dakier's words, the world tilted on its axis, the same way it had the day Brenna learned of Henred's death. Hearing her brother's name, in the same breath as the word *killed*, stole the air from her lungs. Her tongue was dust against the roof of her mouth.

"You...killed...Henred?" She wasn't quite comprehending what that could mean, or how. "My Henred?"

Dakier had already taken several steps away from her. As quietly as possible, he said, "Yes."

"How?"

"I..." It was obvious that he didn't want to say, but didn't dare decline her request, either. His chin tucked down in shame, loose strands of black hair obscuring his face. "It was during the first battle I was in. He and I were facing off, and I shot him. We were quite a distance apart, and when I fired my rifle, I couldn't see who it was."

"It mustn't have been him," Brenna said hurriedly, feeling like she could breathe again for the first time in minutes. Obviously, Dakier imagined his worst fear due to the trauma of battle. She had heard experiences like that could play tricks on one's mind. "I'm sure it was some other Barkurian soldier who looked like him. That's all."

He swallowed hard, hanging his head even farther and reaching into the covered chest pocket of his uniform. He pulled out his hand, closed into a fist, and slowly—excruciatingly slowly—let his fingers fall away.

Brenna's throat went dry again at what lay there—a lock of red curls tied with green yarn in a four-leaf-clover knot. It was meant to be good luck, the final token she'd left for her brother.

It really was Henred.

Dakier had truly killed him.

And that was when she screamed. The cry was like a wolf's, guttural and raw, pure sound supplying her meaning while words failed her.

She reached out and swiped the lock from his hand. It was too good to touch him.

He didn't try to stop her, not at all, but he made the briefest second of eye contact, like he was soaking in the rage as it pummeled through her. Like he agreed that he deserved it.

She hated it, hated him, and hated that he could see her. She hated that he would be noble and understanding after what he did.

As if her pulse had a raging will of its own, she reached out and slapped him across the face so hard that her palm stung.

Reeling, she took a few hasty steps backward, staring at her throbbing palm, now spread wide mere inches from her face. She didn't know she was capable of striking someone, and she wished she'd never found out.

Thick, wet teardrops fell onto her bodice, spreading out in dark splotches against the green fabric, and when she looked up, Dakier's image became a watery fog. Until then, she hadn't realized she'd been crying.

"I—"

"Brenna—"

"Don't you dare say it will be okay!"

Dakier took a single step closer, and she retreated further. She was overcome with disgust at the mere thought of him trying to rectify this somehow, and even more disgusted at herself at how quickly she'd turned to violence. Her back hit Steffi's armoire, and atop it, one of her many priceless vases began teetering. Brenna and Dakier both lunged to catch it, but in avoiding colliding with each other, they missed. The fragile porcelain shattered against the floor with a deafening crunch.

"Aye, someone's in there!" a man bellowed from outside the door, and Brenna's eyes snapped to Dakier's.

It was the guards. Of course they wouldn't have stopped searching for an enemy soldier after he disappeared near the queen's own chambers. From the sound of it, they were waiting in the hall outside for when he reappeared—which Brenna could've predicted, if she hadn't lost herself to her grief and rage. At the moment, three bolted doors stood between them and the guards, but it wouldn't be long before they broke them down.

"Brenna, it's okay," Dakier said, keeping his voice low. "Just hide. They'll take me to the dungeon with the others, and everything will be fine."

But Brenna knew that wasn't true, and from the resignation in Dakier's face, he knew it, too. They might've taken his captain for interrogation, leverage, or both, but he was an ordinary soldier in the queen's private bedroom. They would shoot him on sight, and she would lose him, too. Not in the way she'd already lost him, where she simply never wanted to see his face again, but in the most permanent way possible.

"Hurry, come with me," she said with a sniffle, rushing to the opposite corner of the room. She wiped her eyes, still thick with tears, and stuffed herself behind Steffi's massive canopy bed before she could think better of it. The queen's walls were covered in thick ornamental drapes, and Brenna frantically sifted through them, searching for the hidden break between the fabric panels.

The crack of splitting wood reverberated through the space. From the sound of it, the first door of the three was already down. Dakier stepped closer to the door, looking ready to surrender the second the guards made their way through.

From outside, the guards jeered while Brenna entangled herself in the folds of the draperies.

"Just give up, you urchin!"

"There's nowhere to run, you Tibedese filth!"

Finally, Brenna's fingers found purchase at the edge of the cloth, and she yanked it aside. Behind it, a loose piece of the wainscoting led to a secret passage—an emergency escape from the castle in the event the monarch was threatened. As her chief lady-in-waiting, Brenna was one of the few people who knew of its existence. She was forbidden from revealing it to anyone at all, much less a foreign soldier, or even using it herself in the event her own life were endangered. If anyone found her in the current state, she was as good as dead, so she didn't know why she was risking this for him, of all people.

Still, she slid the mahogany panel to the side, and light poured into the darkened passageway beyond. Dakier watched her, his soft eyes shooting wide as he understood her plan. She meant for him to escape, while she would close the panel behind him. After all, her position allowed her to be in the queen's room, so she could simply say he'd attacked her and escaped.

With a resounding crack, the guard's axe sliced through the door panel, the silver blade jutting into the room before he pried it free.

One more strike and the last door would come down.

A tear streaked down Brenna's cheek.

"Go," Dakier mouthed, not daring to make a sound as he stared at the passageway.

But she shook her head, mouthing back, "Please."

Dakier's eyes shone with recognition, his pupils darting left and right. No time remained to weigh his options. If he didn't leave now, they'd both face trouble, and she knew he wouldn't chance her getting caught.

In a few long strides, he crossed the room and ducked into the opening. Before he could utter another word of protest, Brenna slid the panel back in place and let the curtains fall, masking the secret exit once more.

Thinking fast, Brenna raced over to where the vase had crashed and collapsed to the floor next to it—and the choice wasn't made a moment too soon. With a final swing, the axe blew a sizable hole through the door, and a uniformed arm reached in to turn the knob. When the group of guards rushed in, Brenna looked up at them in what she hoped passed for a daze and rubbed at her forehead as if she'd been struck.

The youngest guard, a sandy-haired man who didn't look much older than Brenna, hurried over to her. He knelt down, looking her over with genuine concern. "My lady, are you hurt?"

"No, I—I don't believe so. A man ran in," Brenna said with a forced stammer, allowing the chivalrous guard to help her to her feet. His kindness sent a twinge of guilt through her for deceiving him, but she carried on with her plan, regardless. "I tried to—to hide, but he shoved me and I fell, and then he ran off."

"Did you see which way he went?" another guard asked.

"I think he went that way." She pointed toward the bathing chambers, another falsehood that would lead them farther from the secret escape passage.

The guards shared a curt nod before running through the double doors she'd indicated, all except for the youngest one, who kept supporting Brenna with one arm.

"I'll be all right," Brenna said in the same shaky voice, still playing the part of the stunned lady-in-waiting.

Gingerly, he released her. He waited a second to confirm she wasn't about to topple over before hurrying off after the others.

And then Brenna was left alone, wondering if Dakier had made it out unseen, and wondering why she'd helped him escape at all.

15

Dakier

As Dakier stepped into the tunnel, Brenna clicked the panel back in place behind him, and he realized her plan a moment too late. She intended to stay back and cover for him, even knowing what he'd done to Henred.

She was honestly too good for this world.

He was standing in a small antechamber, a few feet long and illuminated only by a sliver of light emanating from the queen's chamber. At the end of the passageway was a bend, beyond which he assumed was the rest of the escape route. Brenna's fate on the other side weighed heavily on his mind, but he couldn't return to the bedchamber and risk exposing her. If the guards were with her, they might conclude that she was the one who showed him the path.

With no better option, Dakier continued as fast as he could, holding his breath against the musty stench of the unused corridor. He supposed that anyone fleeing was meant to take a lantern with them, because not far past the turn, the route became pitch black. Even with a moment to let his eyes adjust, he could see nothing in the true darkness. Without his vision, he would have to rely on touch to guide his way, a prospect that left him ill at ease.

At least the walkway was narrow. He could drag both his hands against the stone walls on either side, which gave him some comfort as he navigated. After the initial turn, the path stretched on in a straight line, and he traversed what felt like a mile before anything changed. Then, in the distance, the glowing outline of another door beckoned him forward.

When he reached it, Dakier crouched down to the wood, hovering his ear a half inch from the surface. No hint of movement came from within.

He could wait and see if the path onward led to safety, or he could guarantee his escape now. It reminded him of a proverb from the sacred scripture—*A quail in the hand is worth two in the sky*—and that reminder was enough to make his decision. Without another moment's hesitation, he pushed against the panel.

Nothing happened.

That was strange.

Next he attempted to slide it, imitating Brenna as best he could. Still, nothing.

Rearing back, he kicked, his boot splitting the wood cleanly down the center. Brightness blinded him as light spilled into the corridor, and he blinked furiously as his eyes adjusted enough to scan the room.

It was another chamber, one that looked almost exactly like the queen's, with lavish draperies lining the walls and a strange, short, fenced platform raising a massive canopy bed. He couldn't help but smile at the luck of ending up in a bedroom. It was better than walking into a guard tower for certain.

Then, abruptly, he realized that the room wasn't empty. Its occupant was staring directly at him, mouth hanging agape.

Instantly, Dakier recognized him. A slight boy with sandy blonde hair, the one who'd wielded the snake—Prince Eoghan.

And from the look on his face, the prince recognized Dakier, too.

"It's you," Eoghan breathed before his gaping mouth snapped shut, his curiosity giving way to fear. He darted around the desk he'd been sitting at and brandished a letter opener. "Stay back. I'm warning you!"

"I'm not going to hurt you," Dakier said, but there was no point in remaining in the escape tunnel now that he'd been seen. He stepped into the bedroom, holding his palms up in surrender. Eoghan hadn't called for the guards yet, so that had to be a good sign.

The prince gulped audibly, though to his credit, he didn't back away another step or lower his makeshift weapon. "What are you doing here? Why aren't you with the Tibedese delegation?"

It occurred to Dakier that in discovering Eoghan could wield, he gained leverage over the royal family, since the wielders of old were forbidden from reproducing under the Kerafin Pact. And on top of that, Barkurian culture had always been suspicious and critical of the wielders, who largely hailed from their rival A'slenderia. Prince Eoghan wasn't just any Barkurian, either. If the royal family were hiding a whole line of wielders, that could change the fate of the war.

Since the truth going public would be so damning, Dakier was sure if he threatened to reveal his secret, the prince would let him leave. He might even release Pereira and the others, if Dakier demanded it. But blackmailing the boy felt so despicable that a wave of shame washed over him for merely thinking it. It would escalate the conflict that had cost Henred his life—and made Dakier into a killer.

Unless I was a killer inside all along.

Dakier shuddered, banishing the thought from his mind. No, he absolutely could not think that way. Deep down, he feared if he fully considered it, he might convince himself it was true.

"Your secret's safe with me," he blurted. His palms were still splayed on either side of his head, though his elbows sagged with relief at the admission.

Eoghan's left brow curved into a dramatic arch. "What secret?"

Dakier cursed himself. He never should have said that, but he was too focused on his moral qualms to think straight. He hadn't even considered that Eoghan might not know he could wield.

But then again, how could he not? The prince brought ore to the smithy. Surely he knew its significance. Perhaps Eoghan was being facetious and going along with the secret being safe, but his tilted head and slack jaw suggested genuine confusion.

"You know," Dakier began, trying to think of a subtle way to put it, in case Eoghan was being coy on purpose. "The snake."

"The snake?" Eoghan repeated, before his eyes widened as the implication hit him. "The snake." The edges of his mouth stretched up into a shaking smile that he badly failed to suppress. He discarded the letter opener onto the desk and walked back around it, the instinct to protect himself evidently abandoned. "It worked. I can't believe it worked! I'm actually a wielder! "

With a funny little squeal, he jumped and pumped his fists in the air. It was like he forgot he wasn't alone until his eyes landed on Dakier. "Wait, how do you know it worked?" the prince asked.

A few minutes ago, Dakier was elated that he hadn't waltzed into a guard tower, but he had to admit, this situation was a bit trickier to navigate. He glanced at the thick door behind Eoghan, identical to the one that guards had just broken down to reach him. "It was slithering around in the courtyard. Now that you know, you must be more careful."

The prince's jaw had gone slack a moment before, but now it fell to the floor. "It was *alive*?"

Once again, Dakier had taken things for granted. This time, it was the knowledge that wielders could form far more than metal objects. They could wield life itself. Dakier himself only really knew about it because of Feniel's stories while they worked together. But of course, not everyone spent time alongside a master wielder-in-hiding who loved to drop crucial information in the form of fables. "There's no time to explain."

"Right." Eoghan nodded, taking the news of his newfound powers the way any child would—extremely well. "So, why are you in my room?"

Come to think of it, the prince had also adjusted remarkably well to the notion of him bursting in from a secret tunnel.

"I didn't mean to come to your room in particular," Dakier explained. "I was fleeing through the tunnel, and went through the first exit I found." He hoped Eoghan wouldn't suspect that Brenna had been the one to lead him to the escape route. Though it went against his better judgment, Dakier offered a quick lie, deciding the Creator would forgive it if the intent was to protect Brenna. "I happened upon the tunnel by chance. A stroke of luck, unless you turn me in."

"I wasn't planning to turn you in, but now that you told me I wield the ore, I'm *really* not," the prince said bluntly. "Unless you try to attack me!" He waited a second, like Dakier might attack right then, before he deemed it safe enough to continue the conversation. "But why were you fleeing at all?"

The prince was lucky that Dakier came through the hidden panel rather than an actual attacker, as he feared Eoghan would stand no chance defending himself. With an inward sigh, Dakier recounted the events of the evening as succinctly as he could, trying his best to answer the prince's requests for detailed descriptions of the Barkurians he'd seen rounding up his unit.

"Let's go to the dungeons then," Eoghan said when all his questions had been answered. "I bet that's where they're keeping the prisoners."

Dakier cocked a brow. "You want to go see them?"

The prince nodded emphatically, like what he meant was obvious. "Of course! I'm a prince! If they're not supposed to be there, I'm going to free them."

Dakier had to admit, he was impressed with the kid's bravado, as unassuming as he seemed. But when Eoghan made for the door,

Dakier realized with a jolt that he meant to leave him, a foreign soldier, alone in the royal suite. "What would you like me to do to help?" he hedged.

"You can't help. They'll just capture you," Eoghan answered, as candid as ever. "Just go back in the tunnel."

Dakier sighed, weighing his options. As much as he wanted to be of assistance, Eoghan was right. For his unit's sake, he had better lie low and figure out a more covert way to help them. So, with a bow of thanks to the prince for letting him go, he headed back into the darkness.

16

Brenna

Moments after the first group of guards disappeared, Steffi raced into the room, with a half-dozen more guards trailing in behind her.

She rushed over to Brenna immediately. "Are you alright? When I heard that an enemy soldier fled into my room, I was so frightened you might be here."

"I'm fine," Brenna said, forcing her best reassuring smile as Steffi eyed the shards of porcelain littering the carpet.

"Did he...hurt you?" Steffi grew quieter as she asked. Brenna knew what she was implying—every girl's worst fear in this type of situation.

"No, no, don't worry," Brenna assured. "It was nothing like that, thank the Creator."

Steffi let out a breath, with genuine relief that touched Brenna's heart. With the stately way she always held herself, Steffi proved herself to be every bit the queen, despite her age. This unexpected display of kindness, however, showed the mature ruler she was coming into.

The queen's trust was an honor, and she'd betrayed that trust when she showed Dakier the emergency escape route. It had been a hasty decision, and now she'd betrayed her beloved country again.

But she couldn't stop there.

"Steffi, we need to go to the dungeons," she said, pulse suddenly alight at the prospect. "They've taken the Tibedese delegation as prisoners."

Steffi's chin jutted forward in alarm. "Who has?"

"I—" Brenna was about to answer before she realized that she wasn't sure. Was it Lord Walsh? She'd assumed it was him, but once the name reached the tip of her tongue, she realized Dakier hadn't specified. "I'm not certain. Members of our government."

"Eoghan and I both came down with stomach aches and retired early for the night. I wonder—" The queen's pupils scanned from left to right, like she was mentally scrolling through a list of questions to ask before she settled on a command instead. "Nevermind that. Lead the way. I've never been to the dungeons."

Brenna's brows shot up. "Never?"

Steffi shrugged before dipping her forehead toward the door, her bottom lip quivering ever so slightly. "He never imprisoned me there."

Brenna sucked in a breath as she took in the meaning—when Steffi imagined being imprisoned, she immediately associated it with General Taregh. Those memories were fresh on Brenna's mind as she led the queen through the halls and down the winding stone staircase that led deep beneath the castle.

When she reached the archway that led into the dungeon, Brenna halted, trying to make sense of what lay in front of her. At the far end of the space, the Tibedese envoy was locked in a large cell, but the peculiar part was several additional people standing outside the bars. Lord Ovach, Lord Walsh, and Lord Byrne all faced her direction, but a smaller figure had his back to her and Steffi—Prince Eoghan.

"I demand you release them at once," Eoghan said in his high-pitched voice, still years away from deepening. "Imprisoning a foreign delegation in this manner goes against the stipulations for civilized warfare as formalized in the Kerafin Pact, Section Five, Mandate Forty-Six."

Brenna raised her brows, impressed that the prince paid so much attention to the lessons he incessantly complained about.

"These men violated the terms of honor in the first place by plotting an attack on the queen," Lord Ovach retorted, his mustache twitching with indignation.

"That is more than enough cause to detain them," Lord Byrne chimed in.

"That isn't true," Eoghan argued immediately. "I have word from a reliable source that they were ambushed unexpectedly at the welcome gathering this evening."

"On whose word?" Steffi asked, stepping into the light to make her presence known.

"Oh, Steffi!" Eoghan heaved a sigh of relief. "Thank the Creator. Please explain to your cabinet that there's been a misunderstanding."

"*Eoghan*," the queen hissed. "I'm sure our esteemed lords can justify the allegations."

Brenna's eyes widened as her head whipped to Steffi. The queen held her shoulders back in an exaggeratedly stiff posture, while her gloved fingers kneaded one another. Her bottom lip quivered just the tiniest bit, and Brenna recalled it shaking the same way moments ago when she mentioned General Taregh. With a pang of sadness, Brenna realized why Steffi was suddenly abandoning their plan and siding with the lords—she was afraid of them.

"Certainly," Walsh agreed. He drew a letter from his inner breast pocket. "It was addressed to me directly, warning me of the true intentions of the Tibedese. The note was left anonymous, naturally."

Lord Walsh crossed the dungeon and handed Steffi the folded piece of parchment. As the queen unfolded the page, Brenna peered over her shoulder to read along, but her heartbeat screeched to a halt when she caught sight of the lord's left hand. It had a smudge of green ink all along the heel—the exact clue Brenna had been looking for. Lord Walsh was the one who'd been threatening her.

"Your Royal Highness," Brenna whispered, trying to remember her manners as best she could in her frazzled state. "Might I have a word, please? Immediately?"

Steffi stiffened, her pupils darting between her lady-in-waiting and the lords. But then she folded the letter back together and nodded. "Give us a moment."

The queen walked back down the same stretch of hallway they'd just come through, and Brenna followed after, immensely relieved that Steffi was finally listening to her. "I trust this is about the situation at hand," the queen said as soon as they were out of earshot.

"Yes, of course." Brenna gave a fervent series of nods. "I know I should have told you sooner, but I've been receiving letters threatening me to keep quiet about the truth of the war, and I just realized Lord Walsh is the one who's been sending them. I bet he's the one who orchestrated this trap for the Tibedese, too. He had fresh ink all over his hand, so he could've written the letter he gave you himself."

Steffi blinked once. Twice. "I can't free the Tibedese magistrate."

Now it was Brenna's turn to blink. Isn't that what they had come down here to do? And did she not care about Lord Walsh threatening Brenna to keep quiet?

"Hundreds, maybe thousands of innocent people have died for nothing so far in this war," Brenna said, keeping her voice as low and even as she could, "and you haven't called for peace yet despite it being well within your power. My own brother was killed defending our country—for nothing."

"I have lost people, too," the queen said, her voice now much smaller than normal. "My own parents, lest you forget. But it is not so simple. A monarch must consider the good of the country above their own wishes."

"I apologize for my boldness, but you requested me specifically as your lady-in-waiting, because—as I recall—you felt I was the only one you could trust after General Taregh's treason," Brenna said, her wide eyes imploring Steffi to listen. "So, please, trust me now. A false imprisonment will only make everything worse. It will escalate the conflict you're trying to resolve."

Steffi swallowed hard. "I cannot admit to a false imprisonment on behalf of Bar Kur, just like I can't admit that it was one of our own who murdered my father rather than Inigo Farro." She sighed, her voice thick, like she was fighting back frustrated tears. "Not only would it weaken our nation's position globally, but if I'm the one who proclaims it, I fear the public will revolt and try to come for me and my brothers." A single tear fell, curving down Steffi's round cheek. "After all they went through, I just can't bear for either of them to come to harm."

Brenna's chest ached. She was right. Steffi had changed her mind about freeing the Tibedese out of fear for Eoghan, but that couldn't be the end of it. She just had to think—

"I've got it," Brenna said as quickly as the idea came to her. "I can tell everyone in secret! You'll tell the lords you fired me, and I'll leave the castle."

"What?" Steffi's tone shot up an octave. "Why?"

"That way, I can spread the word on my own." Brenna struggled to keep her voice low as excitement welled inside her. This was a good plan. It could actually work. "Nobody out in the city knows who I am, so they won't associate me with the monarchy. I'll get the people on your side so you can make the pronouncement."

The queen studied the toes of her slippers as Brenna awaited her answer with bated breath, but then she gave a reluctant sigh. "We can try."

17

Katiel

Katiel woke after another night of fitful sleep, her thoughts torn between her gnawing hunger and the impending trial.

She padded across the unnecessarily large suite to the dressing area and opened the ornate armoire. To her surprise, the wardrobe now included a dozen A'slenderian-style fashions. A smile crept up her face at the chance to wear something comfortable, and she quickly slipped into a mauve, long-sleeved frock and a pair of wool stockings to protect against the crisp early-morning air.

After grabbing several breakfast pastries from the kitchens, Katiel wound through the dreary depths of Karolinum alone, wondering why this palace had next to no windows and cursing herself for getting up so early to begin with. After her mortifying introduction to the court the night before, she'd made plans with Anton to practice wielding at dawn, but as she walked across the dewy courtyard, she realized it wasn't even dawn yet. She decided to wait under the willow tree, expecting him to waltz in any minute, but the minutes stretched into nearly an hour while the chill pricked at her cheeks.

"You didn't wait on me, my wielder?"

Katiel could practically hear Anton's smirk as he emerged behind her. She knew what he meant—that he'd expected her to wait in her room and walk there together—but she wasn't about to acknowledge her mistake when she'd been shivering for so long.

"I *have* been waiting."

"My apologies," he said, his tone playful as he stepped in front of her. "Though if it's any consolation, I'll have you know that I've been up all night crafting the perfect weapon design for the first trial."

She shook her head. "There's no time. The trial is the day after tomorrow."

A single, thick eyebrow shot up to his hairline. "Good thing it takes mere seconds to wield."

Katiel bit her lip. She wasn't going to respond to that. He should know as well as she did that there was something wrong with her abilities, and the last thing she needed was him rubbing it in.

"I call it the gauntlet," he said, shifting his feet from the brief silence. He unrolled a blueprint and presented her with a sketch of what looked to be a large metal glove, drawn above an outline of a complex gear system. "The inner workings here will multiply the impact when I strike, while turning the opponent's force against them if I use it to block. I'm certain most of my cousins will stick to tradition with the Drezchy double axes, so I've designed this to use their strength to my advantage."

Anton was smart; she had to give him that. Perhaps even a genius—though she would never, under any circumstance, say so aloud.

"How is it powered?" She hoped the thoughtful question would impress him, then immediately scolded herself for caring.

He flashed his row of stark white teeth. "You're going to wield it to power itself."

Katiel practiced until sundown for the entirety of one day and then the next, only stopping to sleep for a handful of hours and wolf down some breakfast before she returned to practice again. Anton stayed with her nearly the entire time, sketching on a checkered blanket while rotating through every lounging position possible.

With Anton by her side, giving her tips and encouragement, she made a full gauntlet by the end of the second day, but it didn't function. Anton would be better off going into the trial empty-handed than carrying a heavy, useless metal glove, and Katiel's heart pounded just looking at her failed creation.

In desperate need of a break from the gauntlet, Katiel thought back to the more accessible chair for Nev. She hadn't touched the blueprint since Anton first showed it to her, but the chair gave her less anxiety than the gauntlet—likely because no one's life was on the line if she failed to wield it.

She studied the drawing again, trying to come up with a plan. Typically, expanding the ore was much easier than shaping it, so perhaps that's what she'd been doing wrong. Perhaps, to help her feel more in control, she could try expanding the ore into the intended shape rather than keeping the steps separate. It was worth a try, at least.

Reaching into her pouch, she pulled out a tiny fleck of ore and placed a single speck on her fingertip, trying again to form a functioning compass. She inhaled, slow and controlled, but this time, she visualized the base of the shape, with more and more tiny pieces added to it. To her surprise, her imagination manifested before her open palms. At a slower speed, the miniscule additions would have looked like no progress at all, but at this pace, an object appeared to be rapidly woven on an invisible loom. It was so different from the near-instantaneous shaping that had worked for her before.

When the compass fell into her hands, the needle sprang for true north, and Katiel released a little squeal of joy. For once, she felt like she was actually in control of the ore, rather than blindly hoping it might bend to her wishes. This was a reliable, tangible process—something she could replicate.

"What are you smiling about?"

Katiel turned to face Anton. When she saw his face in the hazy dusk, she couldn't help but grin wide enough to show all her teeth. "I found a technique to control my wielding."

"Good girl."

Warmth rushed to Katiel's cheeks, and Anton winked. Just like that, she was back at the riverside on the way to Halstat, dazzled by him.

But that was how she'd gotten hurt once, and she couldn't let it happen again. So, she changed the subject. "I think I'm ready to wield the chair now."

He cocked a brow, the smirk never leaving his lips, and she blushed again despite herself. "Go on, then."

She nodded, pulling out another morsel of ore, but at the last moment, she let her hand fall away from her mouth. "Do you really think I can wield such a complicated machine?"

"If anyone can, it would be you, *Geführtchen*," he said, calling her the familiar nickname—the Aslen word for *wielder*—for the first time since Ballynach. His eyes bore into hers, clearly aware of how him speaking her native language affected her, and heat simmered in Katiel's chest. "You can do anything. You. Anything. Just try."

Katiel worried her lip, looking down at the ore on her palm. "Should I say the command aloud as I wield it?"

Anton nodded. "If you wish."

His dark eyes never left hers, and it was as if, for only a moment, he transferred his self-assuredness to her.

Katiel inhaled the ore and exhaled using her new method of concentration. The cloud of dust expanded only slightly and then attached to the shape before her, one tiny particle at a time. In less than a minute, the chair hovered fully formed before her, surrounded by swirling ore dust that kept it a few feet off the ground.

As peculiar as it felt, Katiel kept the chair suspended in midair, trying to hold on to the mental tether she felt as she was wielding, and said, "Adhere to the will of Princess Ananevia Alexandrina Minevechy of House Dvorsky."

Though she had no way of knowing if the command had worked, Katiel released the creation, allowing it to cascade softly to the ground of its own accord.

The finished product was identical to Anton's drawing. Like Nev's usual chair, the frame was wicker, with black velvet cushions upholstered on the seat and back, but that was where the similarities ended. Her normal chair had large wheels, with long spokes and thin tires, like the wheels on a carriage. Instead, the new one had continuous tracks attached to the base, which Anton had likened to a caterpillar because of the many segments. The tracks themselves consisted of linked, rectangular metal plates, each attached to a spoke that could expand or contract at will thanks to the magic of the ore.

"Is this similar to what you imagined?" Katiel asked, trying not to get her hopes up that she'd actually managed such a difficult feat.

Anton, however, held no such reservation. "It's perfect! Let's take it to her now."

"Isn't it getting quite late?" Katiel protested. "She might be asleep."

Anton scoffed. "My sister never sleeps."

He lifted the chair and set off at his typical break-neck pace, nearly running across the lawn and down the dimly lit halls with Katiel scurrying to keep up. She found herself doing a lot of scurrying after these siblings lately, and she would much prefer that both of them slowed down.

When they reached the door she assumed was Nev's, Anton set the chair down, and Katiel forced herself to keep from panting as she waited for him to open it.

He swept an arm toward the door. "After you."

While she knew him to be the type to barge right in, Katiel instead knocked lightly.

"Harder." He looked down his nose at her and had the audacity to wink.

She shot him a pointed scowl before knocking again, indeed much harder this time. Faintly, she heard Nev's voice say, "Come in."

Despite all her instincts, Katiel turned the doorknob and let herself in, but stopped short when she saw what lay inside. Other than a small canopied bed tucked into the far corner, Nev's suite was less of living quarters and more of a full-fledged laboratory.

Jars, canisters, and small glass tubes covered a long wooden counter, each filled with liquids of every color and labeled with letters that meant nothing to Katiel. At the far end, Nev poured a clear liquid from a tube into a graduated beaker, holding her nose close to the specimen in concentration. A gray collared coat completed the effect, covering her from her neck down to her ankles and wrists.

She didn't so much as glance up when she heard the door click. "May I help you?"

Anton smirked. "That's no way to address our guest, sister. She's quite spent from wielding for you."

Nev's gaze snapped up. "Katiel." She placed the tube in its metal ring and backed away from the table. "I take it you were successful, then?"

"Well, I—" Katiel began, but it seemed Anton's enthusiasm couldn't wait as he stepped aside to reveal the wielded all-terrain wheelchair he'd left in the doorway.

"There's only one way to find out."

Nev's eyes widened as she took in the contraption, a difficult feat considering the thick safety goggles she wore. "You mean for me to use that?"

"Yes, of course." Anton nodded vigorously. "We've made it just for you."

Though the concerned frown never left her face, Nev raised her elbows to be level with her shoulders. It was evidently a silent signal that her brother recognized, because he lifted her small frame by her upper arms and expertly transferred her to the new creation.

"There," Anton said, stepping back to survey the invention now that it bore the princess's weight. "Is it comfortable enough?"

The princess cleared her throat and shuffled to adjust herself in the seat. Though she said, "Yes, quite," she began picking at her cuticles the second her brother stepped back.

"As a wielded machine, the chair is designed to move as you will it," Anton explained. "Simply think of what you wish for it to do, and the chair will obey. Whether you need to climb stairs, dodge an obstacle, move quickly over rough terrain—it's designed to go anywhere you would wish to go."

Nev's brow crinkled in disbelief, but then she steeled her face into neutrality and looked straight ahead. Katiel imagined the princess was about to give a silent command, and anticipation radiated through the air as she waited for Nev to roll forward on her own.

A beat passed, but nothing happened. Katiel immediately scolded herself for believing that she could make such a complicated machine work of its own accord.

Then, so slowly that she almost missed it, the chair inched forward. Nev hadn't moved a muscle, yet it kept rolling until it picked up speed. Then she turned a sharp corner and headed straight for a footstool that blocked her path. Just before it rammed into the stool, the chair halted, and the tracks split up into several spindly, metal legs that stuck out on either side and stepped over the stool like a spider might.

"You did it," Nev said, her eyes bright as she came back over to them. "This will make getting around the castle—the city, everywhere—so much easier. I'll be able to go across the sea with you in this," she said to Anton, and then gasped as if a new thought occurred to her. "I have to try the stairs."

Nev soared out the door and down the empty hall at full speed, the spokes transforming instantly back into normal wheels. Anton flashed Katiel the warmest of smiles, and she returned it as they both hurried after his sister, earning quizzical looks and wide eyes from the servants they passed.

They headed into what Katiel assumed was a ballroom from the opulent, five-foot-tall chandeliers evenly spaced across the elaborately painted ceilings, which featured landscapes and battle scenes on each coffer. Nev radiated confidence as the chair climbed one of the two grand, curved staircases, increasing her pace with each step the chair's spider legs conquered. Anton and Katiel walked to the top of the other side to meet her, and when the princess reached her, she didn't hesitate before enveloping Katiel in a tight embrace.

While Nev said nothing else, the gesture alone meant the world. Katiel had finally used her abilities for good.

But all the while, an unjust war raged across the sea.

Fate had placed her in this strange position within this strange court, and she knew it couldn't be a coincidence. She may have done something good, but now it was time to do something great.

18
Katiel

A WIDE SMILE WAS plastered on Anton's face throughout dinner, and whenever Katiel made eye contact with him across the table, it grew even wider. She knew he was proud of her for successfully wielding such a complex machine, and she wished his praise didn't mean so much to her.

She wished it didn't mean *anything* to her, but it did.

Anton may have betrayed her trust, but since she'd come to New Drezchy, he'd been nothing but kind. Katiel knew he had his own responsibilities, yet he made her feel like she was the only person in the room—in the palace, even. After Alfien and Anton both hurt her, Katiel had carefully shielded her heart, but Anton's thoughtfulness toward her—toward his sister and Simeon—was slowly chipping away at the ice there, bit by bit.

Tomorrow, he'd be risking his life without the protection he'd asked her to wield, yet he showed no frustration toward her. The gift for his sister genuinely seemed to be more important to him. Perhaps he didn't think he'd live through the first trial, Katiel realized with a pang, so he was relieved that the invention had been completed while he could see it.

"Katiel."

She jumped at the sound of Nev's high-pitched voice. From her place across the table, the princess looked at her expectantly, and Katiel stopped cutting her roast duck. With Anton's seat vacant, the two of them were alone in the dining hall, and Katiel realized she hadn't even noticed him leave.

"Have you truly not been able to wield the gauntlet after all this time?"

Nev's doe-eyes narrowed with uncharacteristic focus, and Katiel sucked in a breath. Did she think Katiel was sabotaging him on purpose? The princess's occasional prickliness might suggest it, but it couldn't be further from the truth. Regardless of their own personal history—and the complicated emotions the prince stirred in Katiel at present—she'd given her word to help him win this tournament, and she wouldn't let him down if she could help it.

"I have not," Katiel admitted, forcing herself not to hang her head.

But Nev's matter-of-fact tone bore no hint of suspicion. "It's your mind. Your anxiety level is too elevated when you think of the tournament to wield properly."

Katiel coughed. "My mind?"

"Of course." Nev nodded, like it was obvious, while Katiel's thoughts were reeling. She normally tried not to dwell on her feelings, but with someone pointing it out so directly, she couldn't help but confront the truth. "I've been trying to create a calming tonic for you in my laboratory, but I haven't succeeded in making one without potentially adverse effects."

Katiel recalled the sight of Nev mixing vials of various chemicals into a beaker, her goggled eyes drawn close for a precise pour. "That's what you were making? An anxiety tonic for me?"

"Yes, I was working on it when you came in earlier," the princess replied, as if it were the most casual pastime in the world. "Anton must not die tomorrow."

Katiel's heart raced as a painfully clear image of Anton, weaponless, speared in the center of the plaza, came to her mind. If he died tomorrow—if that gruesome picture became reality—it would be her fault.

“I’ve also been working on a blood transferring apparatus with Simeon,” Nev went on, “in case he loses too much blood. That one has been more successful, though I don’t know how to—”

“Excuse me.” Katiel abruptly stood, the princess’s medical musings doing nothing to calm her frazzled state. “Please accept my sincerest apologies. I’ve begun to feel quite unwell, and I think I had better lie down.”

Nev’s thick eyebrows shot up. “Oh, of course,” she said. “Please go, and don’t hesitate to come by when you’re feeling better.”

Katiel gave a slight curtsy and turned to leave without another word. Tears prickled her lashes as she rushed down the hall, but she didn’t pay the questioning looks from the servants any mind. She simply went into her room and locked the door, in desperate need of a moment to gather herself.

She would have flopped on the bed, too, if there were not an unexpected envelope lying atop the duvet.

Immediately, she picked up the blank envelope, wondering if Brenna finally replied to her last letter about the Drezchy court. But when she popped open the seal and pulled out the note, it wasn’t her friend’s bouncy scrawl that dotted the page.

No, it was all straight rows of tiny, neat calligraphy—her father’s handwriting.

My dear Katiel,

I hope this letter finds you safe and well, darling daughter. Alfien has returned to the valley and told us of your adventures. I understand you've taken up an esteemed position in New Drezchy. Please note that I cannot say all the details that I wish to until I see you in person.

Know that your mother and I are so very sorry we kept things from you. I am personally filled with regret that I did not look deeper into your questions before you left. Perhaps we could have sought out the correct path together if I had listened. If you come home, you have my word to help in your efforts. Please come home.

Mother sets out a place for you at dinner every night, and rest assured you are never far from our thoughts.

Katiel had never known her father to be so wordy, but the letter stretched on and on, regret seeping into her with every word. Father might've helped her if she'd only given him the chance. She thought she had, but she hadn't—not really. Her parents were so overprotective, and her only explanation was that they didn't trust her. After she learned of her ability, she'd thought that they'd hidden it from her after realizing she was somehow defective.

But maybe, just maybe, they wanted to protect her because they loved her, and the thought of anything happening to her was too much to bear. A single, salty tear trickled down her cheek. She hated—absolutely hated—herself for not returning home to them. They could've figured this out together.

Wiping the tear, she read on.

I want you to remember that the Drezchy have always been at odds with our kind. They will use you with no respect for the boundaries of the condition. Stay safe, please. Never trust them. Whenever you need anything, never forget that you have the power within yourself to create it.

Please, whenever you are ready, come home. Your mother and I miss you so very much.

We love you.

Father

P.S. — I'm sure you'll be happy to hear that Alfien has fetched Gunnel and returned her home. She isn't the same though—she's constantly braying—and I think she may run away to look for you if you aren't back soon.

Katiel couldn't help but smile. Her father's thoughtfulness to mention Gunnel was touching—more thoughtful than she'd been in running away.

But it might all be for nothing if she couldn't thwart King Vadim's efforts and end this war. There was no more time to waste. She had to wield the gauntlet.

If she didn't, Anton would be killed while Katiel helplessly watched from the sidelines. A slew of scenarios played out in her mind—scenes of Anton being shot or speared or maimed—and she suddenly recognized the merit of Nev's observation with painful clarity. Just as the princess had said, her anxiety was keeping her from wielding.

She almost wished Nev had given her the tonic in its current form, despite the adverse side effects, but she knew the princess would never agree to it. If she didn't want to lose him tomorrow, Katiel needed to find another way to calm herself.

Katiel had been trying to clear her mind, but perhaps she should instead fill it with positive thoughts—with memories that calmed her.

She forced herself to think of her parents, of baking with them and knitting wool and playing card games with them by the fireplace. She remembered her excitement during her first visit to Brenna's house, when she was just a little girl, and kissing Anton for the first time in the misty forest.

For a second, her mind stood entirely blank, and her chest rose and fell slowly. She almost never felt this calm, and she seized the moment, drawing out a piece of ore from her pouch. She drew the speck up to her lips, gently inhaling and focusing only on the pleasant thoughts.

When she exhaled, a dazzling cloud of ore surrounded her once again, expanding to the correct size for the gauntlet. The cloud hovered at her fingertips, waiting to be formed.

She visualized the gauntlet as Anton had designed it—a single piece of platinum in the shape of a large glove, with a hidden mechanism built into the back of the hand that would amplify and reverse the direction of any force that hit the knuckles, effectively turning any opponent's strike against them.

The ore fell into place one piece at a time as Katiel visualized the shape, the dust suspended in the air before her eyes. She drew her hands closer and farther apart, leading with her fingertips as she crafted the shape to the measurements from the blueprint, firmly etched in her memory after the days of failed attempts.

But this wasn't one of them.

She opened her eyes, and a complete gauntlet landed in her outstretched palms. It was designed to only work only for Anton, but she didn't need to test it to know it would obey his command. She could feel the magic within the object—it was perfect, formed exactly as intended.

Before the princess spoke up, Katiel had never considered that she might struggle with anxiety, but as she turned the fully formed gauntlet over in her hands, she knew Nev was right.

With every painful thought Katiel had, her instinct was to shove it away, to never think of it again. Anxiety was no different. She was ashamed to worry as much as she did, fearful others could tell when her thoughts were racing and jumbled. She was fearful of what her loved ones would think if they could read her mind.

Except Anton.

He predicted her moods and actions so well that it was like he *could* read her mind. She knew without a shadow of a doubt that he could tell when her senses reeled, yet he still wanted to be around her. Actually, he seemed to enjoy being around her, even then.

He wasn't like Brenna or her parents or anyone else who she loved. He wasn't positive about everything, and he didn't always do the noble thing. In fact, sometimes, he wasn't even good.

And strangely, she liked that.

No, she loved that.

She loved *him*.

The realization hit her with such sudden clarity, her skin tingled all over, her arms and bare calves breaking out in gooseflesh.

She'd been pushing him away all this time, but she knew, deep down, that she didn't need to come here. There were other ways to help with the war effort. On the ship, she hadn't come up with the plan to be court wielder just because she wanted to end the war—she could admit that to herself now. She wanted to protect Anton.

His smile, his genius, his kindness, the warm spark she felt every time she was in his presence—in her eyes, he was perfect.

Katiel Salzbruck loved Anton Alexandrei Gregorovich of House Dvorsky.

And she would let herself feel it just this once—in case he died tomorrow.

19

Anton

Though it was several hours past midnight, Anton was still poring over the gauntlet prototype in his study. He'd decided at the last minute to try his hand at building his own, but since ore was the intended power source, the effort had quickly proved futile. Now he was mindlessly tightening and loosening the same screw, fighting hard not to drift off.

With each twist, he convinced himself that he could get the design to work with the slightest adjustment, though he knew that was preposterous. It was just that he needed something—anything—to occupy his mind before the trial, and he refused to sleep away his last night among the living. Simeon had long since fallen asleep on the chaise, his open book still propped on his chest, and the last thing Anton needed was to be alone with his thoughts.

Thoughts of tomorrow, of his uncle watching him fight his cousins, filled his mind. His uncle, who had rendered him weak and scared and small on his darkest of days, haunted his thoughts. Vadim would be watching from his place of safety, while Anton battled for his life, even if it meant taking others' lives in exchange. He would become a monster like his uncle—like the monster he'd witnessed himself become in this very court.

That gear *did* appear to be fitted a bit too tight.

Rap.

A knock sounded on his door, once.

Rap.

Anton's jaw clenched. That vermin better not have come to his quarters again. He thought he'd solved this problem all those years ago.

A glance at Simeon confirmed his friend hadn't stirred, so Anton made for the door in two long strides.

"Yes," he all but growled.

But then a soft, unexpected voice trilled, "Anton?"

Katiel.

One of his cousins must have come after her, like he'd been worrying they would. Or worse—his uncle.

He slung open the door, ready to throw her behind him. "Katiel, are you—"

But she stood there alone, looking fine. She looked better than fine—gorgeous, more than anything—but more importantly, not hurt or even panicked.

No, her perplexed expression made it clear that he was the frazzled one, an embarrassing misstep caused by the impending trial.

"Am I interrupting something?" She eyed his mussed hair, a blush rising to her cheeks, and it occurred to him that she might actually think he had another girl over.

"Certainly not," he said, fighting a scoff as he locked eyes with the tantalizing girl before him. It was like she honestly didn't realize what she was doing to him. "May I help you with anything, *Geführtchen*?"

At the nickname, the center of her lips pressed together like she was trying and nearly failing to hide her teeth. "I completed the gauntlet."

Sure enough, in her hands was a large metal glove, exactly as he'd pictured in his design. The fact that she distracted him enough to miss it was just embarrassing. He should've been more careful, setting her up to discuss this out in the open hallway, and he hastily waved his hand toward the interior. "Come in."

She stepped in, and he fastened the column of locks strewn down the side of his door. "Do you want to try it now?" she asked.

"Of course. Simeon, would you mind coming this way?" Anton joked, considering there was no way to test it without causing considerable damage to whoever he fought.

Katiel caught sight of the scholar, slumped on the chaise face-down, still sound asleep with his mouth hanging ajar and his neck crooked at an angle that would surely hurt when he woke. She laughed then, her light eyes sparkling, and regret seeped through Anton.

He wished he'd simply told her the truth back in Ballynach rather than stealing from her. If he had, she might have given him the ore freely. She might have even agreed to serve as court wielder without him having to deceive her at all, and he would be free to kiss her when she looked at him like that—instead of how they were now.

"I did not think ahead to make a test rig," he admitted, regretting that he didn't foresee the obvious need. "So, I have no way to verify that it works without destroying something."

She shrugged, her lip curling down. "We'll see if it does tomorrow morning."

He wagged his eyebrows, hoping a joke would bring back her pretty smile. "Let's hope I don't die."

Instead, she locked eyes with him as the color drained from her face. "I hope you don't, Your Highness."

Anton swallowed hard.

He had royally ruined things between them. And if he didn't live through tomorrow, he could never make it right.

20

Brenna

Brenna hurried up the spiral staircase to the main level of Ballynach Castle and walked to her room as quickly as she could without drawing suspicion. There, she filled a satchel with as many of her possessions as it would hold—which turned out to be almost all of them. She lost most of her things in the train crash on the way to Ballynach, and a few dresses and jewels that the queen had gifted her were all she had left, along with an ink well, a ream of parchment, and several quills. Unfortunately, she had no coins or food, but hopefully she could trade some jewels for what she needed.

Since Steffi was going to tell the lords she'd been fired, Brenna needed to exit inconspicuously so as not to run into any of them on her way out. And seeing as she was already in the queen's chambers, the solution was obvious—and exciting. She could take the same escape tunnel as Dakier—which she had, admittedly, always wanted to check out. It would get her out of the castle unnoticed, and hopefully, Dakier would still be near the outlet, so she could make sure he'd made it out alright.

Except she shouldn't care about that anymore. Or at least she worried that she shouldn't.

Either way, she reasoned, it made sense to take the tunnel. So, she grabbed the lantern from her writing desk, headed in, and secured the panel back in place behind her.

Winding through the narrow stone tunnel was as eerie as she had imagined, and when she at last reached the unlocked door at the end, she had the sense that a great adventure was about to begin.

The door opened inward, which was a particularly bad design for an escape tunnel, and instantly, she saw nothing but the blinding amber glow of the twilight street. She squinted and inched forward, but immediately, a carriage horn honked, and she jumped back.

This must be the very back of the castle, then, which bordered a busy avenue. When the street cleared, she hurried across it, but just as she reached the other side, Dakier caught her eye.

He stepped out from behind a crate in front of one of the many shops and nodded to her. Despite what he'd done to Henred, Dakier had waited for her, and she debated whether she should turn away and leave him behind.

If she did, she knew he wouldn't fault her for it. She could never see him again if she preferred, but no matter how wrong it was, her heart ached at the thought.

Besides, he was like a brother to Katiel. As an enemy soldier with no contacts and no money, he'd never get out of the walled city alone. She *had* to help him, for her best friend's sake.

With every rationalization, Brenna found herself inching closer to him. And before she could regret her decision, Brenna grabbed Dakier by the bicep—which, to her irritation, was attractively large—and hauled him down the nearest alleyway.

"Brenna—"

He'd had the good sense to stay silent until they were out of view of the castle, but once they were alone in the alley, it seemed his reason was wearing thin.

She spun around, the heel of her impractical court shoes landing with a resounding *clack*. "We are not friends, and we are not talking."

Not that they were exactly *friends* before she found out he killed her brother, but she refused to acknowledge that they'd ever been anything more.

"Then...why did you want me to come with you?" Dakier asked, taking the awkward tone of someone knowing the other might explode on them at any moment.

But even that question was too close to arguing for her liking. "I need your help. Are you going to help me?"

She didn't bother saying what with. Either he was in, or he wasn't. She didn't have the patience to explain her plans, lest it sound like she was begging.

But Dakier didn't hesitate before he said, "I will."

THE FACT THAT BRENNA hadn't explained her plans to him had nothing—absolutely nothing—to do with her not having much of a plan at all.

She knew she needed to tell the public the truth about the king's assassination, about Inigo Farro, about all of it. She knew she needed to get away from the castle, and she knew that however she decided to spread the truth would likely involve wandering the city in the dead of night.

And that's where Dakier came in. He was imposing and muscular—curse him—and she would feel much safer sneaking around the city with him than she would alone. Once they made a quick stop by Jay's city apartment for Barkurian-style clothes to help Dakier blend in, he could remain discreet enough to trail her through the city.

But beyond that, she had no plan.

She set off in the direction of her brother-in-law's flat, but after a good half hour of winding through alleyways and backstreets, her surety faltered. Either the buildings all looked the same or she was leading them in circles, but either way, she needed to hurry before a bystander noticed the two of them together and confronted them. Though Dakier now clutched his army-issue cap and jacket in his arms, leaving him in only a white knit undershirt, boots, and thick brown pants, the outfit combined with his strong Tibedese features still gave the impression of a foreign soldier.

At first, Brenna thought the growing darkness was due to the late hour alone, but soon, the clouds overhead gave way to rain. It started as a sprinkle, but within mere seconds, the light rainfall morphed into a torrential downpour. The pavement darkened immediately, the raindrops too large and incessant to leave a single dry spot between them.

Brenna's poof of curly hair—currently fashioned in a half-up, half-down style to tame the volume—instantly flattened, the front-most waves falling into a curtain of red across her face. With a huff, she pushed it aside, but it was difficult to see anything beyond the wall of rain that separated her from Dakier. Now she understood why the streets were so empty tonight. If she'd been able to go outside earlier, when it was still daylight, she might have noticed the dark clouds forming over Ballynach as well.

In the alleyway, there wasn't so much as an awning to use as cover. She turned to face Dakier, whose hair was as soaked as hers. His clothes were, too, to the point the undershirt was effectively see-through, and she looked down at her own dress in a momentary panic. Thankfully, the deep emerald shade combined with the corset kept things modest.

"Brenna." He cupped his hands over his mouth, trying to be heard over the cacophony of rainfall around them. "I think we're lost."

"Oh, really?" she shouted, rain literally pouring into her mouth as she did. She spit the water on the street. "What should we do? Get a room somewhere?"

Dakier's chest rose, water pouring over his eyes and streaming off his nose. "No reputable inn will take a Tibedese soldier."

"Then we won't go anywhere reputable."

The area they'd wound up in already wasn't the best. In the distance, rowdy revelers sat outside a pub, shouting and clinking pints of ale even in the middle of the downpour, so Brenna shrugged and headed in their direction. Now-futile drying lines crisscrossed overhead like Bar Kur Day pennants, and she vaguely recalled passing through here once before with Katiel and their three Drezchy companions. When the dirt pouring across the street increased into a narrow brown stream, she scanned the area, chose an establishment marked with nothing but the word *LODGING*, and headed inside.

In the nondescript wood-walled foyer sat a lone, two-seat sofa and a short, fierce-looking woman behind a desk.

"No waiting for the rain to clear," she barked immediately when they walked in, puddles pooling around their feet. "Either book a room or get lost."

Brenna stole a quick glance out the tiny window to confirm that the downpour hadn't let up in the slightest before leaning closer to Dakier. "What do you think?"

He hesitated, his eyeline focused on Brenna's dripping hair. "We could go back. Or at least you should. I don't want you to catch a cold."

She knew he was avoiding mentioning the castle within earshot of the innkeeper, but before Brenna could respond, the woman approached with a mop in hand, about to shoo them off like a pair of alley cats.

"In or out!"

"I don't have any money," Brenna said, unclasping one of the annoyingly heavy emerald studs she wore. "Will you take this?"

Brenna half expected the innkeeper to demand the other one, but instead, the woman grabbed the earring from her hand and replaced it with a key and a pile of linens.

"Third floor, room five."

"This is honestly better than I expected," Brenna said when they reached the third-floor hallway, a narrow space lined with a surprising number of doors on both sides. "There's not a rat in sight."

Dakier eyed a mysterious pile in the corner that Brenna desperately hoped was mud. "I think that's human excrement."

Brenna shrugged. "That's still better than rats." Then she recalled that she was furious with him and shouldn't be speaking to him any more than necessary, and turned her back pointedly as she unlocked the fifth door down.

Inside was a tiny corridor as bleak as the lobby, with soft light from the streetlights outside pouring in through the grimy window. Fortunately, it lacked the filth of the hall, but unfortunately, there was only one narrow mattress stuffed into the corner on a creaky-looking bedframe.

"I'll remain outside," Dakier said immediately.

Brenna had a feeling he was going to offer as much even if there were two beds, remembering his stringent ideas of propriety from their stay in Linden. "Please, spare me," she said with the most disdain she could muster. "I want you nearby for my protection, nothing more."

He nodded. "I'll sleep on the floor then."

Dakier was clearly willing to do and say whatever he thought might make things up to her, and she could hardly bear it.

"We should both sleep on the floor," she said, eyeing the bare mattress. They both knew what sort of place this was, and what sort of situation the innkeeper almost surely thought they were in. A foreign soldier and a finely dressed woman staying alone together overnight—the thought made Brenna cringe.

"At least let me remain outside while you get out of your wet clothes," Dakier said gingerly, "before you catch a cold."

"There's no need," she argued. "I have nothing else to wear." She looked down at her soaked garments with a shudder. The court dress's many layers weighed a good ten pounds with all the water, and her thigh-high stockings clung to her legs like wet parchment. "I'll have to sleep in this."

"No, here, this would be better, at least." He sat his hat and jacket on the floor beside him, and before she could say a word of protest, he peeled off his plain undershirt as well.

Her eyes widened as she looked away, but her heart was hammering in her chest. Even a brief glimpse had confirmed how perfect he looked, with lean muscle coiling around every inch of him.

"Since I was holding my jacket across my chest, the shirt is practically dry," he went on, holding the fabric out for her to feel.

She gave the cloth a quick tap, and discovered that he was right. With a kind, bashful smile, he pressed the shirt into her hands, before the door clicked shut behind him.

Brenna heaved a sigh as she shrugged out of her soaked dress, draping the garment over the rickety footboard of the bed to dry. For a moment, she let herself revel in the absence of the corset, the lack of the painful boning that cut into her hips.

Then, sucking in a breath, she slipped the soft knitted shirt over her head and let it fall. On her it was more of a dress, coming almost to the knees and hanging loose all around. She had never worn a dress this short—not even close—but when she called him back, she didn't feel as exposed as she should have.

With any other man, she would've been terrified to be so close, with them both wearing so little. But Dakier was so kind, so trustworthy, that she felt oddly comfortable.

"Thank you for the shirt," she said, keeping her eyes locked on his face, though even that too was drawing her in. "I truly don't mind if you want to take the bed."

"Brenna, I'm so sorry it ended up like this," he said, forgoing the bed discussion completely. His soft tone confirmed he was feeling it, too—the lingering aftertaste of what remained between them.

Dakier was achingly beautiful, standing a foot from her with his black hair slicked back from his face. A raindrop fell from the tip of a single wave onto his bare chest. Her eyes followed it as it trickled down the sharp ridges before darting back to meet his gaze. The dark irises blazed darker, like they had when they danced at the Bar Kur Day festival mere weeks ago.

With just a second of eye contact, her heart was already curling in on itself. She opened her mouth and then snapped it closed. Then she looked away, head suddenly heavy as memories of Henred flooded back to her—hugging him close at their father's funeral; splashing each other in the rice fields as kids; leaving him after a fight the last time they spoke—without saying goodbye.

Brenna met Dakier's dark, soulful eyes, and her throat burned. Dakier killing her brother was a tragic accident, but she still felt like such a traitor to be friendly with him.

"What is it?" he breathed, then sighed as realization dawned. "You can't even look at me."

Salt coated her tongue when she swallowed, the hint of a tear prickling at her lash line as the truth fell from her lips.

"When I look at you, all I can think of is him."

21

Anton

"Begin!"

Uncle's voice bellowed through Vincencim's central plaza, reverberating off the famous twelve-faced clock tower and the stone edifices of the surrounding buildings.

He'd given no speech or warning, like Anton had expected, but rather waited for the ten competitors to take their places in a wide circle before he yelled the abrupt command. It was yet another way to keep them on their toes, Anton supposed, and another way to put strategists like him at a disadvantage.

It was no matter, though. He was scrappy, and he could run circles around his cousins. Though the abrupt commencement left him little time, he had to make a decision—would he run and wait for his cousins to pick each other off? Or stay and fight?

His first instinct was to run, undoubtedly. It was the smart move, though perhaps not the wisest. His aim was to become the people's ruler, and they watched in droves from balconies and temporary stands erected around the plaza's perimeter. He couldn't show weakness in front of them if he meant to earn their respect.

No, he would remain. He had the gauntlet, and the slight thrum within it told him the magic was working. He would fight—but he was going for the easiest mark first.

Ferenc had never been a good fighter. Though he wasn't much bigger than Anton, he'd brought double-axes—a classic Drezchy weapon and the inspiration for the nation's motto, "The axe speaks the loudest."

While the axes were surely powerful, Ferenc wouldn't be able to wield ordinary ones effectively, and as far as Anton knew, none of his cousins had procured any magical weaponry. Already, Ferenc wobbled as he tried to lift both heavy blades at once. The falter made him an easy mark, and Anton took his chance, lunging toward his cousin with the gauntlet outstretched. Gasping, Ferenc dodged the blow only a second before the metal collided with his jaw.

His bark of laughter suggested he hadn't expected Anton to strike first, but that was the pure foolishness that made him the weakest link. Anton had always used whatever he could—usually, his intellect—to gain power in this court, and a more worthy adversary would have known it.

Anton let that raging bitterness fuel him as he struck again, making contact first with Ferenc's left arm and then with his chest on the second strike. Ferenc was tougher than expected—Anton would give him that—since he was still on his feet after being hit. With the gauntlet's endowed magic, the blows must have felt like being kicked by a horse.

Gripping his upper arm in pain, Ferenc took off in a sprint for a side street, clearly hoping Anton would go for someone else. But it was another foolish move. Splitting off from the group made Ferenc an easier target, and Anton was faster.

Ferenc zagged through the streets to lose him, but it wasn't long before he came to a dead end. A flash of panic contorted his face as he whirled around to face Anton. His eyes darted above Anton's shoulder, and it was that momentary tell that sent Anton spinning on his heel.

Down the alleyway, Ferenc's sister, Cezary, stood still, her brown eyes blazing. In her outstretched arm, she pointed a pistol straight for Anton.

She fired, and Anton reacted on instinct, shielding himself with the gauntlet. Without a moment to spare, he raised the metal fist, and the bullet ricocheted off the magically imbued, heat-seeking surface. The bullet flew to the far right, landing in the stone façade of a nondescript building. But before Cezary could shoot again, Anton charged at her, gauntlet first, striking her squarely in the abdomen.

Cezary cried out in pain and fell back, but by the time she hit the ground, Ferenc had already crawled back to his feet.

Ferenc swung at him, but as predicted, the axes' weight proved too much for him. His strikes were slow and easy for Anton to block. With the gauntlet to redirect and multiply the impact, his cousin was thrown back by the force of his own strikes.

When Ferenc swung the axes again, instead of blocking, Anton punched him squarely in the face. With his cousin disoriented, Anton struck again—once, twice. He stopped counting, clenching his jaw as every part of him cringed at the senseless violence.

After only a few strikes, Ferenc fell to the ground, and Anton faced a sickeningly familiar choice. The same choice he'd faced for years in choosing whether to execute the criminals brought before the court.

He pressed his eyes shut and dealt the killing blow.

Behind him, Cezary screamed.

Anton wasted no time before turning to her, her reverberating screech echoing within him. The pistol had landed out of her reach when she fell, but he wasn't allowed to touch it without breaking the rules of the trial.

Anton hesitated, debating if he had the nerve to finish her off. He knew he was supposed to. That was the purpose of this competition, after all—to place the fiercest candidate on the throne. At this distance, he could end her with a single strike of the gauntlet, but the thought of killing a cousin distracted by grief was too much to swallow.

Instead, he kicked the gun hard, sending it spinning down the street, and took off, racing for the plaza. The final six standing would advance to the second trial, and out of ten starting, the odds weren't terrible. With any luck, Ludvig and Signy would have eliminated enough others for the trial to conclude upon his return.

But when he got back to the plaza, Anton found he hadn't been so fortunate. In the center of the square, two of his cousins lay unmoving on the pavement—Havel, the middle sibling of Cezary and Ferenc, and Agneska, Ludvig and Signy's youngest sister, blood pouring from a bullet wound in her chest. The latter was the work of Halina, he already knew, and she reeled on Anton the second he came into view.

On the far end, Ludvig, Signy, and their two brothers, Yaro and Inek, turned toward him as well, leaving no one at their backs but the spectators in the makeshift stands. He was surprised that the four were working together. They were so close—especially Ludvig and Signy, the two eldest—that he'd expected them to split up so that none of them would need to eliminate the others. He supposed they were prolonging the inevitable, then.

Knowing them, they'd consider it a horrible dishonor to die in round one, whereas Anton saw the entire Conclave for what it was—an unnecessary tragedy all around, with no honor to be found.

Then Halina fired her revolver, tearing him from his thoughts.

He planted his feet and extended the gauntlet directly in front of him, as he had with Cezary, letting the heat-seeking surface find the bullet intended for him. Only this time, he tilted the fist to point straight at her.

But Halina saw what he was up to before her bullet even made contact, and she used the half-second of warning to leap aside. Even then, it narrowly missed the tip of her long, red braid. Instead, the steel cascaded into the back of Inek, who stood a few feet beyond.

He let out a pained cry as he fell forward, his weighted double swords flying from his hands. The crowd roared and cheered, but amid the noise, a small shriek caught his attention.

Beyond the square, the dark spires of Karolinum rose high above the stands. The balcony she stood on was barely visible from the distance, but Anton knew from the tone alone that the shriek had been Katiel's.

Unlike the crowd of Drezchy, she was not celebrating. No, the display of violence had clearly revolted her.

Hopefully, her vantage point had blocked her from seeing him kill Ferenc in the side street. He could only imagine the disgust she'd feel toward him if she witnessed that.

"Aye, ex-crown prince," Ludvig called to him, snapping Anton back to attention. "Don't spend too much time looking at your pretty wielder now."

Anton let his gauntlet hand drop to his side, baring his chest. "Better than looking at your ugly mug."

"She's nice looking." Ludvig smirked. "Might have some fun with her once you're dead."

"She would never."

The brute had the audacity to run his tongue across his teeth. "I'm not asking."

Anton's vision seeped with red, knowing exactly what Ludvig meant.

He swung at his eldest cousin, making direct contact with his chin. The mammoth man staggered back, swiping at his jaw. He hid his momentary grimace with a condescending grin, but Anton had seen it. Ludvig should've died from the full force of the gauntlet, but he was fine. Katiel had imbued the weapon to follow Anton's will, meaning he'd held back.

Not for Ludvig, but for her. Because he knew she was watching, and in her eyes, he wished he could be someone better.

"Of course, you'd rely on some moronic machine," Ludvig sneered, "because you're weak. You always have been."

"This is my invention. Designed precisely for *moronic* opponents."

Anton struck again, and Ludvig blocked the blow with both blades doubled up, though his hands slipped down the handles as he struggled to hold on.

"The axe speaks the loudest," his cousin said, repeating the mantra Anton heard many times before.

Idiot.

"This conversation is over," Anton growled. Then he doubled down, striking his cousin repeatedly, the same precise blows he'd dealt to Ferenc.

The man fell back, his pupils swimming as his head collided with the pavers.

Ludvig was down. A single strike would end his life.

All Anton saw was red. He didn't even see a human being lying there, not anymore. Ludvig's death would truly, truly bring a smile to his face.

But suddenly, his arms were yanked back, his reflexes kicking in too late to dodge the grasp. It was Yaro and Cezary, turning him around until he faced Signy.

The tall woman's nose twitched in anger as she looked down at him.

He strained against them, trying to free himself. In this position, the gauntlet was unusable. With his arm twisted at this angle, the weapon only weighed him down, but he dared not drop it and leave himself defenseless.

"Uncle called the Conclave to save us from a weak king," Signy said, projecting her voice toward the crowd. "So, let us eliminate him."

And with a fierce swipe of her blades, Signy slashed two deep gashes across Anton's chest.

22

Katiel

A COLD SWEAT BROKE out on Katiel's brow as she watched the trial, the palms of her hands slick where they gripped the wrought-iron rail.

Her focus was glued to Anton whenever he was in sight, and when he disappeared down a side street, she hardly breathed. From Katiel's side, Nev stole assessing glances at her, but it was hard to care about what she might be thinking. People were dying in front of her, out in the square, and a whole crowd of people did not move to help them. Even worse, they cheered whenever a contestant perished. Katiel truly couldn't understand it. None of these people deserved to die. They were all astonishingly vicious; it was true, but none of them had entered this competition of their own free will. Their birthright alone had landed them in this disaster.

The competition was so brutal and gut-wrenching, she could hardly stand to watch. But she absolutely could not bear to take her eyes off of Anton.

He moved with a grace that no one else had, swiftly evading each strike from his barrage of cousins. The others were able to work together with their siblings, but Anton held his own against them. With every lithe stride, he was beautiful.

And Katiel was helplessly watching his fate unfold.

A female cousin with a red, slicked-back braid fired a pistol at Anton, and Katiel screeched despite herself. In the momentary lapse, she thought he might be killed, but he used the gauntlet to deflect the bullet with a chilling calm.

This was what he was accustomed to—where he thrived, it seemed. It was like she had never known him at all.

And she hadn't, not really. She still didn't. He'd taken her life force, and then he'd taken her heart, and she still didn't fully know the man that she senselessly cared for.

But then a sudden flurry of movement drew her eye. Someone else—Ludvig, she realized—had fallen, and now the others were turning on Anton. She couldn't make out the exchange of words at this distance, but then two others grabbed him, each holding a single arm and rendering him defenseless.

A shrill ringing sounded in the courtyard as a pair of swords cut across his chest.

Katiel heard the noise before she realized it was her own scream, this one louder than the first and piercing everything. The spectators gathered on the balcony turned to glare at her, eyes full of disdain.

They were shaming her for pitying someone they saw as weak, but she did not care about that for even a moment. She must get to him. She wasn't even sure why—she just absolutely, resolutely must.

Katiel rushed off of the balcony, across the parapet, and down the spiraling stairwell of the connecting turret. She clutched the fabric of her skirts, her heeled boots clacking against the steps as she swiftly descended.

At the ground level, an archway let out directly into the square, and Katiel pushed through the masses, weaving between gaps in the crowd. She halted at the very front, unsure if rushing over to Anton would somehow disqualify him—though that hardly mattered if his life was on the line. But she was spared from further mental debate when someone called out loudly enough to be heard over the murmurs of the crowd.

To her surprise, it was Sera who stepped into the center of the plaza. In the square, the false keeper raised her voice to a shout, yet somehow kept her inflection as dry as if she were speaking about mundane weather patterns.

"Six contestants remain," she called to the spectators. "The first trial is hereby commenced."

From the standing section of the crowd, Simeon darted forward, straight for Anton, and Katiel hurried after him.

When they reached him, Anton was lying in an ever-growing pool of blood. His eyes were squeezed shut, though the strained rise and fall of his abdomen confirmed he was alive, and his gritted teeth confirmed he was conscious. His black jacket and waistcoat were completely soaked, and Katiel pushed back her revulsion at the overwhelming amount of blood. Meanwhile, Simeon, unphased as ever, unbuttoned Anton's vestments and pushed the fabric aside.

A clean *X* was cut into Anton's chest, the flesh now ghastly pale as a waterfall of blood poured from the open wound. Katiel only glimpsed the gruesome sight for a second before Simeon covered the wound with a large cloth. He pressed against the area to staunch the bleeding, and Katiel rushed to help, pushing her full weight onto the wound.

"He was not supposed to die yet," Simeon muttered as if to himself, before he looked up at Katiel and barked, "Now wield!"

"What?" Katiel managed, her mind instantly going back to the moments before the train crash, and then again to the time they were chased by a Barkurian policeman. Simeon always seemed to think she could wield whatever she needed at the most stressful times, though since his amnesia hadn't recovered, he likely didn't remember his pressuring her to wield at either of those events.

Simeon was no more patient now. "Wield something to save him!"

Katiel's mind spun, coming up with nothing other than the fresh memory of that horrid *X*. "Like what?" she tried to ask, though the question came out as more of a cry.

"A healing tonic," Simeon said, voice strained with the force he was applying. "A tonic to staunch the bleeding."

"Right," Katiel said with a surge of fresh panic.

Wielding metal solids was the easiest, since the ore was already a metal, and her skills were unreliable even at that. Forming other solid materials was trickier, and she'd only succeeded at it once, with the cloth and wicker parts of Nev's chair. But a tonic, a liquid—that would be impossible for her.

It should be impossible, and yet—

Standing this close, Katiel could see with stark clarity the pallor of Anton's skin, the color drained from his face. His hands looked as if they were carved from ice, so pale they were nearly translucent.

He'd lost so much blood, and he was still losing more. Slick redness pooled around Katiel's boots.

Something thrummed in her heart—something like panic, but sharper and needier. It was like the ore was crying out, desperate to be released.

She'd only felt this sensation once before, when she'd wielded the gun that she killed Taregh with, having known it was the last possible moment to save Brenna.

The ore was on her fingertip. Her hand drew to her face. Inhale, exhale. A glass vial formed between her palms.

She was wielding, and yet she wasn't. It was her hands, her life force, but her mind had left her completely. It frightened her to be so out of control, but she couldn't stop now. The vial contained a liquid, glowing faintly blue, just as her subconscious thought a healing tonic should.

She was acting too quickly to think, too rashly to worry that this would harm him instead of help. He was on his last breath, and she needed to act before the next trial began with only five competitors, after all.

Dropping to her knees, Katiel poured the contents of the vial across the wound.

Before her eyes, Anton's chest began to swell. The bleeding stopped almost instantly. The skin was knitting together.

Unable to stomach another moment of the horrific injury, Katiel looked away. But Simeon was staring at it, mouth agape in such a way that said he was going to write down everything he saw at the first opportunity for the sake of science. All the while, Anton remained unresponsive.

She watched his face, waiting for a fleeting moment that stretched into hours in her mind. He lay with perfect stillness, and Katiel had the gnawing sensation that she was watching a corpse.

But then, a muscle ticked in his jaw, nothing more than a flicker of movement.

Another beat passed, Katiel holding her breath as a stillness fell over them both. The tonic had to work. It *had* to heal him. She had willed it to.

Miraculously, his eyes drifted open. The color returned to his cheeks. And then locked eyes with her so fiercely that Katiel came back to reality.

She was kneeling above the man who was supposed to be her employer. His sister might already see through their attempt at a professional relationship, but the entire court would, too, if she didn't compose herself.

With a long, steading exhale, she forced herself to stand and turn around without another word, making a beeline for Karolinum's nearest gates. She was prepared to push through the crowd, but this time, they parted for her.

Once in her chambers mere moments later, she slunk back against her door, taking the first proper, deep breath she had in days.

And Katiel remembered then that it was her birthday.

23

Brenna

The next morning, Brenna hailed a carriage, paying the driver her remaining earring to take her to Jay's apartment. She might not have been able to find the place on foot, but she remembered the address.

With a pang, she wished Katiel had been there to navigate. They surely would've found the apartment before the rain.

She hailed the coach for one, and Dakier slipped in after her, ducking to avoid being spotted in the driver's mirrors. They didn't speak all throughout the ride, lest the driver overhear, but it wasn't long before they reached Jay's apartment.

Brenna led the way up to the third-floor flat, bracing herself to explain to her brother-in-law why Dakier needed to stay with them—and expecting a good deal of push back. But to her surprise, the tiny, one-room apartment was empty, with clothes and belongings strewn all about, like Jay left in a hurry. The suitcase was missing from its normal spot beside the bed, and she remembered then what he'd mentioned at the welcome party for the Tibedese delegation—Derenta had called him back to Fir Kelt early.

Brenna secretly hoped it was an announcement about another niece or nephew coming, but this also meant that she'd be alone with Dakier for the duration of their stay. Not long ago, this situation would have given her butterflies, but now, she didn't know how to feel.

She set down her carpetbag and started tidying up the place. But after a few moments, the silence between her and Dakier grew uncomfortable, so she forced herself to speak to him while she made the bed. "I have a plan."

Dakier pushed a chunk of hair back from his face, still standing awkwardly by the door. "That's good." She stared at him for a beat, and he added, "How can I help?"

"You were supposed to ask what the plan was," she grumbled.

She knew there was nothing he could say that she *wouldn't* be mad at, but what could she do, really? He killed Henred after making her fall in love with him. He told her, even knowing how she'd react, and had been so intolerably kind every second since. It was almost enough—almost—for her to consider that his actions had been appropriate for the situation. Soldiers were supposed to kill soldiers on the opposite side during a battle. Henred could've killed him just as easily.

No, she couldn't think like that. Not yet. Intolerably kind—that was Dakier exactly. And he had no business being that way to her now, especially not while the strangeness of last night still lingered.

"I want to let everyone know the truth," she explained. "I was thinking of printing it in the paper—telling the world the truth about Inigo Farro the same way that Taregh's boss spread the lie initially."

"It's an idea," Dakier said, "but you know they would never print that."

"That's why I'm going to sneak in." She knew she didn't have to tell him her plans, but after last night, she felt slightly closer to him again. Not to mention, she had no one else to tell. "I'm going to sneak in and print it at night. By the time anyone realizes what's happened, it'll be too late. The truth will be out."

Personally, she thought the plan was fool-proof, but Dakier looked anything but convinced.

"Queen Stefana may be young, and your friend, but I don't know that even she could turn a blind eye if you get caught."

Brenna waved off the notion, but decided against telling Dakier the entirety of the plan she'd concocted with Steffi. As much as she hated keeping secrets, since it involved the queen, she figured she should keep the details—like Steffi pretending to fire her—to herself. "It's not like she'd have me executed."

Dakier rubbed a hand across his chin. "Banished, maybe."

Brenna shrugged, thinking banishment would suit her just fine. She could go live in the Yule Valley, like she wanted, anyway. And the Barkurians would be forced to sign a peace treaty. She'd be welcome in A'slenderia again, and everything would be fine.

After another moment's consideration, she smirked, feeling closer to ending the war than ever. "That's a risk I'm willing to take."

Brenna left Dakier in Jay's apartment as she scouted the streets, searching for a suitable print shop to infiltrate. She needed a place with a big, open window, or maybe a swinging door that didn't lock. Those would be easy enough to break into without any damage.

Or at least, that's what she pictured when she set out. But it was becoming obvious that she'd find no such thing, or at least not as easily as she'd hoped.

Nearly every street corner in Ballynach was home to a newsboy or girl, waving the paper around and hollering at passersby about the headlines. The corner nearest Brenna was no exception, which gave her an idea.

The little girl in a dirty dress noticed Brenna before she could speak.

"Want a paper?" she squeaked, the paper she waved dwarfing her in size as it accidentally unfurled. She hastily folded it back. "Sorry 'bout that. Want a paper, ma'am?"

Brenna raised her eyebrows. She certainly wasn't old enough to be called that, and she idly wondered if she seemed like a full-blown adult to the young girl.

"Aye, I'll take one," she said, "if you'll tell me something. Where do you get your papers?"

"Same place everybody does," the girl said, like Brenna should know. After a second, she seemed to think Brenna was a little slow, and started emphasizing each syllable. "The Eternal City Gazette? You know...the paper press. Where we buy the papers? Didn't you sell any when you were a kid?"

Brenna shook her head. The girl was clearly too young to realize that not everyone had the same childhood experiences, a mistake Brenna used to make herself. A mistake she still made from time to time, if she were being honest.

In the years before her *da* passed, Brenna's childhood had been a happy one. Sure, their house had been the smallest one around, and most of the children in her school called her strange. But she had her siblings and loving parents to keep her company, and letters from Katiel and travels to look forward to. When the school bullies ganged up on her to poke fun, her heart was always in A'slenderia, dreaming of adventure far away from Fir Kelt.

And when Da started disappearing more and more, she didn't know where he'd gone. She only learned after his death that he'd been frequenting the pubs, and she didn't know how to feel about it. But she always had something exciting on the horizon to distract her from the problems at home. First it was friends, then the letter and the war and Dakier all mixed into one.

The young girl coughed, drawing Brenna back to the present. She eyed the paper that Brenna was now clutching. "You going to pay for that?"

"Absolutely." Brenna grinned as she unclasped her emerald necklace, surely the most expensive piece she had on.

In response, the girl snatched the pendant from Brenna's hand and tucked it down her dress, her gaze darting around in an apparent attempt to make sure they hadn't been spotted. As if on second thought, she added, "I can't make change."

"Don't worry about it," Brenna assured, "but since I paid a little extra, can you take me there? To the newspaper print shop, I mean?"

Such a request should've piqued the girl's suspicions, but she didn't ask any questions. Instead, she gave a cheerful, "Sure!" and skipped off.

Brenna followed her, winding through damp alleyways and mostly abandoned cobblestone streets.

"Where are your parents?" Brenna asked, her curiosity overcoming the need to avoid drawing suspicion. "Are they alright with you selling newspapers all day instead of going to school?"

"I don't have any parents," the girl replied, no hint of pain dampening her tone. "Well, not anymore. They died when I was little."

"Oh," Brenna said, trying to hide the pity in her voice. The girl was still little, even if she didn't think of herself that way. She couldn't be older than eight years old. "Who do you live with now?"

"Oh, just the other kids. We usually sleep out behind the shop."

Brenna's heart sank at the revelation, but they reached their destination before she could offer any words of comfort.

The fumes pouring out onto the street hit Brenna's nose before she saw the place. The open windows showed workers milling about, resetting the blocks on the typesetting machine and feeding stacks of freshly pressed paper.

Above them, a broad sign read *ETERNAL CITY GAZETTE,* referencing a nickname for Ballynach she hadn't heard in ages.

"Here's the place," the girl said, her voice brimming with pride.

Brenna placed her hands on her hips, a smile drawing to her lips with the thrill of finally doing something productive toward the war effort. "Let's go in. After you."

"I've never been in there." The girl shook her head, suddenly a bundle of nerves. "We get our stacks out back. The boss leaves them on the stoop."

The wording sent a pang of remembrance through Brenna, thinking of "the boss" who commanded General Taregh, someone she had no more information about now than she had weeks ago. But unless this boss was Drezchy, she was going to disregard the phrasing as a mere coincidence. Focusing instead on the task at hand, she turned from the young newsie with a shrug.

"After me, then."

Brenna opened the glass-paneled front door, the girl keeping close enough to the back of her skirts to be hidden from view.

"Can I help you, miss?" the nearest worker asked, ink-stained fingers clumsily removing his cap. He thought she was a lady, she realized, which was surely due to her fine clothes. From the way he stared at her face and then averted his eyes with a flush, she almost got the feeling he found her pretty as well.

All the workers were young men, and the one who'd addressed her was decently handsome, with shaggy brown hair flopped across his forehead. She could work with this, she thought. She could do something she hated—flirt with him.

Although she really could've given her opening line a bit more thought beforehand.

"I, uhm," she stammered, "really like newspapers."

"Oh, of course," the man said, a fresh blush creeping across his cheeks. "You're in the right place, then. We print the paper right here."

He definitely thought she was pretty then, considering she'd been about as conspicuous as possible. She stole a glance down at the little girl, who rolled her eyes. Even a child could tell she was up to something.

"I find them fascinating," Brenna said, her attention turning back to the worker. She purposefully twirled a red curl around her finger, the same way Katiel always did without realizing it. "I've always wondered how the machines work and everything."

"It's a pretty slow day around here," he said, despite his scowling coworkers bustling around the shop. "I can show you, if you'd like."

She refrained from clutching a fist in triumph. Instead, she demurely agreed, like she never would've expected such an offer, and he showed her how to operate all the machines, from the typesetter to the letterpress. Admittedly, it was all straightforward enough that she probably could've figured it out herself, but she would have no time for trial and error when breaking in at night.

During the demonstration of the letterpress, he encouraged Brenna to try it for herself, and she enthusiastically agreed. The impression lever was much harder to pull than she'd expected. It took both arms, and her billowy sleeve snagged on the roller, causing the end of the lever to collide roughly with the back of her arm. Brenna grimaced as the rough wood tore the top layer of her skin, but thankfully, the man giving her the tour didn't notice.

When he was done with the tour, he walked her outside. Though the conversation lulled, he seemed to linger, like he wanted her to say something else.

"What time do you get off?" she ventured, despite having no intention whatsoever of seeing him again.

"Six in the evening, seven days a week," he said. He was clearly proud of his hard work, though Brenna felt sorry for him not getting a day off.

"I take it you don't work through the night, then?" she asked with a little forced giggle. The question might be risky, but it would be worth it to have confirmation of when the stop would be empty.

"No, sure don't, miss." He chuckled before his face grew solemn. "Though we did once, right after the assassination. You know, that of our beloved king."

Brenna nodded, the irony of all she knew about the topic weighing on her.

The man, who hadn't yet given his name, asked, "Might I see you after work, by chance?"

"Not today, I'm afraid." Brenna squirmed, her act wearing off. She hoped it wouldn't hurt his feelings when she never returned. "Some other day, perhaps."

"Certainly." He smiled. "Hope to see you soon, then."

With that, he tipped the cap he'd been awkwardly clutching the entire time and headed back inside. The newsie was glaring up at her with arms crossed, clearly unimpressed with Brenna's scheme.

"Anyway, I got to get back to it, lady."

Lady. Another indicator that the girl thought Brenna to be a bona fide adult, rather than the insecure teen she admittedly was. Even though she risked drawing too much attention with every minute she dawdled, she felt particularly uncertain about letting the girl go back to her life on the streets.

Brenna got what she needed. She knew the location of the print shop. She had even found out that the back door was guarded only by a bunch of small children. It wouldn't be too hard to slip past them in the night and set up her article in the press. Judging by the frantic pace of the shop, the paper would be out with the damning news long before anyone noticed the front page had changed.

The plan would work, but hesitation gnawed at her. She couldn't leave the girl like this, though she couldn't very well take her back to Jay's apartment either. There was barely room for her and Dakier alone, and besides, they weren't fit to care for a kid. With the plans they had coming up, they'd likely be fleeing sooner rather than later.

Then it hit her—Mara had said the keepers, the protectors of the ore and the old religion, ran a ward for the needy in Ballynach. Mara had even mentioned it was right next to the secretary of war's office. When she had no money and nowhere to go, Mara had found help there, and Brenna was sure they could help the little girl, too.

"Do you want to sleep someplace else?" Brenna asked, before she could come to her senses and change her mind. "Somewhere safe."

The girl's eyes opened wide, but in lieu of an answer, she simply nodded.

Brenna would have to pass by the government offices to reach the ward, and she knew she shouldn't risk the lords of the cabinet seeing her. But Brenna couldn't go on without knowing that this girl was safe, so she led the way with her head held high.

When they arrived at the ward, the girl eyed the unassuming building, which blended in among the surrounding brick facades. Brenna nudged her on, though, and the young girl took a brave step forward.

"Thank you, ma'am," she squeaked, the words escaping her as her tiny hand closed around the doorknob. "I'm Nellie, by the way."

"Goodbye, Nellie By the Way." Brenna smiled at her own joke, fully aware of how bad it was, and gave a little two-finger salute as she turned to leave. "You should invite the other children, too, when you see them."

Nellie nodded, a boisterous grin stretching across her face, and as Brenna walked back to Jay's flat, she couldn't help but smile as well.

The next time she saw Steffi, she planned to suggest allocating some extra funds to the children of the inner city. But first, she had an article to write.

24

Dakier

Dakier paced the length of the cramped, one-room apartment, a slew of worries running through his mind.

Though he expected her an hour ago, Brenna hadn't returned from her scouting mission. It sounded pretty straightforward—find a newspaper printer, look for a way to break in, and leave. It was illegal and dangerous, but she insisted on going alone, and Dakier was trying to support her choices as best he could—even if that meant waiting in utter agony until she returned.

As each minute ticked by on Jay's wall clock, he took a step closer to the door. Surely there would be no harm in changing into some of Jay's spare clothes and going out to look for her, although that seemed an awful lot like stealing.

Another glance at the clock confirmed it was now past eight in the evening.

He could borrow the clothes just this once.

Dakier swiftly changed into the most casual ensemble he could find—a plaid suit and a matching burgundy shirt. The length was fine, but the cut was so tight he worried the seams might tear if he lifted his arms. It would have to do, though, for Brenna's sake.

With his decision made to go search for her, he opened the door, but just as he crossed the threshold, a red tumbleweed pummeled into him. He fell to his back with a resounding rip—the shoulders of his obnoxious collared shirt tearing at the seams.

For a split second, all he could see were Brenna's big brown eyes. Her pretty face was less than an inch from his, encircled in a flurry of fiery curls. But she let out a little squeal at the eye contact and jumped off of him, straightening out her tawny skirt as she stood.

"What's happened?" Dakier asked. "Are you hurt?"

"What?" She scrunched her nose, the gesture particularly endearing on her overly expressive face. "Of course not. Everything's great. I found the place."

"A newspaper printer?" Dakier said, suddenly aware of the nature of the conversation. He reached above her to pull the apartment door to a close. "Perfect."

Despite the good news, Brenna's eyes lacked their usual sparkle, and he realized why with a pang. She couldn't be happy around him. She hadn't even teased him about his too-tight clothes. With him—with her brother's killer—she couldn't be herself.

Once she completed this mission and didn't need his help any longer, he would never bother her again, no matter how much he wanted to be near her. If the day ever came where she could visit Katiel again in the Yule Valley, he would make himself scarce.

"Well, it's getting late," Brenna said, stepping toward the washroom. "You can take the bed, and I'll take the divan."

"Oh, no, I insist—"

"It makes more sense. I'm a foot shorter than you, at least."

As she spoke, she raised her arms to straighten her hair, and Dakier gasped. The whole sleeve of her dress was torn, ripped from the shoulder to the buttoned cuff at her wrist. Without thinking, he rushed over, cradling her elbow while he inspected the skin beneath. The length of her arm was sliced through along the back, tiny droplets of blood prickling the dark fabric.

"You said you weren't hurt."

"I'm not," she said, despite the obvious injury. "I'm fine."

"Did someone do this?"

He asked it without thinking, suddenly seeing red. Of course, a woman couldn't go out in the city alone. The ruthless men out there were despicable, disgusting cretins without any honor.

"No, it was a printing press."

She didn't recoil from his touch, which brought him nearly as much relief as her explanation. It was a simple accident, nothing more. Still, he made a mental note to accompany her for the next phase of her plan. Just in case she had more trouble with the press.

A knock rapped against the door, sending a loud pang through the room and a jolt up Dakier's spine. They'd been speaking right next to it, and Brenna could be in horrible trouble if anyone overheard the plan.

"Alright, let's say it was me who—" he started.

But Brenna opened the door, plastering on her friendliest smile before she'd even seen the visitor. Standing there was a teenage girl, holding out a tray covered by a silver cloche. Brenna quickly took the parcel, thanked her, and shut the door.

"I ordered food delivery from next door on my way in," Brenna said with a wag of her eyebrows. "I thought it would be more discreet than going somewhere—and apparently Jay has a tab there."

Brenna halved the food—the typical Barkurian staples of steak and potatoes—and passed him a plate with his portion, though Dakier noticed she'd actually given him well more than half. He was tempted to comment on her thoughtfulness, but he sensed Brenna wasn't much for compliments just then.

Instead, he asked her about what had happened to her and Katiel once they'd parted ways, and she launched into every detail as they ate. The shadows grew long as he listened, and by the time Brenna finished relaying it all, the lingering light in the apartment was swathed in gray. At some point, they'd seated themselves opposite each other—she on Jay's made bed and he on the velvet divan—and Dakier shook his head as he mulled over the harrowing details.

Brenna and Katiel had been so incredibly brave. They could've died five times over in their efforts. He should've been there for them—even if it meant he was a deserter. They'd met Inigo Farro, and they'd released him from prison. And yet Brenna stood before him as humble as ever, acting like the exact same girl he'd met in the valley years ago.

After telling him everything, Brenna seemed lighter, as if an invisible weight lifted from her shoulders. She clearly hadn't had a soul to confide in, and he hated that staying in Ballynach had made her so alone. All her actions were for the good of others, but it wasn't fair to her. After surviving all that, she should've gone back to Fir Kelt to take some time to process, and he was just about to say so when she surprised him with a new question.

"How do you know Eoghan?"

"The prince?" Dakier clarified, his stalling made obvious by how unusual the prince's name was. "Honestly, it's a long story."

Even in the apartment's growing darkness, he could see Brenna's mouth quirk up. "I just told you a long story."

He looked down at his lap, hoping to hide the way his heart fluttered in his chest. "Very well."

He told her all the details—from the blacksmith's shop to arriving in the prince's suite—assured that Eoghan's secret would be safe with her. But when he finished his tale, the first thing that came out of her mouth shook him to the core.

"Dakier, isn't it obvious?" Her tone brimmed with impatience, like she was surprised she even had to say the words aloud. "Eoghan isn't the wielder. It's you."

25

Anton

Only the Drezchy court would throw a ball when they should be holding a funeral.

It was a mere two days after the harrowing first trial, and Anton was in no mood for dancing. Normally, he enjoyed these functions. Flirting with girls at court was a diverting way to pass the time, and a ball lacked the violent rituals of other court gatherings.

But on this evening, the only girl he wanted to dance with was the same one he'd promised to remain professional toward. And the way she looked tonight made that remarkably difficult.

She'd gotten ready with Nev, and his eyes kept flitting to the doors despite himself as he waited for her to arrive. It made no sense, considering he vowed not to talk to her that evening unless necessary. But when she finally appeared beneath the arched double doors, it wasn't just him who took notice. Every eye in the ballroom turned to her.

The wielder wore a flowy frock in a deep indigo, with several sheer panels draping around her shoulders and hips. Her hair was styled into an intricate crown of braids, with tiny crystals dotted throughout the blond plaits. She looked like a goddess even as she bashfully tipped her chin to avoid the crowd's gaze, and Anton was suddenly extra pleased that he ordered the last minute A'slenderian fashions for her.

He leaned leisurely against the far wall, feigning indifference lest anyone note his reaction. While he had little memory of her healing him as he fell in and out of consciousness, he was concerned the display might have put a target on her back. To avoid anyone targeting her further, he would keep his distance.

But the second Katiel and Nev settled in, a gaggle of male courtiers flocked to them, and Anton rolled his eyes as he made his way to the refreshments table. It was high time for another drink.

ANTON DOWNED HIS FULL glass of wine in one gulp, the evening already halfway through. Though he tried to dance and talk with Nev to occupy himself, it was impossible to keep his mind off of Katiel, and now he had to watch her dance with his prick of a cousin.

Of course, Ludvig would pick an A'slenderian girl who didn't know what to expect for the Roulensk, the most intimate traditional dance of all. They spun across the dancefloor, her back pressed against his brawny chest, and Anton suddenly regretted his decision to give her space for the evening.

It would've been a different matter if Katiel actually liked Ludvig. If she wanted to date his vapid cousins, Anton could respect her wishes. But the uncomfortable glances she shot back at Ludvig—like she was pretending to see if she had the steps right, while deliberately inching away from him—pained Anton to no end. It was nothing like the way she had once looked at him, before all the idiotic things he'd done.

He still held sway as the former crown prince. He could storm over there and break them apart, and bar anyone else from dancing with her.

No, that would make him look desperate. He could perhaps say it applied only to court wielders, but she was the only one, so that would still be obvious. He could—

Abruptly, the song ended, yanking Anton from his thoughts. The musicians took an intermission, and mercifully, Ludvig bowed his head and stepped away from Katiel. Anton didn't know when his feet started moving, but in seconds, he was in front of her, hands clasped behind his back.

"How are the festivities treating you?" What a doltish, formal thing to say.

"Very well," Katiel answered, her full lips curling into the tiniest smile. "How are you feeling? This seems like a lot of movement with your injury."

"Nonsense. I feel as good as new," he lied, before adding, "but I wouldn't be standing here without you." He forced a cough, his nerve waning. "May I see your dance card?"

"Oh, of course," she said, holding her wrist out to him. She was supposed to untie the ribbon and hand it to him, and he tried not to notice how cute she was sticking her arm out instead. "Did I do it incorrectly?"

"Erm, no," he stammered, trying to regain a semblance of composure. "I thought I might steal a dance with the newest member of our court."

She scrunched her nose, like she was trying to remember who the newest member was, and he wrote his name by the remaining Roulensk before she had the chance to reject him. She could refuse to dance with him, of course, but no one else could write their name there now, so at least he wouldn't have to witness anyone else trying to press against her.

Anton barely refrained from writing his name across every other blank line as well before he walked away, but it turned out not to matter. After he spoke to her, no one else asked her to dance, and he smiled despite himself. At least his subjects had not forgotten to fear him in his absence.

As the night wore on, he danced with everyone who passed him their dance card, just to pass the time. They were all faces he recognized from court, though none of them stood out to him in particular. Over the years, he'd trifled with a few of the court girls, but no one came close to Katiel. Trying to charm her when they met had been a fool's errand. She'd bewitched him beyond sense, and—

"Your Royal Highness?" asked the girl he currently danced with, a brunette named Evna, who looked up at him warily. "Are you feeling alright?"

Anton jogged his memory and vaguely recalled a conversation with the brunette before he left for A'slenderia. But then Katiel moved into his periphery, and he forgot to answer her as the song ended. Evna stormed off in a huff that he knew he deserved, but all he could think about was the next dance—the second Roulensk.

Katiel approached him, and the smooth words he'd prepared vanished when she said, "Your name is written on my card for this song."

Like she didn't know him. Like they hadn't just travelled through three countries and two continents together.

Like she wasn't the girl he thought about every waking hour since he met her.

And curse him if he didn't say, "Same here."

Idiot, idiot, idiot.

"It's this one again," Katiel said, twisting her mouth into a little scowl as other dancers started moving. Hopefully she was making that face at the memory of dancing with Ludvig, and not at the thought of dancing with him.

Anton clasped his hands behind his back. "Is that alright?"

"Yes," Katiel said stiffly, holding out her petite, white-gloved hand. "It's alright."

Anton momentarily found the awkwardness excruciating, but the moment passed as he led her into the throng of dancers. When they stopped, she didn't turn around, instead fidgeting with a small curl that had broken free from her braid. "I'm not familiar with any of your country's dances."

"It's no matter," he said, gently twirling her around until her back was to him. "I'll lead you."

"But I'm not a very good dancer," she said, tucking her chin to hide her blush.

He dipped his head until his lips were a breath away from her nape. "Trust me, Katiel. All you need is a good lead."

Then he grabbed her left hand and held it straight out to the side, and she melted against him.

As he placed his other hand on her hip and started gliding through the steps, they were transported into a different world—one where they could be together. In this world, he never learned to fear their closeness, and he never convinced himself to steal from her. He'd tricked himself into thinking he had to, when actually, he was terrified of his feelings for her. But the wedge he'd tried to drive between them hadn't remained for long.

He wondered what it would've been like to grow up in the Northern Mountains with her, like that irritating Alfien had. Anton knew one thing for certain—if he'd been lucky enough to know her all his life, he never would have let her go.

But then she leaned closer to his chest, and a sharp stab of pain from the freshly healed wound tore him from the reverie. He must have flinched despite his best efforts, because she turned her head in alarm.

"Anton..."

The listless sound of his name on her tongue sent a different sensation through him, and his breath hitched as he looked down at her. Her chin grazed her bare shoulder, and her lips lingered dangerously close to his own.

"Anton, about the trial," she continued. "At the end, when I saw you like that..."

The second stretched into hours as he waited, anxious to hear the confirmation he wanted—but hadn't expected—to hear.

"It killed me."

Anton swallowed hard. He longed to kiss her, to feel her bite his tongue again, and to see what other surprises lurked beneath her sweet façade. He allowed his nose to brush her cheek ever so slightly, the promises he'd made on the ship—and the lurking courtiers surrounding them—temporarily forgotten.

"I must admit, I thought the dance with Ludvig might have killed you, judging by your face."

She giggled in the same, soft way she always did, and he found himself saying some other, brainless thing to elicit the sound again.

"I take it you don't fancy men that look like thumbs, then?"

"No!" She rewarded him with a boisterous laugh that she quickly covered with her free hand. Then, as if she couldn't help herself, she added, "Why did you have to say that? Now I will never see anything else."

Anton laughed, the real laugh that he usually reserved for Simeon and Nev in the rare moments of happiness he held onto in this palace. Most in the court had likely never heard it, and he suddenly became aware of the eyes on him.

If he carried on like this, it would be obvious what he felt for his court wielder. Some might have already guessed that he fancied her, and he had to admit he was tempted to show her off. But this display—it was too much. If he revealed the depth of his feelings to these vultures, it could make her a target—a pawn to lure him with—and that thought was crushing.

So, he did what he had to do.

When the dance ended, he didn't ask for another, vowing to avoid her for the rest of the fete. Their hands parted as he pulled away, and the heartbroken look in her eyes threatened to end him. Here he was, worming his way into her trust again, only to hurt her moments later.

He could walk away for the moment, and he told himself to walk away for good—but deep down, he knew he couldn't.

Even if it ended them both.

26

Katiel

STANDING BEFORE THE GILDED vanity in her ostentatious suite, Katiel combed out her braids faster than necessary. Her braided updo had started pulling at her scalp hours ago, and after the trying evening, she couldn't get free of it fast enough.

Going to a ball in a royal court should have been a dream come true, a magical soiree like she'd read about in novels during her long hours watching her flock. Instead, she'd felt socially obligated as a new member of court to dance with anyone who asked her, even Ludvig, who she'd just watched exhibit brutal violence two days prior.

The terrible circumstances had robbed any semblance of joy from the event, save for her one dance with Anton. After her panic at the thought of him dying, the dance itself made her feel more in love with him than ever. But then he avoided her for the rest of the night, dancing with girls and chatting flirtatiously with others, his mouth drawing close to their ears to be heard over the music. The mere thought made her grit her teeth, but she refused to dwell on it. All she had to focus on was helping him get the throne so he could declare peace with Kerafin, and then she could forget about everything and everyone in this dreadful court.

Abruptly, a sudden commotion came from outside her room, and Katiel stilled, stopping the brush in the middle of her hair. It sounded like glass breaking—followed by a thwack and a pained groan—coming from the direction of Anton's room.

Instantly, she was on her feet, rushing into the hallway. Across from hers, the door to Anton's suite hung ajar. There was no light coming from within, but she could have sworn the racket came from that direction. As silently as she could, she crept up and peered through the narrow gap.

Inside, Anton's room was dark save for a single beam of moonlight streaking in through the two-story windows along the far wall. The library area opposite her was empty and untouched, with not so much as a candle out of place.

Next to the bed, a glass inkwell and a bronze clock lay shattered, leaving black ink and cogs strewn about the wooden floor. Her pulse quickening, she squinted into the darkness. The dim lighting delayed her comprehension of what she saw, but when the edges sharpened, she gasped.

It was Ludvig, looming over Anton's black-draped, four-poster bed. One of Ludvig's hands pressed against Anton's mouth, and the other clutched the hilt of a dagger. Anton's eyes were wild, locked on his opponent as if daring him to go through with it—to actually kill him.

Anton gripped his cousin's wrists, arms straining to keep Ludvig's weapon at bay. Even with the effort, the dagger's point grazed the center of Anton's chest. His strength was amazing given the size of his adversary, but if another minute passed as they were, the prince would die of suffocation before the dagger was necessary.

At the alarming thought, Katiel flicked out a particle of ore from her teeth, expanding and shaping it in one swift motion. A thin iron chain sliced through the air and whipped around the front of Ludvig's thick neck, the chain links clinking together as it pulled back to choke him.

Katiel didn't even have to grab the metal. The chain constricted on its own, with an invisible, mindless force designed to strangle the nearest person until she called it off. Immediately, Ludvig coughed as the chain yanked him off the bed, his arms flailing as he released his cousin and the dagger both to claw at his neck. The discarded weapon clanged against the wooden floor, and Anton sucked in a ragged breath.

Ludvig reared back, his fingers clutching the chain as it pulled tighter, but his efforts proved futile. He looked around himself in every direction, frantically searching for the source of his assault and completely missing where Katiel stood in shadow.

Anton's gaze, however, snapped to her. The corner of his lips turned up, and something like exaltation flared in his dark eyes. Heat flushed across her cheeks when she met his possessive stare, distracting her a moment too long while a man's life lay in her hands. Quickly, she mentally relinquished the chain, which fell to the floor in a heap around the brawny man's shoes.

At last, Ludvig noticed where she stood, mere feet away.

"You," he said, piecing together the rescue as if in a daze.

"Leave," she replied, trying to summon an authority she did not feel. "Consider this a warning."

Ludvig's eyes narrowed. "I thought we got along, court wielder. Am I not as much of a prince of our court as he is?"

Katiel ignored the bait, trying to maintain her commanding tone. "I will not warn you again."

The prince's jaw ticked, like he had to physically restrain himself from speaking. Her warning was clear—she had almost killed him and, next time, she would. But the look in his eyes—like he might try his attack again—suggested he didn't believe her capable of it. If only he knew, Katiel thought with a pang, that he wouldn't even be her first kill.

At last, Ludvig stormed out of the room without a second glance, and Katiel waited, heart racing, until his footfalls faded away.

With a trembling hand, she closed the heavily fortified door—which, strangely, did not appear to have been tampered with—and turned back to Anton. "Did you not think to fasten any of your ten locks?"

The prince chuckled, a rough sound, before flicking on the lantern mounted above his nightstand. That was when she noticed what he was wearing—or rather, what he was not. He was sitting up in bed, the sheets thrown off, wearing only a pair of silky black pants with the rest of his skin exposed. She could see every outlined muscle of his torso and arms, from his square, surprisingly broad shoulders down to his sharply defined abdomen. Between the angled indents of his hips, a thin line of dark hair trailed from his navel to below his low-slung waistband.

"My eyes are up here, Katiel."

The words sent a burning blush across her cheeks, but despite what he said, when she looked up, he wasn't looking at her face, either. She suddenly became acutely aware that she was wearing only her white long-sleeved nightdress, and her wavy hair billowed down her back. Having her hair released from its braids almost made her feel more exposed than the thin material of the gown.

"What happened? Why didn't you lock the door?" she asked, trying to reel the conversation in before her mind wandered.

"I was distracted earlier." He sighed, sitting up straighter. "It gave Ludvig a fresh opportunity to come for me. I haven't forgotten the locks in years."

"What do you mean?" She truly had no idea what he was talking about. "What happened earlier?"

Anton bit his lip in hesitation, and it took all her effort to keep her eyes focused on his. "Do you really want to know?"

"Yes." She closed the distance between them until she was under the heavy canopy and perched on the edge of his bed.

"It killed me seeing you tonight, dancing with other men," he admitted, eying her hand, resting on his mattress mere inches from his. He swallowed hard, like saying the words aloud gave him a fresh surge of jealousy. "Dancing with my infernal cousins."

"I am not yours to claim, Anton," she huffed, though she could not deny that it killed her, too, seeing the drones of girls fawning over him, elbowing each other out of the way to write their names on his dance card, and looking pitifully at Katiel while she stood on the sidelines. If they only knew all the time she spent alone with the prince in the past few months.

"I know you're not, and I know it's unfair of me." Anton raked a hand through his messy hair, his beauty dazzling her more than ever. He remained propped on an elbow as he leaned toward her, and every ridge of his taut abdomen contracted with the movement. "What kills me is that, at one point, I almost thought you could have been—that you might have wanted to be—before everything that happened in Bar Kur. Before everything I did."

You mean, she thought drily, *before you tricked me, used me, and stole my life source.*

"Katiel, that day that I stole the ore—I knew, deep down, that it wouldn't work."

"Then why did you leave?" she whispered.

Anton looked past her, before meeting her eyes again and pushing a stray wisp of hair behind her ear. "Because I was a coward. I thought I was tricking you, but the truth was, I felt something that night that I'd never felt before—never even dreamed of feeling. Love."

"Anton," she breathed, soaking in the warmth that she couldn't put into words. Relief swept over her, at the admission that, despite all her misgivings, she'd been desperate to hear.

He loved her, and she loved him.

She loved his smile, his creativity, his reassurances, his warmth, his determination, and his willingness to admit when he was wrong. His kindness, despite the cruel world he was raised in, amazed her.

But she didn't get the chance to say so before he went on, desperation coating his voice. "That feeling terrified me, so I ran, but I wish I'd never left. If something would have happened to you with Taregh..." He hung his head, and she knew his regret was sincere. "I told myself I was being strong. That caring for someone was a weakness. But the truth is, before I ruined everything, I wanted you to be mine—only mine."

Katiel's stomach flipped at the way his jaw clenched when he said *mine*—at the possessiveness behind it. "And what about you?" she ventured, keeping her tone barely above a whisper. "In this fantasy, would you be only mine as well?"

"Of course. Absolutely," he answered, his throaty voice brimming with conviction. Anton watched her hair draped around them, like he longed to run his fingers through it, and she desperately hoped he would. "There's no one like you, Katiel. No one can compare."

Her cheeks heated, hearing the words she had longed for without realizing it. She wanted him to kiss her, but he didn't ask for anything—yet his pupils were so dilated that they nearly erased the mahogany ring of his eyes. No, she was the one who said they should keep their distance, and he was respecting her request for the moment.

She would have to be the one to start something.

She bent down and pressed a long, gentle kiss to his lips. When she leaned back, she drew a slow finger down his exposed torso, and then his hands were on her, gripping her thighs. He pulled her closer until she hovered above him, her knees on either side of his hips, and then he dipped his head to bring his mouth to her neck, tracing a ravenous line of bites up to her jaw.

He was hungry for her, and she loved it. She loved *him*.

After the last time they kissed, she was grateful they hadn't gone further, since she knew she had no reason to trust him. But this time, she reasoned, was different. She loved him, and he could die at any moment during the Conclave. He almost had tonight, right before her eyes. So she decided to take things further, in case this night was the last one they had.

She pulled back from the kiss and reached down, soft fingers toying with his waistband. But to her surprise, where she expected to see his eyes darken in anticipation, they flew open wide as panic overtook his features. His fingers clamped around her wrist, and she gasped as he nearly pushed her arm away.

"Anton?" she started, sudden hurt pulsing through her at the unexpected reaction. "Did I do something wrong?"

"No, of course not," he answered hurriedly, shaking his head as if to physically clear it. He flexed and unflexed the offending hand, though he now gripped nothing but air. "Forgive me. I must have had more wine than I realized earlier. I'm not myself this evening."

Though he seemed entirely sober, Katiel wasn't going to argue, lest her words reveal how close she was to tears. She backed off the bed and stood up, eyes cast down in embarrassment.

She did want to argue, though, or at least to get an answer as to what she'd done wrong. Hadn't he just said he loved her? Perhaps she'd only been hearing what she wanted to hear, and it made sense if he didn't. She was a commoner, and he was a prince; she was average, and he was gorgeous.

With a sigh, she turned around, assuming his silence meant he wanted her to leave. But the second she did, he said, "Katiel, please wait. Please."

Hurriedly, he crossed the tall bed and slung his legs off the side. He clasped her wrist again, far gentler this time, and she let him pull her closer until she was standing between his thighs, his dark eyes level with her own.

The silence hung between them, Anton's face pained as he fought for an explanation. But then he placed his finger under her chin and drew her face up to his.

"Stay with me?" he asked simply, his parted lips a breath away from her own.

And though she couldn't wrap her mind around what had just happened, she couldn't deny him when he looked at her like that. So, she said, "Of course," and let him guide her down until she was pressed into his side.

He lay on his back, and she snuggled closer, pressing her cheek in the crook where his chest met his shoulder. She wanted to ask again about what had happened, but being close to him relaxed her beyond all reason. The air held a sudden chill that she hadn't felt since she'd left home. It was like she was exactly where she was always meant to be, and before she worked up the courage to ask him anything, she drifted off to sleep.

27

Dakier

Dakier reeled, Brenna's proclamation playing on repeat in his mind.

"What do you mean it's me?" Dakier shook his head. "I can't be a wielder. There are a thousand reasons why that makes no sense."

"But," Brenna countered, raising her index finger in the air, "you only need one reason why it does. And besides, the whole wielding thing doesn't make much sense in the first place. It's *magic*."

With the word *magic*, Brenna wagged all of her fingers in front of her face, as though she were pantomiming sparkles. But despite how adorable Dakier found the gesture, her explanation was far from convincing.

"Seriously, why do you think that?" he prodded. "I know you. You pick locks. You solve the most obscure riddles as if they were nothing. I know you've already considered every angle."

Brenna looked down, and a light blush cropped up under her freckles that she was clearly trying to suppress. "I didn't realize you noticed all that."

"Of course I have," Dakier said without thinking. "I notice everything about you."

Brenna's eyes locked with his across the cramped room, and Dakier couldn't look away, even as he nervously rubbed the back of his neck. He hoped the sentiment came across as sweet, but he worried it sounded more like what a strange man creeping in the shadows would say. "Not that I'm, you know, *watching* you. Because that would be odd. I just mean I notice you, when we're talking or interacting—"

"Dakier." Brenna sighed, but the tiniest hint of a smile played at her lips. "Let's focus on the wielder thing."

He nodded, and she leaned forward from her perch on the edge of the bed, as if the rationale were bursting from her.

"Think about it. Eoghan was holding the metal with tongs, but you were the one who inhaled the ash. You were the one who caused a huge swirl of dust when you coughed. Doesn't that sound strange to you? You must have expanded the ore, just like Katiel does, but without realizing it."

"It was strange, sure," Dakier conceded, "but it must be a coincidence. I don't keep a necklace like Katiel does or anything that might have ore hidden inside it. My mother wasn't a wielder. I never knew my father, or anything about him, but I'm guessing he wasn't from the Yule Valley."

"See, you didn't know him!" Brenna exclaimed as if that alone confirmed her theory. "Maybe he was a wielder after all. And anyway, *you're* from the Yule Valley. I mean, do we really know wielding is passed down from parent to child? Katiel, her parents, and Master Larinne all grew up in the same place. Plus, I always had an uncannily peaceful feeling when I was there. It could be something about the place itself."

Dakier took another bite of his now-cold dinner roll, just so he would have something to do with his hands while he mulled it over. Right from the first time he'd set foot in the valley, he'd felt that sweeping sense of calm himself. He'd assumed the sensation was from finally being away from his toxic home environment, but if there was one place in the world that was truly magical, the Yule Valley would be it.

"As for the ore," Brenna continued, "Katiel's parents gave her that necklace as a good luck charm *while traveling*. She wore it constantly when away from the Yule Valley, but I remember her taking it off sometimes at home. Doesn't that tell you something?" She locked eyes with him, her round, brown eyes brimming with excitement. "My current theory is that the ability is transferred environmentally—and you lived there long enough to become a wielder, too."

It did make some sense, he had to admit, though not everything was adding up. "But what about the Kerafin Pact?" he asked. "That treaty prohibited wielders from having children. Why would the writers of the pact have bothered if it wasn't inherited?"

Brenna's mouth twisted into a half moon while she considered. "The wielders could have let them think that, even if it wasn't true," she said at last. "According to Mara, Katiel's parents are old enough to have been around when that pact was created. If the Salzbrucks were as famous as Mara claimed, they might have even been there when it was signed. It didn't stop them from having Katiel, though, and maybe they knew it wouldn't stop them one way or another from making more wielders, because wielding *isn't* passed down hereditarily."

Dakier's chest swelled with hope at the idea, before it deflated as another thought came to him. "If that were the case, Feniel would have to have known about it. He wouldn't have brought me there."

"Or maybe that's exactly why he brought you there!" Brenna jumped up from her perch at the edge of the bed, sending her red curls bouncing. "Outsiders never stayed there other than you—and me. Think about it—how did you meet Feniel in the first place? How did you hear about such a far-off opportunity at all? He could've picked you to make more wielders."

In her excitement, she reached out to grab Dakier's hand. He sucked in a breath at the contact, but then she noticed what she'd done and flinched away.

"Does that sound right to you?" she asked, her voice growing quieter as she inched back to the bed. "Did it seem like Feniel picked you?"

Dakier swallowed, forcing himself to think back to the day he met Feniel. He hadn't thought of it in so long that the memory was fuzzy at first, but then it came back to him, all at once, as clear as if he were reliving it.

When Dakier met Feniel, it was a typical workday in Jinensin. He was thirteen, and he'd moved to the city from Pizemac years prior after his mother married his stepfather and uprooted them. Now that he thought about it, that day with Feniel stood out as one of his only happy memories from his time there.

That day, he was framing a building for his stepfather's carpentry business. As usual, his stepfather had found fault with his work, no matter how hard he tried, and punched him squarely in the face, right there on the job site. His cheekbone and eye throbbed as he finished the shift, and the second he was told he could go on break, Dakier walked a block away to the tiered fountain in the center of town.

It was meant to be a wishing fountain, but he didn't have any coins, so he dunked his head in the clear water instead and let himself rest in the coolness for a moment. His hair swirled around as he took a deep breath and then stood, slicking his wet hair back. A second later, he realized how strange that must have looked, and he craned his neck self-consciously to see if anyone noticed. But among all the townsfolk in the busy central square, only one person looked back at him.

A tall, slender man with a neatly trimmed, snow-white beard watched him from behind a market stall, concern etched in his bushy white brows. Though his skin was only mildly crinkled, Dakier instantly got the impression that he was ancient. It was something about his eyes, so blue and still and deep. When Dakier met his stare, it was like he was peering into the very bottom of a crystal-clear well.

He looked A'slenderian, Dakier thought, though it was common enough to see people of all nations in a city as large as Jinensin.

"Is everything alright, son?" the man asked, and Dakier realized then that the man had come closer. They were only a couple yards apart, near enough for a normal conversation, and Dakier swallowed back his discomfort.

"No, sir," he said, before realizing he'd meant the opposite. "I mean, yes, sir. Everything is fine."

"Is that so..." the man mused, briefly glancing back at his wares before he met eyes with Dakier again. Then he stepped behind a nearby market stall and lifted a wrinkled hand, beckoning Dakier to come along.

Dakier frowned, but followed him, anyway. His stall was covered with an assortment of cheese rounds on one side, and a slew of wool scarves and blankets on the other.

"Do you know any old Aslen stories?" he asked, and Dakier shook his head at the unexpected question. Then a warm grin crept across the old man's face, perhaps the most genuine smile that Dakier had ever seen. "Would you like to?"

He really ought to be getting back to work, and already his delay had likely earned him another beating. But honestly, by that point, he was used to it, and he did want to hear the story, so he nodded.

The man started by introducing himself as Feniel Salzbruck and then launched into a long, interesting tale about a woman named Ilga, who used magic powder to craft an object that could transport her to any place she wished. It didn't have the happiest ending—the townspeople ended up exiling Ilga—but it was entertaining enough, and at the end, Dakier thanked him heartily.

"That was great," he said honestly, debating if he should shake the man's hand. "I'll be thinking about that one for a long time. But I better be getting back to work."

"What kind of work do you do?" Feniel asked, then went on before Dakier could answer. "I'm looking for farmhands at my livestock farm in Northern A'slenderia. It's far, but I'd offer room and board, plus fair additional pay."

Dakier's eyebrows shot up. Right off the bat, that sounded amazing. His stepfather always said he couldn't wait until he didn't have to support Dakier any longer, and Dakier would love to be free of his stepfather's cruelty. He didn't know Feniel at all, but he figured he couldn't be worse, so Dakier took down his information and wrote to him a few weeks later to accept. It was a serendipitous exchange, just two strangers meeting at random. Or perhaps it wasn't as random as Dakier had always thought.

"Well?" Brenna prodded, bringing Dakier back to the present. "Did it seem like he chose you?"

Dakier realized that he'd started pacing, so he stopped himself and turned to Brenna, who leaned forward expectantly from her perch at the edge of the bed. "Honestly, it did."

She gave a little gasp and clasped her hands in front of her chest, like it was taking all her effort to refrain from clapping. "So he could've hidden the ore for you like he did with Katiel. Can you think of anywhere they might've put it? The sole of your shoe, or sewn into the lining of your clothes, perhaps?"

"Not really," Dakier said, shaking his head as he ran through each possibility. "I've worn only army-issued attire since I arrived at Fort Cajetan, and I've been fine."

Brenna's face fell at the dead end, and part of Dakier wanted to end the conversation there, reassured that he didn't possess this ominous newfound ability. But there was one possibility, however small, that nagged at him. "There was one thing..."

"Yes?" she asked, her chin tipping up to him in anticipation.

"When I arrived in the Yule Valley for the first time," he began, unsure of how to explain it, "I had a badly chipped tooth, and after a year, Feniel brought it up and offered to put a crown on it. I suppose raw ore might be inside that."

"Ooh, let me see," Brenna said, rushing up to him. He obliged her, awkwardly opening his mouth and tilting his head back to reveal the silver crown toward the back of his upper right canine. "How'd you chip your tooth?" she asked, raising up onto her tiptoes to inspect it. "Was it a horse? I bet it was a horse."

"My stepfather, actually," he admitted, rubbing the back of his neck and looking anywhere but at her face. "He was incredibly violent, always finding fault with me, and he threw a horseshoe at my face one day and chipped it."

"But that could've killed you!" Brenna gasped, moving a step closer to him. "That should have never, ever happened to you."

Even as he looked away, she let her fingers fall against his forearm. "I'm so sorry, Dakier," she breathed, kindness lacing every word, and he forced himself to meet her gaze.

Though he'd never once talked about these events outside of his prayers, seeing her sweet eyes waiting for him to go on made him realize how much he'd longed to tell her. "I suppose that's why the idea of pacifism in the scriptures resonated so much with me. It made me feel more confident that what he'd done was wrong, but now..."

Dakier's throat burned as he trailed off, refusing to finish the sentence.

Now he was just like his stepfather. Worse, even—he'd become a killer.

It was the thought that had plagued him for weeks now. But Brenna saved him from having to voice it, seeming to read his mind as she took a step back and softly shook her head.

"You aren't like that, Dakier." She swallowed hard, and he stepped away, too, sensing that the moment and the conversation were both over. "You're nothing like that."

28

Brenna

The next two days passed uneventfully, and no word came from Steffi about the captives.

Alone with Dakier in the cramped space, Brenna focused on writing her article and avoided talking as much as possible, for Henred's sake. Since Dakier had no loose ore with which to test out his newfound abilities, he kept busy reading an adventure novel of Jay's. But they couldn't keep to themselves all the time, and Brenna kept slipping into easy conversation with him before remembering she wasn't supposed to like Dakier anymore.

Brenna told herself she was waiting to print the story until every word in the article was perfect, but she knew that wasn't the only thing holding her back. Truthfully, she was terrified that spreading the truth to the people of Bar Kur would somehow do more harm than good, but after two full days of procrastinating, Brenna's impatience finally won. It was time to either abandon her plan or take action, and she'd never been one to give up without a fight.

"Dakier," she said abruptly, still seated at Jay's writing desk. She'd been thrumming her fingers against the surface, completely lost in thought, and Dakier had dozed off while sitting upright against the wall at the opposite end of the room. "Dakier." She repeated his name until he jolted awake, knocking the open book off his lap and onto the floor. "It's time."

"Are you sure?" he asked, shaking his head as he rose to his feet. He stole a glance at the narrow window, from which sunlight still poured into the tiny apartment. “I thought the plan was to wait until nightfall.”

“I’m sure.” She pulled her satchel off the nail in the wall and tightened her already-tight bootlaces. “Now is—now’s as good a time as any.”

She held back the rest of the thought—that if she didn’t leave now, she might chicken out for good. But knowing Dakier, he’d likely figured that much without her having to say it. He always seemed to know what she was thinking.

“Do you want me to come with you?” He rubbed his hands together as if he were washing them, the hope that she would agree clearly written on his face. “To keep watch? In case something happens.”

In all honesty, she wasn’t even considering going without him. The newspaper shop wasn’t in the nicest part of town, and she shuddered to think of walking there alone in the dead of night. She actually wished she’d put her pride aside and let him come along the first time.

But she hadn’t forgiven him, so she said, “Fine,” with a pointed *Hmpf* and headed out the door.

“SAY, WHATEVER HAPPENED BETWEEN you and that lass who came by the other day?”

Brenna pressed her back against a brick wall, hiding around the corner from the Eternal City Gazette. They’d arrived just before sunset, and now she and Dakier were biding their time, waiting for the last of the workers to leave—the very same workers who were now chatting as they locked up for the night. While technically they could be talking about anyone, Brenna was pretty certain she was the lass in question.

"Who?" a second male voice asked.

"Oh, don't play dumb with me. You know, the short one with a million questions?"

Brenna's cheeks burned, feeling Dakier's gaze on her, but she refused to look at him. She hadn't disclosed exactly how she got the information she needed, but he had to know it was her they were discussing.

"Aye, fine, you got me," admitted the second man, his tenor confirming he was the one who showed her around the shop. "I waited for hours. She might've been a pretty fine lass, but she never showed."

Brenna's blush deepened, worried Dakier would disapprove of her standing up some random worker.

"Don't judge me," she whispered, peering around the corner to ensure the men were gone. "It was just a bit of innocent reconnaissance. All I did was talk to him."

When she turned back to him, Dakier met her gaze with a slight smirk. "I'm not judging."

It honestly *was* humorous, but Brenna, unready to laugh with Dakier just yet, fought back the smile that tugged at her lips. Without another word, she walked off down the alley, heading for the gazette's back stoop. Dakier stayed on her heels, his movements impressively quiet as they ascended the short flight of stairs.

To pick the lock, Dakier passed her his A'slenderian army knife without missing a beat. It was the type that housed twenty different gadgets in a single tool, and as she flicked through the overwhelming number of options, she wished she'd thought to practice this ahead of time. At last, she settled on a corkscrew that looked promising, but just as she did, Dakier reached forward to turn the handle.

It was already open.

Mischief danced in his eyes as he locked them with hers. They both knew this was the kind of comical mistake that Brenna lived for, but she refused to enjoy the moment with him, as much as she wanted to.

She stepped gingerly into the shop, which was far darker than the twilight-dusted street they'd come from. The good news was that if anyone found her there past close, they likely wouldn't be able to recognize her in the darkness.

The bad news was she could hardly see a foot in front of her, which made finding the right printing press difficult. The worker she'd flirted with the other day had shown her the press that printed the front page, and that was the one she needed. She didn't have time to switch out the entire paper, and she was determined to make as big an impact as possible—though that would be impossible if she couldn't see.

Brenna sighed and reached for her satchel to retrieve the spare candle and match she'd brought. She hadn't wanted to use them, but she quickly struck the match and transferred the small bloom to the wick, then tossed the match to the floor and stomped the flame out with her boot. She would have to be even quicker now, because if someone walked past, the glow visible through the wide front window would surely give them away.

"Come with me," she whispered to Dakier, thinking that she needed him to hold the light for her more than she needed him standing guard, and he nodded and followed as she bumbled around the shop. When she found the front page press at last, Dakier took the candle without her having to ask, holding it above the press so she could use both hands to rearrange the letters.

Brenna held her breath as she pulled on the wooden lever. This time, she kept her arms clear of the jagged edge that had cut her before, and the typesetting apparatus opened without a hitch. Then she took a deep breath and started rearranging the letter blocks into the article she'd crafted.

The only productive thing she'd accomplished over the past few days was writing the perfect article. Every sentence had to be just right, from the gripping headline to the minute word choices, but in the end, she was pleased with the result. She'd never been much of a writer, but somehow the words had come to her when she needed them most. And after reading and re-reading the missive so many times, she knew each word by heart.

Her fingers flew through the task of setting the front page, and it was finished before she knew it. She wiped her hands on her skirt in satisfaction, but noticed a moment too late that her palms were covered in ink. Even in the dim candlelight, she could clearly see two swathes of black streaking down the front of her only dress.

"Dang it," she said, about to wet her thumb to rub it off.

Then, out of nowhere, a voice boomed from the street outside. "Who goes there?"

Whether the voice belonged to a concerned bystander or a night watchman, she didn't know, but whoever it was, she'd rather not get caught. As the front doorknob rattled, she snatched Dakier's wrist and dragged him with her.

She dashed across the room blindly, stopping only when her nose was an inch from a corner. It wasn't the exit, as she hoped, but it was the best hiding place she could find. She crouched behind the nearest press, and Dakier hastily ducked in behind her. The space between the wall and the press was narrow, and Dakier's chest pressed against her side to accommodate them both. They were so cramped, she could feel his heart beating against her ribcage, and Brenna tried to ignore how her heart fluttered at the contact.

She hoped the man who'd spotted them would assume the glow he saw was a trick of the light and move on. But as the creaks in the floorboards grew closer, it became clear they'd have no such luck.

"I know you're in here," the man crooned. Probably a night watchman then, she reasoned. "Come out wherever you are."

She glanced at Dakier, who pressed a finger to her lips, and she sucked in a sharp breath. It was clear from his expression that he meant the gesture innocently, but her cheeks blazed nevertheless.

"Why don't you come out now, and save us all the trouble?" the night watchman asked again.

Despite Dakier's warning, it seemed like the wrong call to stay silent—because the last thing she needed was the man getting close enough to arrest her. She shook her head once, hoping to alert Dakier to her plans, and then sprung up, grabbing an open ink pad from the nearest press.

"Gladly!" she cried as she threw the pad, ink-first, in the man's face.

"What the—?" He clamored with his hands as he tried to make sense of what hit him, and it was all the distraction Brenna needed.

She didn't look back as the two of them raced out the door and onto the street.

29

Brenna

The next morning, Brenna hung her head as she left the apartment.

Sure, she felt lucky that she and Dakier made it back to Jay's apartment without being followed. Their identities hadn't been discovered, and she was relieved she hadn't gotten arrested again. But she'd still failed at her one chance to publish the truth.

She finished rearranging the front page, but the workers would have surely checked the pages extra carefully after hearing about the break-in. The Eternal City Gazette would likely increase security after last night's episode, and if word spread around town about an intruder messing with the presses, every newspaper in Ballynach would have their guard up.

Brenna had no ideas left, and for the first time since she'd found Mara's letter, she truly wished she'd never obtained it. Uncovering the truth had made absolutely no difference in the end. Defeated, she meandered aimlessly through the bustling city, too downtrodden to worry that anyone might be looking for the perpetrators of the print shop intrusion. Eventually, she headed back, only to find that Jay's street was as abuzz with activity as the rest of the city had been.

Amid the throng, a newsie on the corner caught her eye, and Brenna decided a number puzzle would be the perfect thing to brighten her spirits. This girl appeared to be much older than Nellie, but Brenna still tossed her an extra coin that she'd borrowed from the spare change cloche Jay kept on his desk.

The girl passed her the paper with emphatic thanks, but Brenna frowned as she realized it was the Eternal City Gazette. This very copy would have announced the truth about the war if she hadn't failed so miserably.

With fresh annoyance, she shoved the paper into her satchel and made a beeline for Jay's apartment building. There were a peculiar amount of pedestrians for the hour, well past the morning commute to work, and she had to bob and weave through the crowd. Just as her heel landed on the first step, a young woman slammed into Brenna, knocking her satchel off her shoulder and onto the pavement.

Brenna grumbled as she bent to pick up the scattered contents, sending a scowl in the general direction of the woman, who hurried off without so much as an apology. But when Brenna caught sight of the front page, she froze.

It was just like that day back in the Royal Kelt—a day that seemed so long ago now—when she first saw Inigo Farro's face on the front page of the local paper.

This time, his photo was absent, but his name was still there, emblazoned in a bold headline.

Inigo Farro Innocent – Barkurian General the True King-Killer

It was the headline she wrote.

She barely restrained herself from letting out a cheer, right there on the apartment stoop. The plan had worked. *Her* plan had worked. By some stroke of luck, her article was there in its entirety, printed on the front page of the most popular paper in the city.

Reading the morning paper was a daily staple for most Barkurians, and it was already almost noon. By now, everyone in the capital would know the truth.

In the article, she'd detailed nearly everything that happened—from General Taregh framing Inigo Farro to incite a war with Tibedo, to the kidnapping of the then-princess Stefana and the princes, as well as the tragic death of the late queen. She'd left out the parts about Katiel and the wielders, as it was irrelevant to what the public needed to know, and she obviously wasn't about to incriminate her friend.

Brenna had signed the article anonymously, of course, but she'd chosen a fitting pen name—*the Loyalist*.

It was an homage to Mara's pen name in her letter, a way to honor the keeper and all she'd done. Though Mara wasn't there to see the truth come out, Brenna hoped that wherever she was now, she would be at peace knowing her efforts weren't in vain.

Looking around the street with fresh eyes, Brenna noticed that most of the people buzzing about were holding newspapers. They pored over them, pointing and animatedly talking to one another. They talked about the truth—about the discovery of what really happened.

She'd done it. Steffi could call for peace now.

Just like that, this fight would be over.

The war would finally end.

30

KATIEL

"INGENIOUS," ANTON MUTTERED AS he reviewed Katiel's latest revision to his blueprint.

It was a design for an underwater breathing device, one of the tricks he planned to use in case the final battle was held by the coast. In the weeks since she had arrived, her skills had improved enough to finish all of Anton's necessary inventions. Now they were working on fail safes in case of unforeseen conditions, and honestly, Katiel was so worn out, she was tempted to cut the day's practice short.

They were on a picnic blanket, spread out in the grass at the far end of the gardens. Unaccustomed to the stifling heat that graced New Drezchy that day, Katiel had placed it under the willow tree for shade, which Anton, wearing his typical full suit, teased her mercilessly for.

When he finished reviewing the design, he grinned up at her. "This should work perfectly."

She wanted to smile at his praise, but her worries kept her mind drifting elsewhere—to the state of their relationship.

The ball had been days ago now, and to her surprise, Anton hadn't asked her to stay over with him or even kissed her again since. During the days, they were back to their old rhythm, wielding prototype after prototype of his inventions with only the mildest of flirtations interspersed. That night together, she'd been willing to accept his explanation that he wasn't feeling like himself.

Now, she knew there had to be something more, and her mind went to all the worst possibilities for an answer. Perhaps he was trying to trick her again somehow and taking things further than kissing was a rare moral line he would not cross. Or perhaps she was simply not attractive enough for him—which, unfortunately, was the most likely option as far as she could see.

He was a prince, a genius, and quite possibly the best-looking person she had ever seen. Meanwhile, there were millions of girls like her in the world, and hundreds in this very court, vying for his attention. The idea that he was in love with her, of all people, didn't make sense.

"Anton," she said abruptly, before she could think better of it. "Are you still interested in me?"

He cocked his head back as he looked up from the blueprint he'd been editing, his thick eyebrows arching up toward each other. "Am I?"

It was a question and an answer and yet told her nothing. "I'm serious," she insisted. "Are you interested in *me*, or interested in having a court wielder win you the crown?"

Anton sat up straighter and set his quill on the grass beside him. "You. Of course, you." He stared deeper into her eyes, like he might find an explanation there. "Is this about the other night?"

The sincerity in his voice almost made her feel guilty for wondering if she should trust him. Almost, but not quite. His profession of love had meant so much to her, but it would destroy her if it were all a ploy for power. While it was agonizing to ask him to confirm her fears, she wanted to hear the truth now rather than later. So, she settled on simply saying, "If you do not desire me, I understand. We can remain professional going forward."

"What?" he asked with a scoff, tossing the blueprints to the side. "Katiel." He grasped each of her arms, just above the elbow, like he was holding her in place—even though she wasn't trying to leave. "Katiel, if you knew how much I desire you, it would embarrass me. Humiliate me, even. You're all I think about."

The corners of his jaw clenched when he said it, but Katiel didn't know if she trusted his answer. He seemed to think about a lot of other things—the competition, overthrowing his uncle, and unique designs for violent weapons, to name a few.

"You don't believe me." He sighed and raked a hand through his umber hair. "Of course, it's about the other night. I wanted to tell you the truth about what happened, but...Shall I be honest now?"

That was it, then. He had not been honest. Bracing herself for whatever hurtful thing he was about to say, she said, "Please do."

"I—how do I say this," he stammered, his voice dropping an octave despite them being entirely alone in the clearing. "Something happened when I was younger, and when we were together, my mind began playing tricks on me. After the attack from Ludvig that you stopped, and all the killings with my family...it was like I was suddenly back there, in that moment, instead of with you, and I lost my senses."

Katiel blinked several times, trying to make sense of what he was implying, and sorrow overcame her as understanding dawned. He wasn't repulsed by her. He needed support, and she'd assumed the worst. "Anton, I'm so sorry—"

"But you didn't do anything wrong," he hurried to explain. "I've trifled with girls before, but I never undress. I, well—I want to keep myself closed off, I suppose. Normally, I say that right away, but I thought that with you—"

"Anton, you don't have to explain yourself." Katiel reached out, grasping his hand in hers and forcing him to look her way. "Truly. I'm sorry. I shouldn't have assumed I knew what you wanted."

He shook the thought away with a flick of his wrist. "No, honestly, you didn't misread me. I thought since I loved you—since I love you—it would be different, but it wasn't." He paused for a beat, and then muttered bitterly, "Yet another thing he's robbed from me."

The strangest look passed across his face, like he had not meant to tell her that. Like he was ashamed, and even scared of what she would think. Yet there was also an edge to his tone, an edge that she had heard before, every time he had mentioned his uncle. Suddenly, all the little comments Anton had made about him clicked into place.

"King Vadim?" she clarified, sensing that he wanted her to know.

He swallowed hard and nodded. "Don't worry. It's been many, many years since he bothered us."

A muscle in his jaw ticked across the sharp bone as he looked beyond her, and Katiel's heart sank further with the haunting implication, considering Anton was only eighteen now.

"But please don't tell anyone of this," he added. "Especially not my sister. It would crush her to hear of it."

"Yes, of course," Katiel promised, squeezing his hands a little tighter. She willed herself not to tear up, trying to be as supportive as she could. But she sensed that he did want to talk more—that he'd been waiting for someone to talk to—so she ventured another question. "Is that why you became the Ghost?"

He nodded before the apparent weight on his chest poured out all at once. "At first, I blamed myself. I thought it was some sort of cosmic punishment, or I had brought it on myself somehow. But when I found out it happened to someone else, too, I snapped out of it. I outsmarted him—taught him to fear me—so he wouldn't bother us again."

Katiel swallowed, heart full of despair at what he'd had to go through. She imagined he might be referring to any of his cousins as the other victim, but she would rather comfort him than pry any further. "You could outsmart anyone."

He smiled woefully. "I appreciate that, but I understand if you don't want to be with me any longer, now that you know."

"Oh, no," Katiel said immediately, horror-stricken that he would even imagine such a thing. "That would never affect how I feel about you. Never. What happened was not your fault."

"I meant," he clarified, looking anywhere but at her eyes. "I understand if you are no longer attracted to me."

She wondered if she sounded this ludicrous to him when she asked if *he* still desired *her*. Her constant longing for him might as well be written across her forehead in ink. "Anton, nothing could ever change the way I see you," she assured, his openness allowing her to say what she truly meant as well. "The way I feel about you is what I imagine an addict feels about opium. Less of a want and more of a need."

The corner of his mouth crept up, but the light did not quite meet his eyes. "You always say the most wondrous things." He leaned over her, pushing a stray lock of hair behind her ear. She waited for him to continue as she looked into his chocolate eyes, watching the constellation of emotion swarming there. "But I don't want to be your opium, Katiel. I want to be your everything."

Her heart fluttered at his words, and she caught his hand before he could remove it. She held it tight against her cheek—like she might hold on to him forever. "You could be."

He leaned toward her, and she tumbled onto her back, her fall cushioned by the soft grass beneath the blanket. She pulled the lapels of his jacket until he hovered above her, and he grinned down at her as she brushed her nose against his. "Thank you for being here for me, Katiel," he whispered against her lips.

But she didn't have time to kiss him before another voice in the courtyard said, "Oh, gross."

Anton drew back, and Katiel jerked upright. The spell the prince had cast on her vanished, leaving only mortification in its wake.

Simeon stood not ten feet away from them, his back turned pointedly. "When you said you sometimes practiced wielding outside, I didn't realize that was a euphemism."

"It wasn't," Anton said, righting the collar of his jacket as Katiel tucked her skirts back under her knees. "You can turn around. We're clothed."

"Good for you," Simeon drawled sarcastically as he spun around, his eyes still squeezed shut. "Not like I've been looking for you all morning or anything."

Simeon, who had turned toward the willow instead of them, looked like he was having an argument with a tree. Anton met her gaze conspiratorially, and Katiel couldn't help but snicker.

But her gleeful mood sobered as Simeon said, "The king has carriages waiting outside—one for each of you. The second trial has been set for today."

31

Katiel

"You and me. Together."

Anton reached over to squeeze her hand as he whispered the words, and Katiel felt a surge of optimism despite the dire prospects before her.

They were standing at the edge of an arena, awaiting the second trial. As to what sort of arena it was, she couldn't be sure. Once Simeon had roused them, they'd been blindfolded with thick, black swaths of fabric and led into separate carriages. An earthy scent of juniper wafted to her nose, telling her she was in some sort of lush field or forest, and judging from the distance traveled, they were just outside of Vincencim. The solo ride hadn't lasted long, but it still gave her time to mentally prepare for the ordeal ahead.

The second trial's rules were simple. Of the six remaining competitors, the last two standing would advance to the final round. Each competitor was allowed to bring in one champion to aid them in their efforts. Katiel was serving as Anton's champion, clearly, but as for the other five—neither she nor Anton knew yet who they'd chosen. Once a competitor was eliminated, their champion was required to exit the arena at once, and the others were barred from harming them at that point. Officially, they weren't supposed to harm the champions at all, but Katiel would be on her guard, regardless. There was no punishment worse than death—and the Conclave's winner could pardon himself besides—so she didn't imagine Anton's cousins would spare her if their lives were on the line.

Katiel thrummed her toes within her boots and twirled her hair with her free hand. It felt like ages since she'd been led to her post beside Anton, waiting for some unknown signal to start. She was about to ask him if he knew what it would be when a horn sounded. A nameless valet removed her blindfold in one swift stroke, revealing the place where she was about to fight for her life.

Before them lay a hedge maze, stretching as far as she could see to the left and right. Directly in front of them, a single, imposing entrance inviting them into the eerie labyrinth, with no other discernable breaks in the tall, continuous hedges. The narrow path between the shrubs seemed to stretch on endlessly, and it looked nearly impossible to traverse with any speed. Spindly, twisted roots protruded from the packed dirt walkway, and thorny branches jutted out at odd intervals. The hedges themselves towered as high as a two-story chalet, and opposite them, a crowd was gathered on a grassy, circular berm.

The king was watching nearby, Katiel was sure of it, and the evil man now filled her with even more disgust than before. She had to do everything possible to help Anton win, for the good of this country and for Kerafin. The last thing the continent needed was a disgusting worm like Vadim ruling it.

Twilight was already creeping up on them, and it wouldn't be long before darkness fell. Gas lamps periodically jutted out from the top of the hedges, but with the dim light they provided, Katiel feared tripping on a root or mauling herself in a bed of thorns.

In the distance, as if from the mist-shrouded mountains beyond the maze, the horn sounded a second time, and she knew without being told that the second trial had officially begun.

Anton cut a glance down at her, a blaze burning in his dark eyes. "Are you ready?"

She let go of his hand to free both of hers, and patted the pouch of raw ore that was tied at her waist. "Ready."

Katiel's blood was electric as they wound through the maze, her feet seeking out clear spots along the pathway. Anton led them through like he knew where he was going, but she kept a mental tally of the twists and turns to help backtrack lest they find themselves lost.

"I'm forgetting myself already," Anton muttered, halting so abruptly that they nearly collided. "Can you wield the featherlight shield and the drawback blade?"

"Of course," she said, angling her back to him in case someone came up the path while she worked.

She wielded both easily, having practiced these inventions enough times in the days prior to commit them to memory. But to her surprise, when she presented them to him, he pushed the shield back in her direction. "For you."

She had no time to process before he turned and ran on ahead, and she could only hope he was heading in a safe direction. At every crossroads, he took a left, and she trusted he had a plan—though she wished she knew for certain.

The greenery rushed by, and Katiel felt weightless as raw adrenaline coursed through her. They'd been running for ages when Anton stopped on his heel ahead of her and abruptly leapt into the hedge itself. Brambles nicked at the long sleeves of her dress as she scrambled in after, but she worried that if she stopped to ask what he was doing, it would already be too late.

Katiel peered between the branches, blinking the maze back into focus. Down the winding path stood Yaro, one of Ludvig's younger brothers. Though Yaro was smaller in stature than the eldest, he was just as muscular and, according to Nev's court run-down, twice as dense.

"That's Emil with him," Anton supplied quickly, before the two men spotted them. "His closest friend since childhood. He must've gone with the 'choose who you can trust' route."

Katiel let the statement sink in. Yaro had a childhood friend who he trusted with his life, just like her. It humanized him—far more than she was comfortable with.

But before she could react, Anton charged out of their hiding place, the drawback blade drawn above his shoulder.

The surprise attack was all it took to overtake Yaro, and in a single stroke, Anton drove the sword through his chest. As designed, the prongs along the sides of the blade extended, sending barbs deep into Yaro's abdomen. He screeched—a guttural bleat not unlike a dying goat—and Katiel watched helplessly as he collapsed to the ground. The weapon hit the dirt before his body, forcing the prongs deeper. Even in the silence, his haunting cry echoed in her ears. Katiel was going to be sick.

Blood pooled around him, soaking through his tunic. Though his eyes remained open, it was clear he was gone. An entire life had ended in a single strike, and Katiel could hardly contain her disgust. This grotesque, vile death was due to a weapon of her own making. The rising bile stung her throat, but she swallowed it down, hoping she could somehow take the memory with it.

Emil stood by his friend's side, making no move to exit the arena, as his role required. He was clearly in shock, and Katiel was reminded of her and Brenna. She shuddered at the mere notion of Brenna dying in front of her, and yet she was responsible for someone else losing a friend in the same manner—a man's life gone, as if it were nothing.

Anton reached for her, his voice thick with sorrow. "Come on."

He held his hand out to her, palm up, but for a moment, she couldn't take it. Where Anton had stood, all she saw was the murderer who'd just sliced through his cousin.

She looked up to meet his gaze, her hand still hovering above his, and found his soft, doe eyes imploring her to understand. He had to do it, they seemed to say, and she knew that was true. Yaro wouldn't have shown him mercy if their roles were reversed. No one had ever shown Anton mercy, but she could.

He was the Ghost, but he was also one of the kindest men she'd ever met. And so Katiel took his hand, holding tight to the murderer she loved as he led her deeper into the maze.

Her heartbeat was rapid and languid at once. A thunderclap cracked above them, signaling impending rain. Her face was already slick from tears, and her resolve strengthened as the narrow pathway turned into a veritable deluge. Nothing mattered anymore, so long as she made it out of this alive. Not just alive—she had to get out of this with Anton by her side. Otherwise, she might end up like Emil.

A few strides more and she saw it—a break in the hedges up ahead. That meant they'd reached either the open center portion or an exit from the maze itself. Anton lingered before he entered the open space, his curt nod in her direction confirming it was the former—and they weren't alone.

"Anton," a woman's voice crooned from inside, the bitterness in it spiking the hairs on the back of Katiel's neck. "Look who I brought."

32
Anton

Anton whipped around the corner to find the speaker—Cezary—standing in the circular clearing in the center of the maze with her hands on her hips.

In his periphery, he saw Katiel about to rush around him, and Anton shifted his body to block her from Cezary's line of fire. His cousin raised an incredulous brow, her dark curls bobbing as she mockingly shook her head, and he realized what he'd done.

Katiel was his weakness. He knew that, but letting his cousins know—

"I thought you were the genius, Ghost," Cezary chided, "and yet you keep revealing your secrets."

"Oh, I—" Anton started to retort, but Cezary cut him off.

"Eh, eh," she tutted, and Anton gritted his teeth. "I'm still talking. And I'd like to reveal one of my secrets, too."

From the half of the clearing still drowned in shadow, a man stepped into the light, and an involuntary gasp fell from Anton's lips.

He recognized this man. He'd *mourned* this man.

Of all the court wielders he'd known over the years, Xabius was the one who Anton had been closest to—other than Katiel, naturally. He'd looked up to every court wielder, but Xabius in particular always paid him special attention, wielding tiny, complex contraptions to keep him occupied during tedious state affairs. Assembling and disassembling them served as a precursor to his earliest inventions, but Xabius was executed by order of the king when Anton was still a child—or so he thought.

The elderly man in a deep violet robe stepped up to Cezary's side, his bushy eyebrows hanging so low they almost blocked his eyes completely. With a long gray beard and shaggy locks falling across his forehead, he was the stereotypical image of a wielder of old. Complete with an olive robe, he looked exactly like the illustration of Jurgen in Anton's most treasured A'slenderian folklore tome.

"Look at our little Anton now, Xabius." Cezary crossed her arms, rocking her weight from one leg to the other as she barked out a harsh laugh. "He's not the crown prince anymore. But he's still little."

It was obvious she was goading him, but Xabius remained impervious, a reminder of the idol he'd been to Anton growing up. Upon seeing him now, the wielder's eyes held a sadness so profound that Anton had to look away.

Katiel drew in close, and the hairs on his neck stood on end as her breath hit the exposed skin above his collar. "I thought you said there were no more court wielders."

Cezary smirked, clearly having heard Katiel's whisper. "There aren't. Except him. Word was he escaped his execution, but our dear old uncle couldn't let that embarrassing news get out."

"So, you ran off to hide." Anton crossed his arms as he held Xabius's gaze, feeling a twinge of guilt about squaring off against his childhood hero. "That truly is a surprise."

"You've grown into a man," Xabius said simply. A fondness fell from his lips as though he truly couldn't help himself, and Anton swallowed the lump forming in his throat.

But Cezary wasn't feeling so nostalgic. "Yes," she sneered, "he's the *man* who murdered my little brothers in the last round."

The sadness in Xabius's sagging eyes only doubled at that, and Anton couldn't help but snap, "Enough talking. Let's settle this between us, then."

Cezary winked, but the hatred in her stare was unmistakable. "You first, cousin."

He stepped back, closing the distance between himself and Katiel. "Let me handle him."

"No, let me. I'm here to help you." Katiel's mouth squeezed tight, but there was a fierce determination in her stare that he hadn't seen before. "That's the only reason I came all this way—to help you."

Anton shook his head, knowing—and hating—that she was right. As much as he wanted to protect her, a fellow wielder stood a better chance at defeating Xabius than he did. "To go against him, you must wield whatever comes to mind as quickly as the thought passes. Can you manage that?"

In reply, she wordlessly passed off the featherlight shield and stepped in front of him.

Then she lifted her hand and blew onto the fleck of ore in her open palm.

A vortex of dust swirled around them, the flecks glinting as they spun. Her elegant hands shifted, crafting her target with zeal, like she'd finally come into what she was born to do. Though the merit was not his to claim, pride swelled in his chest all the same.

But a second later, panic washed over him. With this newfound confidence, Katiel was challenging Xabius, a master wielder who'd earned countless victories in duels. She was risking her life for him, and Anton hated that he brought her here. But he had to honor her decision, even as Xabius readied himself to strike.

With a deft twirl of a single hand, the aged wielder expanded the ore and formed it into an axe, the classic type favored by Drezchy warriors. No doubt, this was a requirement of Cezary's for her champion. The Xabius who Anton knew would never make such an impractical choice for a duel, but leave it to his moronic cousins to honor tradition even when their lives depended on it.

Immediately, Xabius passed off the axe to Cezary, who took the weapon with a smirk and charged for them.

"Don't stop," Anton shouted, winding around Katiel to block them both with the shield. "I've got it."

His cousin swung at him with impressive force—much more force than she physically could manage, were it not for the wielded weapon with perfect weight distribution—but the strike was futile. The featherlight shield was wielded as well, and could easily block the attack. She struck again and again, but the axe was useless. Grunting in disgust, she tossed the weapon into the hedges, retreating the twenty feet back to where Xabius actively wielded what Anton could only assume was another weapon.

Anton glanced at Katiel, hoping to catch a breath, but she thrust the pistol she'd been wielding into his hands. He followed her eyeline to Cezary, head ducked as she conferred with Xabius, and Anton was surprised that his cousin would make such a foolish mistake. Cezary knew better than to let her guard down while dueling with him, and yet, it was hard to bring himself to attack her when she wasn't even looking.

"Now," Katiel whispered, and Anton couldn't help but gape at her. Killing someone—anyone—was the last thing Katiel would ever want, and he wondered at what his court had turned her into in such a short time. "Anton, now."

He gulped and did as she instructed, telling himself it was to protect Katiel. There would be plenty of time to feel guilty later, when they'd survived.

He raised his hand, finger on the trigger. He wasn't a fantastic shot—he hadn't practiced on the training field with Sera in years—but at point-blank range, there was no way he would miss.

But just as he fired the round, Xabius glanced up. When he saw him there, pistol drawn, the wielder launched into action, his decades of experience showing through. Anton realized now that he hadn't been forming a weapon at all, but a shield of his own. It was as wide as the path through the hedge maze, and Xabius raised the metal into place before the bullet reached them. The bullet ricocheted off the surface, careening sideways into the hedge.

Anton cursed under his breath and leaned over to Katiel, drawing his lips close to her ear. "We're at a stalemate with ordinary weapons. We need something else. Let's try the—"

"Anton, look out!" Katiel screeched.

He whipped his head up to see Cezary charging him once again, this time brandishing a sapphire-hilted dagger. He was so foolish, making the same mistake as Cezary had moments before. If he hadn't become so obnoxiously moral, he would have already taken her out when he had the chance.

Just before his cousin reached him, Anton squared his stance, ready to take her on, but Katiel leaped sideways at the last moment, apparently about to push him out of the way. In the clash, Cezary's dagger sliced down the length of Katiel's arm in a single swipe.

Katiel collapsed to the ground, and Anton felt a surge of panic course through him. Clearly, that was no ordinary dagger.

Acting on pure adrenaline, he picked up Cezary's discarded axe and sliced the blade toward his cousin. In his rage, he barely nicked her, but it was enough for him to push her back a few paces.

By her side, Xabius drew his hand to his mouth, preparing to wield. But before he could, Anton surged forward and wrapped his fingers around the wielder's amulet. Xabius gasped as Anton wrenched the chain from his neck, and Anton tucked the pendant in his pocket. As expected, the out-of-practice wielder couldn't last even a second without his source, and the elderly man crumpled to the ground, immediately immobilized and gasping for breath. When Cezary spun to him in alarm, Anton seized the moment to check on Katiel.

She was lying flat on her stomach, the pitiful sight enough to send Anton into a blind fury. But she needed him, so he crouched down to her and placed a gentle hand on her back.

"I'm fine," Katiel mumbled, the weakness in her voice betraying her words. She tried to push up onto her hands and knees, but one of her elbows buckled in the attempt, sending her face into the dirt path.

No, no, no, no.

Anton launched forward, grabbing her and hauling her into his arms. To put distance between them and Cezary, he carried Katiel to the far end of the open space. Gently, he lowered her down into a seated position, propping her back against the hedges.

"Don't bother," Cezary called across the clearing, spinning her dagger by the hilt in triumph. "The blade's poison-tipped. With a gash like that, she's done for."

The malice in her voice, Anton knew, was for him alone. She was making him suffer in the way he'd made her suffer, by hurting those most dear. It had been thoughtless, detestable of him, to reveal to her—and everyone at court—that Katiel was important to him.

"Stay still," he ordered, ignoring his cousin as he gingerly turned Katiel's arm to survey the wound. Beneath the blood-soiled shreds of her sleeve, the deep gash ran from her wrist to her elbow. It was shallow, just enough to break the skin.

"My hand," she said, the words thick with the pull of unconsciousness. "I can't feel my hand."

"Stay with me." He leaned over her, shaking her shoulders as roughly as he dared in her fragile condition. "Keep yourself awake."

In desperation, he pressed his lips to either side of the wound, sucking out the poison as best he could before he spit it onto the dirt.

"That won't work," Cezary drawled as she stalked over to them, leaving the helpless Xabius lying in the grass. "I'll let you get up, though, to make it a fair fight. Unlike some people," she added with a bite, "I don't strike cousins who can't defend themselves."

The words stung, he had to admit. Cezary had every reason to hate him for what he'd done to her brothers. He didn't blame her.

Suddenly, his cousin let out an ear-splitting shriek, followed by a horrific squelch. Anton whipped around to the sound, shifting closer to Katiel as he assessed the new threat—Ludvig.

Beneath his oversized foot lay Cezary, unmoving on the ground, with her glazed eyes still open. The brute pressed his boot into her abdomen for leverage as he dislodged his axe from her skull and wiped the blade clean with the edge of his tunic.

The sting of bile rose in his throat upon seeing Cezary's lifeless eyes, but Anton forced himself to look away, even knowing he'd never forget the sight as long as he lived. Ludvig, on the other hand, bore a satisfied grin as he turned his attention to Anton, still bent over Katiel.

"Figures I'd find you like this," Ludvig said, exaggeratedly crossing his arms. "Though I have no idea what she'd see in someone so scrawny."

Katiel was still breathing steadily, so Anton got to his feet, blocking her with his wide stance in case Ludvig tried to harm her. "I'd prefer it if you spoke less," Anton said, forcing a false yawn. "It's like conversing with a mule."

He wiped the trickle of poison and blood from his tingling mouth with the back of his hand, about to fire off a second insult, but then a thought occurred to him. With Cezary and Yaro eliminated, they might be the only competitors left. "Where are Halina and Signy?"

"Halina murdered Signy," Ludvig replied bitterly, his care for his sister making him far more relatable than Anton was comfortable with. "So, I killed Halina. Just like I'm about to kill you."

His cousin took up a fighting stance with his axe bared, while Anton raised a brow. Ludvig wasn't the brightest gaslamp on the street, but surely he understood the rules of the tournament. "Then we're the only two left," Anton said. "The second round is over."

"Or I could end you right here," Ludvig replied, shooting a quick glance toward Katiel as he edged closer. "It should be easy, now that you don't have your little wielder to save you."

Anton frowned, making a show of looking from left to right. "That's interesting. I don't see a champion with you at all." He paused, scratching his chin for effect. "Perhaps no one was willing to spend that much time with you?"

The jab was disappointing—he knew he could do better—but from the sneer on Ludvig's face, Anton still struck a nerve.

"Oh, I have a champion alright," Ludvig ground out, tossing his axe between his hands. "And it's someone I picked out especially for you."

Anton's veins turned to ice as a broad-shouldered young man wearing wire-framed glasses stepped out of the maze-cast shadow, his hands clasped in front of him and his face entirely passive.

"Simeon?" Anton asked, cocking his head to the side as he looked between him and Ludvig. "I thought the champions had to agree to help their sponsor."

But his friend tilted his head down to sneer at Anton over the rim of his frames, unwavering in his cool demeanor. "I did agree," Simeon said, with a bite to his voice that Anton didn't recognize. "But I'm not surprised you didn't figure it out. You've always underestimated me."

33

Katiel

Katiel squinted at the scene before her, trying to make sense of it all through her poison-induced haze. Anton and Ludvig stood opposite each other, which made perfect sense...but Simeon was there as well.

At first, she thought Ludvig's champion might have been someone who simply looked like Simeon. With his tan skin, close-cut black facial hair, and thick glasses, she assumed it had to be someone else, but then he turned and gave her a better look. It was definitely Simeon, Anton's closest friend, who had traveled throughout A'slenderia and Bar Kur with them before he lost his memory in the harrowing train crash. Perhaps that had something to do with him working with Ludvig—but what, she couldn't say.

"I don't understand," Anton was saying, echoing Katiel's thoughts. "Why would either of you want to work together?"

"Simple," Ludvig said, his small mouth stretching into a sinister smile. "He promised to let me keep the crown when I do this!"

Katiel tensed, her confusion at the statement overtaken by Ludvig charging toward Anton with the poison-tipped dagger in hand.

Look out!

She tried to scream the warning, but she couldn't move her lips. The lingering effects of the poison left Katiel immobile, and she helplessly watched as Simeon lunged forward. He swiped the dagger from Ludvig's grasp as casually as if he were plucking a dandelion, before whipping around and plunging the dagger into Ludvig's chest.

Simeon shoved his weight into the blow, and the blade sliced clean, burying itself to the hilt.

"Oh, thank the heavens," Anton breathed, and Katiel inwardly cheered, overwhelmed with relief that Simeon was here to help. Then the scholar pushed Ludvig off of his blade, and a torrent of blood poured from his chest where the dagger had been.

Katiel momentarily closed her eyes, hoping she could somehow erase the image from her mind if she looked away fast enough. But when she opened them not a second later, the scene was somehow cast in shadow.

The color drained from Ludvig's face, surely from the immense blood loss, and Anton stepped closer to Simeon as he gestured in her direction.

"Can you help Ka—?" he started to say, but just as suddenly as he'd attacked Ludvig, Simeon was upon Anton, the same dagger poised at the prince's back.

Clearly feeling the tip, Anton froze, and his friend tutted from his place behind him. "Underestimated me again, Anton."

Simeon's low voice was laced with venom, a stark change from his normal demeanor.

The recognition that washed over Anton's face was immediately followed by pure confusion. He tried to turn and look at his friend, but Simeon halted him, jutting the blade in closer.

"Eh, eh, eh," he chided. "Stay right where you are."

Katiel sucked in a breath, trying to piece together what was going on. She tried to muster enough strength to crawl to them, but her body was still entirely numb.

"Simeon..." Anton drew the name out, clearly searching for the words. "I don't understand."

"What's not to understand?" With his free hand, Simeon flicked an imaginary speck of dust from the shoulder of his brown suit jacket.

With one hand remaining on the dagger, Anton should have been able to evade his friend's grasp, but he didn't budge. The only explanation was that he didn't believe Simeon would hurt him.

"The Conclave was an effective way to weaken the throne," Simeon continued, "but none of the Dvorsky can survive. It's nothing personal. You're by far the most tolerable of the lot."

Anton craned his neck in an attempt to look at him again, but Simeon flexed his grip in warning.

"I still don't understand," Anton said, the words coming out choked in his strained position.

"There are a lot of things you don't understand," Simeon said, his mouth twisting into an eerie grin. "Starting with the fact that you've known 'the boss,' as you called him, very well all this time. And he certainly wasn't Vadim."

Anton's brow crinkled as he looked between his friend and cousin. "Ludvig? The mastermind behind a continental war? There's no way."

"Not him, you dolt!" Simeon snapped back, his cool façade momentarily cracking before he sniffed and leveled his tone once again. "Me. It was me. I was the mastermind. I was 'the boss.' I've been planning everything out, all this time, and you never once suspected me."

Katiel's eyes widened. She couldn't have heard that right.

"I always hated that nickname, by the way," Simeon said, still holding his dagger to Anton's back, yet conversing as if they were having a chat over afternoon tea. "Leave it to that moron Taregh to give me such an insipid moniker."

"No," Anton said, forcefully shaking his head. "It can't be. I refuse to believe it."

If she could have moved her neck, Katiel would've nodded along. She couldn't believe it either. There was a palpable love between these two lifelong friends, an almost familial bond that she could feel on both sides whenever they were together. Katiel knew it couldn't be a mere manipulation.

But Simeon only scoffed, his contempt focused on Anton alone. "Use that big brain of yours and *think.* You made me your emissary. You gave me signing permissions on the royal accounts and allowed me to seal letters in your stead on the Dvorsky letterhead. You made me the second-in-command of your ship, for Creator's sake, and you never even suspected me!"

"I *trusted* you," Anton spat. "There's a difference."

"You never paid attention to anything I was doing, and it cost you." Simeon jutted the dagger forward the slightest bit. Anton winced in response, but since he was still standing, it might not have pierced the skin.

"First, I got in the king's ear," Simeon continued, "hinting at how noble it would be to call a Conclave until he eventually thought it was his idea. I meticulously convinced him how much it would increase his power to be free of all the other royals, when really, it would only weaken the throne enough for me to take over."

Slowly—but strangely—it started making sense. Anton's offhanded comments from the past few weeks rushed back to Katiel, the gears finally clicking into place.

There's just one thing that doesn't add up: how my uncle came up with such an elaborate plan, considering he's an absolute idiot.

Simeon's the smartest person I've ever met.

"Then," Simeon went on, "I orchestrated Sera and Nev's breakup with some convincingly timed misunderstandings, and encouraged Sera to get away to A'slenderia. Once she was gone, I used the royal letterhead to write to her as Nev—I am quite skilled at forgeries, you know. Sera went along with everything, even corresponding with General Taregh of Bar Kur and trailing after Mara, just to win back her precious Nev, because Sera thought your sister was 'the boss.'"

Simeon tsked, as if a misguided bid for love was somehow worse than a deliberate bid for war. "And that just left you. All we had to do in A'slenderia was find some ore for me to experiment with, and my plan would've been complete. I even pointed out Katiel's necklace that day in the tavern. But you just had to mess it up with your usual antics and start a fling with the first girl you saw. It was terribly hard to eliminate those girls with you always lurking around. In fact, I had to fake amnesia to get you to listen to me and leave them, and by the time we finally left Kerafin, it was nearly too late."

Simeon shot a glare in Katiel's direction, his poised dagger never wavering, and she felt she was going to be physically ill. All the revelations swirled together with the poison to form a nauseating concoction in her mind, too clouded to form a single coherent thought. Simeon hadn't just known the truth from the beginning. He'd orchestrated everything, from swiping Katiel's necklace that very first day to the train crash.

"Then why did you become Ludvig's champion?" Anton asked, the question coming out hollow. "Why not just let him finish me off in the final round?"

"Because he was the strongest competitor," Simeon said, his voice still void of any emotion, "and I needed to ensure that I was the one to kill you."

Anton opened his mouth as if to speak again, but no words came out, or at least nothing that Katiel could discern. She grunted, straining against her weakened limbs to reach them and hoping Simeon didn't truly have the heart to go through with it.

But then, Simeon's lips moved, and Katiel could swear he said, "I'm sorry."

Right before he drove the blade deep into the back of the man she loved.

Anton didn't make a sound.

Simeon yanked out the dagger, wiping the blood off on his trousers like it was nothing more than a rain-soaked umbrella. Anton fell forward, arms splaying futilely to catch himself before he crashed into the dirt, while his former friend looked on with an uncontainable smile, like this was all a game to him. Like he hadn't just murdered his lifelong friend.

She squeezed every muscle in her body, trying to run to him, trying to move at all, but all she felt was the same dull sting of the poison throbbing through her veins. Anger coursed through her, driving out every rational thought as she watched the love of her life lying limp for the second time.

In that moment, Katiel hated Simeon, and she truly wanted to end him.

Never once had she even come close to thinking such a thought before, and the thorns of shame crept up on her, pricklier than the maze they were standing in. She could understand now how these people became so vicious—one horrible encounter, one hateful thought at a time.

"As for you," Simeon said, turning to her with a snap of his fingers. "Guards."

From the edge of the octagon, two burly men stepped into view from the shadows. It took Katiel a second to register they weren't coming to collect Anton, but her.

She shrieked, trying again to will herself to stand, will her arms to lift, and will her muscles to obey her command. But it only took a few paces before two Drezchy royal guards were upon her, lifting her between them while pinning her hands to ensure she couldn't wield. Internally, she gave a wry scoff—as if she would even know what to wield in this situation—but it did give her hope. If Simeon had instructed them to do that, then he must think the numbness would wear off soon.

Aloud, all she could muster was a weak demand. "Let me go."

Simeon didn't bother with a reply. Instead, he took up the poison-tipped dagger and walked over to her. As he lifted the dagger to Katiel's neck, he emotionlessly said, "You're going to feel a pinch. Can't have you regaining movement in the carriage ride."

Katiel's brows knitted together, unsure what he was referring to, but the thought was fleeting as the tip of the blade pricked her skin.

"Don't worry, though," Simeon said as he removed the metal from her flesh. "A minute amount such as this won't kill you, or at least, I don't believe it will."

The promised pinch was followed by a burn, starting at her neck and thrumming throughout her body. It set her pulse alight, but she clenched her jaw, refusing to scream.

Katiel was choking on air. There was nothing reaching her lungs. It was worse than drowning, where at least the grim cold of water could fill her.

Now, she felt absolutely nothing.

And Anton was lying there, unmoving, just out of her reach.

A thousand memories flashed through her mind, all the times she'd had with him and all the times she longed to still. Him staring at her that night in the tavern, him laughing with her across the campfire. Coming to the Yule Valley with her one day, meeting her parents, traveling somewhere new for the first time together.

His smirk, his strong hands, the cashmere musk of his cologne. Staring down his nose at her in that heavy, heady way of his.

All that was gone, and a single tear trailed down her cheek at everything that could've been. The worst part was, she hadn't realized how horribly, completely, and irrevocably she loved him—until it was too late.

34

Dakier

Dakier gulped as he surveyed the crowd before them.

The last time he was in a crowd like this in Bar Kur, he'd been punched solely for his nationality and fled. He'd gone unnoticed so far thanks to Jay's Barkurian-style suit—which he had to walk carefully in to avoid ripping any more seams. His only consolation was that they stood toward the back of the group, so few people would see if he did.

Not a full day had passed since Brenna's article was printed in the Eternal City Gazette, and already a rally had been called in King Stefan's Square to address the situation. Brenna seemed to think it was going to be good news—maybe even a call for peace already—but Dakier feared the worst. He tried his hardest to convince Brenna to lay low for the day, but she wouldn't relent. She was going to this rally with or without him, so he decided it had better be with him—even if that meant his odds of getting beaten up today were unusually high.

A temporary podium had been erected in the center of the square, with little wooden staircases leading up to it on either side. Atop it stood a small-statured, balding man with a gray mustache, shifting his weight nervously from side to side. Dakier recognized him as being one of the lords he'd seen at the welcoming gathering-turned-ambush.

"That's Lord Ovach," Brenna leaned into his side to mutter. "He's probably the least irritating cabinet member."

Dakier quirked a brow. "Is that a good thing or a bad thing?"

"Eh." Brenna shrugged. "I was hoping it would be Steffi."

"Does that mean we can leave?" he half-joked, shooting her a tentative smile.

Brenna only scowled at him. "You can leave. I'm staying."

She crossed her arms, but Dakier was saved from having to think of a clever retort. Another man who he vaguely recognized walked onto the podium, this one burlier and gruffer. He took center stage as the mustachioed lord scurried off to the side.

"Lord Byrne," Brenna muttered, the implication clear that this lord was one of the most irritating.

"We've called you all here today to address—"

Lord Byrne began his statement confidently, the picture of a practiced statesman. But several people in the crowd began shouting over him the second he opened his mouth, drowning out his booming voice. He was obviously trying to address the news about the war's origins, though what he had to say about it remained to be seen.

What was apparent was the Barkurians' stance overall. From all the voices clamoring at once, a clear theme emerged: pure and utter denial.

"Those no-good Tibedese at it again!"

"They're framing our general."

"Our lovely queen would never stoop to such lowly conditions—kidnapped or not!"

Dakier scowled at the last shout, though he couldn't see who it had come from. By his side, Brenna's shoulders slumped.

"They—" she said softly, as though speaking to herself. "They don't believe it. They don't believe Inigo Farro was framed."

"Brenna..." Dakier began, but he may as well have been invisible. Brenna's eyes were glued on the lords, waiting for what they would do next.

It took several minutes for the crowd to die down enough for Lord Byrne to speak again. "As you all have very well heard, an anonymous article was published in the Eternal City Gazette this very morning and set the entire city astir."

"Anonymously, mind you," Lord Ovach chimed in, high-pitched voice ringing out over the massive crowd.

"Rest assured that, on behalf of Queen Stefana, we are looking into these matters and into the allegations," Lord Byrne continued, his bellowing voice rising to the brink as the voices of the crowd yelled over him again. "Do not worry yourselves. While a thorough investigation will be conducted, if these matters were true, the informer—the *Loyalist*, as it were—would come forward himself to substantiate his claims."

"Allegations!" someone called indignantly.

"Whoever pulled this stunt should be hanged!" another cried.

Dakier's eyes went wide. He needed to get Brenna out of here—now.

He looked down, about to say so, only to find an empty space where Brenna had been.

She'd already made it to the outskirts of the crowd, weaving around the people to get to the front. She seemed to be heading for the lords, and Dakier found himself speaking despite her distance away.

"No," he started to say. "Don't—!"

But Brenna had already run up onto the stage.

35

Brenna

Brenna had reached her breaking point.

The lies sickened her past the point of self-preservation. If the anonymity of the article was the problem, she wasn't about to leave this place without revealing her identity to the masses.

She raced around the edge of the crowd, making straight for the wooden steps leading up to the podium. Faintly, she heard Dakier call out to her, but the potential consequences were the farthest thing from her mind. Her bitterness over Henred's and Mara's deaths had been simmering for weeks. At last, it had boiled over into a scalding rage, and she was ready to let herself burn.

There was no turning back as she launched herself up the stairs. Before she knew it, she was standing atop the podium with the two lords watching her, mouths agape. In the crowd, hundreds of faces stared back at her—thousands, even. Her heart thrummed in her chest, seizing in sudden terror at the size of the audience.

Dakier still stood among the crowd, teeth gritted and eyes wide. He looked terrified, and she fleetingly regretted holding onto anger toward him all this time. The look on his face left no shred of doubt of how much he cared for her.

As the lords waited in stunned silence, Brenna frantically tried to remember what she wanted to say.

"It was—" she started, far more weakly than she had hoped. She tried again, shouting to be heard even by the farthest stragglers. "It was I who wrote the article."

A gasp sprang up, like the audience was one person. Then the murmurs grew louder, but she went on, projecting her voice as much as she could.

"My name is Lady Brenna Malley." She paused, sucking in a deep breath. "I was there that day, facing off against General Taregh. He tried to kill me to cover up his deception, but everything I wrote in that article is true. It's all true!"

She looked over the crowd, expecting to see the people murmuring to each other, mulling over her words. Instead, the mob seemed to be inching closer, the scowls deepening on the anonymous faces in the sea of red hair. People were looking straight at her, trying to make eye contact while shouting curses that she couldn't make out from the stage.

Then one shout rang out, louder than the others.

"That's the queen's lady-in-waiting!"

For a moment, the people hushed, and then Brenna's face fell as the cries grew indignant. The roaring reverberated in her ears and drowned out everything except a clear message—their fury was now targeted at her.

For one foolish moment, she actually thought that her admission would be enough—that putting a face to the article would be all it took to persuade the people of its credibility. She saw now that she was being as naïve as ever. These people didn't want the war to end like this, with Bar Kur admitting its mistake and calling for peace. Brenna didn't know how they *did* want it to end, though, and perhaps they didn't either.

"And you call yourself a Barkurian!" an anonymous voice belted from the crowd.

"I'm just as Barkurian as any of you!" she spat, her rage resurfacing with a vigor. She pointedly grabbed a clump of her fiery hair, grateful for her stereotypical appearance. "This"—she gestured now to the crowd—"isn't what it means to be Barkurian. We don't call for unjust and unnecessary wars! It's our own people's lives who are on the line in this."

All this time, Lord Byrne had been watching with his arms crossed, as if waiting for her to dig her own grave. But now, he snapped his fingers, and a royal guard climbed the stairs on her side of the stage.

"Tibedo poses no threat to us!" Brenna projected her voice, clamoring to get the words out before the guard could drag her away. "They want peace! We, the people, just have to agree to it so that the queen knows we're behind her. This rally"—she swept her arm once more—"isn't what King Stefan would've wanted. He was everything that it means to be Barkurian. He stood for honesty, integrity, and justice, and we can, too!"

"Integrity, ha!" Lord Byrne finally interjected, projecting his voice so all could hear. "Tell them how you broke our laws and freed Inigo Farro."

Brenna stuck up her chin, keeping her head held high. "I freed Inigo Farro because he was innocent, and I would do it again."

Her breath caught, another spark of hope flickering as the expressions of the crowd shifted. Momentarily, she wondered if she won them over, but then the shouts began anew.

"Traitor!"

"Traitor!"

The cry rang out, echoing the chant until the group found their rhythm.

Brenna's skin went cold, the blood draining from her face.

Traitor. Traitor. Traitor.

Lord Byrne lowered his voice as he said, "Seize her."

Behind him, Lord Ovach cowered, uneasy—apologetic, even—but he kept his mouth shut.

Without missing a beat, the guard closed in, grabbing Brenna's arms and pinning them behind her back far more roughly than was necessary. She didn't try to resist. She knew this was a risk, and she would go with them willingly. Since Steffi had encouraged her to write the article, Brenna knew the queen would release her.

Then, out of nowhere, the guard slammed her down on her stomach, her forehead colliding with the wooden platform, and she let out an involuntary yelp at the impact. Her head spun, blurs of black flying across her vision.

Just as suddenly as she'd been knocked down, the weight on her back lifted, pulling her arms with it, and she went rolling across the stage. A blur of burgundy soared above her. She scooted back away from the skirmish, trying to make sense of what she was seeing.

Before her, Dakier straddled the guard, pinning the large man to the ground between his thighs. He held the man's wrists, rendering his arms immobile at his sides. Dakier, the genteel farmhand and reluctant soldier, had tackled him to the ground.

For her.

"Run!" Dakier shouted as a second guard ascended the stairs, but Brenna wasn't about to leave him in such a state.

Frantically, she scrambled, surveying her surroundings for anything that she could use to help. Byrne and Ovach stepped back, out of harm's way. The latter held up his hands in front of his shoulders in surrender, and when Brenna met his eye, she could've sworn he winked.

He was telling her to go—telling her to run—echoed by Dakier's repeated shouts.

But she couldn't abandon Dakier. It was two against one—maybe more, if any of the bystanders involved themselves. Definitely more, once more guards arrived.

Yet Dakier was holding his own.

The man below him wrestled one arm free and struck Dakier, his fist colliding with Dakier's ear as he ducked to the left. The second guard lunged for him from a standing position. For a moment, Brenna feared Dakier would be ripped in two, but he leapt to his feet at the last second, sending one guard tumbling into the other.

"We should be going," Dakier said, swinging Brenna into his arms like a groom holding his bride.

Brenna squealed as he jumped off the back of the stage. They hit the cobblestone, his knees bending low to take the brunt of the impact, but then he peeled off at incredible speed, earning a fresh gasp from the people left in their wake.

She knew he was fast, but she didn't know he was *this* fast.

He set her down and grabbed her hand as he weaved through the narrowest alleyways he could find, but she didn't object, holding tight to him as she ran with all her might.

He paused after he turned down an alley cloaked in shadow, still not letting go of her hand. Neither of them dared to move for minutes, lest someone who trailed them remained lurking nearby. Brenna was pretty sure they'd lost anyone following them, but she supposed it didn't hurt to be cautious. In the meantime, every point where her body had made contact with him while he'd held her was buzzing.

"That was exhausting," Dakier said as he finally released her hand. His definition of exhaustion must have been very different from Brenna's, though, because his breaths came out steady and controlled, with no sheen of sweat on his brow.

Brenna looked around at the nondescript alley. "Where did you take us?"

"I just ran blindly," Dakier said, rubbing at the back of his neck. "I think we're in the same area we wound up in after the rainstorm."

"Aye, you're right," Brenna said, her head swiveling as she surveyed their surroundings. "Do you think you could get us to the hostel? That might be a good place to hide out and think of a plan."

Dakier nodded and headed down the alley, Brenna following as quietly as she could to avoid detection. It turned out they were only one block from the hostel, and when they entered the lobby, the innkeeper was as unbothered as she'd been the first time around. She didn't even tell them which room was theirs. Instead, she plopped a key in Dakier's hand and went back to her newspaper—the Eternal City Gazette.

Brenna knew she desperately needed to sort things out with him, and more than needed, she wanted to. She wanted to be friends with him again, at the very least.

As they made their way up the stairs and down the hall, she hastily tried to plan what to say. Brenna took a deep breath as they crossed the threshold into their room, but Dakier spun around to face her at the same moment, his words coming out all in a rush.

"Brenna, listen—I'm sorry if what I did just now made things any worse for you. Truly, I don't know what I was thinking, tackling a royal guard." He combed a hand through his hair, huffing more than he had while sprinting. "And I know I went against my vow of nonviolence...again..."

Until that moment, it hadn't even occurred to her that his defense of her went against his belief in pacifism. As the full weight of what he had done set in, she struggled to find the words to express her gratitude. "You...you attacked them. For me."

"I couldn't watch them harm you." He shook his head. "When he slammed you down, something came over me. I couldn't let you get hurt."

Brenna stepped closer. "Thank you." A smile spread across her face as she looked up at him. "It means a lot that you would do that for me."

Dakier drew in a breath, his gaze never leaving hers.

"I would do anything for you."

His dark eyes shone with complete sincerity, and she knew he meant it. He truly would do anything for her. It was what she needed, what she had always wanted in a partner—someone she could rely on through anything.

He stood so close, yet she wanted to be closer. All it would take was a stroke of her finger against his cheek, a tilt of her head, and her lips would be on his.

But even though every fiber of her being was telling her not to, she turned away and said instead, "Let's leave Ballynach at nightfall."

36

Anton

"Anton, stay with me."

A light pressure rapped against his cheek, a palm—

Anton blinked groggily, trying to open his eyes, but it felt as if his eyelids were made of sand, slipping just beyond his control.

The hand slapped him again, harder this time. "Stay with me, Anton. Wake up."

His head pounded, and a strange pressure weighed on all sides of his chest, as if a snake were actively constricting around his abdomen. An unsettling mixture of mud and damp sand soaked into his suit in splotches, and Nev's pale face hovered above him.

"Oh, thank it all," she muttered as the darkness around them slowly settled into shapes.

Rectangular hedges surrounded him in every direction.

The maze. He was still in the Creator-forsaken maze.

The distant crowd was gone, an eerie silence hanging over the arena that was filled with shouts and jeers not long ago. Judging by the position of the full moon overhead, little time had passed since Simeon had stabbed him.

"Where's Katiel?" he croaked out, sending a searing pain throughout his back and ribcage.

"You need to flip over," Nev said, ignoring his question. "You have a punctured lung. I need to administer a healing tonic to the wound."

Anton sucked in a breath before he pressed his hand into the ground for leverage. Nausea wracked over him in waves even with the minimal motion, and his chest felt like it was completely empty. He squeezed his eyes shut as he gave a final push, before he said, "I can't."

"Never mind," Nev said, her flexing jaw betraying her even tone. "I could try to flip you, but I'm not confident it won't reopen the wound. Open your mouth."

His sister lifted a glass flask filled with a glowing cerulean liquid, and Anton let his head fall back as he parted his lips. Even the simple movement was excruciating, but the chemical sting of the tonic as it moved through his body was far worse.

The tendrils of his muscle and flesh ripped into threads, only to weave together again in the span of a second. To cry out in pain was the deepest dishonor, but the burn was such that he was tempted. Only when he felt a drop of blood trickle from his mouth did he realize he'd been biting his lip, but then he clamped down harder to distract himself from the agony coursing through his veins.

This time tomorrow, he told himself, this feeling would cease. In less than an hour—less than five minutes, perhaps—it would be over. He had to focus on enduring it for only a moment longer—

And just like that, it was gone, the shocking ache replaced by a blissful nothingness.

Gingerly, he sat up, reaching toward the wound at his back before he thought better of it and jerked his fingers away.

"Judging from your relatively minor blood loss, I've assessed that the puncture was deep enough to cause internal injury while sealing the exterior, but you mustn't touch the wound," Nev warned, and Anton turned to see her anew. She was sitting on the ground in front of her new chair, her small frame engulfed by her layers of tulle skirts flailed wildly around her. She must have flung herself out of the chair in her haste to get to him, and she maintained the sense of urgency, answering his next question before he even had to ask. "When I saw them leaving the maze, I rushed in to find you."

"When you saw who leave?" Anton asked, his heart pounding.

Nev's eyes shot off to the side, and Anton felt his chest constricting again, now for a far different reason than being stabbed in the lung.

"Who, Nev?"

"Katiel," she whispered, staring unfocused at her cuticles. "They carried her out. She looked so..." She paused, reached up to place her hand over his as if it could cover up the unwelcome memory. "She didn't make it."

"She's..." The stationary maze began to spin around him. "I thought I saved her. I thought I drew out all the poison."

Nev shook her head. "I don't know. I didn't see that part. I just saw guards carrying her limp body out of the maze."

Anton leaned forward, his open palms smacking the ground as he closed his eyes.

"She saved you again, you know," Nev went on, moving her hand to rest on Anton's shoulder. "It was her wielded healing tonic formula from the first trial that I replicated and kept handy for today, and I couldn't have made it to the center of the maze with my old chair. You know how it was going over roots—"

Nev was softly stroking his upper arm, trying to reassure him even as her own breath caught every few words, but he was no longer comprehending what she said. He was fully immersed in his thoughts, and one rose above the rest.

Simeon did this.

Simeon prevented him from saving Katiel. He kept him from tending to her, kept him from being there with her in her final moments.

Simeon, his lifelong friend, one of the precious few people he loved in this world, had betrayed him in the worst way imaginable. And now Katiel—no, he wouldn't let himself think of Katiel. If he didn't think of her, she could still be frolicking in a field somewhere in his mind, and he couldn't bear to imagine anything else.

Instead, he got to his feet and helped his sister back into her chair before he said, "I'm going after him."

"Going after who?" Nev asked, pushing up with her arms to adjust herself into a more comfortable position.

"Simeon."

He gritted his teeth as he bit out the name, but when he caught his sister's eye, there was a strange glint there.

"Simeon?" she repeated.

"Yes, Simeon. *My* Simeon," Anton added bitterly. "This is his doing. The Barkurian king's assassination, that Tibedese man being framed, inciting Uncle to call the Conclave—all of it. He admitted it himself."

Nev paused, briefly pulling at the edge of her cuticle before she returned her hands to her lap. "I know."

Anton stepped over a tall root jutting across the path, his sister's admission hitting him only after a delay. But then he stopped in his tracks and whirled around to her so abruptly that his calves collided with her knees.

"What did you know?" he asked, ignoring the fresh ache along his shins. "Why didn't you tell me?"

"I knew he started the war," his sister admitted, unable to meet his eyes. "When Sera returned from Kerafin just after you, she figured out the truth and told me, but—"

Anton waited, trying to control his ragged breaths, but his cheeks burned when she didn't continue. "But *what*?"

"But I didn't tell you because I wanted him to reclaim our lands!" she shouted, flinging both hands in the air in frustration. "Uncle didn't let me take the title of crown princess just because of my condition. Uncle didn't let me participate in the Conclave. Do you really think he would've taken the Blood Raven in a few months? I certainly didn't believe it, and neither did Simeon. The Conclave was just an excuse for more cruelty, and yet the Drezchy public loves him!"

Anton didn't need any more reminding of their cruel uncle, and if his own sister would defend Simeon after he literally stabbed him in the back, then Anton really didn't care to discuss this further. But he needed to know everything Nev knew before he left.

"I get it. We all hate the king," he said through gritted teeth, "but what does that have to do with taking over Kerafin or reclaiming our homeland?"

"Don't you see?" Nev exclaimed, her hands flying through the air for a second time. "What is the one thing our dear Vadim promised year after year, but never made any move to do? Taking back our homeland. Simeon wants to be the king, and you never wanted it, and he's certainly capable. This is the best way to overthrow our Uncle Vadim for good, and establish a new monarchy with the public's support."

"So, you lied to me?" Anton shook his head, unable to believe what he was hearing. "You helped him try to take the throne from me behind my back?"

"I didn't help him," Nev insisted, though she couldn't meet his eyes. "I didn't know he planned to hurt you. I just didn't tell you what I'd learned."

"Some sister I have," Anton spat, turning on his heel and storming down the hedge-edged path.

"It's not like you asked me!" Nev called after him. "Ever since you've returned—even before you left—you've been treating me like a project to fix, instead of like a sister. Like my condition is so inconvenient to you that you had to intervene without even asking me what I wanted!"

Anton stopped short. The nausea that now roiled in his gut wasn't from a stab wound, or even from the inescapable grief that threatened to overtake his mind if he lent it another thought. It was from this painful truth resonating with him, the truth that had been present in every off look in his sister's eyes that he'd tried to ignore.

Whenever something good came into his life, he always ruined it. Now Katiel was gone, and he was losing his sister, too.

All he could think to shout was, "You're right!"

Nev pushed her head back, her open mouth snapping shut. Whatever she'd been expecting him to say, it clearly wasn't that, and honestly, he didn't blame her.

"You're right," he went on, taking a small step closer to her. "I'm sorry that I treated you like a project to fix...I didn't realize it before, but now that you say it, I can see what you mean. I always do that. I've destroyed every relationship I've ever had, but the woman I love just died, and I need you right now. You're the only person I have left."

Nev was silent for a long moment. "You loved her?"

Anton nodded, wetness dripping down his face that he refused to believe was tears. Perhaps it was a surge of perspiration, concentrated only below his eyes.

"I still do."

"Oh, Anton," Nev said, coming closer and wrapping her arms tight around his middle. "I'm sorry. It's not that I'm not grateful for your help, for what you *both* did for me—"

"No, I understand," Anton said. And though he longed to remain like this, remain in this one moment of peace and let her comfort him as he grieved Katiel for the weeks and months and years to come, he knew he couldn't rest yet.

Anton had a good idea of where Simeon would head next—back to Kerafin. His former friend had proven that he didn't mind ending innocent lives in the quest to get what he wanted, and despite Nev's reasoning, Anton was far from on his side.

Mere weeks ago, he might not have cared. After all, the continent had done little for him, other than exiling his people to a penal colony.

Selfishly, all he wanted was Katiel back in his arms, but if he couldn't have her back, he could at least be someone like Katiel, who cared deeply for even the strangers around her. She had sacrificed everything in her quest to stop this war, and he had to see it through for her sake.

Anton set off again, searching for an exit from the winding maze, with Nev following behind him. Finally, when he spied a break in the hedge, he breathed a sigh of relief and stepped into the field that adjoined the empty viewing berm and the rows of tents for spectators.

"I'm going after Simeon," Anton said, setting his jaw as he turned back to his sister. "I know you sympathized with his plight, but do not even think of trying to stop me."

"I won't. I don't agree with how far he's taken things." Nev woefully shook her head. "I imagine he'll return to Kerafin, now that he believes the Conclave to be over."

Anton nodded, encouraged that she'd come to the same conclusion. "I'll make for the coast."

"You can use a horse from the carriage I took here," Nev offered. "And I'll go back to Karolinum, to try to intercept any correspondence between Vadim and Simeon."

"It's a solid plan," Anton agreed, and his sister led him to a nearby building that he could only assume was the carriage house. In minutes, the horse was saddled and ready to go, with Nev coming up behind to wish him good luck as Anton took the reins.

He edged the horse into a gallop, and after a few long hours, reached the familiar port. The day he'd landed with Katiel, the harbor had been bustling with sailors and shipwrights, but now, it was a ghost town. The eerie emptiness raised the hairs on Anton's arms, but he halted his steed with a forced calm.

The typical merchant ships were nowhere to be seen. In fact, the sole vessel at port was an imposing royal navy vessel, a larger and more elaborate version of the type Anton had last chartered to Kerafin.

Anton inched closer, then ducked behind a crate and narrowed his eyes to survey the clipper more closely. The hull design took on a new life as he noted the unusual angle of the front-most joints, and the position at which the craft floated in the water—notably higher than a ship of its size should be able to.

Anton gritted his teeth. This was *his* ship design. He had devised a plan for a wielded clipper that could traverse the sea in days rather than weeks, and Simeon must have stolen it from his room. Assuming Simeon had found Xabius before the second trial, the wielder would've had plenty of time to go over the plans and create the mercurial craft. Only his closest friend could have found the design in his heaping mess of inventions, and Anton mentally added this theft to Simeon's tally of secrets—a list that seemed to be growing by the minute.

On deck, sailors were raising the sails while dockhands loaded the last of the crates. There was no sign of Simeon, but that stroke of luck likely wouldn't last for long. If Anton was going to make a move, he would have to do it now.

And in true Ghost fashion, he crossed the gangplank and slipped onto the ship unnoticed.

37

Katiel

She assumed the carriage would take her back to the palace, but to Katiel's surprise, when the vehicle halted, a nameless guard dragged her out into Vincencim Harbor, the port she'd arrived at weeks ago.

Though the ride had taken hours, the poison hadn't fully left her system, and he had to carry her to her destination—which turned out to be a ship's stateroom, not dissimilar to the one she'd stayed in on her last voyage. She still couldn't move a muscle below her neck, so the guard placed her on the narrow, quilt-covered bed that took up most of the tiny stateroom. The icy prickle of dread lessened slightly at the familiar accommodation, but then exploded again when the guard closed the door behind him. She hadn't a clue what Simeon had planned for her, but she knew it couldn't be good.

Her mind raced with so many possibilities that she couldn't focus on one. Already, the ship swayed beneath her, indicating they'd set sail. Their destination had to be Kerafin, but she dreaded what he would do with her once they arrived. He might try to force her to wield a weapon—to subdue the people of the continent, perhaps—but surely he knew she would never help him kill innocent people. She would rather die.

Although, if that were to happen, at least her soul could reunite with Anton's.

At the mere thought of him, a hard lump welled in her throat. Tears prickled just behind her lashes, but they never came. She hadn't cried since being carried from that cursed maze, and deep down, she knew why. It was because she hadn't fully let herself believe he was gone.

He'd been stabbed in the back. He'd fallen lifelessly to the ground. Recalling the image felt like a knife was being thrust into her own heart, yet denial crept up on her again, clouding her vision. Somehow, she hoped Simeon had spared him. He was his friend, after all.

If he was gone—if that's what these cruel Drezchy did to their closest friends—then they would have no mercy on her. She couldn't fall into her grief now and mourn Anton. Instead, she needed to think like he would have in her position. She needed to escape.

Strangely, she wasn't tied down. Though the effects of the poison lingered, she imagined it had to wear off at some point. She had to formulate a plan now, so that she could leap into action once the movement returned. If only she could clear her mind and think—

Soft footfalls sounded outside, and before another thought could register, the stateroom door burst open. Simeon, with his wide frame, engulfed the space in shadow as he stepped inside, his normally ignorable presence now more imposing than any of the Dvorsky cousins.

Katiel gave a cursory flex of her jaw, testing if she could move it at all, and licked her chapped lips.

"What do you want with me?" she croaked. She hadn't spoken in hours, and the effort of uttering a single sentence left her feeling even weaker.

"What do you think I want with you?" Simeon asked, reaching for a wall-mounted cabinet above the headboard that Katiel hadn't noticed. He began drawing various items from it—tubes and flasks and beakers. They were the same items Nev had in her laboratory in the palace, which Simeon must have stocked on board for this very purpose.

Katiel longed to bite out an angry remark—to demand how Simeon could do this when Anton had done so much for him—but she held her tongue. If she didn't voice what happened to Anton, she could hold on to her foolish hope that he survived.

"I do not wish to play your guessing games," Katiel said instead. She added as much derision as she could manage, though Simeon didn't seem to notice.

The scholar pulled up a stool by her bedside, and then lifted a long surgical needle to his eyes and flicked at the liquid-filled glass chamber at the top. "To remove air from the mixture," he explained blandly, as though the flicking were more alarming than the six-inch needle about to pierce her flesh.

It was clear Simeon was nothing like Taregh, a weak-minded man who she'd tricked out of information with a simple insult. Simeon was competent and calculated enough to pull all the general's strings, while weakening Bar Kur in the process. But Katiel could be calculated as well, when she had to be, and she knew Simeon had to have his own weaknesses, even if they were hidden deeper under the surface.

"Don't you want to know what I'm doing?" Simeon prodded.

The question reminded Katiel of something Anton would ask, a thought she rejected as rapidly as it came. She needed to stay alert for when she regained feeling in her limbs, and memories of Anton would tear her apart if she let them.

"Fine, I shall tell you," he said, despite Katiel's lack of reply. "This is a concentrated dose of the poison you've already been administered, just enough to keep you sedated for this procedure. Don't worry. You'll be safe, and it shouldn't sting on the way in. If Xabius would've paid closer attention to my notes, the substance in your system would have been refined to the same degree."

"You gave Xabius the formula for this poison?" Katiel asked, the question spilling out despite herself. "Why?"

"Because he asked me to."

It was a non-answer, yet strangely, Simeon said the words with sincerity. The thought occurred to Katiel that, despite the years of planning an elaborate deception, the scholar might not lie outright when confronted.

"Then what do you want with me?"

Simeon lifted Katiel's right arm, the one closer to him, and placed it atop a pillow. Watching him move the limb was beyond disconcerting, the lack of feeling giving Katiel the eerie impression her body was not her own.

"Isn't it obvious?" he asked, tying a thin rope around Katiel's arm. "The ore."

If she could move her neck normally, she would've shaken her head, but all Katiel could muster was a weak question. "What will you do with it? You cannot wield it."

The scholar adjusted his glasses before he lifted the needle again, which was as long as Katiel's longest finger and wide enough in diameter to see the opening from a foot away. Simeon pressed his lips together in concentration before he slid the metal into the back of Katiel's hand. Immediately, a stream of blood rushed into the tube, before he clicked a clamp into place to keep it from pulling more. Katiel imagined it would feel cold where the metal touched her skin, with a rush of warmth when the blood was drawn. Dismally, she couldn't feel anything at all.

"I cannot wield it *yet*," Simeon said, raising his index finger with the last word.

As if in explanation, Simeon hung a cloth bag above them from a hooked metal rod before he jabbed a matching needle in the back of his hand. It was attached to a tube identical to Katiel's, both of which connected to the bag.

The purpose of this apparatus was evident, but Katiel's shock led her to ask the obvious. "You're going to siphon my blood?"

"In a manner of speaking," Simeon answered drily, as though his patience with Katiel's inferior intellect was growing thin. "The bag will create a pressure deficit, which, along with the help of gravity in this position, will allow your blood to transfer directly to me. It's a transfusion of blood, a new procedure that I've invented expressly for this purpose. You see, a few years ago in my research, I came across a discovery."

Katiel waited wide eyed for him to continue. The transfusion, as he called it, had not yet begun, and Katiel could only hope that it would leave her alive in the end. Surely, *surely*, Simeon would not do such a thing outside of the Conclave, but if he could stab his closest friend—

"Growing up a mere librarian's son in the Drezchy royal court, I longed to become something greater," Simeon explained, adjusting his glasses with his free hand. "I longed to step out of Anton's shadow, and I knew I could, you see, if I only thought about it long and hard enough—I was very naïve when I was young."

Katiel thought that, at only eighteen, Simeon was still very young, but she didn't say a thing as the scholar spun his tale.

"It was that foolish optimism that drew me to the wielders. They held the very essence of possibility in their hands. So, once I began my studies, they were my prime subjects. First the court wielders, and then any wielder I heard of passing through the area. There weren't all that many, to be sure, but the descendants of refugees from Kerafin amounted to enough subjects."

An odd itch crept up behind Katiel's ears at being referred to in such a way, like she was less than human. Or perhaps Simeon saw all people as subjects for study. Perhaps since he'd often been treated as less-than by the royals he envied, he didn't see the merit in treating others any better.

"I discovered," Simeon went on, pride touching his voice at the declaration, "that the wielders' blood is fundamentally different from that of an ordinary human. I found it by viewing samples from every specimen on a microscopic magnification device. One of Anton's inventions, actually. The wielders always fascinated us both." He took a wistful pause, and Katiel imagined that possibly—just possibly—he felt remorse. But then he continued without another word about the prince. "At first, I theorized that if I wanted to wield, I had to find raw ore to infuse into my blood stream.

"Under the pretense of aiding me with general research, Nev smuggled meager stores of ore for me from the royal vault, a resource I'd thought completely depleted on our continent. It wasn't much, but it was enough for me to run tests. And what I found was that the infusion of ore into the bloodstream did not have the desired effects. The unique blood of the wielders was not something I could replicate." He halted again to survey Katiel. "I assume you know now where I'm heading with this."

Katiel leveled him with a stare that she hoped was at least vaguely threatening. "You believe if you transfer my blood to yourself, you'll be able to wield."

"Very good."

With his free hand, Simeon removed the clamp on the tubing and grabbed the lever attached to the transfusion apparatus. When he turned it a quarter of the way, Katiel's blood seeped into the clear tube at a frightening velocity. She held her breath, waiting for the discomfort to come, but she still couldn't feel anything. Meanwhile, Simeon continued his explanation like it was all a casual, everyday procedure. Like Katiel could survive any amount of blood loss, which she was most certain she could not.

"It has long been thought that the ability to wield is passed down hereditarily, but I found nothing biological to support that notion in all my testing. One day, in his own studies, Anton came across a key fact that I hadn't paid attention to before—travelers' reports of the unusual water quality in the Northern Mountains of A'slenderia, the region where wielders traditionally hailed from.

"I went down the map, charting out all the hometowns of the known wielders in our library records—Ilga, Oskar, Jurgen, Xabius, your own parents, in fact—and came to an intriguing conclusion. They each grew up in towns with runoff from the largest glacier in the world—the Icemark."

The Icemark—where the Creator was said to have formed all of Endra at the dawn of time, conjuring a universe from nothing but dust.

It was strangely not unlike wielding, Katiel noted before she felt a twinge of shame at the mere thought. Surely she did not, could not, liken herself to a god. Yet the power called to her, unyielding, and that did not seem quite so horrible. Anton had reminded her again and again that she could create anything.

The steady draw of her blood brought her back to the present, the crimson still flowing freely. Some god she was, she thought drily, lying there helplessly as a man stole her power.

"Thus, my current theory," Simeon continued, unphased by the blood-curdling procedure underway before him, "is that the wielder's blood is fundamentally altered after ingesting the ore-laden glacial water for a prolonged period—several years, at least. But I, of course, do not have that long. And that's where you come in."

You could have had that long, Katiel wanted to say. *You could have waited.*

In fact, Simeon could have done so many other things. He could have moved to the Yule Valley and tested his theory over time while devoting his life to science. But he wasn't merely interested in research. After a life of playing second to Anton, he wanted power, and to get it, he was using the only weapon he had—his intellect.

"My theory is that, when the wielder comes into their ability and their blood transforms, they must either continue to drink the water, or keep the ore on their person...but I'm beginning to think you're no longer interested in my tale," Simeon said, pursing his lips into an almost-pout. "Am I boring you?"

"Not at all." Katiel spoke quickly—perhaps too quickly—but she did not want him to stop talking, lest he reveal a crucial flaw in his plan that she might exploit.

"Very well—or rather, *bestien shud.*" The scholar gave a little knowing smile, and Katiel internally seethed that he dare use her language. "I had a feeling you would refuse if I asked directly about the transfusion, so I decided to take the *creative* approach. And, as I discovered after I snuck a sample when you boarded the ship in Afdot Harbor, you just so happen to have a universally transferrable blood type."

He smiled the same way again—a charming, sinister thing—as her blood glugged into the tubing.

Bizarrely, Katiel longed to smile back, and she could not help but wonder if he held a magic of his own, something he had yet to recognize in himself—an ambition that could have been used for good, instead of this...

Katiel's mind was swimming, slipping farther and farther away from her. She ebbed at the edge of consciousness, thoughts blurring at the back of her mind and retreating before they came into focus.

"Simeon..."

"Yes?" he asked blandly.

But she'd already forgotten what she was going to say. It was a suggestion, or a plea to be let go, surely. It was a persuasion she'd constructed when she'd been able to think clearly.

Now her necklace drew her focus—the new one Anton had bought for her—the small, amber heart filled with ore. It was lifting, pulling with a distinct magnetism toward the concentration of her blood.

Tucked into her dress, Simeon could not see it, but Katiel could feel it.

The ore was a lifeforce—*her* lifeforce—and it called out as though protesting the unnatural transfer taking place. Much more than a substance, the ore possessed something that was very like a soul.

And Katiel could feel the movement—which meant she was regaining the ability to feel at all. If she could only hold out longer, she'd be able to escape.

But she'd lost too much blood, and she couldn't think any longer.

38

Katiel

The door creaked open, and Katiel blinked herself awake. It could've been hours or days since Simeon first siphoned her blood—she had no concept of time in the windowless room.

Though she loathed facing Simeon again in this state, she was certain her legs would turn to jam if she managed to work herself upright. The most she could manage was remaining alert, her mind swimming inside itself with even that minimal effort.

Light flowed into the pitch-black room through the now-open doorway, and the sights pieced together as if in a dream. A figure stepped in, dragging a cloak against the floorboards. A swish of long, black hair flashed in her vision.

But Simeon didn't have long hair.

And he didn't wear a cloak.

"Sera?" Katiel cocked a brow, taken back to the first time Sera showed up unexpectedly. In fact, it seemed like that was the only way she showed up at all, and it was grating on Katiel's nerves. "Are you working for Simeon now? He said he tricked you into believing Nev was behind the war."

"I figured out the truth when I returned to New Drezchy," Sera explained, keeping her voice low, "and once I'd learned his secret, it was either join him or find a sword in my own back."

"I see you're back to looking out for yourself," Katiel spat. "Anton didn't deserve the dagger in his back either, but neither of you looked out for him."

Sera clenched her jaw, clearly not expecting this new, bitter side of Katiel. Perhaps witnessing her love murdered and then having her power drained until she was an inch from death had that effect on a person. Though the numbness of the poison had long since worn off, Katiel was still so weak from blood loss that she strained as she pushed herself up to a seated position.

"What have you come for, then?" Katiel asked, biting back a slew of curses. "To do his bidding and steal more of my blood? I must warn you; I do not know that I'll live much longer at the current rate, assuming he wants to keep me long term."

Sera flinched, the words having their intended effect. "Just listen," she said, turning up her palms. "I am begging you."

"Go on," Katiel said flatly. "It isn't like I can leave."

"Now you know of Simeon's role in weakening the continent," Sera began, to which Katiel merely nodded, "but I doubt you know how well he succeeded. All the troops normally stationed at the coast to guard the ports have been moved to the Barkurian border, to try salvaging whatever ground Tibedo can against Bar Kur. Even with the reinforcements, Tibedo is losing badly."

Katiel nodded once again, a humiliatingly difficult feat from her awkward, reclined position. Last she'd heard, the continental war was at a stalemate. The A'slenderian army had kept the Barkurian soldiers from advancing into Tibedo, but their forces weren't large enough to defeat Barkurians entirely. This information was nothing new, and Katiel did not want Sera to witness her in her pathetic state any more than necessary. "What else?" she asked, not bothering to hide her impatience. "What did you learn?"

"He plans to attack a settlement on the coast, a village called Pizemac." Sera didn't fidget, didn't pace the room like Katiel longed to. She'd always been too controlled for that. But a muscle ticked over and over in her jaw, which for her was a terrible sign—and enough for Katiel to believe her. "Simeon doesn't care that it's a civilian settlement."

Katiel sucked in a breath, though even that felt shallow. Her head was still foggy, but Sera's urgency helped her focus. Thinking through it all, one word stood out in her mind—one piece that did not quite fit as neatly in the picture as she would like.

"Did you say 'Pizemac?'"

Sera cocked her head ever so slightly. "Yes...though I'm not familiar with it. Does the name mean something to you?"

It did. Pizemac was Dakier's hometown. Katiel herself had never been there, but from the way he described it, it was nothing more than a small fishing village.

"No," she lied. "It means nothing. I've never heard of it."

"I know it's the nearest port to the mines," Sera supplied. "Officially, they primarily mine for crude oil, but for years, rumors have spread that the mines in south Tibedo actually harvest the ore. It seems Simeon believes it to be true—or at least wants to investigate for himself."

"So, you overheard all this, and you came to tell me. Why?" Katiel asked, her frustration spilling over. Even with her limited mobility, her hands had formed fists without her notice. Her nails drew little crescents of blood on her palms. *A waste of a valuable resource,* she thought bitterly. "Why don't you tell someone who can do something about it?"

"You *are* the person who can do something about it," Sera insisted, her hands clasping and unclasping with nerves. "You're the only person who can."

And with that ominous statement, she was gone. Her silky hair and cloak swished from the space in tandem, and the door swung shut without a sound.

In her delirium, Katiel wondered if she'd really been there at all. Then Anton's words came back to her, the memory now like a loved one's embrace.

You can do anything.

It was the salve she desperately needed.

You. Anything.

She'd never believed him, not really. Sure, she could wield anything made of metal—even other materials, if she trained, but this was the first time she'd truly let the truth sink in.

She could wield anything in the universe—and *anything* was exactly what she needed. If she could wield a magical object to transmit a message to the continent, even across the open ocean, she could warn the people of Pizemac before the city was destroyed.

What she needed was a magical quill, one that would transfer what she wrote directly to the recipient.

The thought of wielding such a creation threatened to fill her with dread—but this time, she let it.

She let the panic come, let every emotion come as it may. Adrenaline, once a detested intruder, was now a tolerated guest, and she let it propel her up onto her elbows. From there, she pushed up to a seated position. Though her vision swam with blotches of ink, she felt invigorated, like a storm had struck lightning through her heart. And it was that lightning that would see her through to the end.

Her racing thoughts, normally a distraction she loathed, now came to her aid. She could run through every possibility, every option in rapid succession.

A letter to the A'slenderian authorities.

But no one would believe her.

A letter to Queen Stefana of Bar Kur, who would believe her thanks to Katiel having saved her from captivity.

But contacting an enemy nation's sovereign first would be treason.

A letter to her father.

Whose only concern would be getting Katiel home safe.

A letter to Brenna.

Who somehow, despite all odds, would figure something out to save the town. Katiel had absolutely no doubt about it—Brenna would find a way. As soon as she thought of it, her mind was set on Brenna. Her dearest friend was the one who Katiel needed to tell—and there was no time to lose.

Fortified by her renewed hope, she jolted herself upright. She swayed on her feet, catching herself on the footpost of the bed with a wobbly hand. Ink clouded her vision again, but she blinked it away.

Her idea was simple. Instead of writing on a sheet of parchment before her, she could wield this quill to write on the wall nearest Brenna, so her friend would be sure to see the message.

Although it sounded far-fetched at first, the more she visualized it, the more the concept solidified in her mind. She could wield it, so long as she had one morsel of ore.

Katiel's hand flew to her collar, grasping for her amber necklace. The tiny heart was still there, the comforting shape distinct beneath her fingertips, and she wondered why Simeon hadn't taken it from her. It was a given that the cunning man had noticed it. Most likely, he wanted Katiel to remain healthy enough for the procedure, but strange as it may be, Katiel could not shake the notion that the scholar was testing her, curious to see what she would do.

She would not be surprised if he had a secret spyhole in the room to watch her, and Katiel self-consciously scanned the walls. Her head craned left and right, but upon seeing no visible porthole or crack, she forced herself back to the task at hand.

Let Simeon test her. Perhaps Katiel would pay for what she was about to try, but the chance to save thousands of civilians wasn't an opportunity she could pass up.

Though she was but one person, she could do anything she imagined. She just had to let herself believe it.

Katiel retrieved the pendant, screwed off the metal cap, and plucked out a speck of ore before she replaced the top and let the necklace fall back against her chest. All she needed was a quill—an otherworldly, enchanted quill.

She exhaled the ore, shaping the white feather quill with the intention of writing on the wall closest to Brenna. If he were in her shoes, she knew Anton would have invented a device that was far more interesting, complicated, and foolproof. Still, this would hopefully be enough to transmit her message anywhere, and that was all she needed.

The completed quill fell into her hands, and she wasted no time before starting to write her message across the floor. As she wrote each letter, it disappeared immediately after, and she dared to believe it was being sent to Brenna as she intended.

She released a sigh at having completed the magical quill with relative ease, but just as she began to write, a scratching noise sounded from outside the room. Katiel froze, not daring to breathe until she was sure the threat had passed. If Simeon or one of his lackeys discovered her like this, Katiel didn't know what they would do to her.

So far, she'd written a single word—*Found*—but as the footsteps in the hall faded into the distance, Katiel decided to forgo the detailed message she'd planned. Instead, she kept the missive short, and in no time at all, she'd scrawled out the full message onto the floor.

Another set of footfalls sounded in the hall, clunky and obtuse. Instinct told her it was a guard, with Simeon's quiet, graceful steps close behind.

Hastily, she shoved the quill under the bed, pushing it all the way back against the wall so it wouldn't be spotted. Thankfully, the message disappeared as soon as it was transmitted to Brenna, and no words were now marked on the floor. At least, she desperately hoped it had been sent to Brenna, and she hadn't just risked everything for naught.

Katiel laid back on the bed, and the door opened just as she closed her eyes to feign sleep. In desperation, she prayed her plan would go unnoticed—and she never prayed. Only when the intruder spoke did she dare to crack one eye open.

"What have you been up to, *Geführtchen*?"

For one second, she let herself imagine that it was Anton standing there, resurrected and coming to save her, and not what it truly was—Simeon, in all his cruelty, using Anton's nickname to mock her.

Yet, there he stood, the unassuming friend behind a continental war, preparing to siphon her blood until she fell unconscious.

39

Dakier

"I'm going to do it," Brenna said, marching up and down the length of the pint-sized room.

They'd been hiding out in the hostel for less than an hour now, and Dakier had thought the plan was to wait for nightfall before they headed back to Jay's apartment.

"What do you mean?"

"I'm going back to the castle," she explained, her skirt swishing above her stockinged feet as she continued pacing. "What was I thinking—jumping up on stage? My plan didn't work. I should just go back and ask Steffi what to do next, rather than hiding out here like some kind of criminal."

"The article worked pretty well, I think," Dakier pointed out, hoping to brighten her spirits. She hadn't hesitated before doing the right thing—she never did—and in his eyes, that was something to be proud of. "All of Ballynach knows the truth about the assassination now, thanks to you, and it will likely spread throughout the country soon enough."

"But now I told everyone it was me!" she exclaimed, splaying both palms in emphasis. "The Barkurian people hate me. They'll probably throw tomatoes at me in the streets for years to come, but I can't hide forever! Without Steffi's help, I won't be able to get out of the city unnoticed. But then if I return to the castle, what will happen to you?"

"Brenna, you don't—" Dakier started to say that she didn't need to worry about him, but a bizarre sizzling noise distracted him. "Do you hear that?"

"Aye." Brenna nodded, eyes narrowing. "It sounds like some kind of massive bee."

Brenna turned just as Dakier did, and they both jumped at the sight. A fire had started in the middle of the blank wall above the bed and was burning its way across the surface. The tiny flame zigged and zagged along the planks, scorching like a lit fuse on a stick of dynamite, but there was no fuse to be seen. A black burned indention was left in its wake.

"What on Endra..." Brenna muttered from beside him.

The flickering path seemed random at first, but by the time it reached the edge of the wall and a second path started below, Dakier recognized it as a cursive script. This was a message.

The letters were languid, curling freely as if someone were handwriting the brief missive before them. Just as the next line of text began, the first line faded, and the second line didn't last any longer than the first.

FOUND THE BOSS

WILL ATTACK PIZEMAC

CAPTIVE ON SHIP

Dakier stepped back reflexively. Pizemac—like his hometown Pizemac?

"It has to be a message from Katiel!" Brenna cried, wrenching Dakier out of his thoughts. "It has to be her."

In her excitement, she grabbed his arm and shook him, but Dakier couldn't tear his gaze from the now-blank wall. "How?"

"The ore!" Brenna nodded ten times fast. "That would make sense, right? It's magic. We didn't know what all it was capable of. She must've figured out how to do *this*."

Brenna swept her arms, indicating the whole wall at once, and Dakier had to admit that it was plausible.

Still, he scratched his head. "How would she know where you were, though?"

"I don't know," Brenna replied with a sigh, trying to piece this puzzle together. "Maybe whatever she made was meant to find me, wherever I was."

The awe in her tone was unmistakable, and Dakier had to admit he felt it, too. While he'd always believed in magic, seeing it in person—it was something else.

Then she turned abruptly, like she'd just realized the location of an item forgotten. "How I read this is: Katiel found the boss, but he took her prisoner. That means she needs our help. Do you know where or who Pizemac is?"

Dakier swallowed back the panic and nodded. "Intimately." He paused, trying to gather his thoughts. "That's my hometown, a small village on the Tibedese coastline. I don't know what they'd want with such a place, but it might be the first town they'll reach in Tibedo since they'd likely be coming by sea."

Without missing a beat, Brenna slipped on her discarded boots and tightened the laces. "Then we have to go there now. We can't even wait for nightfall."

"And do what?" Dakier asked desperately, though he was readying himself to follow her out. Despite his half-hearted protests, he would follow her anywhere.

It was no small thing to leap into action like she always did, but true to form, Brenna shrugged and flung open the door. "We can figure that out on the way."

40
Steffi

Steffi wrung her hands, watching the grandfather clock opposite her as she waited for her last appointment of the evening to let out. The lords were droning on about routine matters of state, but all she could think about was Brenna.

After Brenna printed her story in the Eternal City Gazette, she and Eoghan went out into the city in disguise. Steffi hoped the Barkurian people would be pleased with the news, and give her a chance to free the Tibedese without fear of pushback. Then they noticed the crowd forming in the city center. She and Eoghan edged to the very back to watch the procession unfold, but the last thing she expected to see was Brenna, running up on stage, and then a Tibedese man darting up after her.

Steffi couldn't make sense of what happened, or why he took her, but she just hoped wherever she was, Brenna was alright. Eoghan had tried to reassure her that Brenna was fine, but Steffi had no idea why her brother trusted that strange man, and he only gave vague answers when she pried further.

Brenna hadn't resisted; in fact, she'd smiled when the man lifted her, but what if that was only shock? What if her brother had reassured her off of a silly hunch—he was only a child, after all—and Brenna was in danger? Really, Steffi should have never taken advice from a nine-year-old. She should send out a search party for Brenna this very instant—

The clock struck the hour, and Steffi stood abruptly, even though Lord Byrne was still speaking.

From the other end of the long table, Eoghan raised his eyebrows in silent question, and Lord Byrne's mouth snapped shut mid-sentence. All the advisors hastened to their feet, with panicked eyes as though they'd missed some key protocol—which, technically, they had. No one was supposed to sit while the queen was standing, but she usually gave a bit more warning first. It was strange, having all the men who she'd once looked up to listening to her now, when Steffi felt like she was merely play-acting as her father.

"The meeting is adjourned," she declared in her best estimation of her father's tone. As she rushed from the room, her attendants all remained in place, clearly unsure of how to proceed, but Eoghan jumped up to follow her.

His shoes clacked against the floor tiles as he hurried to catch up. As usual, he was taking any opportunity he could to run indoors.

"Shh," she hissed, looking over her shoulder with a pointed glare.

"Why are you sneaking around the castle?" Eoghan whispered as he came up beside her. "You don't have to sneak. You're the queen."

Steffi pursed her lips and readjusted her grip on her skirt. "I'm not sneaking. I'm hurrying."

Even from her periphery, she could tell her little brother rolled his eyes. "Then why are you hurrying?"

"I'm worried about—" she started to say, but Eoghan cut her off.

"Brenna!"

"Well, yes..." she began, taken aback by his loud exclamation—until she realized what he was looking at.

At the end of the long corridor, Brenna waited around the corner, only her head peeking out as she looked back at them. She pressed a finger to her lips in warning, but Steffi was already rushing over to her, and when she reached her lady-in-waiting, Steffi enveloped her in a tight hug. Eoghan collided with them a second later, wrapping his arms around both of them and squeezing hard.

"We were so worried about you!" Steffi said as Brenna shrugged out of their embrace. "We saw that Tibedese man carry you off—"

"You were there?" Brenna interrupted, eyes darting left and right like she might have been followed. "Wait, never mind. It doesn't matter. I have something urgent to discuss with you."

Steffi straightened, pushing her shoulders back into the unnatural, rigid posture that her governesses had trained her to take until it was second-nature. She wasn't behaving as her father would—running up and hugging his subjects was out of the question for a king—and she forced her voice back into the cold neutrality that she was told befitted a monarch. "I see. Let's discuss it in my chambers, then."

Brenna shook her head, her red curls bouncing across her shoulders. "There's no time."

"I see," Steffi repeated, scanning the grand hall. There was a door to their left, between the smattering of gilded armchairs and tea tables that lined the wall, and she opened it, beckoning Brenna and her brother to follow.

Inside was a small servant's pantry, lined with shelves covered in clean dishes and washcloths, and she pulled the door shut behind them until only a crack of light shone from under the door.

"What is it?" she asked, giving a stately nod that she wasn't sure if Brenna could see.

"I received a message from Katiel," Brenna began, huffing as though she'd run all the way there. "Drezchy forces are coming to attack a coastal town in Tibedo. That's why I need your help. We need to warn them. *You* need to warn them."

Steffi pursed her lips, considering all the options. What would her father do? In times like these, he would usually ask her mother, but thanks to the same evil-doers who now threatened these Tibedese civilians, she was gone as well. And she didn't dare bring up this information to her advisors, since for all she knew they'd all been behind Taregh's treason, as well as threatening Brenna to leave her post.

"Eo?" she prompted, turning to look down at her little brother. "What say you?"

"Me?" he asked at full volume, and Steffi could vaguely make out his silhouette jamming a finger into its own chest. "Since when do you care what I think?"

"Since now," Steffi snapped. "Should I go into Tibedo to warn them?"

"No, of course not," Eoghan and Brenna said at once, with Eoghan adding afterward, "Send Brenna. A simple note won't be enough, but a queen can't go unannounced into the country we're at war with! But if you don't do anything, people will die, and they also might try to blame Bar Kur for the attack. You can't trust half of those cabinet guys, but Brenna already saved us once. So, send Brenna."

Steffi sighed. A world leader was taking advice from a child, and worse yet, he was right. She hadn't wanted to put Brenna in harm's way again, but it did seem like the best option. "Alright. If you would be willing to go, I can order a discreet coach to get you into Tibedo, and you can take a train to the coast from there."

Brenna's silhouette nodded vigorously. "I'll do it. Of course. Thank you." She sounded like she was about to leave before another thought occurred to her. "Oh, and Eoghan—I need your ore."

"Your *what*?" Steffi demanded.

"Heh," her brother said sheepishly as he reached down for his pocket. "I can explain later, Stef..."

"It's okay," Brenna said. "You're not the wielder. It was the Tibedese man."

That statement was bewildering enough on its own, but Steffi's confusion only increased when Eoghan pulled his hand out of his pocket. Even in the dim lighting, she could make out a long chain with a pendant at the end, a clear crystal surrounded by a swirl of metalwork and filled with a glittering gray dust.

He actually had ore—a substance that was completely forbidden on their continent—and on his person at that. She knew little brothers were sneaky, but this was a whole new level. She was about to say as much, since she was practically his mother now, but Brenna spoke first.

"Katiel's necklace!" she exclaimed as she took the charm from him and laced it around her neck. "Where did you find this?"

"I went through Taregh's desk once we got back," Eoghan said proudly.

"But how did you have enough for the snake?" Brenna asked.

Steffi wasn't following that question at all, but Eoghan said, "I only took one tiny piece that I placed atop the ordinary iron I was working with," and Brenna nodded as if that made sense. "I guess your boyfriend blew on it."

"Shouldn't you be going?" Steffi interrupted, though she fully planned to force her brother to explain all of this, in detail, later. "Aren't the Drezchy going to attack at any moment? Just go to the royal stables, and keep your hood up. I'll have the carriage fetch you there."

"Right," Brenna said simply, and the bravest person Steffi had ever met left the tiny corridor without looking back.

41

Brenna

Brenna was sinking deeper, deeper into the depths of the river. The current was pulling her back into the train car, wedging her foot back into its hold, trapping her beneath the surface.

She held her breath, knowing this small bit of oxygen would be her last.

Everything was shapes, blurred by the water pressed against her eyes, but she strained to focus on the sky—

Then she noticed that she wasn't the only one in the train car.

Brenna tried not to move. She didn't want to see her, but her head turned of its own accord, toward the figure.

But it wasn't Mara.

It was her father.

She screamed, forgetting about the air she desperately needed. Her *da* looked just like he had that day in his casket, so still and taut and different. So, she screamed again. And screamed, and screamed.

"Brenna!"

It was Dakier's voice, above her, far above her. But he hadn't been there that day on the train. He'd left them. Why had he left?

The thought woke her. She gasped, her eyes flying open.

In the low lighting, she could make out the strange lines of a narrow space. It wasn't her room in Galvey, or Katiel's room, or her room at the castle.

"Brenna, it's alright."

Dakier's familiar face appeared above her, his lips pursed in concern. A low, red velvet ceiling loomed above, and the faint screech of metal against metal rattled in the distance. Suddenly, reality came back to her. She was in the train car cabin on the way to Tibedo. When she'd fallen asleep, Dakier had been sleeping on the opposite bench a few feet away, but now he was hovering above her, distractingly close.

The events of the past two days rushed back—Dakier whisking her away from the stage, Katiel's astonishing missive, Eoghan handing her the necklace.

But all that evaporated as her mind reverted to her horrible dream—to her father's face, down there in the depths. She hadn't thought of him in so long, and now, even though she was awake, she couldn't get the haunting image from the dream out of her mind.

Henred was the only one who really understood what it had been like to lose their father, and now he was gone, too. Tears stung at her lashes, and she brushed them away in a huff. Dakier grabbed her wrist, placing it in her lap with the gentlest touch.

"Please don't cry."

Dakier's eyes were full of sorrow, like he somehow knew exactly what she'd dreamt. He reached a hand out slowly, and she could tell he meant to wipe the tear from her cheek.

So, she let him.

She hadn't cried when she'd learned the news of her father's death, or when she'd heard that he'd been out drinking again and had crashed Jay's phaeton afterward. When everyone in town scowled at her deeper than they already had, she'd held herself together, trying to stay positive for her *mam* and Henred.

But now that the tears had finally started, she couldn't stop them.

Dakier edged closer and wrapped his arms around her. His wide shoulders completely enveloped her as she let her wet face fall against his chest.

"I'm so sorry, Brenna." He stroked her hair, running his hand across her back. "I'm so, so sorry."

She'd despised him for something he hadn't meant to do, yet he hadn't resented her for it. He'd been nothing but kind and understanding, looking out for her all the while. He was a good person—no, a great person. He was so great she almost wanted to punch him for it. And yet he still wanted to be with her, of all people, and she didn't want to push him away anymore.

When she had felt so, so alone, Dakier proved that she wasn't forsaken. He was filled with kindness, and he loved her. She could literally feel his love in the press of his arms. The weight of his chin rested gently on the top of her head, and she knew, without a doubt, she was safe there.

She peeled away just enough to look at his face, the lanternlight casting shadows in sharp lines across his cheekbones. He reached out, cupping her cheek and wiping a stray tear away with his thumb.

"Do you," she asked in a voice far smaller than she intended, "Do you still love me?"

"Brenna." Her name was almost a sigh on his lips. "When I was gone, I thought of you so much—how brave you were, and how determined. You risked so much without thinking about any consequences to yourself."

He paused, and she worried that he was avoiding admitting that he really didn't love her, or at least, he didn't anymore. But then he went on.

"While horrors surrounded me, you were the good left in the world that I clung to. Memories of you—of all the sweet things you do when you don't think anyone notices—those provided me more solace than anything. I might have been secretly in love with you for years, but I love you now more than ever."

Brenna swallowed, staring into his eyes. They were so dark she could see her reflection, like she was glimpsing his very thoughts.

She didn't want to, but she still loved him. Desperately, and more than ever.

His thumb stroked her face again, this time drawing across her lower lip. Her mouth parted for his on instinct, and she strung her arms around his neck, arching into him. One hand pressed into her lower back, and the other moved to her chin, tilting her face up to him.

Then her eyes were closing, and his lips were on hers.

It was chaste and electric. It was warm and cold and soft and firm and magical.

He didn't try taking anything further, like he knew exactly what she needed. The kiss, the connection. The reassurance that she was loved and protected and not alone.

After what felt like an eternity, she pulled back. When she met his eyes this time, she felt suddenly shy, like they were seeing each other for the first time.

"I should let you get some sleep," he said, his awkwardness reminding her of their first dance together.

He made to stand, to head back to the other traincar bench, but she gently grabbed his wrist. "Please don't go."

Heat flared in his eyes, briefly igniting her curiosity. She would like to see that fire burn freely—the fire that he kept so well contained—and the thought was so foreign to her that she was almost ashamed of herself. But then his words brought her back to the present.

"Are you sure?"

"Yes," she replied, tugging at his wrist as softly as before.

He settled in next to her, wrapping a strong arm around her and pulling her in close. She rested her head on his shoulder, nuzzling her cheek into him as she pulled the blanket over them both. Savoring in the perfect way they fit together, she melted in further, wishing offhandedly that they could stay this way for all eternity.

And when she drifted back to sleep, she didn't have any more nightmares.

42

Brenna

When Brenna awoke, the train had already stopped, and Dakier was shaking her awake.

Dreamily, she smiled up at him until she realized where they were. Tibedo—to her, enemy territory.

Quickly, Brenna plaited her hair and wrapped a calico scarf around the front to avoid drawing unnecessary attention, and held tight to Dakier's hand as they exited the cabin.

The first thing she noticed was the heat in the open-air train station, thick and oppressive in a way she'd never experienced. The simple building was beautiful, with textured walls the color of fresh cream, with tiled accents in shades of orange and red.

She followed Dakier across the dirt road to a carriage rental booth and dropped his hand to hang back while he made the arrangements. He spoke for a moment with the clerk in Tibedese—a notably attractive language when spoken with his deep baritone—before he turned back to her.

"Bad news." Dakier ran a hand through his hair. "We're still a good ten miles away from Pizemac, and they're out of phaetons."

Brenna wracked her brain, scanning the booth for any alternative. It looked like they were out of just about everything, save for the horse at the far end of the corral. Safe to say, the graying steed, who reminded her of the horse Simeon rode to Halstat, had seen better days.

"Can we ride that one?" she asked Dakier.

He translated the question to the clerk, who then began a long-winded reply in Tibedese. It was bizarre, standing there and not understanding a word being spoken. She was in awe of Dakier, who'd learned Aslen within months of moving in with the Salzbrucks. Meanwhile, Brenna didn't speak a word of Tibedese, but she still nodded along like she understood everything.

Finally, Dakier turned to her. "He says we can rent it."

The summary was annoyingly anti-climactic after the long wait, but there was no time to comment on it. Brenna paid the man with the very last piece of her jewelry, and the clerk saddled the old mare. Thanks to a gentlemanly hand from Dakier, Brenna mounted the horse first, while Dakier sprang up with ease and settled himself in front of her. She tried to act casual as she wrapped her arms around him for support and let her cheek fall against his back.

Dakier nudged the horse onward, and Brenna let out a yelp as the creature took off at break-neck speed. Dakier glanced back at her with a grin, and their mutual surprise turned into laughter at their luck. The horse traversed miles of the arid landscape without slowing, and in what felt like no time at all, Brenna glimpsed the coastline in the distance.

Brenna swallowed, overwhelmed by both the magnificent view of the sea beyond the cliffs and the anticipation of what was about to happen. "Do you think anyone in Pizemac will recognize you?"

"Surely not," Dakier said, shaking his head. "None of my family live there anymore, and I was a child the last time I visited. I hardly remember this town at all."

Brenna nodded, trying to hide her disappointment. If the villagers recognized him, it might help in convincing them to flee, but Brenna would find a way to persuade them, regardless. She had no choice. "Are you ready for this?"

Dakier stole a glance back at her, her anxiety echoed in his eyes, as he said, "As ready as I'll ever be."

The mare trotted on into the village, and by the time they reached Pizemac's central plaza, Brenna felt confident that the Drezchy hadn't yet laid siege.

The plaza surrounded a lovely, tiered fountain, its chilly mist creating a heavenly aroma when mixed with the salty sea air. A host of townspeople milled about—a tall man selling adorable pygmy goats, a jolly young woman pushing a pastry cart—and each one caught Brenna's eye. Beside them, a mother laughed as her toddling son tried to wriggle out of her grasp, his aim clearly bent on jumping in the fountain, and Brenna couldn't help but smile at the peaceful scene. These villagers had no inkling that harm was on its way, which hopefully meant there was still enough time to evacuate.

"Brenna," Dakier said, his low tone dragging her from her musings. "I don't think we should go around the city shouting for everyone to evacuate. It could cause a panic."

Brenna wanted to retort that she obviously wasn't going to do that, even though that had been her exact plan. "But 'The Drezchy are coming!' has such a nice ring to it."

Dakier shot her a bemused look, and Brenna's heart warmed.

"Fine, I'll be serious," Brenna obliged, making a show of straightening her skirt. "What do you suggest?"

Dakier checked his pocket-watch. "The magistrate for the coastal region holds a seat in Pizemac, so we could try to warn them first. That building is likely the lyceum, so I say we head there." He indicated the only façade more than a single story tall—a wide, burnt orange building with a clock tower extending above the center. "If we alert the leadership first, they can execute an orderly evacuation. Chaos might delay everyone in getting to safety."

Brenna nodded, finding his hand with hers and giving it a little squeeze. "I'm with you. Lead the way."

His wide smile made her heart flutter like it was the first time he ever smiled at her, and he squeezed her hand in return. "I love you."

In her giddiness, she forgot to say it back, but her mood sobered as they stepped inside the double doors of the lyceum.

Inside, assorted artifacts adorned the stucco walls, and the scents of mint and olive oil permeated the space. A receptionist sat on a cushion behind a low desk, and when Dakier explained the situation, they were, mercifully, taken to the magistrate at once.

A middle-aged woman with long, black hair sat at the far end of a second room decorated just like the first. Her eyes were closed and her legs were twisted under herself, evidently in some sort of meditative pose. When the receptionist introduced them, the magistrate wordlessly opened her eyes, and Dakier took that as permission to launch into the tale.

Brenna couldn't make out a word of what Dakier said, but he was obviously relaying what had led them here and why the townspeople needed to evacuate. As he spoke, the magistrate unwound her legs from their pretzel and stood up, walking around her desk to face them. But when he finished speaking, the woman—who Brenna noted was called Magister Lim, from the plaque on her desk—spoke a single, definitive word, and Dakier's face instantly fell.

"Nao."

"What did she say?" Brenna whispered, though she had a feeling she knew what it was.

Without Dakier having to translate her question, Magister Lim repeated herself in Endran. "No."

Brenna blinked, taking in the abrupt response. "Pardon?"

"We are not evacuating," the leader said, speaking flawless Endran while steepling her fingers under her chin.

So much for a society built on peace, Brenna mused drily, before immediately regretting the snide thought as the leader went on.

"This story you tell—it is too much to believe. You come from the Barkurian capital. We have yet to hear word that the Tibedese delegation arrived safely. Why would I listen to you now?"

"You make a great point," Dakier said, holding up his palms in a sign of goodwill. "I know it all sounds strange. But I am Tibedese. As I said, I was in Bar Kur as a translator for the army. You can trust us. We're here to help."

"No," she said again, turning her back before Dakier could utter another word of protest. "Be gone. You are lucky I let the Barkurian go free after she dares show her face here."

With a snap of her fingers, two guards entered the room to escort them out. It wouldn't help their case to resist, but Brenna couldn't bear to leave like this, knowing that countless lives depended on it. Those kind people she'd witnessed in the square, and countless others like them, would die. No, there had to be another way. If only she could figure it out...

A variety of artifacts decorated the opposite wall, and Brenna squinted as she took a closer look. At least twenty sets of prayer beads adorned the space, like the ones Dakier always carried, and a small, singular bone rested in a wall-mounted glass case. They weren't just knickknacks, but religious relics, she realized. The magistrate must follow the old religion like Dakier, and perhaps that alone could be enough common ground, but—

There.

Amid the variety of beads, there hung a single ornament, larger than the rest. A metalwork piece twisted into a winding hexagon, the shape matching Katiel's pendant and Mara's tattoo. It was the sign of the Keepers.

When Brenna saw it, she knew what they had to do.

"Dakier," she whispered, urgency giving way to frenzy in her tone. "We can fix this. But you have to wield something. *Now.*"

43

Anton

There was nothing Anton loved more than a well-executed plan, and this one was working perfectly.

He'd been hiding out on Simeon's ship for days, biding his time. Lying low had been simple enough. He'd swiped a spare naval uniform from the laundry—mind, the clean laundry—and blended in by posing as a sailor, sleeping in a spare bunk in the crew's quarters and sneaking a bite from the mess hall between meals. With his loose curls slicked back straight and facial hair left unshaven, none of the other sailors seemed to notice that the unfamiliar face among them looked uncannily similar to the prince—possibly because, around him, subjects were quick to avert their eyes.

Simeon, of course, would recognize him right away, but so far, he'd been surprisingly easy to evade. Since Simeon spent all his time below deck working on who knew what, Anton busied himself with tasks out in the fresh air. Assuming Simeon had indeed used his ship design, the voyage was taking longer than it should, and Anton was growing antsy. After all, a deck only needed so much swabbing. All the time, he kept his eyes on the west, toward Kerafin.

At last, this morning, he'd awoken to the sight he'd been waiting for—that tiny sliver of green on the horizon. Land peeked out over the endless expanse of sea.

That meant it was time to put his plan into action.

Anton pulled his uniform cap lower down to block his face before he slipped into the deckhouse. No suspicion came his way, even as he pulled back the hatch to the lower decks and hopped in, foregoing the ladder completely. To the others, he was just another sailor going about his business. Unbeknownst to them, he was on a mission—he was going all the way to the bottom. He wound his way down through the levels of the hold, descending one rickety ladder after another as he went.

He'd seen the barrels of gunpowder being hauled on deck, the cannons being loaded. His relatives had already weakened the continent from the inside out, and now they meant to attack the mainland—but if he could help it, they wouldn't get the chance.

He was going to sink this ship.

One benefit of Simeon stealing his ship's design was that Anton knew the craft by heart. He could easily scuttle it before the crew caught on. First, he would jam the bilge pump, and then tear a gash in the hull with a hatchet he'd swiped from the galley.

On the lowest level, Anton headed to the stern, finding the unguarded bilge pump with ease. In accordance with his blueprints, the pump would empty any excess water automatically without a crew member present. There was no backup way to drain excess water if the pump mechanism were to fail—a flaw in his original design—and Simeon would be left with no choice but to abandon ship.

Looking left and right to confirm no one approached, he opened the latch on the valve box and swung the metal door open. Without missing a beat, he grabbed the toggle lever, which turned the pump on or off, and threw all his weight against it. Raw wood chafed against his palms, but a crack rewarded his efforts, and he stepped away with the lever in hand.

Once he jammed the outlet, the ship would gradually fill up with water, causing it to sink in a matter of hours. Rearing back, he shoved the lever into the outlet valve with all his might, then stood aside to admire his handiwork. The pump wouldn't function anymore, so now he only needed to allow the water to flow in.

He had to be quick about this before any of the crew came down to find him, so he wasted no more time before unhooking the hatchet from his belt. The hatchet's blade found purchase in the wooden hull with a satisfying *thunk*, and he yanked it free before rearing the tool over his head and striking again. It took several more swings before he broke all the way through the thick wood, but once he did, water began pouring in immediately. With only a few more strikes to widen the breach, he decided it was large enough, and fled back up to the main deck.

It truly was the perfect plan. Soon, this end of the ship would fill up with water, which would upset the weight distribution and cause the entire hull to crack in two. The shore was in sight, so he wouldn't have the deaths of his former friend or the innocent crew members weighing on his ever-expanding conscience, but once the ship split, there would be no chance to attack Kerafin.

It was a peaceful solution—a diplomatic solution—and a smile crept to his lips at how proud Katiel would be. The only issue, though, was that the hole could be patched if any sailors realized the ship was capsizing—which meant he was in need of a little distraction.

He set off up the maze of ladders, but when he opened the hatch to the main deck, he was met with an unwelcome sight. A pair of black boots tapped impatiently, mere inches from his nose.

"Your Highness."

Seething, Anton flew up the last few rungs, but when he leveled his gaze with Simeon's, the full weight of the betrayal threatened to crush him. When he'd trusted Simeon with every one of his darkest secrets, his supposed friend sat there listening, knowing the entire time he meant to kill Anton when he got the chance. So many happy memories—most of his *only* happy memories—were now tainted by Simeon's presence in them.

"How have you been, Your Highness?" Simeon drawled, his stare daring the prince to break eye contact first. "Read any good books while you were stowing away?"

Anton scoffed, noting the lingering looks of the sailors passing by. They were moving a bit too slowly, watching him and Simeon a bit too closely, but he didn't mind an audience if it meant distracting the crew until the ship was too waterlogged to recover.

"Considering that you left Katiel to die," Anton all but growled, "I think we can drop the pretense of civility."

"I left you to die as well, you know," Simeon said, removing his glasses to dab at a smudge on the lenses, "but if we're dropping all formalities, I'll be on my way."

Simeon sauntered across the deck toward the row of cannons, and Anton realized with a jolt that they were now within firing distance of the coast. But before Anton had time to react, Simeon wordlessly raised his hand, and a sailor posted at the nearest cannon nodded and lowered the linstock. The cannon fired, rolling backward along the deck before the ropes went taut and the sailors pulled it back into place. In the distance, an explosion went up where the artillery made contact with the village.

Anton charged toward the sailor about to fire the next cannon, but Simeon snapped his fingers, and two large sailors rushed up and wrangled Anton's arms.

"Unhand me," Anton seethed, looking each of them in the eyes with a lethal stare. "I am your prince."

"Sorry, sire," one said sheepishly, even as he continued to restrain him. "We have strict orders from King Vadim to follow Lord Simeon's command onboard."

Anton seethed. Whether Simeon was actually working with his uncle, or simply forging missives signed by Vadim, he couldn't say. His former friend was no longer someone he recognized.

"There are innocent people in that town!" Anton screamed, the conviction in his words shocking even himself. "You can't do this."

"Since when do you care for lost lives, Ghost?" Simeon asked, raising a brow as he casually replaced his glasses. "This has to be Katiel's doing."

"Don't you dare say her name!" Anton spat, stretching his foot toward a lantern held in a nearby sailor's grasp.

His focus narrowed on the target, and his kick struck true. The glass box flew through the air, landing directly on his target—the deck next to the gunpowder barrels. A shatter rang out, shards of glass flying with the impact, and the kerosene poured onto the deck, immediately catching fire from the flame within the lamp.

Following the path of the spilled kerosene, the blaze spread, flashing across the deck in a wall of flame. The path led straight for the ten-odd barrels of gunpowder, just as Anton intended. Next to the line of cannons, one barrel was already open, and the eyes of the gathered sailors locked on the deadly ammunition.

One prudent older sailor rushed over, not waiting for the captain's command. "Quick, move the barrels!"

Most of the crew rushed over, while the two men restraining him took quickened breaths, their eyes darting between their current post and the rapidly spreading inferno a few feet away.

Simeon, still standing opposite them with his arms crossed, rolled his eyes as he addressed them. "I'll take him from here."

The men dropped Anton without hesitation, with one mumbling, "Oh, thank the Creator," as they raced to help staunch the fire. Anton landed shakily on his feet, straightening his lapel to disguise him catching his balance.

When Anton looked up, Simeon reached into his pocket and, in the blink of an eye, drew his palm to his mouth and blew. A small, controlled spiral of ore glimmered magnificently above his hand, and

Anton had to blink five times fast to make sense of what he was seeing.

With the crew distracted, Simeon held an audience of one as he waved his free hand in a single, broad swipe. It was a deliberate, graceful motion, so different from Katiel's sweet, nervous strokes when she wielded. But instead of creating something to help put out the fire, the tiny specks of ore compounded into a fresh lantern.

It was identical to the one Anton had just destroyed, and his former friend held it out to him. "Here," Simeon said, his normally jovial eyes now cold and calculated. "Good as new."

Mindlessly, Anton took the lantern from him. Then he managed to pick up his jaw enough to mouth a single, quiet question.

"What have you done?"

"I wielded a lantern from the ore, obviously, after you ungratefully set fire to my new ship." Again Simeon tsked, as if the raging fire and scrambling crew behind him were nothing more than a swarm of gnats buzzing by his ear.

"What do you mean you 'wielded' it?" Anton drew out the words through gritted teeth, knowing deep down that he already knew the answer.

Simeon shrugged. "Xabius's blood type didn't match mine, but the girl's did, so it all worked out. I have you to thank, truly, for keeping her close until I needed her."

The girl.

A cold sweat broke out along Anton's temples.

"You've been siphoning Katiel's power," he breathed. "You've been keeping her here, on this ship, and taking the power from her. How?"

Simeon's smirk was all the confirmation he needed. "Why don't you ask her yourself?"

The world spun, the sky and the sea melting into a single blue abyss. Anton tried to move, to run below, but his feet were rooted on the spot as the reality of what he'd done set in.

Katiel was alive.

But he had set fire to a rapidly sinking ship with her trapped below deck.

44

Katiel

Days had passed since Katiel sent Brenna her message, days of nothing but sleeping and siphoning. She was grateful that, as far as she knew, no one found out about her warning Brenna, but the extreme blood loss was taking its toll. Even when she was alone, she was too exhausted to move for more than a moment. The hours passed, each the same as the last—forcing herself to stand, perform the basic necessities to care for herself, and head back to bed.

Drip.

An unfamiliar noise startled Katiel from her daze, and she scanned the room for its source. Her neck turned painfully slowly, but then she saw it—a trickle of water slipping in through a crack in the corner of the ceiling.

Drip.

Drip.

A third plunk of water landed on the floor, and then the crack broke wider.

A torrent of water rushed into the room.

Katiel gaped at the deluge for only a moment before she leapt into action. Adrenaline took over as she forced herself to her feet, her aching thigh muscles groaning in protest. She lunged for the door, the simple step taking all her effort as she waded through the ankle-deep water.

She tried to turn the handle, but it wouldn't budge. She knew she was locked in—she'd tried the door every few minutes when she still had her energy—but now, the fear compounded. The walls seemed to close in, the spare space made even smaller, and she fought the urge to cry out.

But there was no time for screaming. She had to focus. She had to escape.

Water was still pouring in through the hole in the ceiling. At this rate, the water level would rise above her head in mere minutes.

Her chest was thrumming. She knew she should wield something to help her, but a moment came and went, and then another. She was stalled, frozen in terror. It was like those dreams where some horrible event was about to happen, and she tried to scream, but no sound came from her open mouth. Now, no coherent thought came to her frantic mind, and the realization only compounded her hysteria.

Her hands flew to her braid, fingers wildly grasping for purchase in her hair. The cold seawater splashed past her knees.

Think.

The walls were too close.

Think.

About to drown.

Think.

The water reached her hips, her soaked skirt like an anchor tied around her legs.

She needed to wield something to break down the door.

She reached for her neck, meaning to draw out her necklace, but her fingers found no chain. Frantically, she clawed at the collar of her dress and at her chest, where the pendant normally rested, but there was nothing there.

Her intense fatigue wasn't due to blood loss alone, she realized. Simeon had taken the ore from her, and in her terror and confusion and sheer exhaustion, she hadn't even noticed. She should've wielded something to help herself escape, a sledge to break down the door, when she'd had the chance.

Now she was on her own. She had no ore and no magic.

She was back to being the simple Katiel from before, the Katiel who was powerless and afraid.

The water poured in faster now; she was sure of it. Or perhaps it was the panic playing tricks on her mind. But it reached her neck, and suddenly, she had to swim to keep her head above water.

She dove below the surface, back to the door, yanking on the handle again with her boots pressing on either side of the door for leverage. Still, nothing.

The last of her air bubbled before her eyes and rose to the surface, the silver orbs disappearing at the top of the deep teal she was suspended in. She followed them up, gasping in a fresh pull of air when she reemerged.

Her head clunked against a solid slab, and she winced before looking up.

It was the ceiling, even as the water level continued to rise.

She was going to die like this.

Her skull smacked into the ceiling again as the water level swelled again, forcing her to crane her neck to keep her mouth out of the seawater.

She was going to die here and sink to the bottom of the ocean.

Her soul might join Anton in whatever came next, but her parents would never find her body.

45

Dakier

"What?" Dakier whispered, trying to keep the panic at bay.

They'd come all this way only to be banished from Pizemac, and from the looks of it, the guards wouldn't wait much longer before they hauled them out.

"Wield. Something." Brenna hissed, jerking her head toward the ornamentation on the wall. Following her eyeline, he saw what she indicated—a wrought-iron keeper symbol at the center of the collection.

According to Mara, keepers were oath-bound to follow the command of wielders, so if Magister Lim were indeed a keeper, Dakier proving himself as a wielder would be the easiest way to change her mind. And beyond that, he'd be lying if he said he hadn't been yearning to try. He had wielded a snake—a living being—by accident, so hopefully he could wield a stationery metal object on purpose.

Without another moment's hesitation, Dakier retrieved a speck of ore from Katiel's recovered necklace and tried to remember the instructions Sera had given Katiel all those weeks ago.

Inhale. Exhale. Expand. Shape.

A foreign pulse thrummed against his fingertip before he inhaled, and when he blew out, a tornado of glittering gray engulfed them all.

Magister Lim's eyes shot wide, and Brenna punched a fist in the air in triumph.

He did it—purposefully this time—but he couldn't stop yet. Forcing his concentration, he pictured himself forging an object just like the one on the wall, visualizing how he would have to turn and curve the pieces with his anvil. All the while, he held his hands out, palms facing each other. Like magic, the shape formed along with the image in his mind.

All at once, it was there, hovering between his palms—a perfect match to the iron symbol on the wall. Then, a second later, gravity set in, and he dashed his hand under the sculpture, grabbing hold before it fell to the ground.

Magister Lim's jaw hung down to her collarbone, and neither of her guards uttered a word.

"You are—" she began but faltered. "You wield the ore. How?"

Dakier shook his head. "I honestly don't know, but right now, that's the least of our concerns. We have to evacuate the town."

"Right." The magister nodded, his status as a wielder evidently overruling her prior concerns. "Yes, we'll evacuate at once."

Thankfully, the village had an evacuation procedure in place. Lim explained that it was intended for inclement weather, but the system was efficient, regardless. Soon, the majority of the townsfolk hauled their belongings in carpetbags, heading in groups to the neighboring cliffs.

"I hope you're wrong about this," Lim said a short time later, dusting off her hands as she walked over to where Dakier and Brenna stood on the beach next to the town. They'd all been doing their part by helping the citizens pack carts for the evacuation, and the streets were finally clear as the villagers left for higher ground. "As much as these folks would hate a false alarm, I'm sure everyone will be relieved to—"

"Look!" Brenna screeched, pointing to the sea.

Besides Brenna and himself, the only people left were Magister Lim and a handful of townsfolk who'd hung back to help. At Brenna's cry, the group whipped around. There, a silhouette disrupted the horizon, and it was rapidly growing. Dakier cocked his head to the side. No ship could travel so quickly—and yet, in only seconds, it was close enough to see each sail.

Brenna gasped behind him. "It's going so fast!"

"Brenna," Dakier said, grabbing for her hand, "We need to run."

"No," she protested, shifting her hand away before he could grasp it. "Think about it. We got Katiel's letter just two days ago. She's probably on that ship right now! We need to find her."

Dakier nodded, pride swelling as Brenna's complete selflessness showed through yet again. "You're right. I'm with you."

"We will come with you as well," Magister Lim added, while several of the townspeople murmured their agreement.

"No, please, go along with the others to the high ground," Dakier insisted. He placed a hand on the magistrate's shoulder, hoping to convey a confidence he didn't feel. "Your people need you."

The magistrate pursed her lips, taking a long pause before she reluctantly agreed. "Very well," she said, clapping Dakier's shoulder, "but we will watch closely, in case you need us."

The ship rapidly approached, and with a jolt, Dakier realized it was on fire. A wisp of dark smoke billowed from the center, and a faint orange glow emanated from the deck. If Katiel was on board, there was no time to lose.

But as soon as Dakier's boots hit the sand to run, a resonant *boom* sounded from the craft.

A flaming cannonball arced through the air. It careened over the port, above the small fishing boats dotting the harbor, and crashed directly into the village.

The artillery exploded on impact, the deafening bang convulsing in Dakier's eardrums. A great cloud of smoke erupted where the laced cannonball landed, and a sickening, acrid scent filled the space between them and the town.

This ruthless attack was exactly what Katiel had warned of, and yet, somehow, Dakier was rife with shock as the clocktower went up in flames.

46

Anton

ANTON LAUNCHED HIMSELF ACROSS the tween deck and into the upper hold of the ship, his legs moving faster than his mind. The entire craft shuddered over and over, and combined with the muffled resonance coming from above him, he could tell that Simeon's men were firing cannons at the shore despite the growing fire. But as much as Anton wanted to stop him from destroying the town, saving Katiel was more important.

The cargo hold was vast, with dozens of separate compartments, and Katiel could be trapped in any of them. He'd already spent far too long trying to repair the bilge pump—to no avail—and by this point, there was far too much water in the hull for him to patch the breach. This ship was sinking, and he had to get Katiel off before it did.

He'd already checked that the deckhouses were empty, which only confirmed his fear. She was being held at the bottom of the waterlogged ship, and every second counted. He descended ladder after ladder, sliding his hands down the sides without bothering to use the rungs. His palms burned against the splintered wood, but it didn't matter.

His thoughts evaporated as he hurried, a single image fixed in his mind—Katiel.

Her sweet, small smile. Eyes full of determination, of unexpected bravery. Her kind, trusting heart.

Anton never should have asked her to be court wielder.

Never in a thousand lifetimes would he do it again. He'd known the trials that awaited her in his homeland. He'd *known* she was walking into the Conclave. Anton had brought her face to face with the greatest monster he'd ever encountered—his uncle. That alone was unforgiveable.

He hadn't been thinking of her, and he hated himself for it.

But as to what he had been thinking of, he couldn't say. It wasn't selfishness, since he still loathed the idea of himself becoming king.

No, it *was* selfish. The true error was hating his uncle more than he loved Katiel. He'd longed to see the king defeated more than he longed to protect her.

When he left Bar Kur, he ran out of fear as much as anything. He feared that things might change—that he might change, and learn to love someone more than himself.

But he had. He loved Katiel more than he'd imagined was possible, and it couldn't be too late. Fate—the Creator, whatever power that be—absolutely could not allow it to be too late for them.

He descended another ladder, and this time, he landed knee-deep in seawater. The frigidity sent a chill up his spine, but as he raced down the corridor, he soon adjusted to the temperature. It was warm enough to survive, at least, if only he could get Katiel out in time.

Through every section of the hold, he screamed her name, but no response came as he made his way deeper into the ship.

As he feared, the last level of the hold was now entirely submerged. He could easily end up trapped beneath the water himself, but it was the most likely place for Simeon to have locked the wielder away if he meant to keep her presence hidden.

So, without another thought, he sucked in a massive breath and pulled himself under.

47

Katiel

Katiel was not going to drown. She wouldn't let herself.

She survived the train crash, the face-off with Taregh, and both Conclave trials. Simeon had drained her blood for days, wearing her down into a shell of a human, but she endured it. She survived every challenge life threw at her, and she was still here.

To her surprise, the water level had stopped rising. Three inches of air remained between the waterline and the ceiling, but already, it was almost unbreathable. Somewhere far above her, a muted roar sounded with a steady rhythm, and the ship's creaks drowned out all else. If she didn't act fast, even the small amount of air she had left would be useless to her.

Katiel wished she had her ore, and then immediately scolded herself. Mere months ago, she hadn't known it existed. Now she relied on it, but she didn't have to. There had to be a way to escape, even on her own.

In the top corner of the ceiling, the small hole remained empty, which meant the room above wasn't yet filled with water. The realization sparked a new rush of energy, and Katiel clawed at the torn edges of the hole with all her might. The raw wood tore into her skin and splintered her palms, but she scarcely noticed, focusing all her energy as she chipped away at the planks. She kicked fiercely to stay at the surface, pausing only to let her weight assist her in prying off the boards.

She was at the edge of exhaustion, but she couldn't stop. She kept clawing, and once the hole looked to be just wide enough, she grabbed the rough edges of the opening and hoisted herself up.

Her head crossed through easily, but her body was trickier. She shoved one arm through to wedge her shoulders sideways, but they caught at the opening. There was no other choice, though, so she kicked and pulled and twisted even as blood trickled out of a small gash above her elbow, mixing with the water in a sickening swirl of crimson.

With a final shove, she placed her palms flat on the floor above and hoisted herself up. Her hips dragged against the jagged edges, sure to give her another series of cuts, but she managed to make it all the way through.

Once her feet crossed over, she flung herself onto her back on the damp floor. Her chest expanded and contracted, and for a few moments she let herself feel every breath. Moments ago, each breath could've been her last, and relief coursed through her at having escaped the hellish chamber. But she wasn't out of the ship yet, so she forced herself to her feet.

She was in another small stateroom, lit by a set of dim, wall-mounted lanterns that illuminated the soaked curtains and bedding. Water sloshed out of the hole in the floor that she'd just escaped through, threatening to take her back into its murky depths, and she backed out of the room before the terror consumed her.

The stateroom let out onto a long corridor filled with nondescript crates and barrels, and she dashed out, hoping the sinking was at least keeping the crew above deck and occupied. The saltwater was creeping up past her ankles and onto her calves, and she knew she had little time left. Already fatigued from ore withdrawal, her thighs burned even more as she ran, blindly searching for a stairwell to the upper levels. After a few agonizing moments, she spotted a ladder hanging down from one side of an open hatch.

Katiel jumped to grab hold and pull it down, but she missed. Her foot twisted beneath her as she landed, and a fresh wave of pain roiled through her leg. But she tried again, and this time, she grasped it, fingers tightening around the bottom rung. She yanked the ladder down fully and flew up it, barely feeling the searing pain in her ankle as the adrenaline coursed through her.

When she reached the next level, her left leg wobbled as she tried to put weight on her ankle. She wasn't sure which way to go, but as she scanned her surroundings, her breath caught in her throat.

A man stood not ten feet away from her—a man who looked exactly like Anton.

Her first thought was that he had to be an apparition, a figment of her imagination conjured by her desperation and lack of ore. Anton was dead. Yes, she'd held onto the nagging feeling that he had somehow survived that final blow, but even if he had, he wouldn't be standing before her on this sinking ship.

But then he said her name, his deep voice thick with amazement, and she knew it was him.

He was here, against all odds. Then her feet were moving despite herself, or perhaps he was coming closer, and she was crashing into him.

When her lips tangled with his, the world was suddenly right again. His large hands, firm and unrelenting, pressed into her back, holding her to him like she might evaporate if he let go.

This time, it was she who broke away. She leaned back just enough to see his face, which was as startling in its beauty as ever. He was drenched, his dark hair hanging wet over his forehead, and she reached up to push a stray wave out of his eyes.

"You were searching down below to find me," she said, as realization dawned. "You came for me."

"Of course." He took one of her hands in both of his and planted a kiss on her knuckles. "I will always come for you. I ran once, but

I'm here now. And I'll never leave your side while you'll have me." Katiel's heart soared, but before she could reply, Anton's mouth fell into a stern line. "But for now, we must make haste. We're not out of danger yet."

At that, he stepped back, pulling on her hand as if to guide her down the hall. Katiel nodded and started following when her ankle turned again, a surge of pain zinging up her leg, and she realized the injury was worse than she'd thought.

"You're hurt," Anton said, swallowing visibly before the rest came rushing out. "Katiel, I am so terribly, terribly sorry. I never should've brought you to New Drezchy. Truly, I tell you, I had no idea what Simeon had planned."

"It's alright," she cut him off, not wanting to think of how much her own lovesick choices had cost her. They were both alive, and keeping it that way was what mattered now. "Let's focus on getting out of here."

No sooner had the words crossed her lips than his large hands were on her waist, lifting her off the ground and into a cradle position, her knees hung over one forearm while the free arm supported her back. The movements were swift and effortless, and she blushed at the surprising show of strength. She clung to his shoulders to lighten herself as best she could, but it hardly seemed necessary. He set off down the hall as though she were weightless. She blushed again, her mind threatening to go down another avenue at the knowledge he could lift her—were they to make it out of this situation.

A stairwell came up on their left, but he passed it, instead heading toward a dead end. "Are we not going up?" Katiel asked, suddenly considering jumping down despite the torn ankle.

"No," he said, his jaw grazing her hair with a shake of the head. "When I was scuttling the ship, I tore a large gash in the hull. It's wide enough to swim out and up to the surface easily, and it's just around this bend. It'll be much quicker to reach than the main deck."

She leaned away enough to look up at him, and his pace slowed as she threw them off-balance. "You sank the ship?"

"I was trying to stop Simeon." A lock of his wet hair fell across her face, and she became aware once again of how close their lips were. "I didn't know you were onboard."

Before she could answer, a loud creak from deep in the ship interrupted her thoughts, reminding her of the urgency, and Anton got the message, reaching for a doorknob to their right. Katiel assumed the door led to the hull breach, but before he could grasp the knob, another deafening crack sounded. This time, the sloshing sound echoed on all sides like an encroaching whirlpool, and the ship tilted beneath them.

Anton stumbled, and Katiel scurried out of his arms. She leaned away to stay upright, and it worked for a moment, until she was crouching sideways, clinging desperately to the soaked carpet as the floor beneath her feet approached the vertical. Anton reached for her, his other holding onto the door trim with white knuckles. She leapt toward him, her fingertips brushing his as she strained to grasp it, but her hand clasped nothing but air as she went spinning head over feet down the corridor. She tucked her chin and covered her head with her hands, hoping at least she wouldn't break her neck as she tumbled down the steep slope.

Suddenly, the ship's titling movement halted, and the floor leveled out beneath her. She leapt to her feet, her torn ankle throbbing in painful protest. In a fight to remain upright on the wobbling surface, she widened her stance, but the floorboards under her seemed to move of their own accord. All at once, they splintered, cracking upwards directly under her, and she screamed, leaping to the side in her confusion.

"Katiel!" Anton cried, reaching out a hand to her from the other side of the crack.

Before she could move, before she could think, the gap stretched wider, and she realized all too late that she'd leapt to the wrong side. The hull had broken in two, with the chasm between the halves separating her and Anton. Mercifully, she could still see him on the other side, gracefully diving into the water out of harm's way.

She waited for him to surface, but where he should've emerged, there was no trace of movement. Her heartbeat hammered anew, but in her moment of waiting her own side rocked, throwing her back from the fractured edge of the deck. Desperately, she lunged for the stairwell beside her, wrapping both her hands around the rail before she got tossed down the corridor again.

For a single, blissful moment, she glimpsed the sky above her, the clouds swirling as she whipped around with the ship, her grip somehow holding until the ship stopped swaying. As soon as the craft came to a halt, she moved her toes to the edge, readying herself to jump. Trapped below, she'd feared she'd never see daylight again, and here she was, a leap away from freedom.

A very—*very*—high leap away from freedom.

It was high enough that a false landing could be her end, but she had no other choice. She took a deep breath, but just before she pushed off, a great beam of wood—the mast, it had to be—came crashing down from above, blocking out the sweet glimpse of sky.

48

Brenna

Brenna's jaw fell slack as blow after blow decimated the quaint fishing village. The pungent scent of sulfur wafted over to her with each deafening boom.

Even from a safe distance away on the shore, she could clearly make out the destruction. The jagged rooflines already appeared altered, the explosion having leveled several buildings in the town center. The clock tower, previously the tallest building in the village, was now nowhere to be seen.

Brenna spun around to face Dakier, whose right knuckles were white around his string of prayer beads. His other hand squeezed hers as he said, "Tell me what you need me to do."

Brenna nodded. "Can you wield something? A weapon? An enchanted boat to get us to the ship as fast as possible?"

"I—" Dakier hesitated, letting go of her hand to wring his together. "I wielded a simple metal shape once, and I honestly think I got lucky. Wielding something more complex could take time, and trying that may delay us more."

"Right, right. Fair enough." She knew how long wielding took Katiel to master, and how sporadic her successes were. If Dakier didn't think he could do it, there was no point in pushing him. The ship was close enough to shore to row to, and they had no time to waste.

Brenna took off for the docked fishing boats, bobbing unharmed beside the ravaged town. "Help me!" she shouted, but Dakier was already by her side, placing a steady hand on her back to lead her into the boat.

She hoisted up her skirt, the tiny craft swaying as she stepped in. Dakier untied the rope from the dock and passed her a set of oars, which she hastily slid into position. She'd never rowed a boat before, but Dakier clearly had, and they were off in no time, speeding toward the massive sailing ship.

Dakier sat with his back to their target, while Brenna faced him, giving her a clear view of the broad ivory sails. The soldier's motions were sure and swift, and though he was clearly making most of the progress, she tried to imitate him as best she could.

The oars were heavy on their own, and Brenna's back groaned in protest with each swipe through the water. But she didn't relent, grinding her boots into the floorboards and clenching her jaw as she rowed faster.

As the ship grew closer, she didn't take her eyes from it, squinting to try to spy Katiel amid the chaos. The first thing she noticed was the state of the deck. The railings were pitched black and charred, as if a fire had recently been put out, which explained the smoke she'd seen earlier coming off the ship. Sailors were rushing across the deck and lowering lifeboats into the water, but she saw no sign of Katiel among them.

Then she noticed the hull. It was lower in the water than it had been when they'd set off, and now, the bow was tilted slightly upward. The entire vessel was off balance.

"The ship..." she said, barely able to get a word out amid her labored breaths. "It's sinking."

"Stay focused," Dakier replied. His own breathing remained steady, as if he rowed across a hundred yards of ocean regularly. "We'll get there. If she's onboard, we'll reach her in time."

"But why is it sinking? What's going on?" Brenna shook her head, craning to see over Dakier's shoulder in case she might glimpse something to explain the situation. "I can't see Katiel."

"Perhaps she already made it off," Dakier suggested, but his tone wavered, and Brenna knew he didn't believe it either.

"If she's a captive, they wouldn't just let her go," Brenna said, frantically scanning the waters surrounding the ship. A few of the sailors had already jumped off the high top deck and were swimming to shore. At the sight of their panicked faces, the memory of the train crash in the river came rushing back to her.

Knowing Mara was trapped below and watching Katiel be carried down the rapids, Brenna had been too afraid to act. She'd been so sure that she couldn't make a difference in a physical emergency that she hadn't even tried. She'd held onto the hope that someone else would act—some other force would intervene—and everything would be alright.

Mara lost her life that day, and Brenna had never stopped wondering what might have happened if she'd jumped in after her. Nightmares of drowning had plagued Brenna since the incident, and the thought of going under the water again threatened to eat her alive. But the thought of not helping someone in need—the thought of Katiel getting hurt—would do more than that. Those thoughts would end her.

"We need to get as close as we can!" Brenna yelled as they approached the ship, trying fruitlessly to steady her clamoring pulse.

Dakier shifted his weight, beginning to turn the boat, when the craft abruptly rocked. Brenna yelped as she flew off her seat and slammed her back against the bottom of the dingy. A great splintering sounded, loud enough to be heard even as a massive wave washed over the side of their tiny craft.

Dakier leapt across her, pinning her to the bottom, her chest nearly flush to his as he used his body to shield her. Even from her place under Dakier, salt water soaked through her dress and hair, but the surge was gone in a blink.

The wave had passed as quickly as it came, and their dinghy somehow, blessedly, remained afloat. Dakier leaned back, offering a hand to help her sit up, and she couldn't help but beam at him. He'd protected her without a second thought.

"Thank you," she breathed, her fingertips grazing his cheek before she planted a quick kiss on his lips.

Her smile didn't waver as she pulled back, but when she noticed the sight over his shoulder, her heart sank once more.

The ship had split entirely in two.

The strange crack she'd heard now made sense. Both halves of the ship were spread out in the water but remained upright, with the mosaic of corridors of the farther half exposed in their direction. The other half—the one closer to them—was still swaying, and just as suddenly as the first wave had come, it fell to its side, sending the wooden mast plummeting toward the other half.

Brenna jumped back onto the floorboard and held onto the wooden seat as the boat rocked violently, thankful at least that their boat remained upright amid the turmoil. But then she saw it—or rather, her.

Katiel was below deck on the far half of the ship, clinging to the torn shards of hull to steady herself as the craft rocked and tumbled. She was looking down at the water, assessing the drop with wide eyes, so she didn't see the mast falling directly above her.

"Katiel!" Brenna cried. "Watch out!"

Katiel snapped her head up, shrinking back as she registered the falling mast, and then she leapt out of the way, diving headfirst into the water. She avoided the deadly impact by mere inches, but the mast landed in the water right where she went under.

With the speed the mast was sinking, Katiel would likely become trapped beneath it, and Brenna sucked in a horrified breath.

Despite the mounting fear of the murky seawater below, she had to try to save Katiel. The memories of the train car swirled through Brenna's vision and clouded her thoughts, but that didn't matter.

All that mattered in this moment was what she chose to do next.

She gulped as she pushed off the edge of the dinghy and dove in headfirst.

Frigid water engulfed her, filling her ears and nose and mouth. Before the train incident, she'd never thought twice about swimming underwater in a river or stream, but now, she had to fight against her panicked impulse to inhale.

She kicked her feet as hard as she could and swept her arms in broad strokes. Even with her skirt tangling around her ankles, she kept swimming, deeper underwater than she'd ever imagined going. Her head threatened to explode with the ever-increasing pressure, but she didn't stop. Fear engulfed her on all sides, horrid scenes of the train crash flashing through her mind, but she pushed them away.

Fear could not suffocate her if she didn't let it.

She could do this. She would reach her friend, or she would die trying.

Though the water was hazy, and the salt stung her open eyes, ahead of her she spotted a figure—a shadow of the right size—and she swam for it with all her might. She reached out to touch the shape and grasped the fabric of Katiel's dress to pull her closer. Even in the clouded depths, she knew the blurred face before her was that of her dearest friend.

Brenna grabbed her friend around the waist and pushed off the sinking mast as hard as she could. Already, she was running out of air, but she couldn't give up now. She closed her eyes and gritted her teeth, focusing on nothing but her kicks.

Then, she felt herself surge faster toward the surface and looked down. Katiel, having regained consciousness, kicked as well, albeit weakly, and Brenna switched positions, now supporting Katiel by the shoulders. The change freed up one of Brenna's arms and gave her the extra power she needed. After only a few more strokes, her head burst out of the water, Katiel's along with it.

Brenna gasped in a huge breath, though she longed to let out a triumphant cry. She'd never missed the air quite this badly, but she hadn't the energy to make a peep.

Dakier was treading water near them, looking all around as though he couldn't tell for certain which way Brenna had gone. When he spotted them, he swam over and looped Katiel's arm around his shoulders. To Brenna's surprise, another person swam with him as well, taking Katiel's other arm from her.

"Anton?"

"There's no time to explain," he said, breathing hard. "Get in."

Brenna nodded and swam the short distance back to the dinghy, hoisting herself inside and turning to offer the others a hand. Once inside, Dakier pulled the ore-filled amulet over his head and strung it around Katiel's neck, and she gazed up dreamily before her eyes fell on Brenna. When they did, she sat up with a wide smile.

"You came."

"And you're alright!" Brenna surged forward, clasping her in a tight hug before she pulled back. "Now, let's get out of here."

49

Brenna

When the boat rammed into the sandy shore, Brenna hopped out first. As her boots landed in the coarse, gray sand, she fought the urge to lie face down and sleep. A light rain had started falling, but Brenna welcomed the salty mist. All of her friends and the townsfolk were safe, and that's all that mattered.

Behind her, Dakier stepped out of the boat, while Anton lifted Katiel over the edge. He offered a chivalrous hand while she found her footing, and Brenna wondered what had happened between them in New Drezchy. Judging from the way Katiel leaned against him for support, he wasn't her enemy anymore.

"I really am glad to see you," Brenna said, voice wavering as she eyed Anton, "but can someone please explain what's going on here? What happened to you two?"

"Katiel was captured," Anton replied, rage biting in his tone even as his hand tenderly clutched Katiel's, "but that doesn't matter now. Somehow, she's safe. You're all safe."

Softness had replaced his typical cocky, inquisitive demeanor, and he angled his shoulders toward Katiel. To her own surprise, Brenna found herself believing that whatever happened between him and Katiel in New Drezchy had truly changed him. This time, he might actually be on their side.

"The people of Pizemac are alright, too," Brenna said. "We got your warning in time, so they fled to higher ground before the first cannon fired."

The dread lifted from Katiel's face for a moment, but then her gaze fell on the horizon. "Not again."

Around them, some of the ship's crew had made it ashore and were jumping onto the sand in relief as she had, paying no attention to their group of four. Brenna was about to suggest they get off this beach in case any of them realized their captive was missing, but Katiel spoke first, her quiet voice ripe with concern. "What is he doing?"

Brenna turned toward the sea, squinting until her eyes landed on a strange sight.

At the bow of one half of the upturned ship, a man stood upright. He was a statue at the helm, not so much as attempting to flee to safety, and his sharp gaze mirrored theirs. A chill shot down Brenna's spine at the unmoving wraith, staring them down long before they noticed him.

And then a second later, she realized that the man's face was one she recognized.

"Is that Simeon?" Brenna asked, cocking her head to the side. She would've expected Anton to have saved him, too, but both his and Katiel's jaws were clenched in anger. "Wait, is Simeon the person who captured Katiel?"

Katiel took another step back, and when her light eyes met Brenna's, they were filled with sorrow. "He's the boss."

A thousand new questions sprang to Brenna's mind, but they all disappeared when Simeon lifted his hand to his mouth. Out of nowhere, a great cloud swirled around him, glistening as it stretched into the rain-kissed haze.

Brenna's mouth fell open, though she didn't dare avert her eyes. "Simeon's a wielder?"

Katiel gulped. "Yes, but—"

But Katiel stopped short as Simeon's wielded creation fell back into his arms. From this distance, Brenna couldn't quite make out what it was, but the object was as wide as Simeon was tall. Immediately, he moved it around behind him and leapt into the air.

Though he should have fallen back down, he didn't, and Brenna realized what he'd wielded—a set of wings. The black wings appeared to move of their own accord as they flapped, and Brenna's mouth hung open as she watched him approach. Dakier stepped between her and the strange, flying man, and she craned to see around his large frame.

Within seconds, Simeon lowered himself to the ground in front of them, and Anton moved closer, his squared shoulders and wide stance doubling his size.

"Simeon, end this now," Anton bellowed, his deep voice carrying across the beach. "You've made your point."

"It really is a shame," Simeon drawled as his feet landed gracefully in the sand, "for the power to remain with someone so slow on the draw." He eyed Katiel, as if he expected her to have already taken up arms against him. "Or should I say—it would've been a shame had you not so graciously shared it with me."

"You shared your power with him?" Brenna asked as the words sank in, her head swiveling between Simeon and Katiel. "That's how he became a wielder?"

"I would never," Katiel replied through gritted teeth. "He took it from me by force."

Brenna gasped, overcome with the terror that Katiel must have felt at the hands of a man they'd all considered a friend. Her first instinct was to wrap Katiel in her arms to comfort her, but she refrained, because Simeon now stood mere feet from them. He removed his wings and tossed them aside before he spoke, the familiar condescension in his voice now laced with a sinister tint.

"You *could* have shared it with me, though. It would've made all this much easier." With a wink, Simeon flicked a stray raindrop off of his shoulder, and Brenna noticed that his burgundy suit remained completely dry even as the light rain continued to fall. "Moisture-repellant fabric. Also wielded. It's lovely being a wielder when you actually know what you're doing—when you've been planning this for a lifetime."

"Why, though?" Katiel demanded. "Why have you been planning this? To get back at Anton somehow? Or to become king yourself?"

"All of the above, I suppose," Simeon said. Before he spoke again, he examined each of them with forced bravado, and Brenna got the feeling he'd been waiting to give this speech for quite some time. "Honestly, who wouldn't want to be king? Born as a commoner, I was never meant to achieve greatness. Yet, I had to listen to this spoiled prince whining about it for years." Brenna quirked a brow. He spoke of Anton as if he weren't there, yet his gaze was reserved only for the prince. "Talk about inconsiderate. He even traveled anonymously in A'slenderia so he could feel ordinary. Who would want that?"

"I had to execute people to get my sadistic uncle to leave us alone," Anton spat, his nostrils flaring involuntarily, and Brenna reeled at all that Katiel had understandably left out of her letters. "Why wouldn't I want to escape that?"

"Leave *us* alone?" Simeon's gaze fell. He looked suddenly smaller as he paced back and forth, forming a semicircle in the sand. "Leave you alone, perhaps. You never gave a second thought about me."

"What?" Anton asked reflexively, his brows knitted together as he mirrored Simeon's slow steps. "I thought..."

"No," Simeon cut him off. "You didn't think. I've always been more capable than you in every way, yet I remained in your shadow. Now, I'll go down in history, while you'll be forgotten. I've surpassed you."

"I still don't understand," Anton said, though his tone had noticeably softened. "Even if this is all a bid to take the throne from me, why would you ever work for that monster? Don't you remember what he's done?"

"Let us get one thing straight," Simeon snapped, a ticking muscle in his jaw cracking his veneer of composure. "*He's* working for *me*. Even if he doesn't know it yet."

Brenna furrowed her brow, a slew of questions halting on her lips as she took in the marked difference between the former friends. While Simeon's expression was full of hatred, Anton's was far kinder, despite the extent of his friend's betrayal.

"I concocted a plan that ends in his death," Simeon all but growled, "with me taking his throne. There will be no contenders left to challenge me as I overtake a weakened Kerafin and become the greatest king New Drezchy has ever known. Does it sound like I remember to you?"

Anton sighed, looking away for the briefest moment. "I admit it; I misjudged how much you were capable of. In reclaiming our homeland, you've achieved the empty promise of every Drezchy ruler for the past century. So end this now. You've won. No one else needs to die."

"I've yet to achieve it." Simeon tsked, head shaking with obvious disdain. "But make no mistake—I will take back our lands and take the rest of Kerafin in consolation. Our dear Vadim most certainly has to die, and I need your little wielder's help to achieve that." He paused and took a small step closer to Katiel. "So if you don't mind, I'll be taking her back with me."

"We won't let you!" Brenna exclaimed, the sudden declaration surprising even herself.

But Simeon's smirk only grew wider as he reached up to cup Brenna's cheek. Her eyebrows rose, until the scholar's lips narrowed into a pout. In a sudden rush of movement, he reached for his pocket, stretched out his hand, and exhaled, whipping his body around to face the water with his arms spread wide.

Ore, thick and dazzling, swirled around them all, a massive torrent that sent Brenna's hair flying into her face and her skirt whipping around her ankles. Beside her, her friends fought against the gale, their hardened expressions ready for a fight. Brenna yanked her curls away from her face, desperately determined to stop him, but the fierce Drezchy was far too quick for any of them.

In a blink, the cyclone of ore lifted and swept past the sand, the tip now hovering above the surface of the sea. Just as suddenly, a sailing ship replaced it, grander than the one that sank and twice the size. Beside it, a row of matching ships formed, stretching along the coastline in both directions.

It had only taken one ship to destroy a town, and in the blink of an eye, Simeon had wielded a full armada. Brenna shuddered. With this power, there would be no way to defeat him.

The scholar turned back to them, eyeing their gawking faces with glee. "Kerafin belongs to me now."

50

Katiel

"Enough!" Katiel shouted, her fury directed at Simeon alone. "This is recklessness. You've already destroyed Pizemac. What will you do with such a fleet—decimate every town on the coast?"

Simeon merely shrugged. "If that's what it takes."

"Where will you go?" Katiel demanded, sweeping her arm toward the sea. "You may now have a fleet, but you have no one willing to sail it."

"You never learn." The laugh that spilled from Simeon's lips was musical, maniacal, and would surely haunt Katiel's memory. "You simply never learn. You have all the power in the world, yet you always underestimate it."

Arms spread wide, Simeon turned back to the ocean, and Katiel's mouth fell open. Though she hadn't seen him pull out a speck of ore, he was once again wielding an object of incredible size. A torrent of ore rose above the fleet, spinning and whirling in a raging storm, yet the surface of the water remained still. Simeon's arms did not move as if molding a shape, instead remaining in their splayed position with his fingers far apart. It was like he wasn't casting the ore into an object at all, but into raw power.

And yet, he did wield. As quickly as the cloud formed, it fell, but no object hit the water. Instead, dozens of sailors appeared on the deck of every ship.

"You can't!" Katiel screamed, louder than she had in her entire life. "You must know you can't form living things. Surely in all your studies, you've learned the tale of Jurgen. To exist will be torture for those beings. Wielded creatures have no souls!"

"I need an army to rule Kerafin," Simeon replied without missing a beat. "They don't need to have souls."

Anton's fingertips grazed her arm as he leaned down to whisper in her ear. "Katiel, I know we need to stop him, but we're outmatched. He might command his forces to take you again."

She nodded, knowing he was right. It was a losing battle. Even if they killed Simeon's henchman, he could always create more.

Katiel wasn't sure if Simeon's abilities would wear off at some point, in which case he'd need to siphon her blood again to remain a wielder. She was certain, however, that she didn't want to wait around to find out.

"It's been lovely, Simeon," she said, even though the statement was categorically untrue, "but we must be going now..."

She backed away, her hand never leaving Anton's, and Brenna and Dakier followed suit beside her.

Simeon laughed, pushing his glasses up his nose. "We'll see about that."

He reached for his pocket, and Katiel turned and sprinted away from him. Running across the sand in boots was a struggle, so she let go of Anton, who she could tell was hanging back for her sake. A quick glance over her shoulder confirmed Brenna was right behind her, with Dakier bringing up the rear.

Katiel hadn't gotten the chance to see what Simeon was wielding, but a second later, a bolt whizzed by, narrowly missing Anton. She risked another glance back to find Simeon in the same place they'd left him, aiming a crossbow at their backs.

But before Katiel could say another word—before she could scream at this person, this monster, that she had considered a friend—the bolt hit the sand mere feet in front of them.

"Run!" Anton yelled. He started a zigzag pattern to make himself harder to hit, and Katiel copied his movements.

They were sprinting for their lives, but even that wasn't quick enough. There was nowhere to go, and even if they could somehow outrun Simeon, they couldn't lead him right to the displaced villagers. Katiel was the wielder, and she had to protect them somehow. While she was unwilling to create an army to match Simeon's own, surely she could think of a trick to escape.

Just then, Katiel noticed a crack in the cliff side, and an idea sprang to her mind. She might not be able to outrun him forever, but she could try to outsmart the mastermind himself.

"There!" she shouted, pointing to the crack.

The four of them hurried toward it, each sliding sideways to make it through. The narrow fissure opened into a spacious cavern. Its ceiling stretched so high that Katiel couldn't see the top, but there was no time to marvel at its beauty. She needed to prepare for when Simeon inevitably followed them.

Reaching for her necklace, she flicked open the top and drew out a single morsel of the ore. In a flash, she wielded a weapon of her own design—a set of double axes, fashioned to strike with the force of an ox while remaining light enough for Katiel to lift with only her little finger. It was a classic Drezchy weapon, poetically chosen for the circumstance. The Conclave may have been cut short, but the third and final battle could now commence.

"Classic." Simeon scoffed, making his presence known as he slipped into the cave. "The born wielder never invents anything useful."

Conceit radiated through the scholar as he drew back, reaching down without taking his eyes from Katiel's. It was obvious what he was doing—retrieving one of the stores of ore on his person, this one tucked into his boot.

His sharp canines gleamed as he stood back up, his powerful stance making him seem five times Katiel's size. "But if it's a fight you want, then I accept."

Without sparing another breath, he wielded his own weapon in the precise, controlled manner Katiel had already come to expect from him. It was a set of double axes—exactly like Katiel's.

Anton, Brenna, and Dakier all took a step forward, like they meant to intervene, but Katiel raised a halting hand. Simeon had stolen her power without permission, and she was the one he was after. She would do this on her own.

Simeon charged at her, a ferocious glint in his eye, and Katiel's first thought was that she made a mistake by attempting to fight him. Yet, when he swung for her, she blocked the strike with ease. With the slightest of movements, she pushed her axes against his, sending Simeon flying backward and sliding in the sand with a thud.

It was obvious what had happened—Simeon had wielded ordinary axes, not having realized the unusual parameters enchanted into Katiel's. For a moment, Katiel couldn't help but smile at him. Perhaps she had learned something from the Conclave after all.

Simeon shot back to his feet and paced in a semi-circle, a condescending smirk plastered across his face. He had realized his error, no doubt, and had already moved onto a new tactic. He was trying to wear Katiel down, to intimidate her.

"I'm surprised you didn't wield yourself a potion for incredible strength," Katiel said, trying to convince herself as much as anyone that she could handle this.

"Brilliant," Simeon replied, with genuine pride that sounded bizarre on his lips. "Now you're thinking."

Katiel bristled at this man thinking he knew her own power better than she did. Admittedly, he might, but the acknowledgement still stung.

Suddenly, Simeon struck, his blades slicing through the air in a cross. The tips clipped both of her shoulders, her own axes held too low to block.

Agony ripped through Katiel, the torn flesh stinging against the salty air. She stumbled back, shaking her head as she pushed through the searing pain.

She may have let her guard down too easily, but her weapons were stronger than his. Even with the shooting pain coursing through her, she held her ground. She blocked Simeon's next blow, and then she struck out on the offensive, her blades swinging dangerously close to his neck.

Simeon's eyes widened at the near miss, and Katiel quickened her attack, axes slicing through the air as fast as her burning arms could muster. With every swing, Katiel forced Simeon back, and she maintained her pace, charging forward until his back collided with the cave wall.

Katiel swiped at both of Simeon's axes, and the weapons went flying, his strength giving out after bearing their weight for so many blocks.

Instantly, Katiel leaned into Simeon, crossing her blades around his throat. "Surrender," she said, biting out the word, the authoritative tone tasting foreign and false on her tongue. "Surrender and accept Anton as the champion of the Conclave and the rightful heir to the throne, and I'll let you live."

"That's the difference between you and me," Simeon said, not one ounce of fear present on his face despite the perilous position. "I'll never surrender, and you'll never kill me. You don't have it in you."

Simeon was a mastermind. Anton had said as much time and time again, yet Katiel had continued to underestimate him. It was a mistake she couldn't make again, not when so many lives were at stake. She could—she *should*—end him right now, and eliminate Kerafin's greatest threat once and for all.

Katiel stole a glance at Anton, weighing the possibilities. His so-called friend had orchestrated an entire allied war to achieve his selfish ambitions, but Anton still cared about him.

He saw something in the scholar, something few likely had the chance to discover, but Katiel saw it, too. Simeon had an astounding intellect, endless capability, and fierce determination. Katiel longed for him to use those qualities for good, and somehow, despite everything, she truly believed he could.

Katiel had ended General Taregh's life without regret, but he would've killed Brenna if she hadn't. With Simeon, he might hurt others in the future, but there was a hope that he could change—and hope was enough.

So, she shifted her weight back and stood, dropping the axes into the sand. "You're right," she said. "I don't have it in me. I am neither a judge nor jury. You'll stand before the A'slenderian parliament, and they will determine a fitting punishment for your crimes."

Simeon cocked his head to the side as he climbed to his feet. "That's what you think? That I'll go with you, just like that?"

"You have no other choice," Anton reached forward, hand closing around Simeon's neck, and slammed his back against the wall. "She let you live, and for that, you should be grateful."

Simeon's mouth twisted into a snarl, about to bite out a retort, but a thundering cascade of crashing rocks drowned out the words. Loose boulders and rubble slid down the sloped walls and tumbled to the ground, and Katiel bolted for the far end of the cavern to avoid getting pummeled.

The others weren't far behind, and when the rumbling stopped, Katiel dared to take her hands off her head and look around. The narrow crack they'd entered through was blocked by at least six feet of solid rock, with some of the larger pieces likely weighing as much as the five people trapped inside combined.

Anton had let go of Simeon in the chaos, and the scholar's neck whipped toward the cave's entrance and back to them. This he hadn't anticipated—that much was clear—and Katiel knew there was nothing Simeon hated more than being taken by surprise.

"What have you done?" he seethed, lunging for Katiel.

She flinched back with the abrupt motion, but just as suddenly, Brenna was behind him, raising one of the fallen rocks above her head and bringing it down against the back of Simeon's skull.

He let out a ragged cry as he fell forward, his arms splaying wildly as he hit the sandy rock beneath them. His glasses shattered on impact, and to Katiel's surprise, Anton dropped to his knees beside the unmoving form, head hanging in despair.

Brenna's face fell as she looked at the others and then back down at Simeon. "I didn't..." she started. "I mean, he was going to hurt you! He already hurt you, so I didn't—"

"Shh," Dakier said kindly, giving her a reassuring smile before he bent down on Simeon's other side. He reached out two fingers to Simeon's neck and waited for a moment. "He's still alive."

"Oh, thank the Creator," Brenna breathed, as if Simeon were a friend—as if he hadn't tried to end all their lives minutes ago. "I just wanted to protect you, Katiel, before he wielded some invention to take you away again. I didn't want to kill him."

"He would have deserved it," Anton mumbled, and Katiel's eyes snapped to his.

It was exactly what she'd been thinking. She wondered when she'd become this person, who decided when someone deserved to die, and actually considered acting it out.

She should've returned home when her father wrote to her, and the thought brought a fleeting tear to her eye. Trapped in this cave, with Simeon liable to awaken at any moment, there was no time for reflection, but she couldn't shake the feeling that her father's words could help her now.

Whenever you need anything, never forget that you have the power within yourself to create it.

Please, whenever you are ready, come home. Your mother and I miss you so very much.

We love you.

Suddenly, it hit her—the obvious hint within the message.

Come home.

You have the power within yourself to create it.

It was as if he'd anticipated this situation. He was trying to tell her that she could get herself home safely, whenever she needed.

"I'll wield us something to teleport us out," Katiel said, bobbing her head as she tried to rally her courage. "Even if we make it through the rocks, Simeon's army will capture us. It's our only chance, as far as I can see."

Brenna and Dakier nodded their agreement, sending a fresh surge of optimism through her, but Anton ruefully shook his head.

"Katiel," the prince said, her name on his tongue still causing her stomach to flip, "in all my studies, I've never heard of a wielder creating a charm to teleport solid objects to a second location, let alone a location on the other side of a solid surface."

Katiel looked up at him, taking a step closer until he was the only thing she could see. "I need to believe I can do anything. Aren't you the one who told me that?"

"I did say that, didn't I?" he admitted, a slow smirk creeping toward his jaw. "Just keep in mind while you're wielding that the destination will be blind. We wouldn't want to escape only to materialize inside the cliff face."

That was a great point. She would need to form something that could allow not only herself, but three other people to materialize on the other side of a solid wall. If they materialized inside the cliff, they would suffocate, but she had no way to test this teleportation theory before trying it with her friends.

She would have to trust her father, and trust that he wouldn't suggest anything that would put her in danger. This was her only chance.

Now all she had to do was wield.

She drew out her ore as anxiety pounded within her chest.

She needed to enchant an object to take them all home, and to do it, the first thing she imagined was a compass, just like the one she'd made on the way to New Drezchy. Even her brief encounter with Alfien mattered—it was the only reason her father had learned of her state and written to her—and she realized that everything had happened for a reason. Nothing had been a coincidence, and her father's letter was proof of that.

With a fresh swell of confidence, she breathed in the ore and exhaled. She concentrated as she crafted the delicate object bit by bit, making sure to focus on the intent—that this creation would take its wielder, and all their loved ones, home.

Within seconds, the compass fell into her palm, its copper face shimmering and inviting. "Hurry!" she called. "Grab on!"

Instantly, Brenna, Anton, and Dakier each put a hand on the compass, while Simeon remained unmoving behind them.

"Ready?" Katiel called, a gust of wind swirling around the four at the mere thought of sending them away.

"Let's do this!" Brenna affirmed, yelling to be heard over the deafening gale.

The wind around them spun faster. Katiel's braid smacked across her face, and for a second, she worried it wouldn't work at all. They could be trapped here with a powerful wielder who could wake up at any moment. But then, Katiel closed her eyes, drowning out every errant thought.

In her heart, wordlessly, she gave the command.

Take us home.

Katiel knew, before she even opened her eyes to check, that it had worked. She was in the Yule Valley.

After a plethora of wrong choices, a few right ones, and countless brushes with death, she was finally, *finally,* home.

51

KATIEL

KATIEL'S FRIENDS STOOD OPPOSITE her in the open meadow, all clutching the compass and gaping at their surroundings. The sheep weren't out to pasture at the moment, but a light shone from her house, confirming her parents were home. Her heart soared, and a wide smile stretched across her face in spite of everything. Not only had the compass worked, but the Yule Valley was the same as it had always been.

"You did it!" Brenna cheered, engulfing her in a crushing hug.

Dakier quickly followed, wrapping his arms around them both. "You made us proud, Katiel."

After a moment, they drew back, and Katiel looked up at Anton, who appraised his surroundings with wonder. If he decided to stay in the valley, she'd have to show him around, but that would have to wait. She was home, and she had forgotten how wonderful that felt.

To her surprise, her parents were already running across the field toward her, faster than she'd seen either of them move in her life. Within an instant, they were both upon her, crushing her into the tightest embrace.

Katiel's eyes welled, and she clung to their arms as hard as she could. Grief washed over her at how much she missed the feeling of being home, loved, and safe.

At last, her mother and father drew back, their tears matching her own. She felt all the words left unspoken, all the proclamations of love and happiness that were sure to follow once they'd all gotten clean and made themselves comfortable inside the cozy chalet.

For now, her parents let go of their crushing embrace, but each kept a hold of one of her hands.

She gave them both a little squeeze back, her lips pulling into a full-toothed smile at the thought of all she had done since she'd left those months ago. "I have so much to tell you."

52

Brenna

"Figures."

Brenna's quip earned her a scowl from several of the Barkurian council members, but won a sly grin from Steffi.

A week had passed since the attack on Pizemac, and the discussion began with the news that neither the Tibedese, Barkurian, nor A'slenderian authorities had been able to locate Simeon. As Brenna had expected, by the time the Tibedese police removed the rubble and searched the sea cave, Simeon had vanished, his wielded fleet along with him. Brenna, for one, still counted their efforts as a victory, since no civilians were harmed. And since he couldn't access Katiel's blood to siphon, Brenna hoped that meant he wouldn't be able to wield any more armadas.

"All evidence suggests Simeon Mendev has retreated," the High Magister of Tibedo began, addressing the group after the formal introductions, "but the threat from New Drezchy remains."

In their company were world leaders, statesmen, and decorated war heroes, as well as Brenna and Katiel. It was the most bizarre occurrence in Brenna's recent memory, which—given all she'd experienced over these strange few months—was truly saying something.

At Steffi's suggestion, the long banquet table straddled the border between Bar Kur and Tibedo, the arrangement symbolic of the peace the queen hoped to broker. While Brenna was journeying to the coast, Steffi arrested Lord Walsh and freed the wrongfully imprisoned Tibedese envoy in a true bid for peace. Given all the wrongs that Bar Kur bore responsibility for—from the initial framing of Inigo Farro to the imprisonment of their magistrate—the Tibedese were understandably hesitant to agree to any propositions. But once they received word from Magister Lim that it was Queen Stefana's lady-in-waiting who warned Pizemac's people of the Drezchy attack, the leaders of Tibedo had a change of heart.

And that was how this meeting came to be—a fantasy that Brenna had only dreamed of. A peace negotiation among the nations of the continent.

"On behalf of Tibedo, I would like to propose a new alliance," the High Magister declared, "with the nations of Bar Kur and A'slenderia both. Given the grievances Bar Kur has committed thus far, Tibedo has cause to demand significant reparations. In lieu of more typical recompense, we ask only for defense against the threat from across the sea. Drezchy forces will return to reclaim their historic lands—of that, we have no doubt—and we are willing to concede that Kerafin is stronger united, regardless of the wrongs committed of late."

Brenna nearly laughed aloud with her elation, but she held her breath, lest this outcome prove too good to be true.

Steffi waited a beat to ensure the High Magister was finished before she rose to her feet. This time, she didn't look at anyone else before speaking, an unwavering conviction ringing through her tone. "It is with much gratitude that the Sovereign Nation of Bar Kur unequivocally accepts this generous offer. We will remove all forces from your border, and move toward preparing to defend the entire continent of Kerafin—Tibedo included—in the event of further action from New Drezchy."

Brenna struggled to keep her jaw from hanging open, and her heart threatened to burst.

She could not believe her ears.

She did it.

They did it.

Applause broke out around the table, and Brenna joined in, her claps ringing louder than all the rest. Katiel beamed at her from her place with the A'slenderian delegation, a full smile that showed all her teeth.

The discussion between the nations continued for hours as the leaders pored over every detail of the peace treaty, but Brenna's mind was fixed on the best statement she'd heard in her life—the war was over.

The war was over—and she and her friends had helped end it.

This marked the shortest war in the history of Kerafin. Everything she hoped for had come to fruition. Henred, her beloved brother, may be gone forever, but his death hadn't been in vain. Without knowing the pain of that loss, she never would've had the courage to publish the article. She wouldn't have dared to stand on that stage and pour her heart out to the masses.

Now, pride swelled in her chest, for she'd achieved her goal. Peace was restored with the homelands of her dearest friends—and yet, Bar Kur was destined to remain a nation at war.

In the impending fight against New Drezchy, she would be no help at all.

Brenna stole a glance at Anton, seated at the table as his country's sole representative. After introducing himself and stating his intention to reclaim the throne and secure peace between his country and Kerafin, he remained silent. His tucked chin spoke only of fear at what was to come, and even Brenna couldn't ignore the growing sense of dread as the fateful meeting drew to a close.

One war was over, but a new war was only beginning—and this time, Kerafin would be ready.

[illegible] broke out around the table, and Brenna joined in. Her claps [illegible] louder than all the rest. Kate beamed at her from her place [illegible] full smile that showed all her teeth.

The [illegible] of the nations continued for hours as the [illegible] pored over every detail of the peace treaty, but Brenna's mind was fixed on [illegible] she'd heard in her life—the war was over.

The war was over—and she and her friends had reached the end. [illegible]

[illegible] knowing the pain of that loss. She never would've had the courage to publish the article. She wouldn't have dared to stand on that stage and pour her heart out to the masses.

Now, [illegible] smiled to herself, for she'd achieved her goal. [illegible] was restored with the [illegible] or her dearest friends—and [illegible] was [illegible].

In the [illegible] fight again [illegible] she would be [illegible].

Brenna stole a glance at Antrim, seated at the table as his country's [illegible]. After [illegible] himself and [illegible]

[illegible]

Continue the Journey

Don't miss the epic finale to the Kerafin Chronicles trilogy, Fate and Frost, coming in 2026 from Storm Hollow Press.

Fate and Frost - Coming 2026

If you enjoyed this story, please consider leaving a rating or review on Amazon and Goodreads.

If you *really* loved it, please consider subscribing to my monthly newsletter at hayleywhiteley.com/subscribe . You'll receive exclusive content and be the first to hear about new projects and upcoming releases!

Acknowledgments

FIRST OFF, THANK YOU, reader, for continuing this journey with Brenna and Katiel through another adventure. I'm so grateful for the chance to share my imagination with you, and I hoped you enjoyed this story!

To my editor, Sarah, thank you for your incredible editing skills. I've learned so much from working with you, and this novel wouldn't be the same without your improvements. To my cover artist, Stefanie, thank you for another gorgeous cover. Your work captured the spirit of the series so well.

Thank you so much to my first round beta readers, Meg, Angela, and Jessica, for your incredible, helpful, and kind insights. Your input had a major impact on key plot changes and helped me so much in improving the storyline into what it is today. Meg, thank you in particular for your extra detailed feedback, which helped me expand many of the crucial emotional moments in the story. Thank you, Ana, for reading the second iteration to let me know areas that still needed developmental improvement.

To Roxane at Glitch in Normality, thank you so much for your insightful sensitivity read for Nev. I'm so glad you liked the novel, and your suggestions were all wonderful improvements to Nev's scenes. Thank you also to Yvette and the Writers with Social Awareness group for help on Nev's plotline and character arc. I also need to sincerely thank every ARC reader and social media Street Team member. Without you, the first book wouldn't have been successful enough for me to publish a second one, so this installment is a direct product of your efforts. I greatly appreciate you being willing to take a chance on an indie author who's just starting out.

Thank you so much to my entire family for your encouragement and support. Nick, I couldn't have written this book without your love and support. Thank you for always being willing to listen to all my ideas, point out possible plot holes, watch the baby a little extra when I had deadlines coming up, and make fun of Anton for no good reason. Hollis, my sweet son, thank you for being the absolute light of my life. Having you beside me makes every day brighter. This is the first book I've started since you were born, and the joy you bring me helped the whole writing and publishing process become more joyful this time around. I should also thank my cats, Maui and Fitz, for being great writing and editing companions at all hours of the night.

Finally, I have to thank Jesus most of all, for every blessing and opportunity in my life.

About the Author

Hayley Whiteley is the author of the young adult gaslamp fantasy trilogy, The Kerafin Chronicles. She earned her Bachelor's in Mechanical Engineering from Auburn University and enjoys using her technical background to create unique magic systems. When she's not dreaming up fantasy worlds, she can be found reading, exploring the outdoors, or watching bad reality television. Hayley lives in Florida with her wonderful husband, sweet toddler, and two crazy cats.

Hayley's latest updates and upcoming releases can be found on Instagram at @hayleywhiteleybooks and on her website at www.hayleywhiteley.com.

www.ingramcontent.com/pod-product-compliance
Lightning Source LLC
Chambersburg PA
CBHW020249030826
48979CB00030B/2668/J